PUP
DETECT

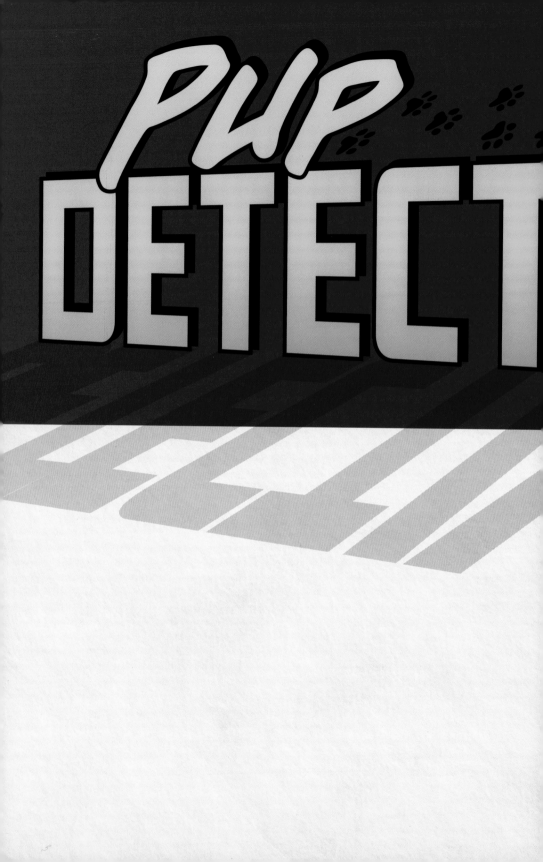

THE MISSING MAGIC WAND

Written by **FELIX GUMPAW**
Illustrated by **WALMIR ARCHANJO**
at *GLASS HOUSE GRAPHICS*

 LITTLE SIMON
NEW YORK   LONDON   TORONTO   SYDNEY   NEW DELHI

LITTLE SIMON
AN IMPRINT OF SIMON & SCHUSTER CHILDREN'S PUBLISHING DIVISION
1230 AVENUE OF THE AMERICAS, NEW YORK, NEW YORK 10020
FIRST LITTLE SIMON EDITION AUGUST 2021
COPYRIGHT © 2021 BY SIMON & SCHUSTER, INC.
ALL RIGHTS RESERVED, INCLUDING THE RIGHT OF REPRODUCTION IN WHOLE OR IN PART IN ANY FORM. LITTLE SIMON IS A REGISTERED TRADEMARK OF SIMON & SCHUSTER, INC., AND ASSOCIATED COLOPHON IS A TRADEMARK OF SIMON & SCHUSTER, INC. FOR INFORMATION ABOUT SPECIAL DISCOUNTS FOR BULK PURCHASES, PLEASE CONTACT SIMON & SCHUSTER SPECIAL SALES AT 1-866-506-1949 OR BUSINESS@SIMONANDSCHUSTER.COM. ART AND COLOR BY WALMIR ARCHANJO, LELO ALVES, JOÃO MÁRIO & JOÃO ZOD • COLORS BY WALMIR ARCHANJO & JOÃO ZOD • LETTERING BY MARCOS MASSAO INOUE • ART SERVICES BY GLASS HOUSE GRAPHICS • THE SIMON & SCHUSTER SPEAKERS BUREAU CAN BRING AUTHORS TO YOUR LIVE EVENT. FOR MORE INFORMATION OR TO BOOK AN EVENT CONTACT THE SIMON & SCHUSTER SPEAKERS BUREAU AT 1-866-248-3049 OR VISIT OUR WEBSITE AT WWW.SIMONSPEAKERS.COM. DESIGNED BY NICHOLAS SCIACCA. GLASS HOUSE GRAPHICS CREATIVE SERVICES ART BY WALMIR ARCHANJO AND JOAO MARIO TEIXEIRA DE ARAUJO. COLORING BY WALMIR ARCHANJO AND RAFAEL RAMOS. LETTERING BY MARCOS MASSAO INOUE. SUPERVISION BY MJ MACEDO/STUPLENDO
MANUFACTURED IN CHINA 0621 SCP
10 9 8 7 6 5 4 3 2 1
LIBRARY OF CONGRESS CATALOGING-IN-PUBLICATION DATA
NAMES: GUMPAW, FELIX, AUTHOR. I GLASS HOUSE GRAPHICS, ILLUSTRATOR.
TITLE: THE MISSING MAGIC WAND / BY FELIX GUMPAW ; ILLUSTRATED BY GLASS HOUSE GRAPHICS. DESCRIPTION: FIRST LITTLE SIMON EDITION. I NEW YORK : LITTLE SIMON, 2021. I SERIES: PUP DETECTIVES ; 5 I AUDIENCE: AGES 5-9 I AUDIENCE: GRADES K-1 I SUMMARY: "THERE'S A NEW STUDENT AT PAWSTON ELEMENTARY NAMED LABRA-CADABRA-DOR, AND HE HAS A FEW MAGIC TRICKS UP HIS SLEEVE. WHEN LABRA HYPNOTIZES RIDER TO TRY AND PULL HIM OVER TO THE DARK SIDE, THE OTHER PUP DETECTIVES WORRY THEY MIGHT HAVE BITTEN OFF MORE THAN THEY CAN CHEW WITH THIS MAGICAL MYSTERY!"— PROVIDED BY PUBLISHER. IDENTIFIERS: LCCN 2020049166 (PRINT) I LCCN 2020049167 (EBOOK) I ISBN 9781534484849 (PAPERBACK) I ISBN 9781534484856 (HARDCOVER) I ISBN 9781534484863 (EBOOK). SUBJECTS: LCSH: GRAPHIC NOVELS. I CYAC: GRAPHIC NOVELS. I MYSTERY AND DETECTIVE STORIES. I DOG–FICTION. CLASSIFICATION: LCC PZ7.7.G858 MI 2021 (PRINT) I LCC PZ7.7.G858 (EBOOK) I DDC 741.5/973–DC23. LC RECORD AVAILABLE AT HTTPS://LCCN.LOC.GOV/2020049166. LC EBOOK RECORD AVAILABLE AT HTTPS://LCCN.LOC.GOV/2020049167

CONTENTS

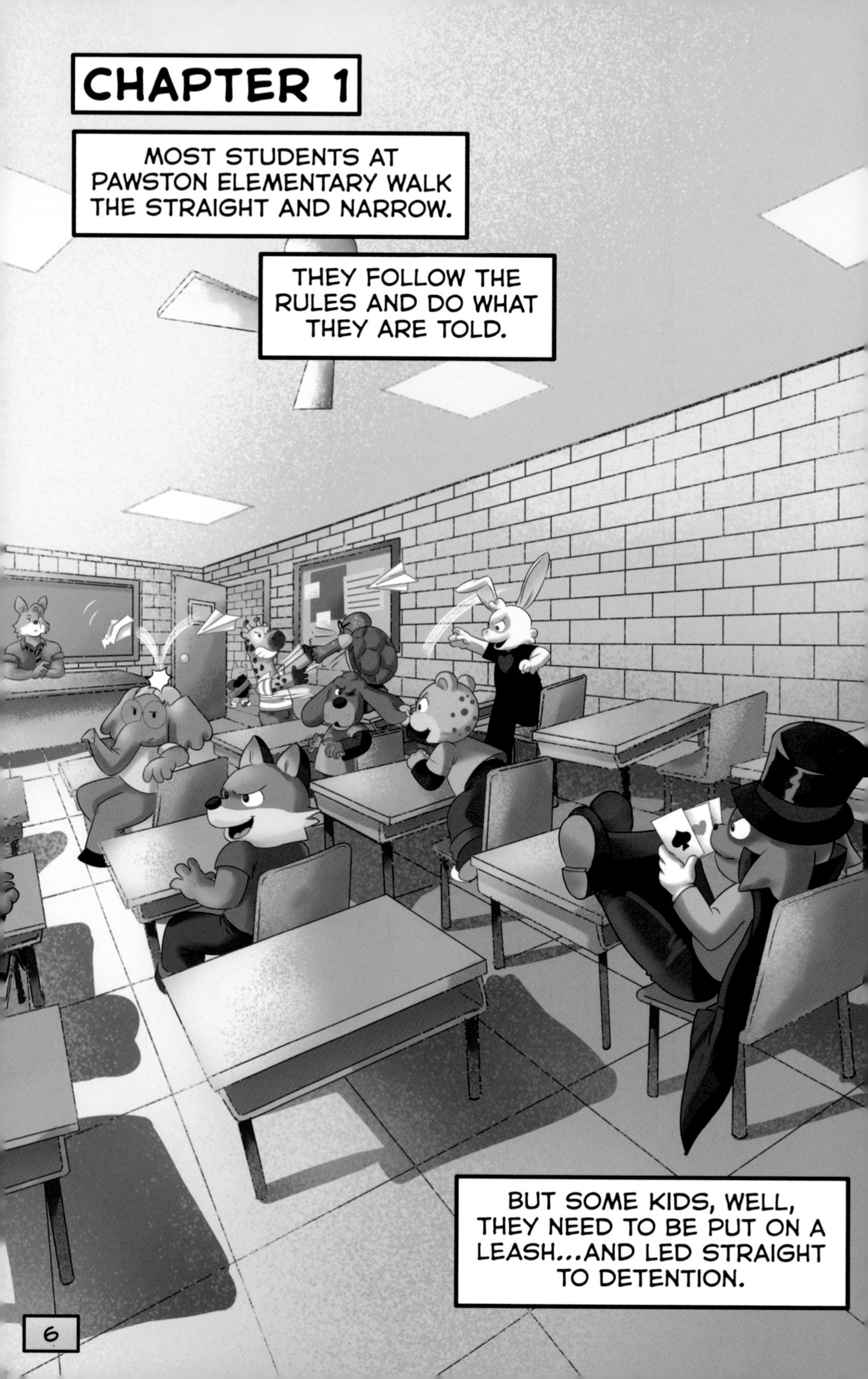
CHAPTER 1
MOST STUDENTS AT PAWSTON ELEMENTARY WALK THE STRAIGHT AND NARROW.
THEY FOLLOW THE RULES AND DO WHAT THEY ARE TOLD.
BUT SOME KIDS, WELL, THEY NEED TO BE PUT ON A LEASH...AND LED STRAIGHT TO DETENTION.

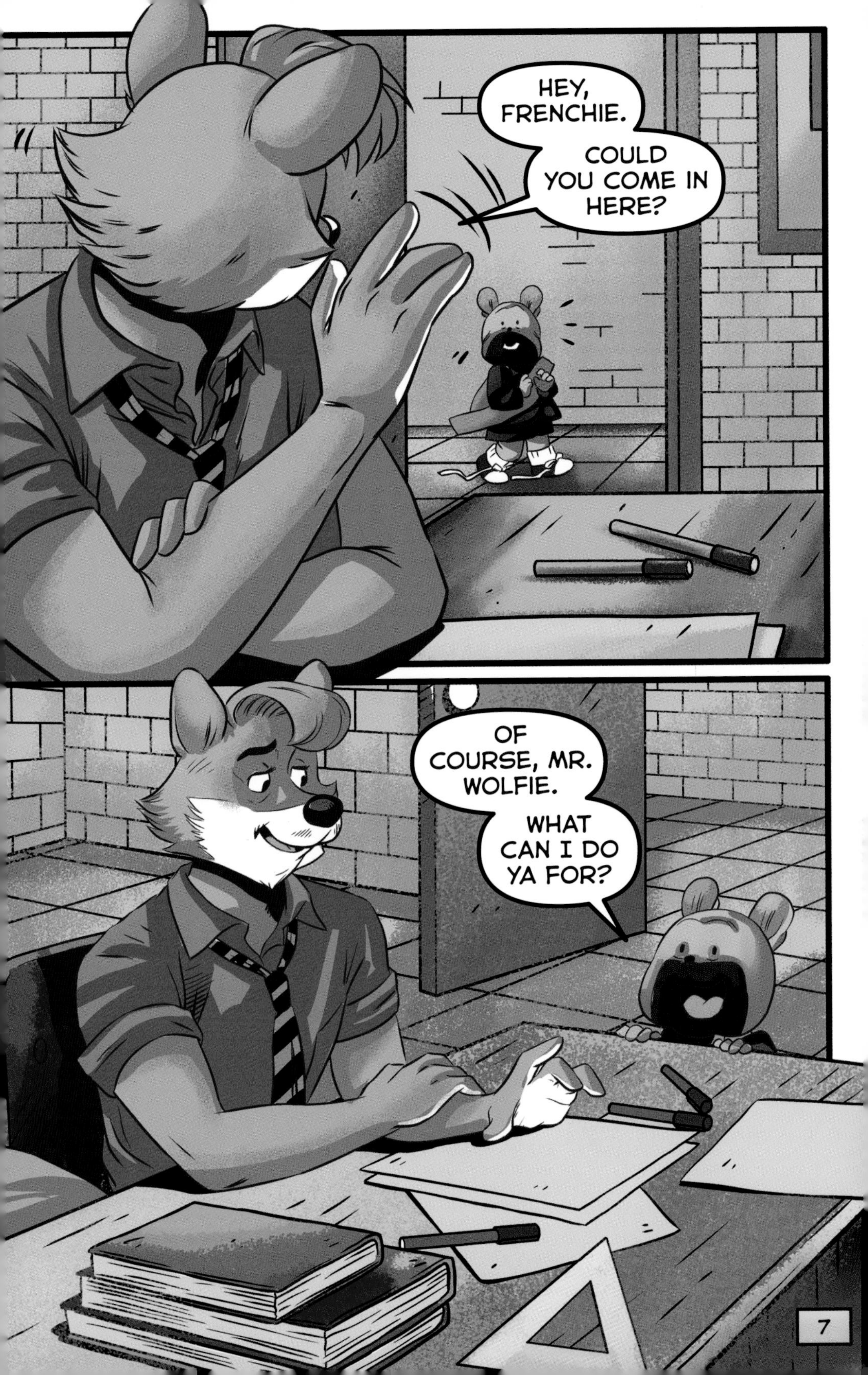
HEY, FRENCHIE.
COULD YOU COME IN HERE?
OF COURSE, MR. WOLFIE.
WHAT CAN I DO YA FOR?

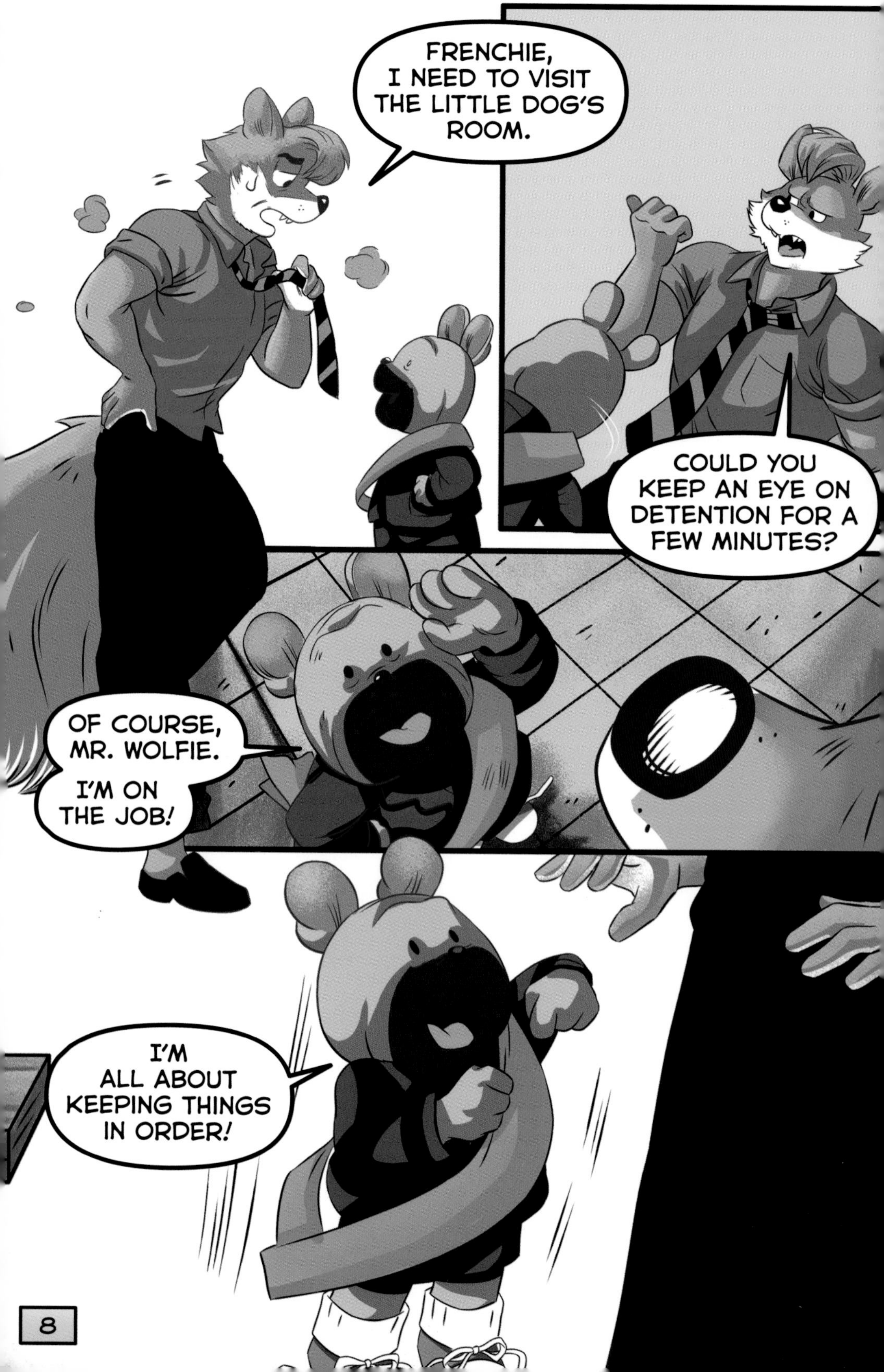
FRENCHIE, I NEED TO VISIT THE LITTLE DOG'S ROOM.
COULD YOU KEEP AN EYE ON DETENTION FOR A FEW MINUTES?
OF COURSE, MR. WOLFIE.
I'M ON THE JOB!
I'M ALL ABOUT KEEPING THINGS IN ORDER!

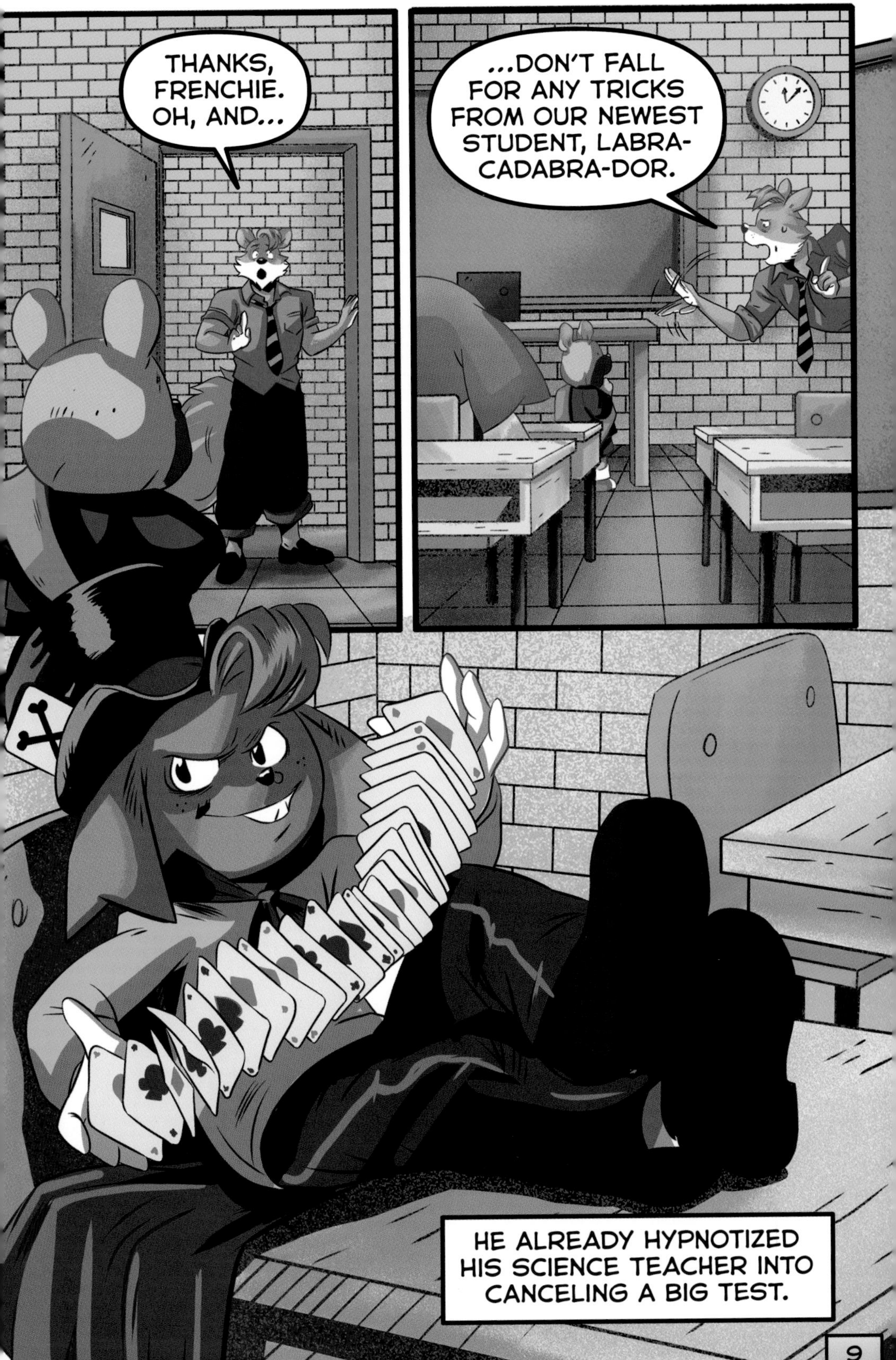
THANKS, FRENCHIE. OH, AND...
...DON'T FALL FOR ANY TRICKS FROM OUR NEWEST STUDENT, LABRA-CADABRA-DOR.
HE ALREADY HYPNOTIZED HIS SCIENCE TEACHER INTO CANCELING A BIG TEST.

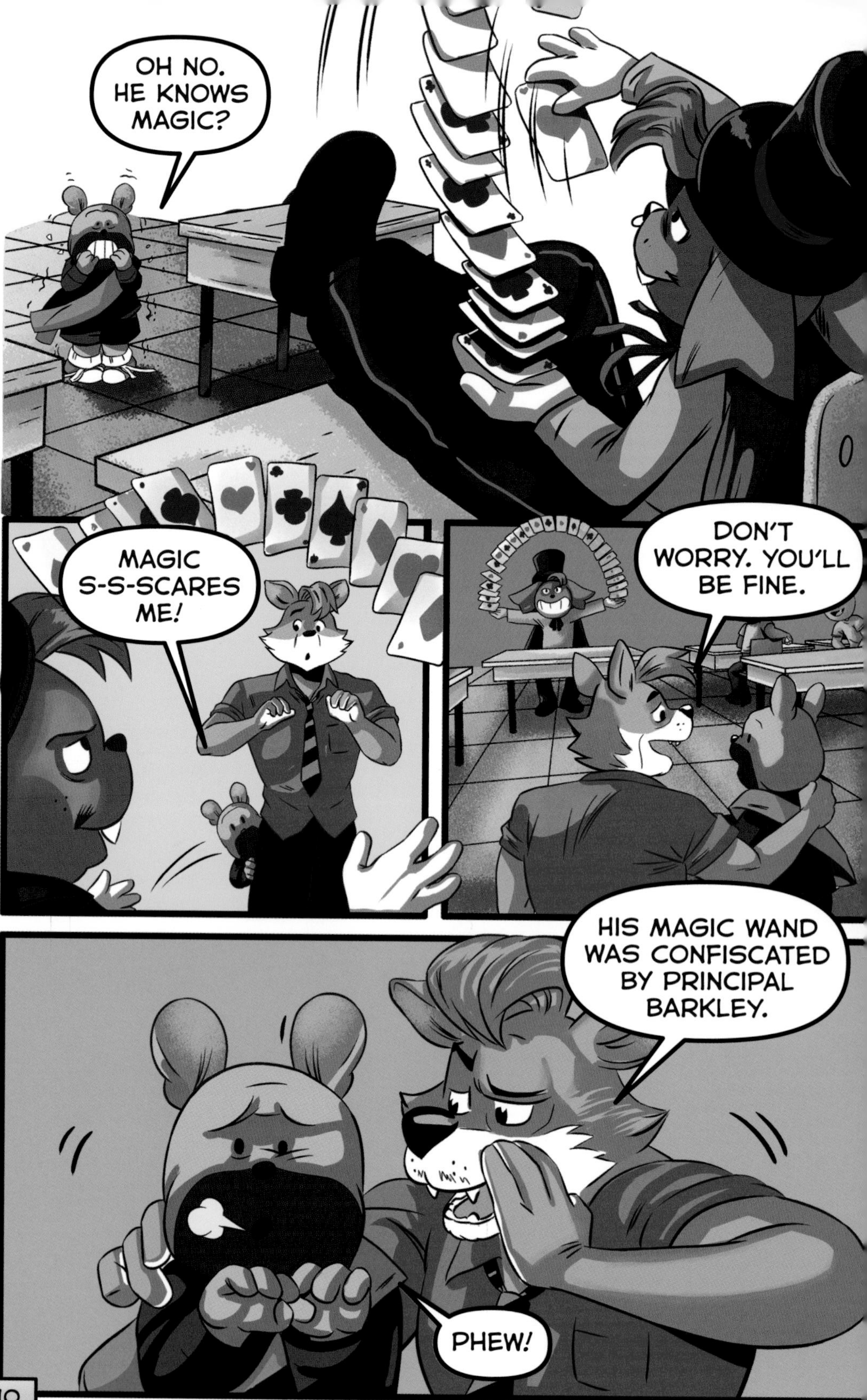
OH NO. HE KNOWS MAGIC?
MAGIC S-S-SCARES ME!
DON'T WORRY. YOU'LL BE FINE.
HIS MAGIC WAND WAS CONFISCATED BY PRINCIPAL BARKLEY.
PHEW!

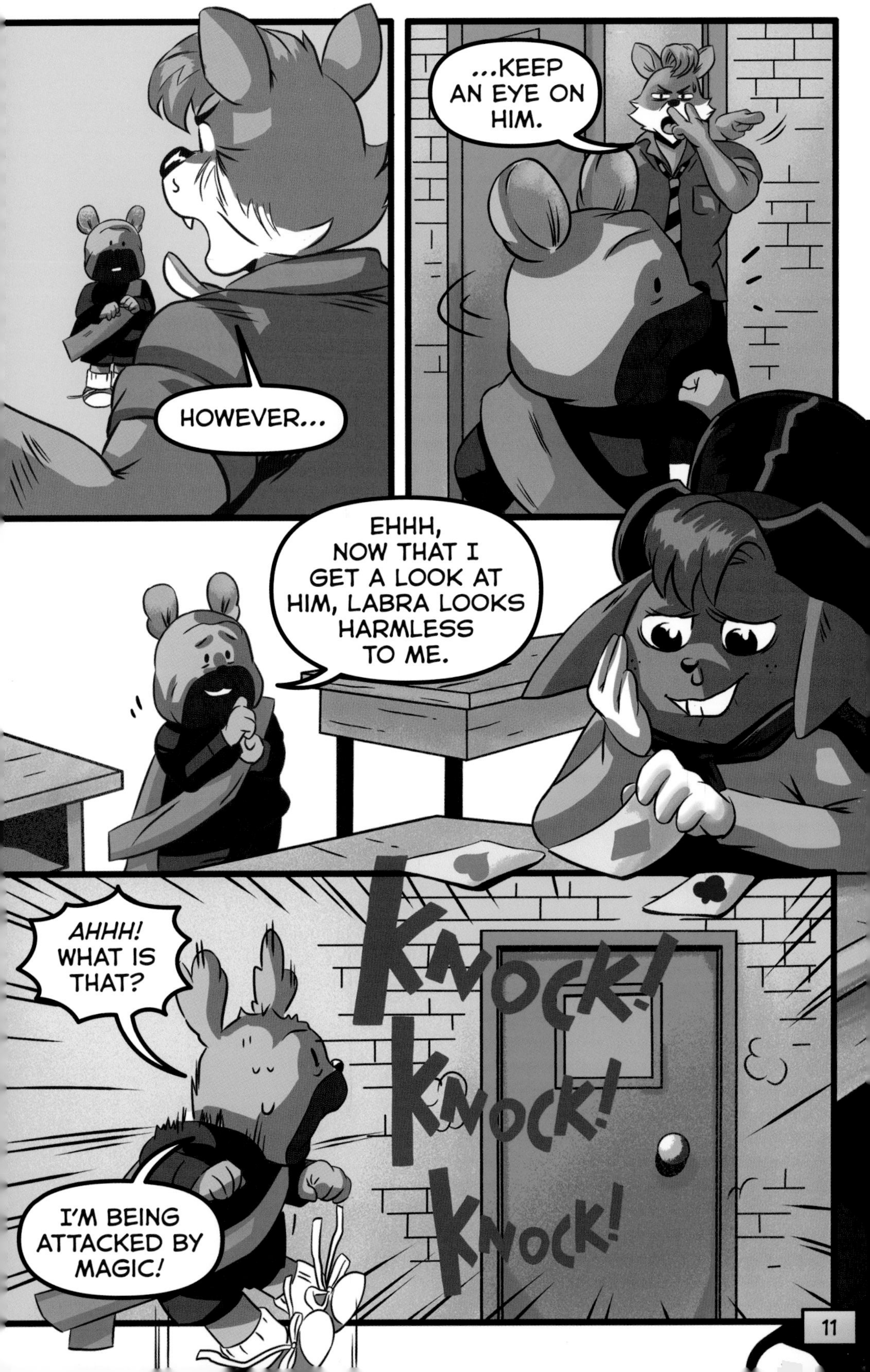
HOWEVER...
...KEEP AN EYE ON HIM.
EHHH, NOW THAT I GET A LOOK AT HIM, LABRA LOOKS HARMLESS TO ME.
AHHH! WHAT IS THAT?
KNOCK! KNOCK! KNOCK!
I'M BEING ATTACKED BY MAGIC!

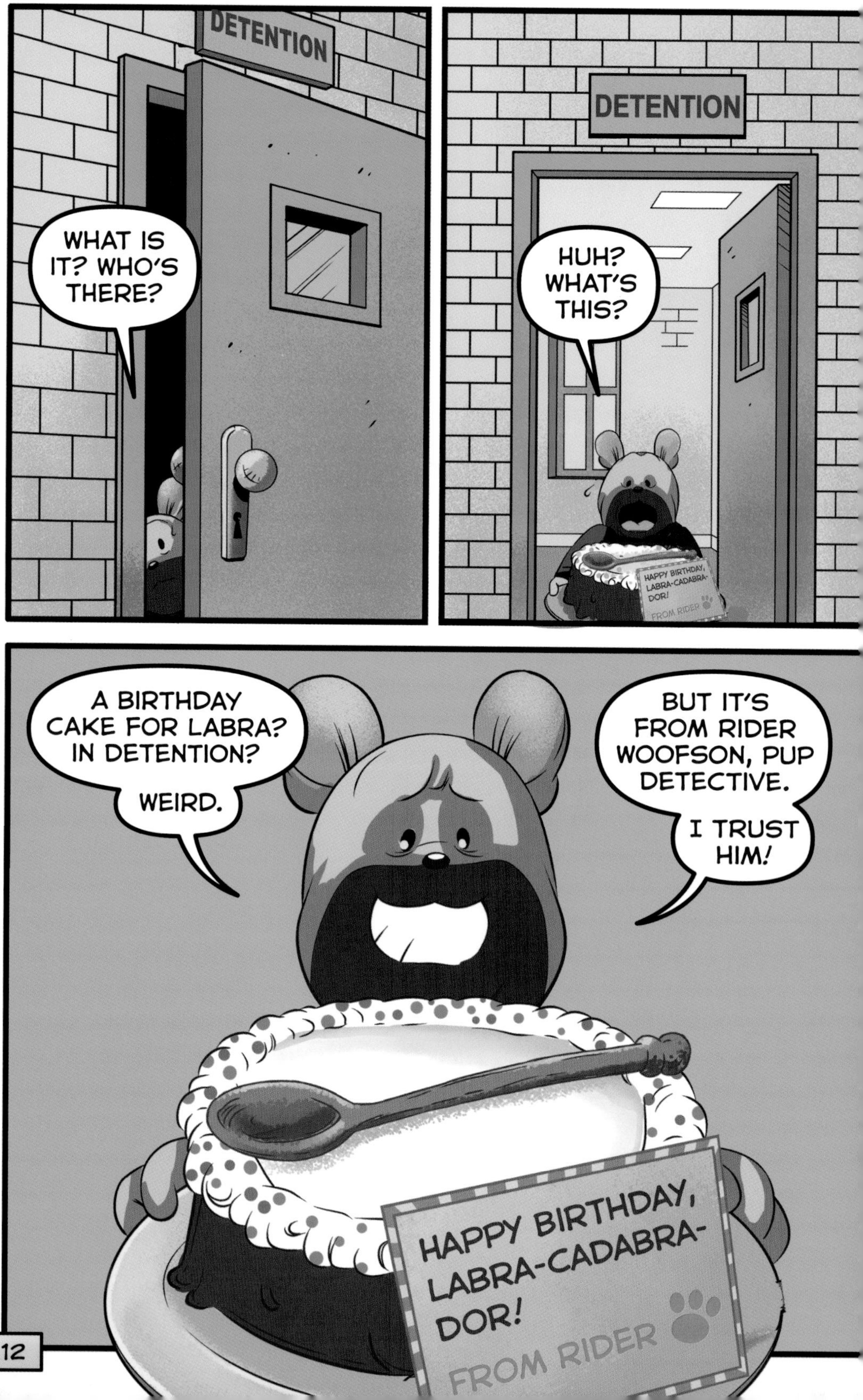
DETENTION
WHAT IS IT? WHO'S THERE?
DETENTION
HUH? WHAT'S THIS?
HAPPY BIRTHDAY, LABRA-CADABRA-DOR!
FROM RIDER
A BIRTHDAY CAKE FOR LABRA? IN DETENTION?
WEIRD.
BUT IT'S FROM RIDER WOOFSON, PUP DETECTIVE.
I TRUST HIM!
HAPPY BIRTHDAY, LABRA-CADABRA-DOR!
FROM RIDER

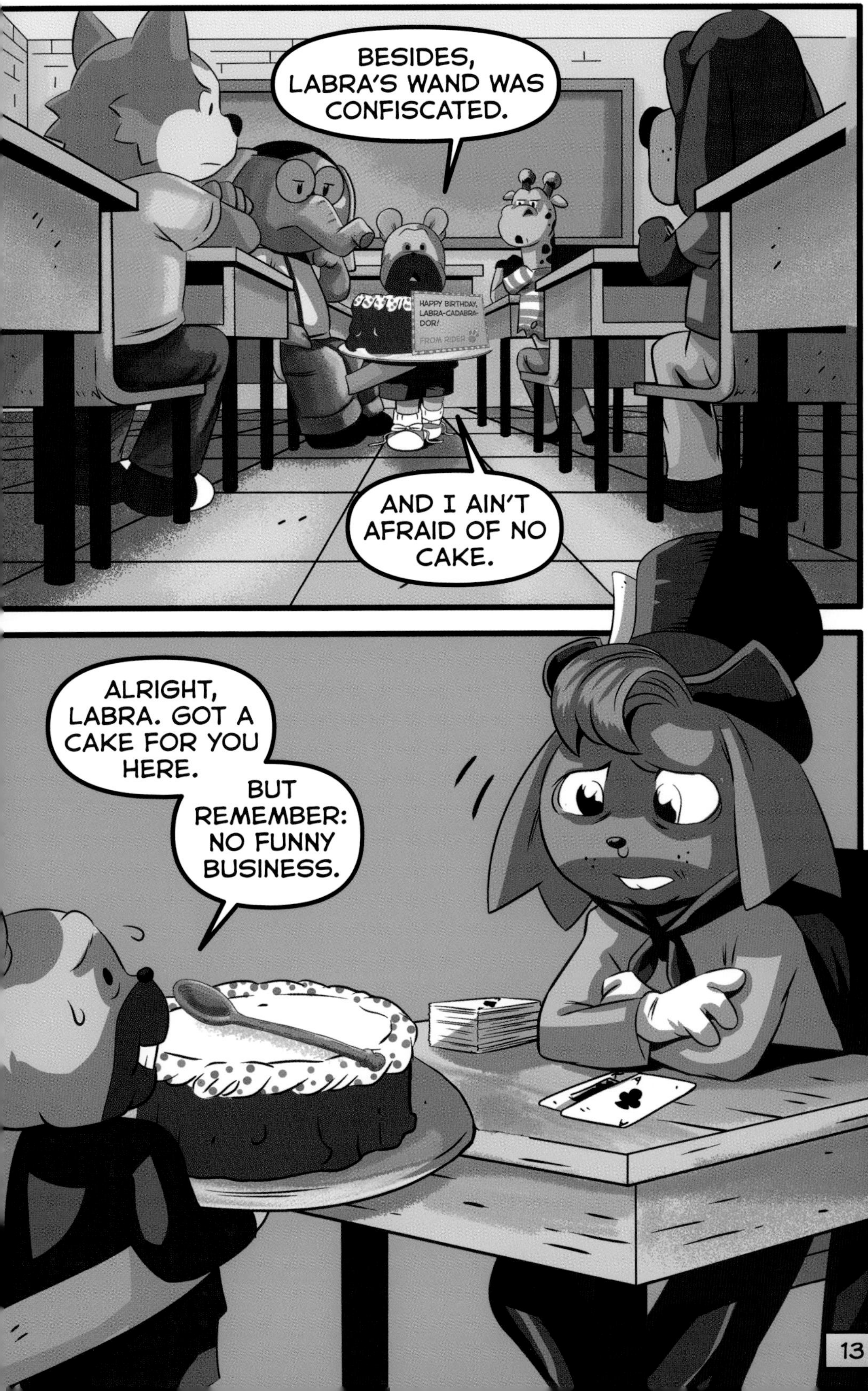
BESIDES, LABRA'S WAND WAS CONFISCATED.
HAPPY BIRTHDAY, LABRA-CADABRA-DOR!
FROM RIDER
AND I AIN'T AFRAID OF NO CAKE.
ALRIGHT, LABRA. GOT A CAKE FOR YOU HERE.
BUT REMEMBER: NO FUNNY BUSINESS.

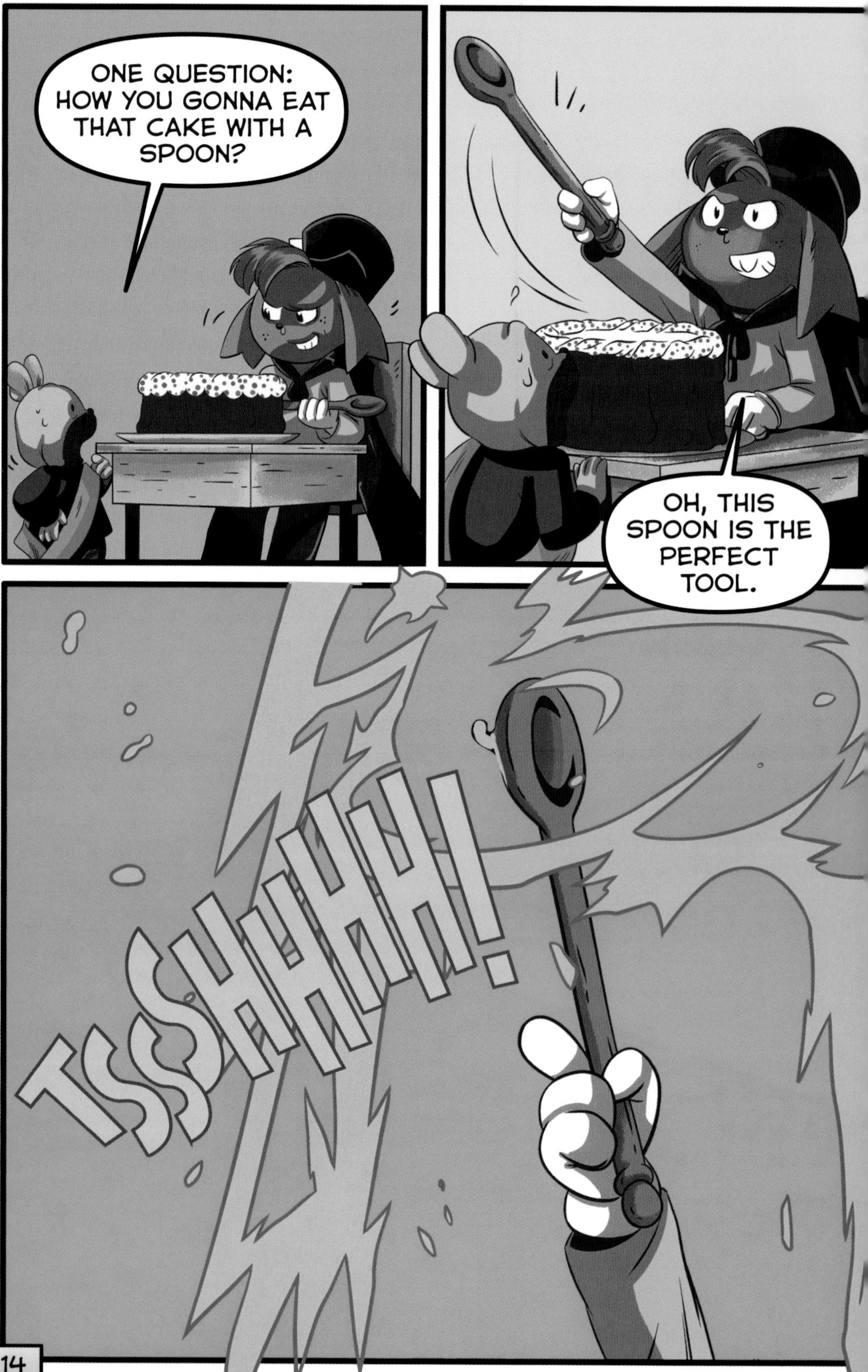
ONE QUESTION: HOW YOU GONNA EAT THAT CAKE WITH A SPOON?
OH, THIS SPOON IS THE PERFECT TOOL.
TSSSHHHHH!

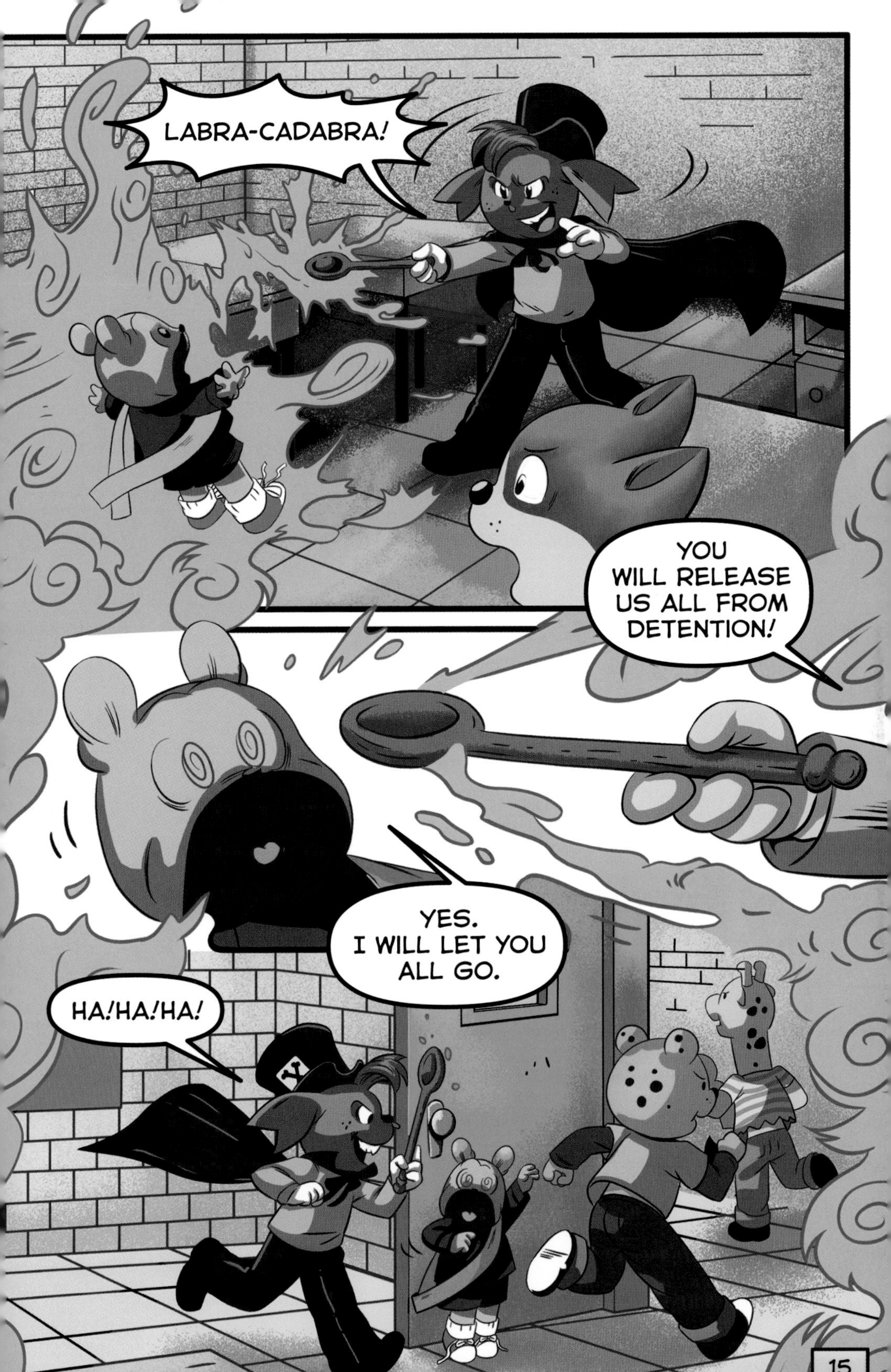
LABRA-CADABRA!
YOU WILL RELEASE US ALL FROM DETENTION!
YES. I WILL LET YOU ALL GO.
HA!HA!HA!

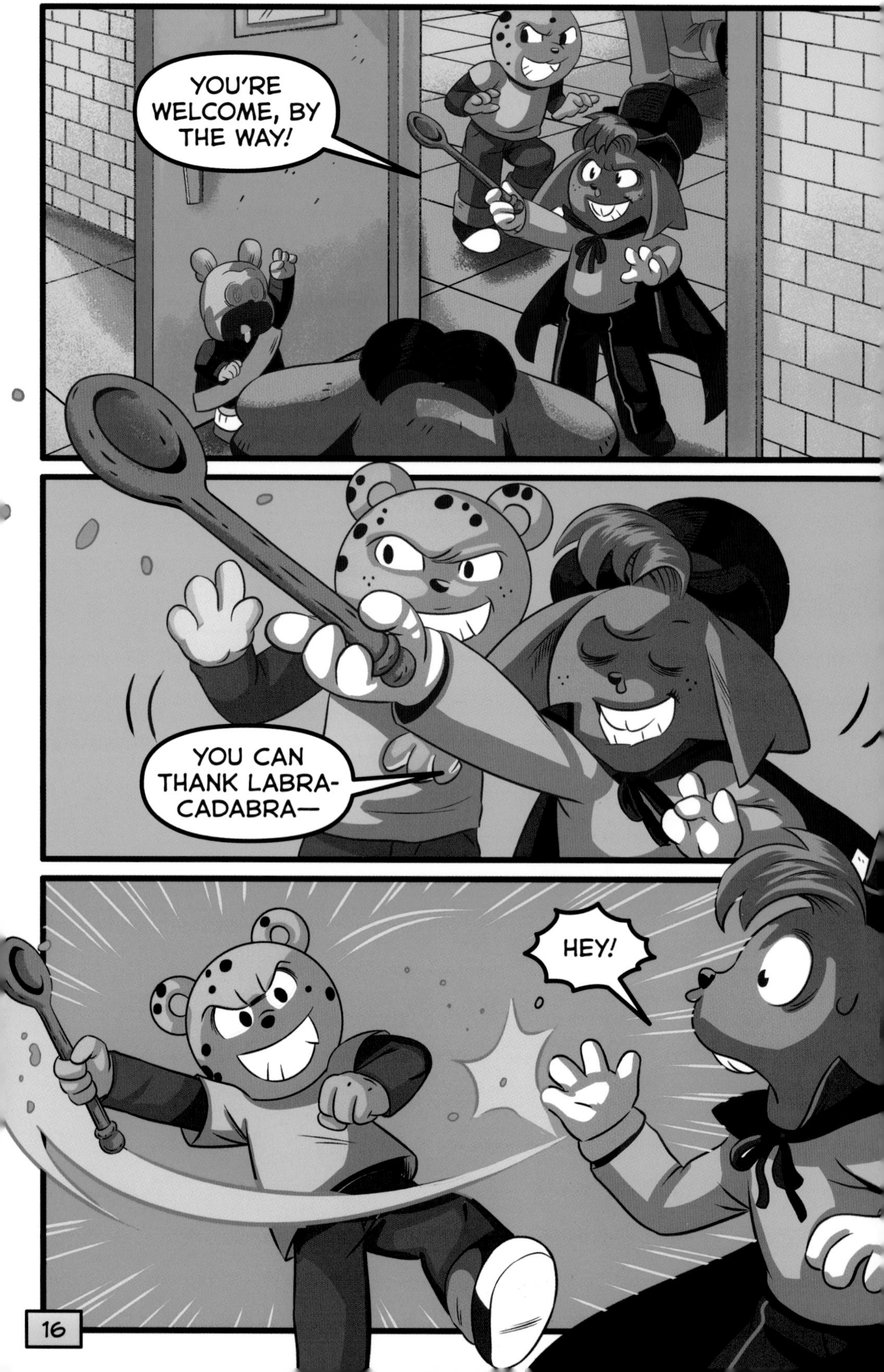
YOU'RE WELCOME, BY THE WAY!
YOU CAN THANK LABRA-CADABRA—
HEY!

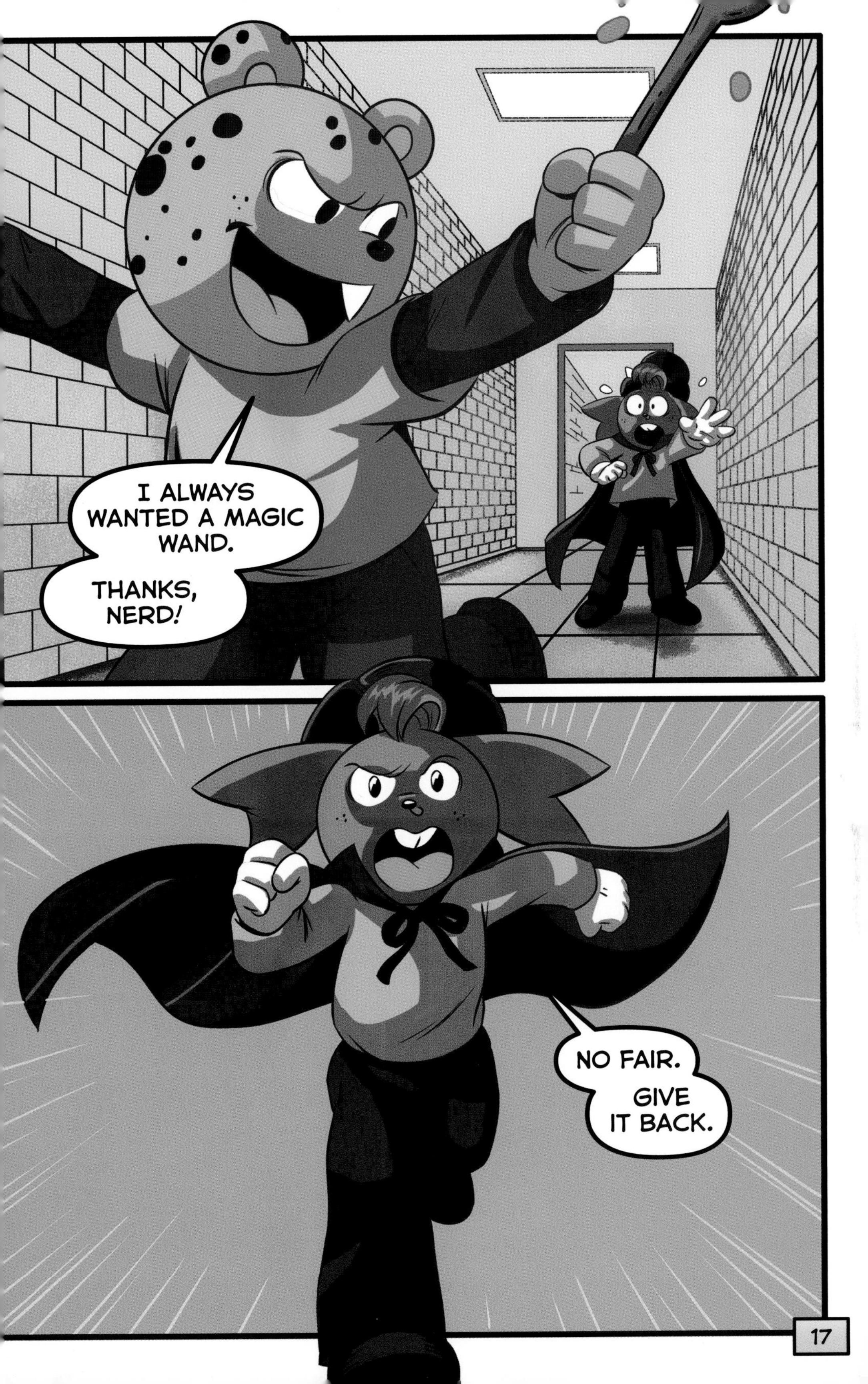
I ALWAYS WANTED A MAGIC WAND.
THANKS, NERD!
NO FAIR.
GIVE IT BACK.

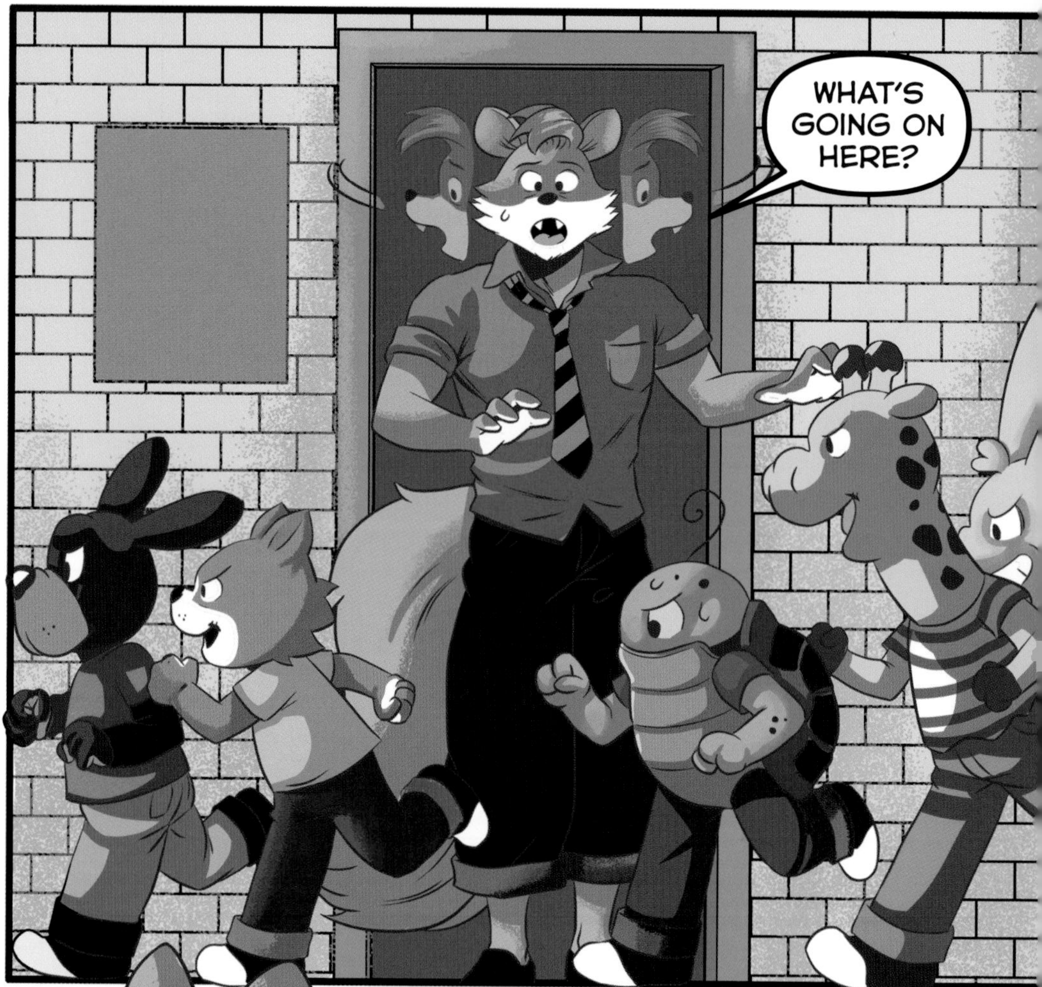
WHAT'S GOING ON HERE?

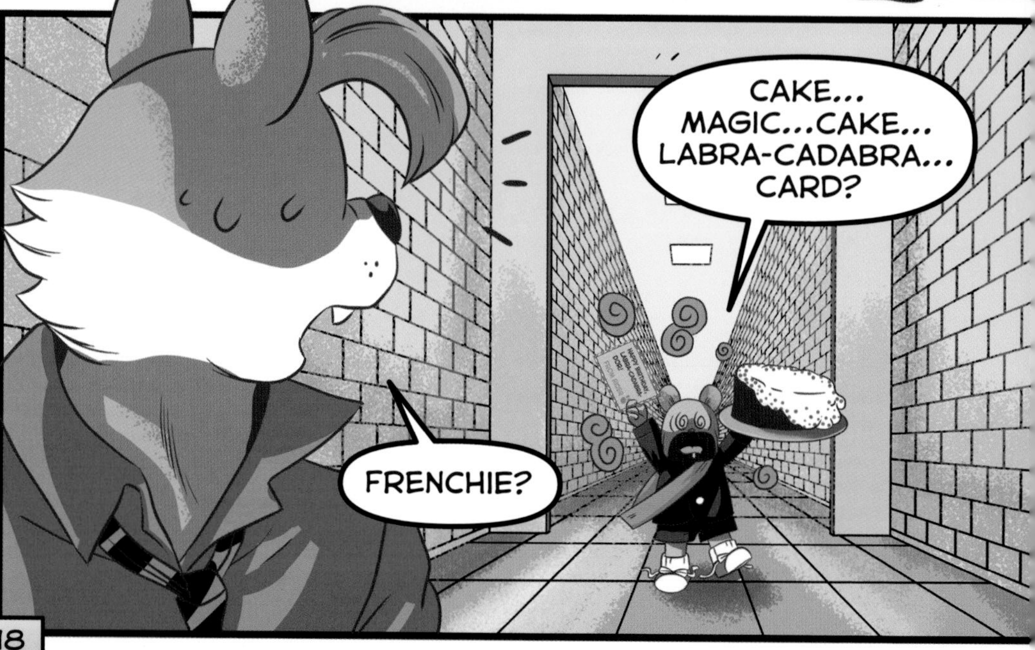
CAKE... MAGIC...CAKE... LABRA-CADABRA... CARD?
FRENCHIE?

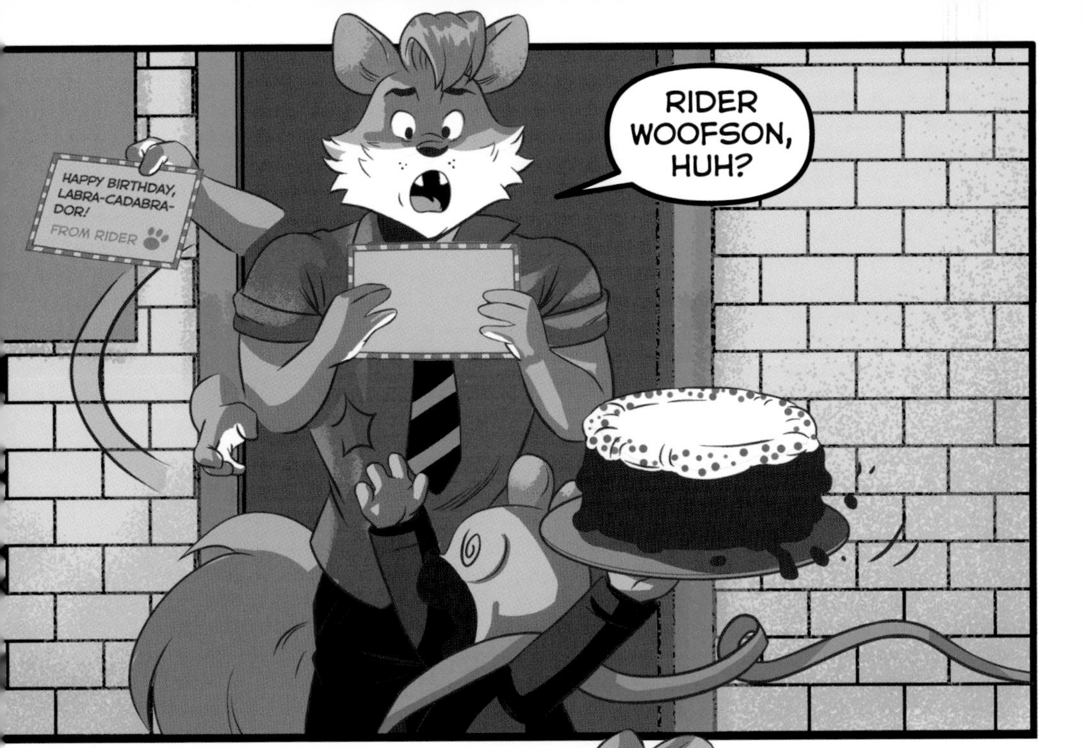
HAPPY BIRTHDAY, LABRA-CADABRA-DOR!
FROM RIDER
RIDER WOOFSON, HUH?

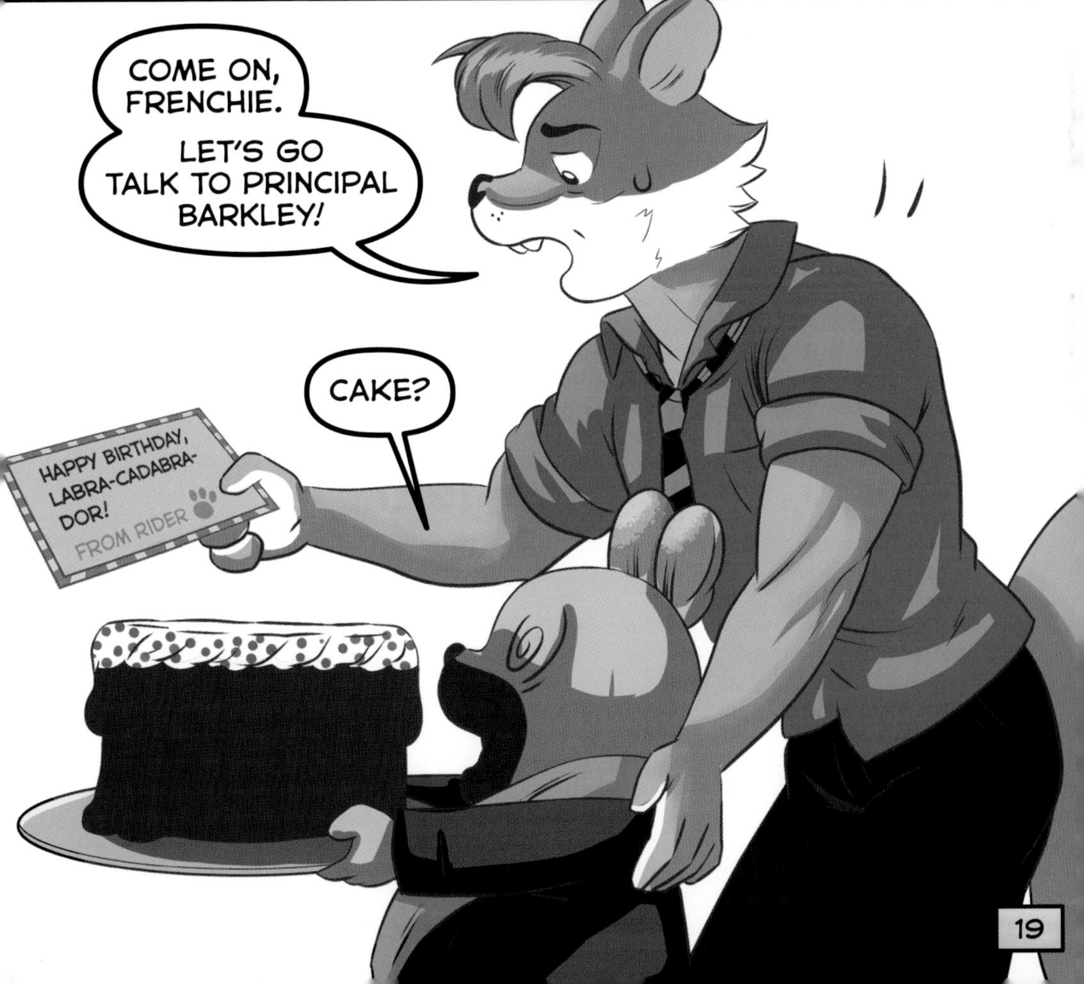
COME ON, FRENCHIE.
LET'S GO TALK TO PRINCIPAL BARKLEY!
CAKE?
HAPPY BIRTHDAY, LABRA-CADABRA-DOR!
FROM RIDER

CHAPTER 2

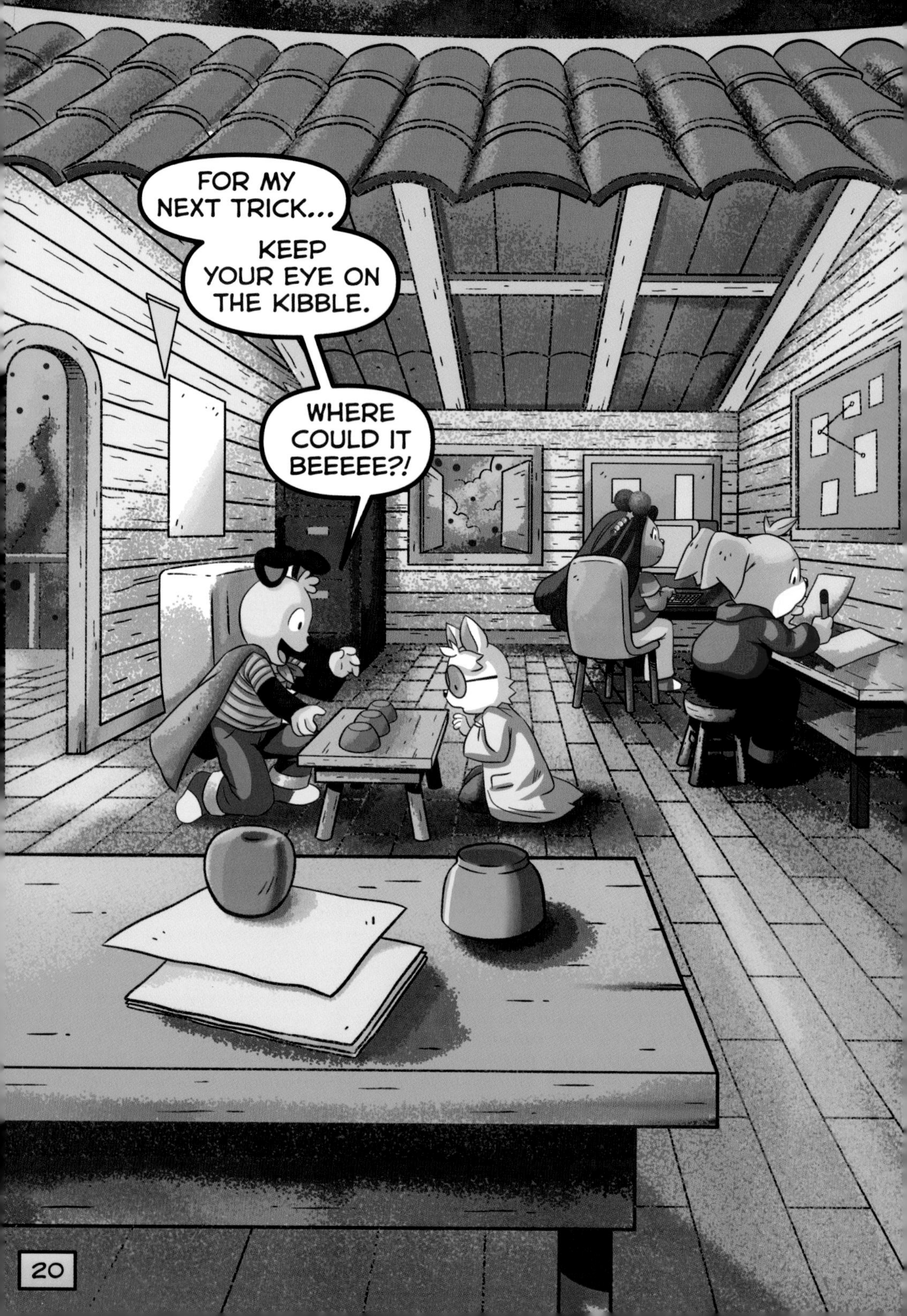
FOR MY NEXT TRICK...
KEEP YOUR EYE ON THE KIBBLE.
WHERE COULD IT BEEEEE?!

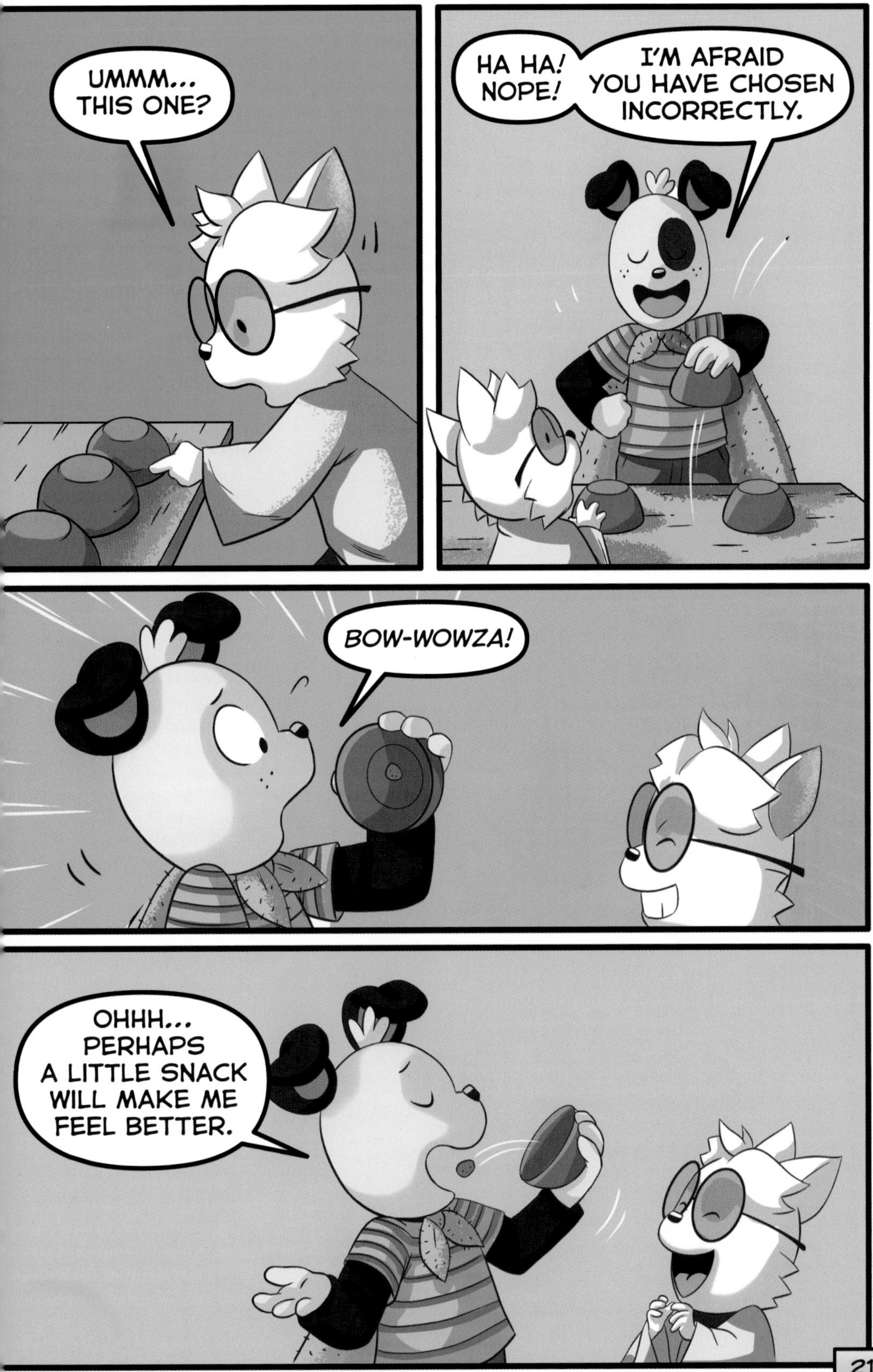
UMMM... THIS ONE?
HA HA! NOPE!
I'M AFRAID YOU HAVE CHOSEN INCORRECTLY.
BOW-WOWZA!
OHHH... PERHAPS A LITTLE SNACK WILL MAKE ME FEEL BETTER.

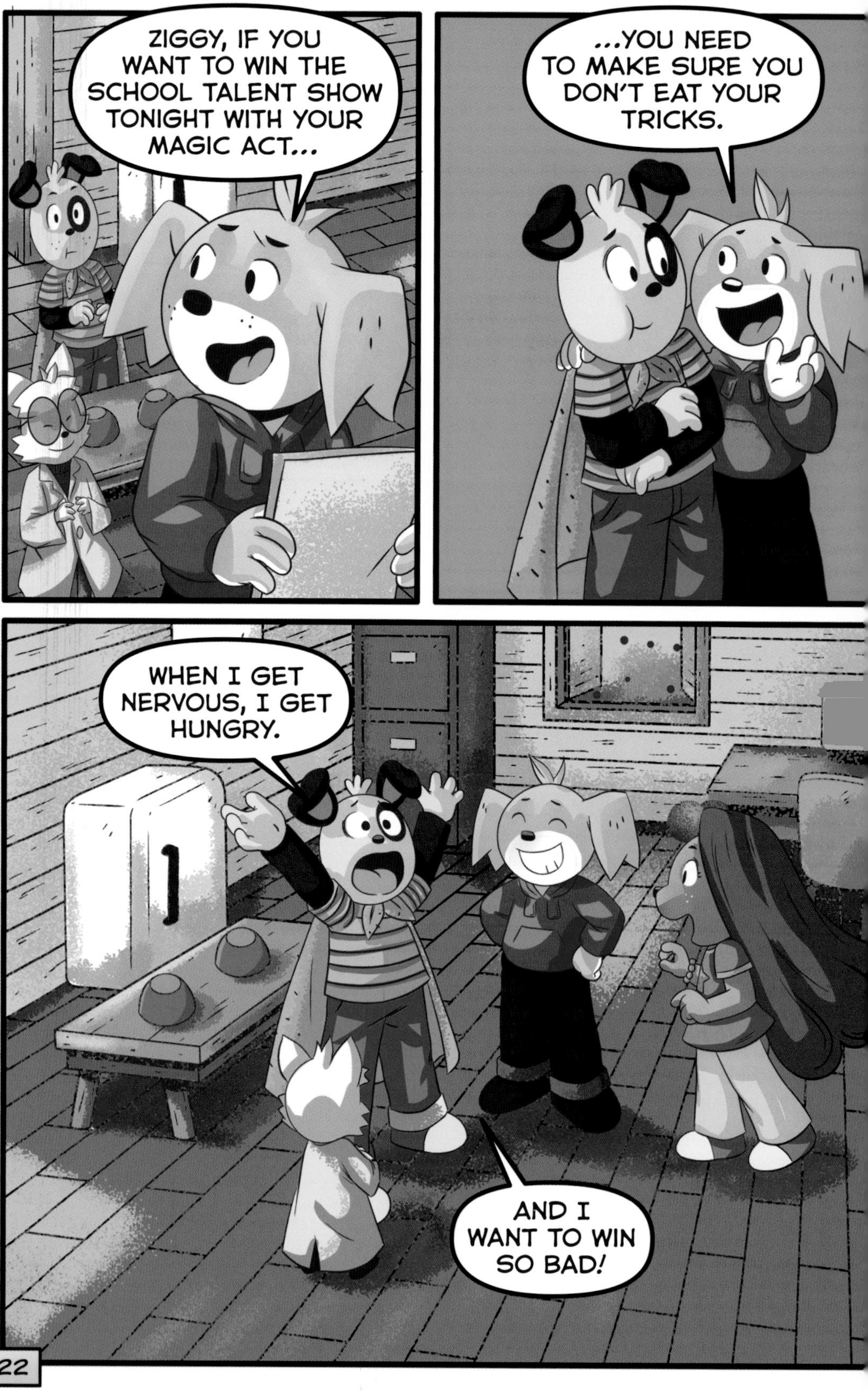
ZIGGY, IF YOU WANT TO WIN THE SCHOOL TALENT SHOW TONIGHT WITH YOUR MAGIC ACT...
...YOU NEED TO MAKE SURE YOU DON'T EAT YOUR TRICKS.
WHEN I GET NERVOUS, I GET HUNGRY.
AND I WANT TO WIN SO BAD!

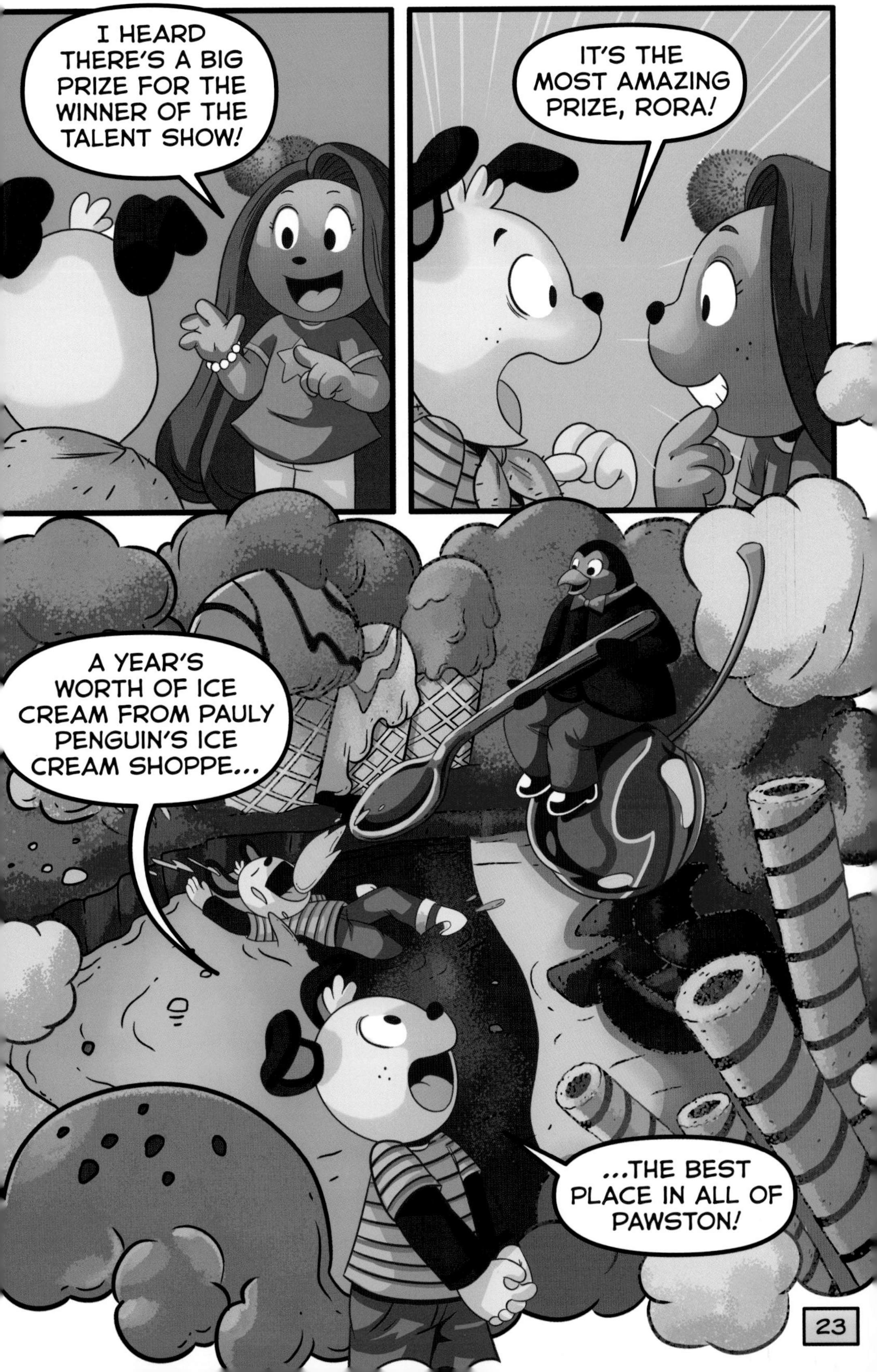
I HEARD THERE'S A BIG PRIZE FOR THE WINNER OF THE TALENT SHOW!
IT'S THE MOST AMAZING PRIZE, RORA!
A YEAR'S WORTH OF ICE CREAM FROM PAULY PENGUIN'S ICE CREAM SHOPPE...
...THE BEST PLACE IN ALL OF PAWSTON!

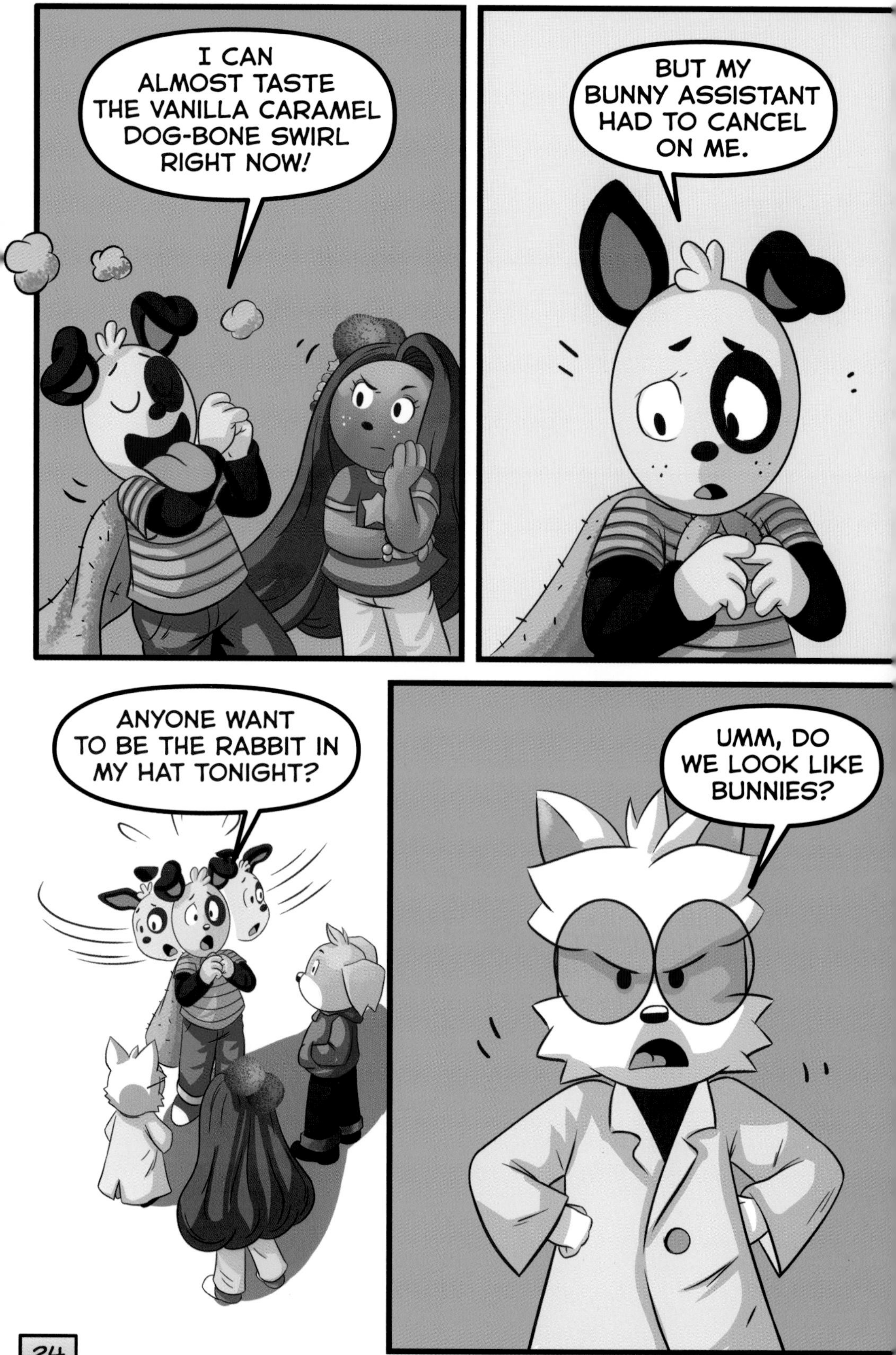
I CAN ALMOST TASTE THE VANILLA CARAMEL DOG-BONE SWIRL RIGHT NOW!
BUT MY BUNNY ASSISTANT HAD TO CANCEL ON ME.
ANYONE WANT TO BE THE RABBIT IN MY HAT TONIGHT?
UMM, DO WE LOOK LIKE BUNNIES?

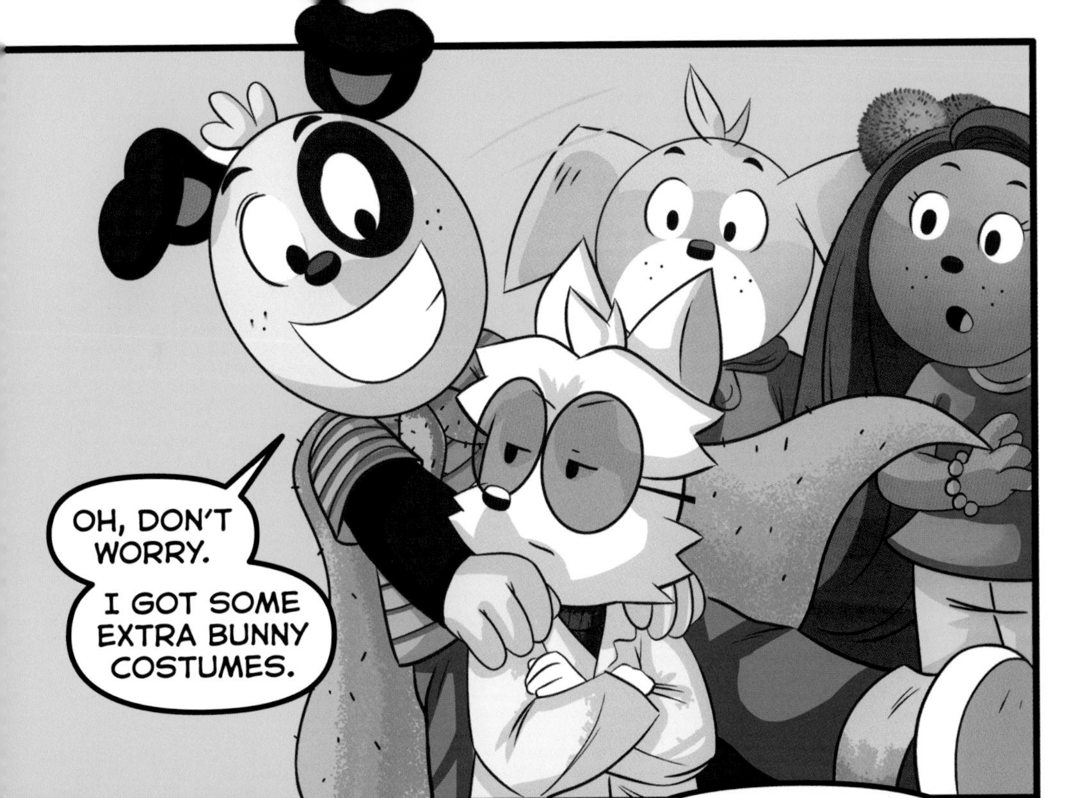
OH, DON'T WORRY.
I GOT SOME EXTRA BUNNY COSTUMES.

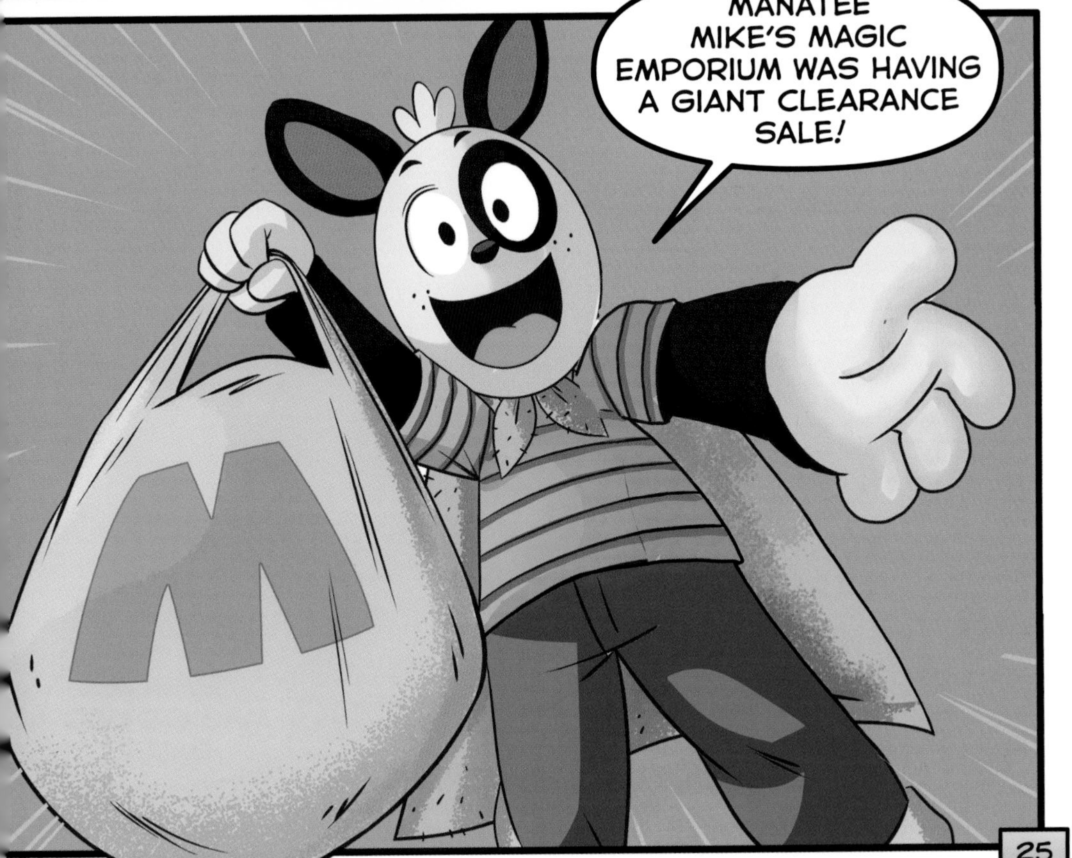
MANATEE MIKE'S MAGIC EMPORIUM WAS HAVING A GIANT CLEARANCE SALE!

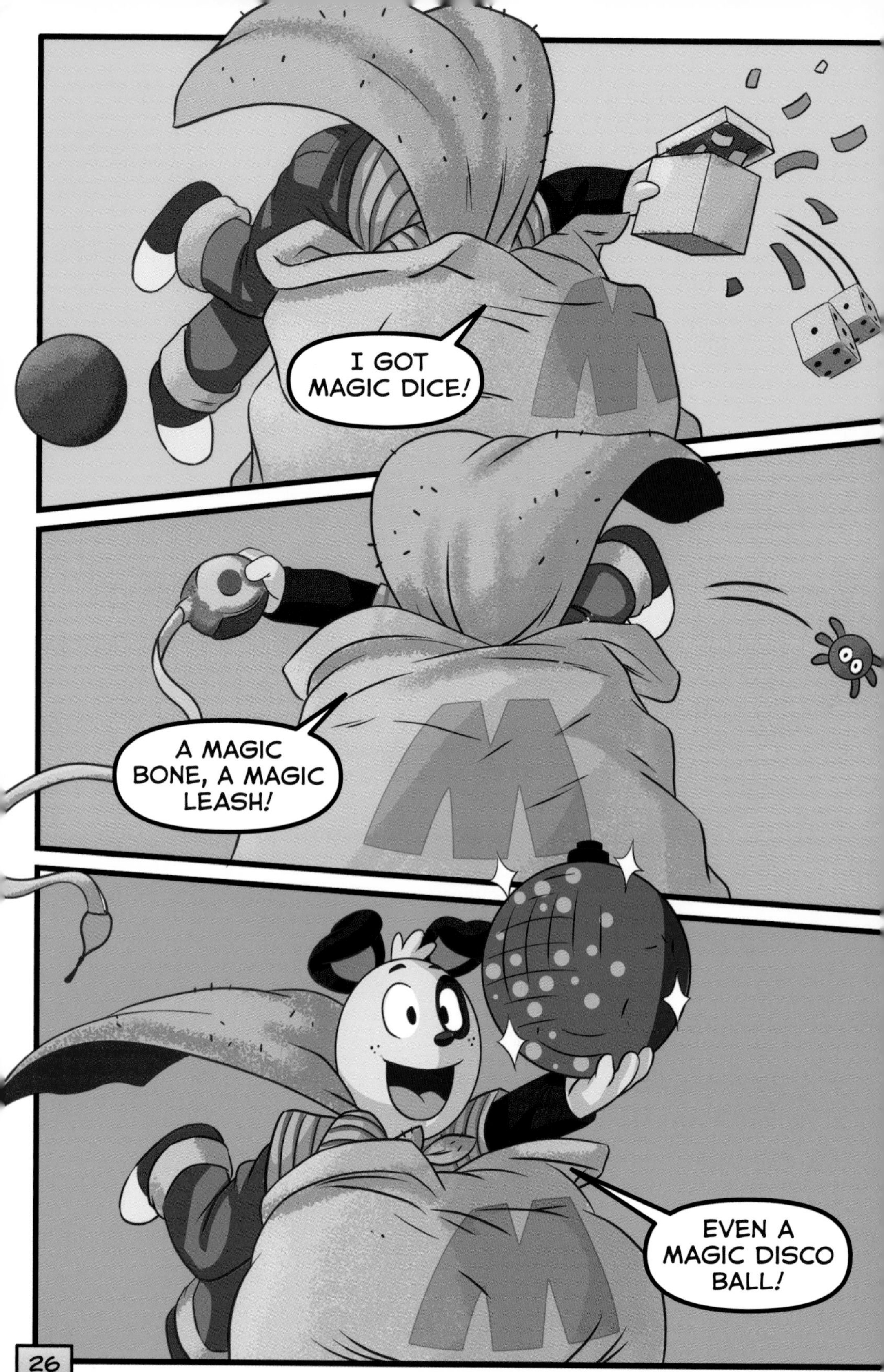
I GOT MAGIC DICE!
A MAGIC BONE, A MAGIC LEASH!
EVEN A MAGIC DISCO BALL!

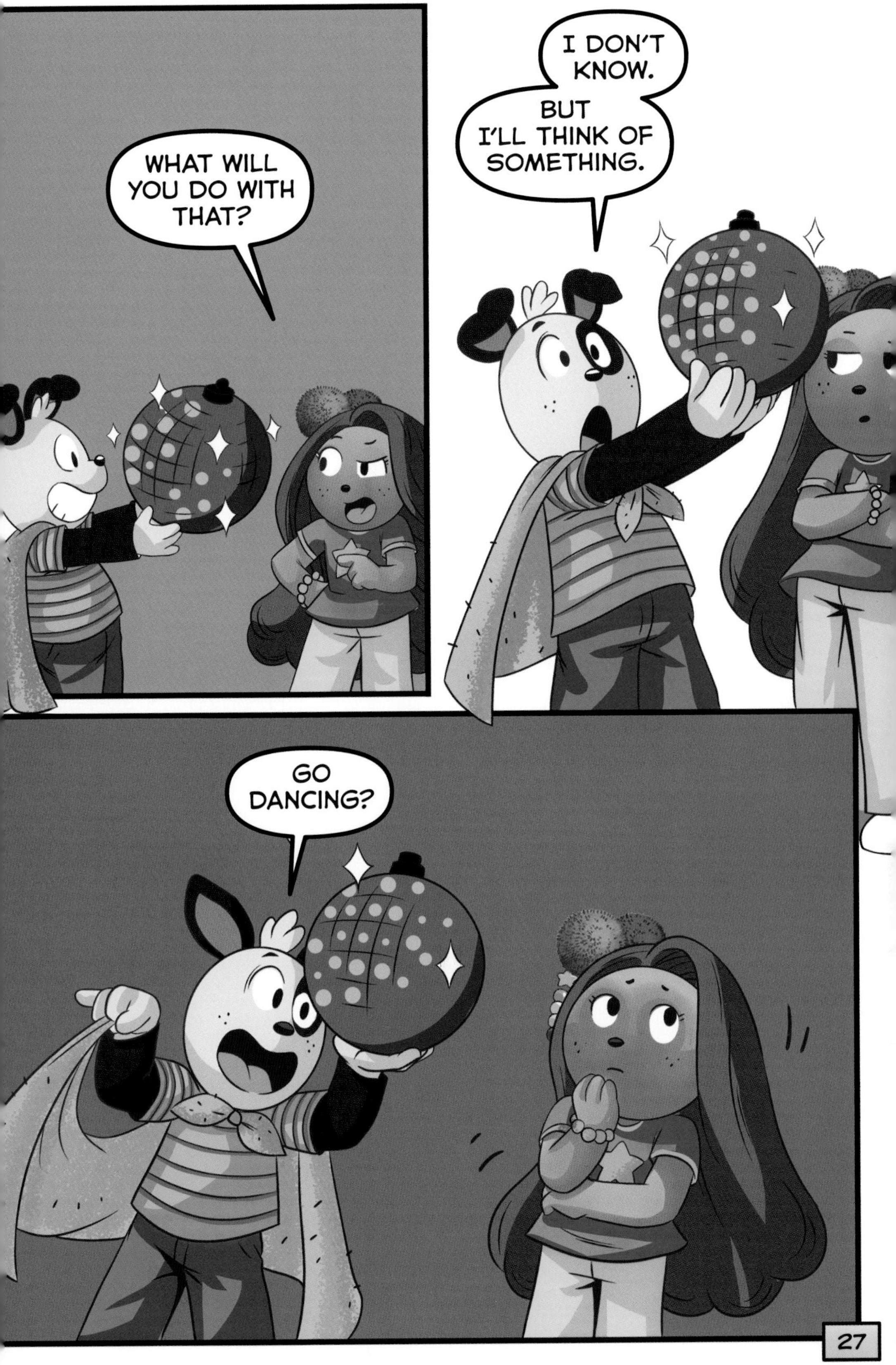
WHAT WILL YOU DO WITH THAT?
I DON'T KNOW.
BUT I'LL THINK OF SOMETHING.
GO DANCING?

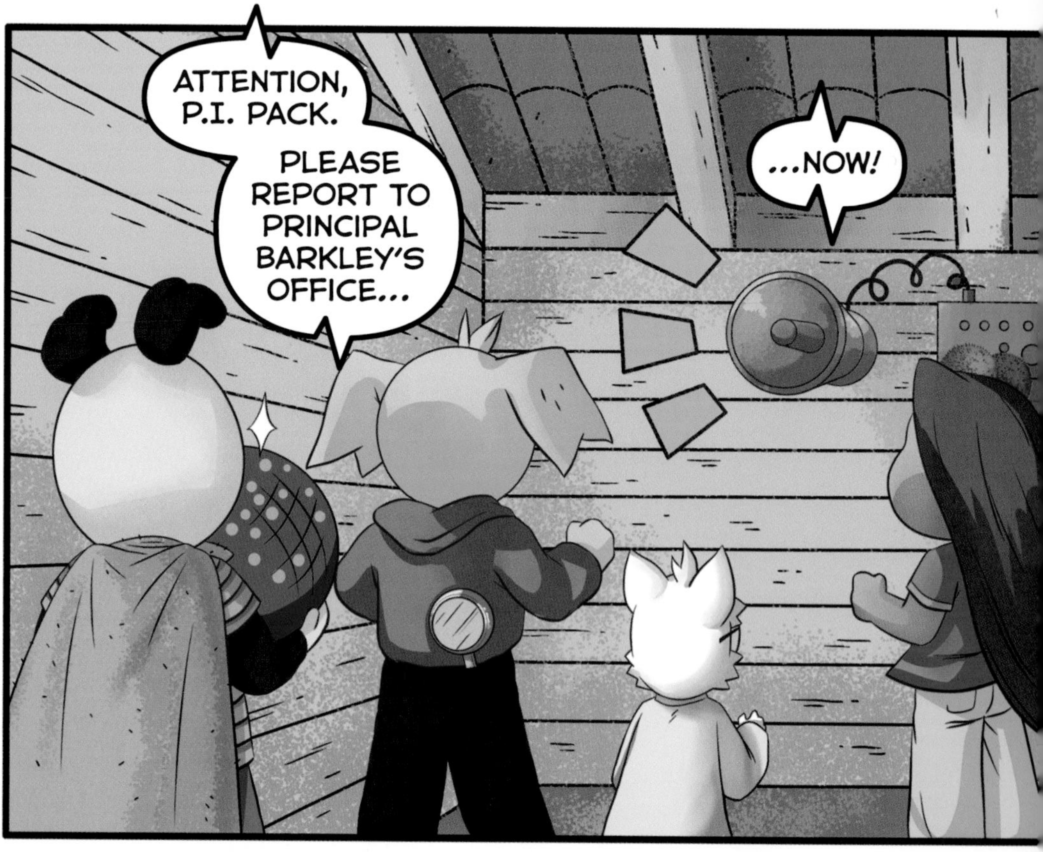
ATTENTION, P.I. PACK.
PLEASE REPORT TO PRINCIPAL BARKLEY'S OFFICE...
...NOW!

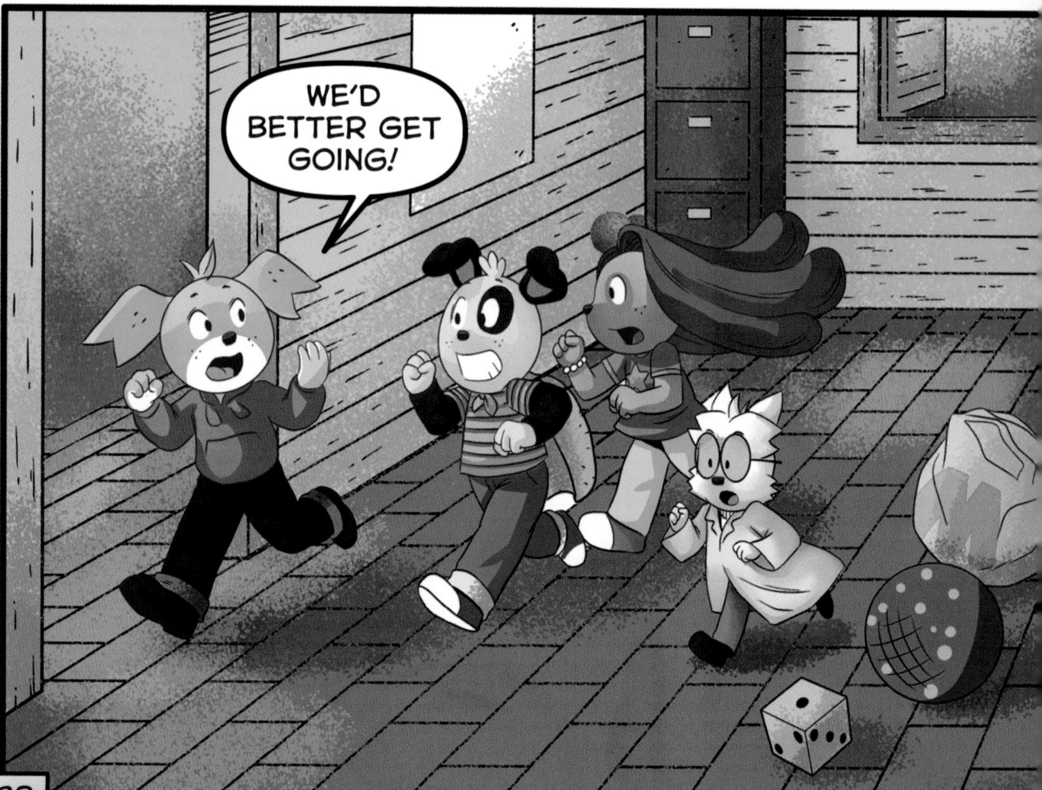
WE'D BETTER GET GOING!

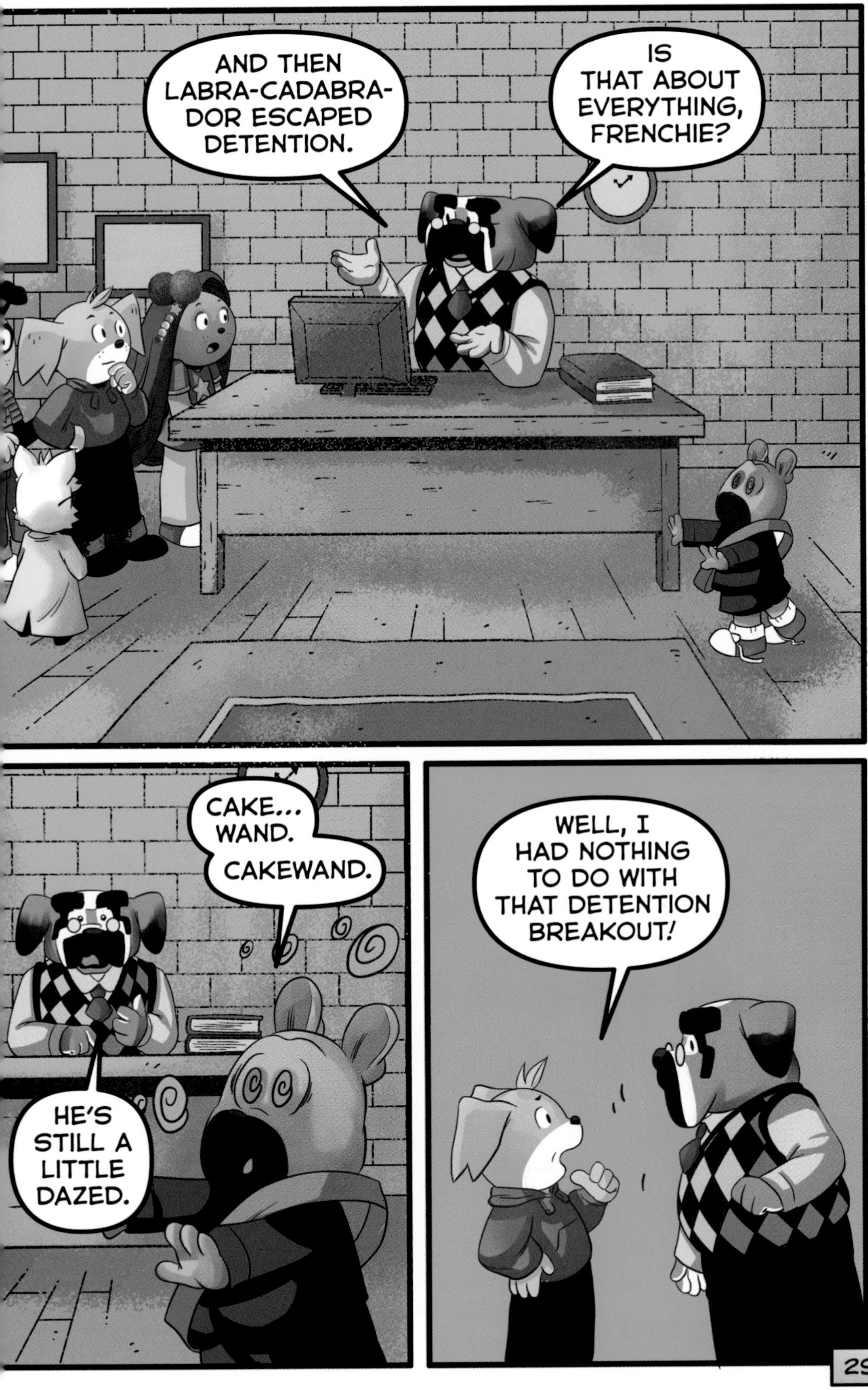
AND THEN LABRA-CADABRA-DOR ESCAPED DETENTION.
IS THAT ABOUT EVERYTHING, FRENCHIE?
CAKE... WAND.
CAKEWAND.
HE'S STILL A LITTLE DAZED.
WELL, I HAD NOTHING TO DO WITH THAT DETENTION BREAKOUT!

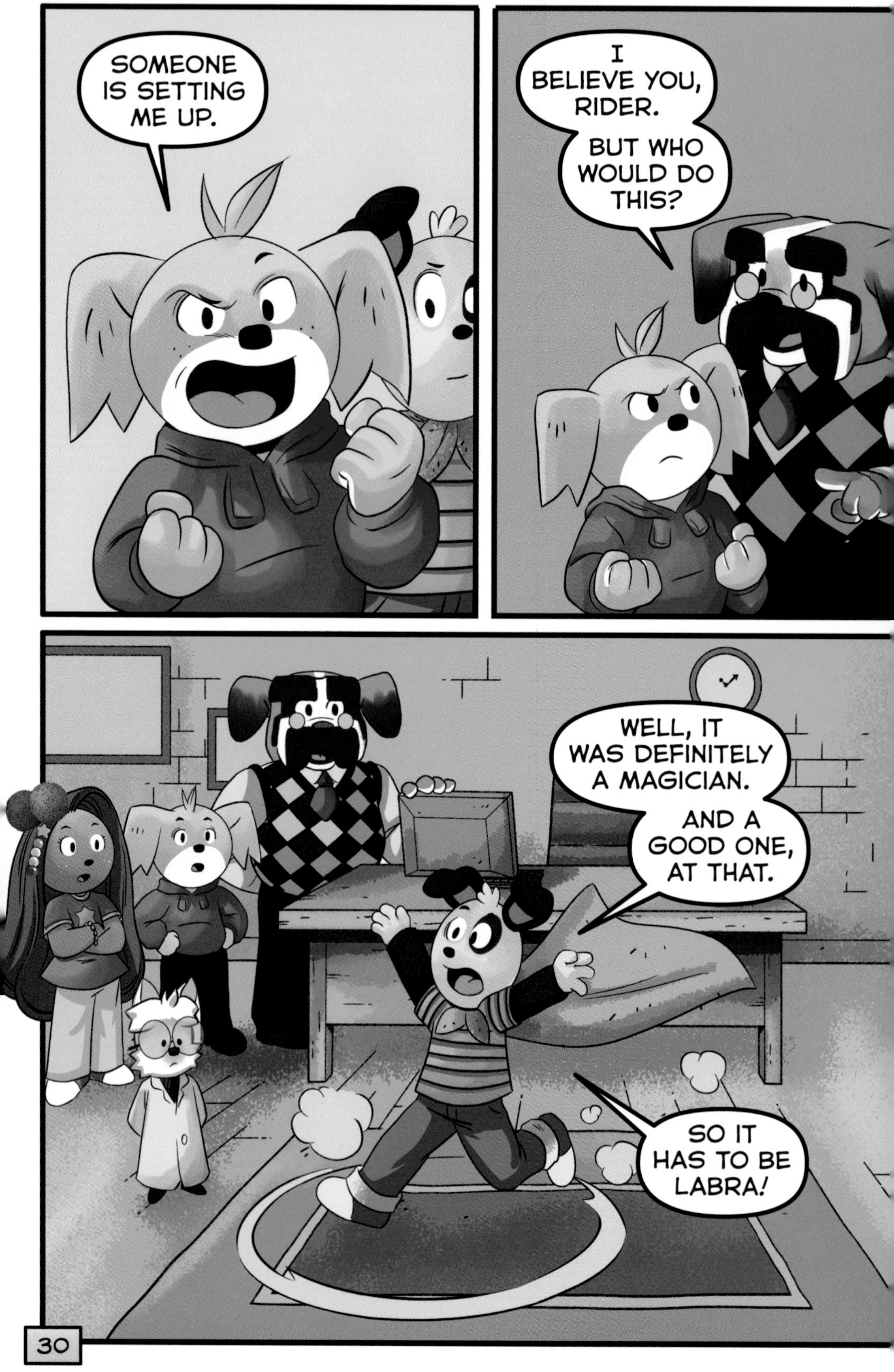
SOMEONE IS SETTING ME UP.
I BELIEVE YOU, RIDER.
BUT WHO WOULD DO THIS?
WELL, IT WAS DEFINITELY A MAGICIAN.
AND A GOOD ONE, AT THAT.
SO IT HAS TO BE LABRA!

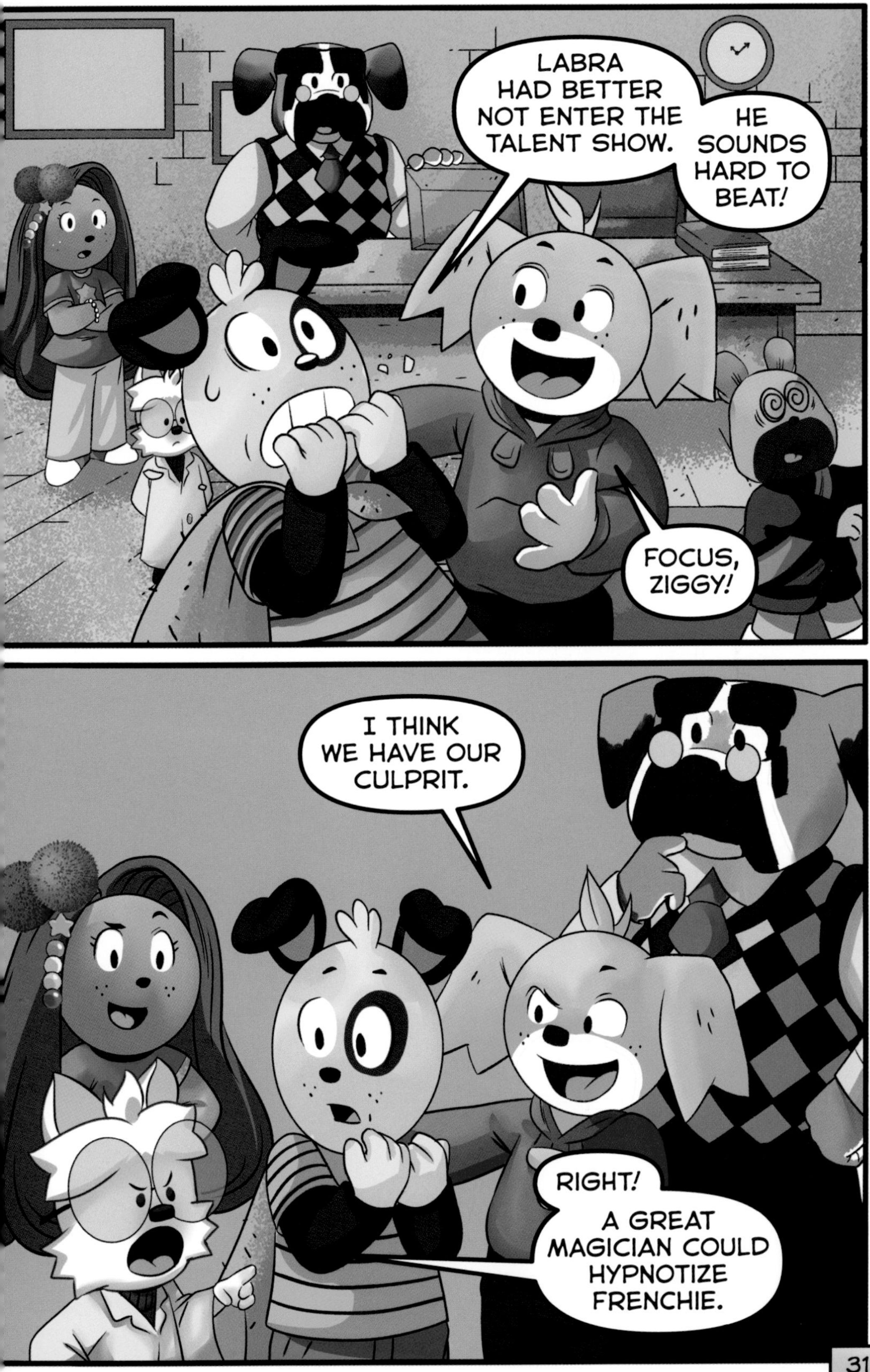
LABRA HAD BETTER NOT ENTER THE TALENT SHOW.
HE SOUNDS HARD TO BEAT!
FOCUS, ZIGGY!
I THINK WE HAVE OUR CULPRIT.
RIGHT!
A GREAT MAGICIAN COULD HYPNOTIZE FRENCHIE.

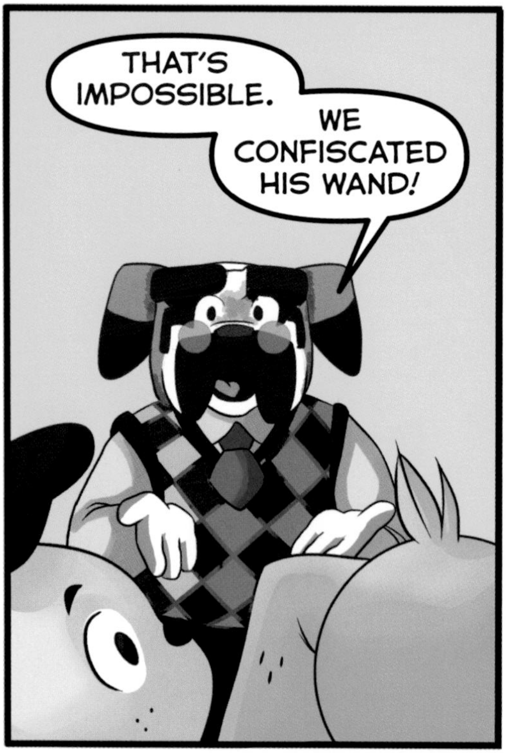
THAT'S IMPOSSIBLE.
WE CONFISCATED HIS WAND!

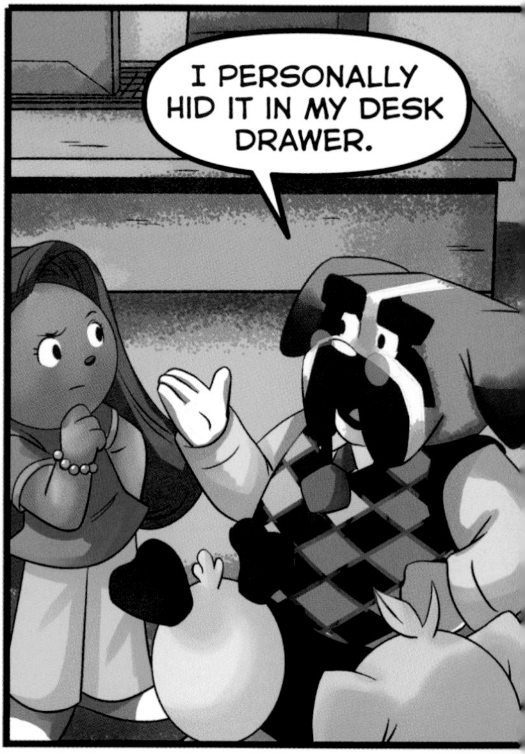
I PERSONALLY HID IT IN MY DESK DRAWER.

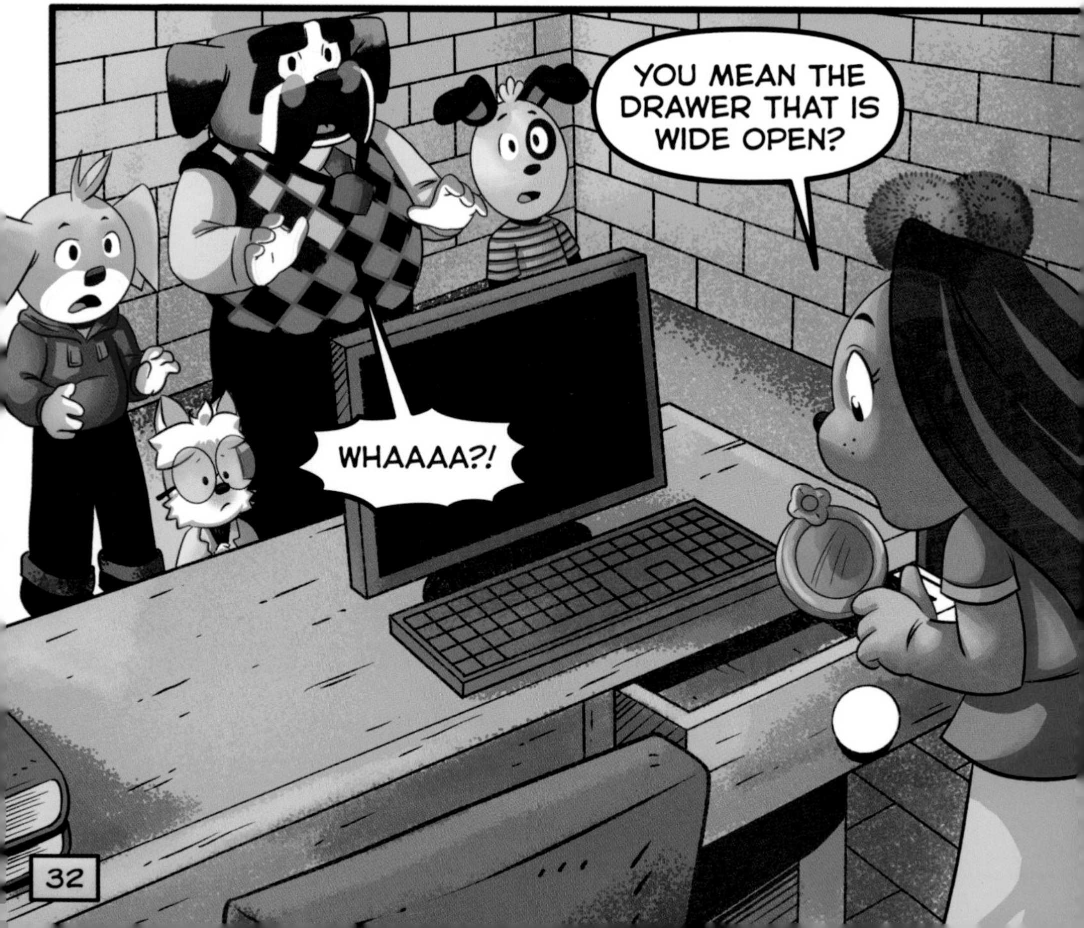
YOU MEAN THE DRAWER THAT IS WIDE OPEN?
WHAAAA?!

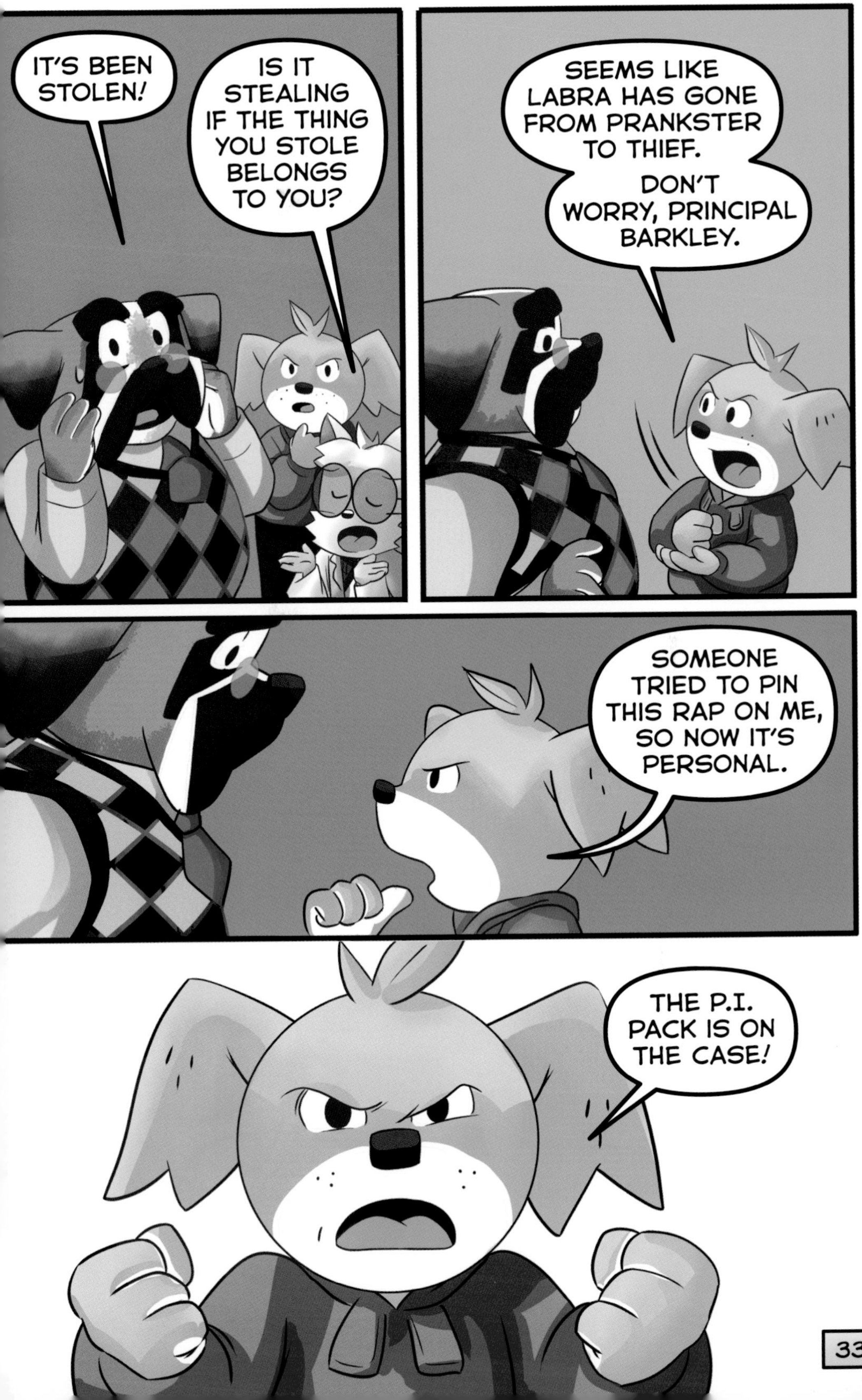
IT'S BEEN STOLEN!
IS IT STEALING IF THE THING YOU STOLE BELONGS TO YOU?
SEEMS LIKE LABRA HAS GONE FROM PRANKSTER TO THIEF.
DON'T WORRY, PRINCIPAL BARKLEY.
SOMEONE TRIED TO PIN THIS RAP ON ME, SO NOW IT'S PERSONAL.
THE P.I. PACK IS ON THE CASE!

CHAPTER 3

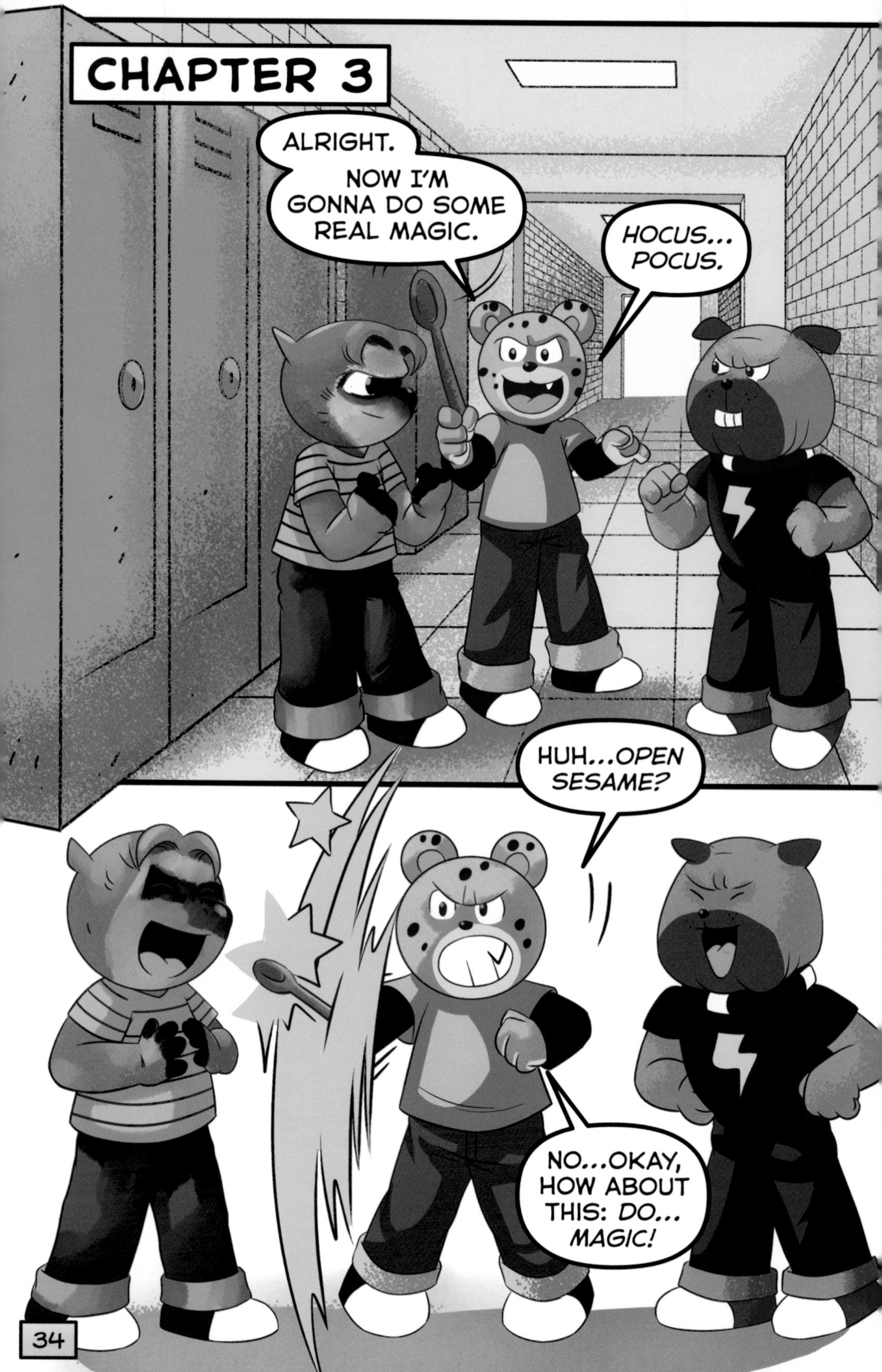
ALRIGHT.
NOW I'M GONNA DO SOME REAL MAGIC.
HOCUS... POCUS.
HUH...OPEN SESAME?
NO...OKAY, HOW ABOUT THIS: DO... MAGIC!

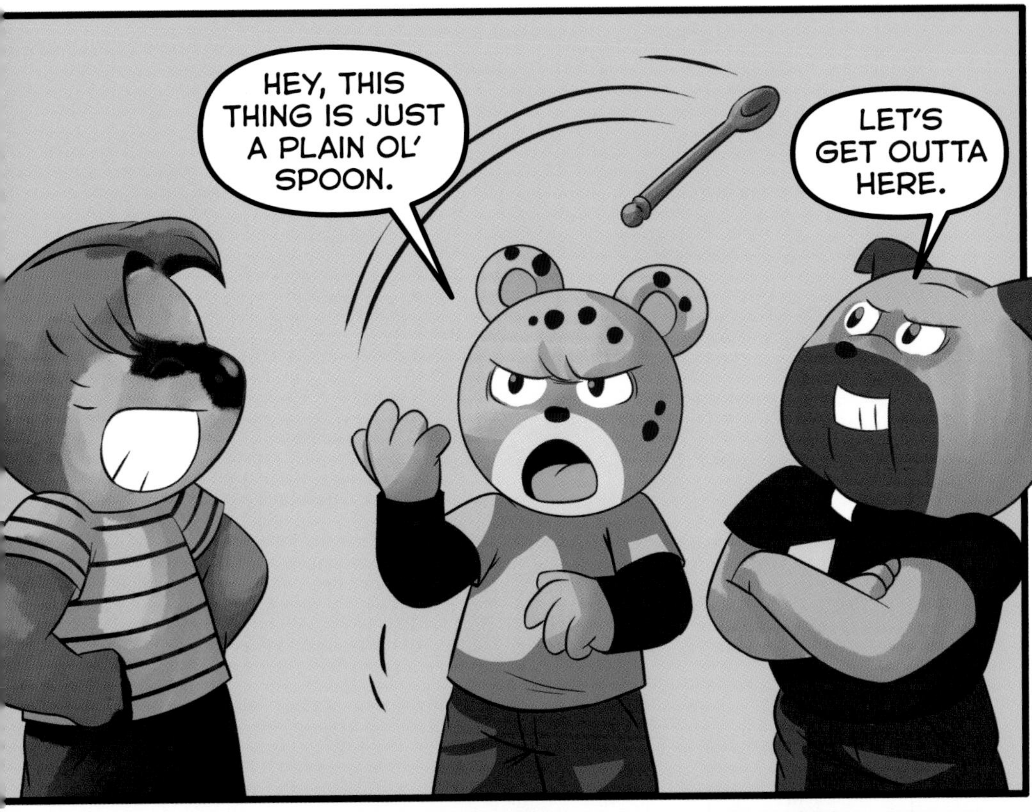
HEY, THIS THING IS JUST A PLAIN OL' SPOON.
LET'S GET OUTTA HERE.

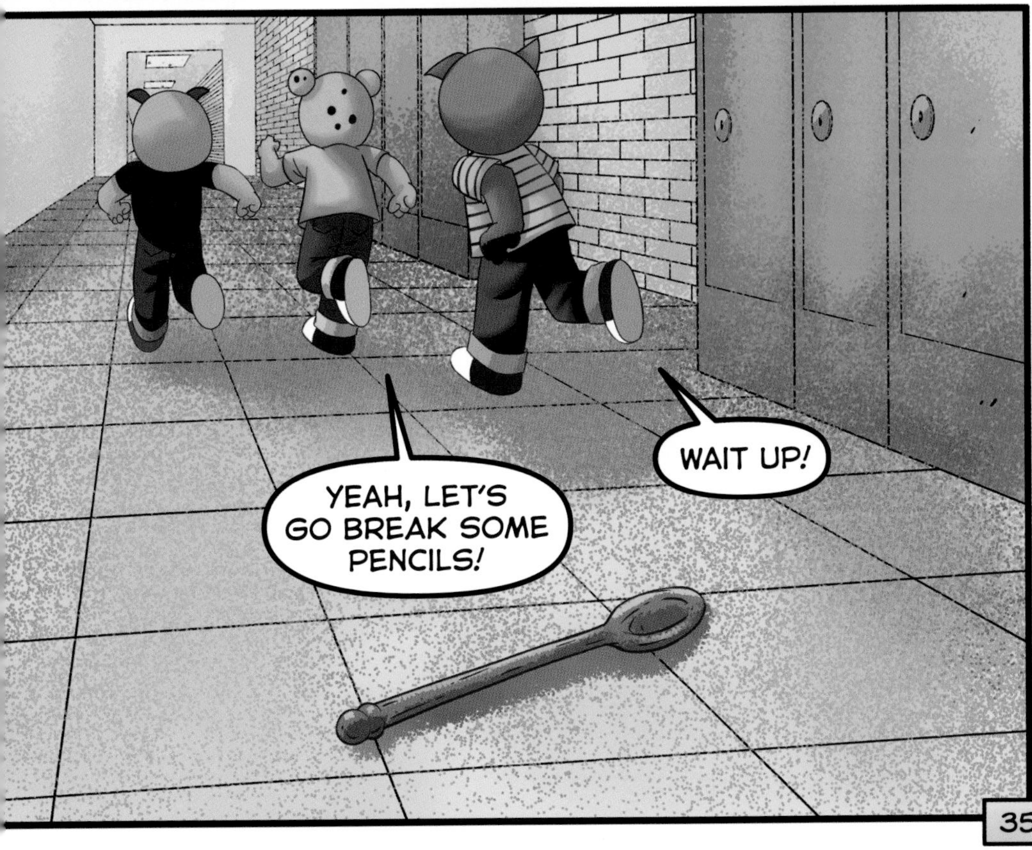
WAIT UP!
YEAH, LET'S GO BREAK SOME PENCILS!

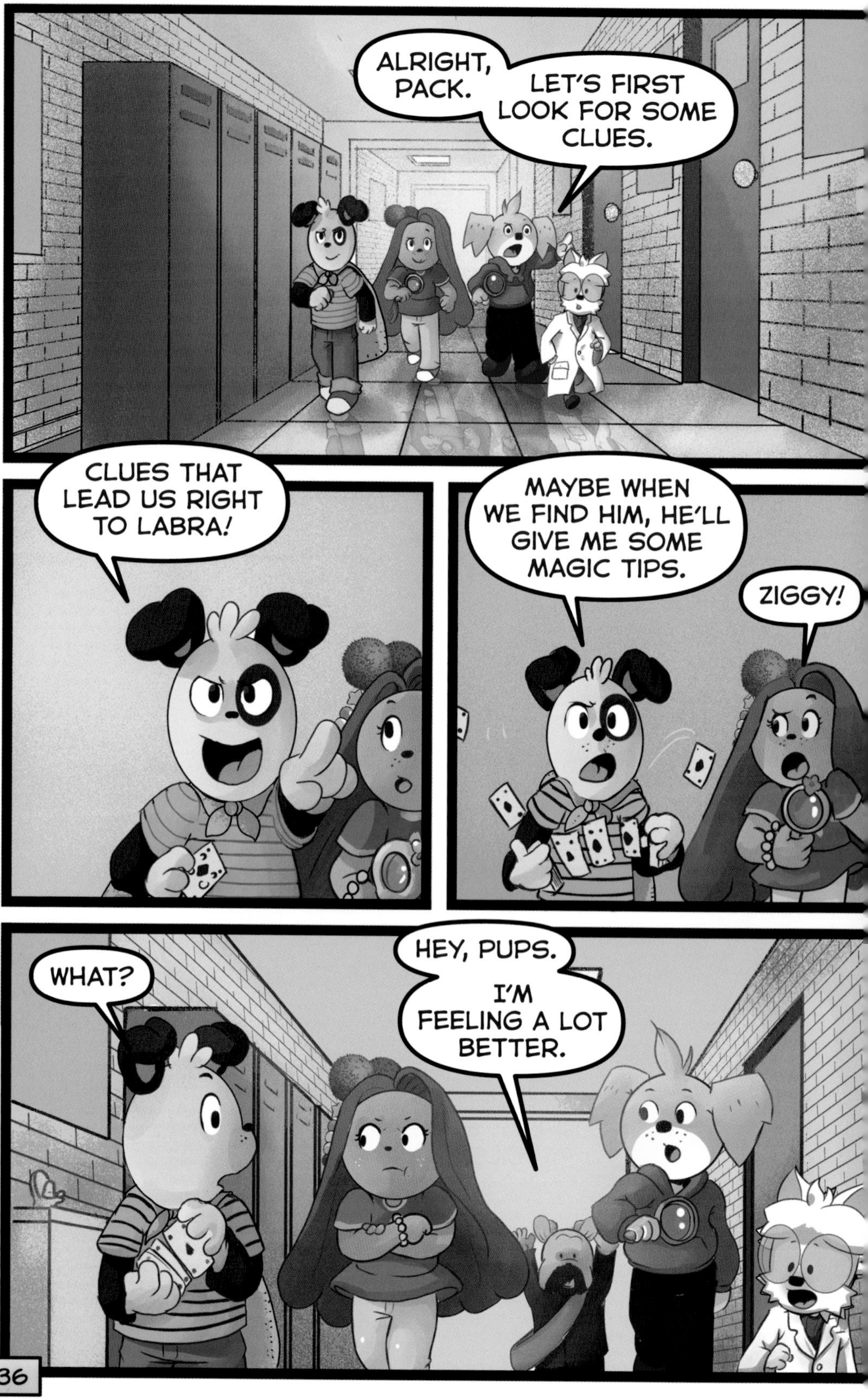
ALRIGHT, PACK.
LET'S FIRST LOOK FOR SOME CLUES.
CLUES THAT LEAD US RIGHT TO LABRA!
MAYBE WHEN WE FIND HIM, HE'LL GIVE ME SOME MAGIC TIPS.
ZIGGY!
WHAT?
HEY, PUPS.
I'M FEELING A LOT BETTER.

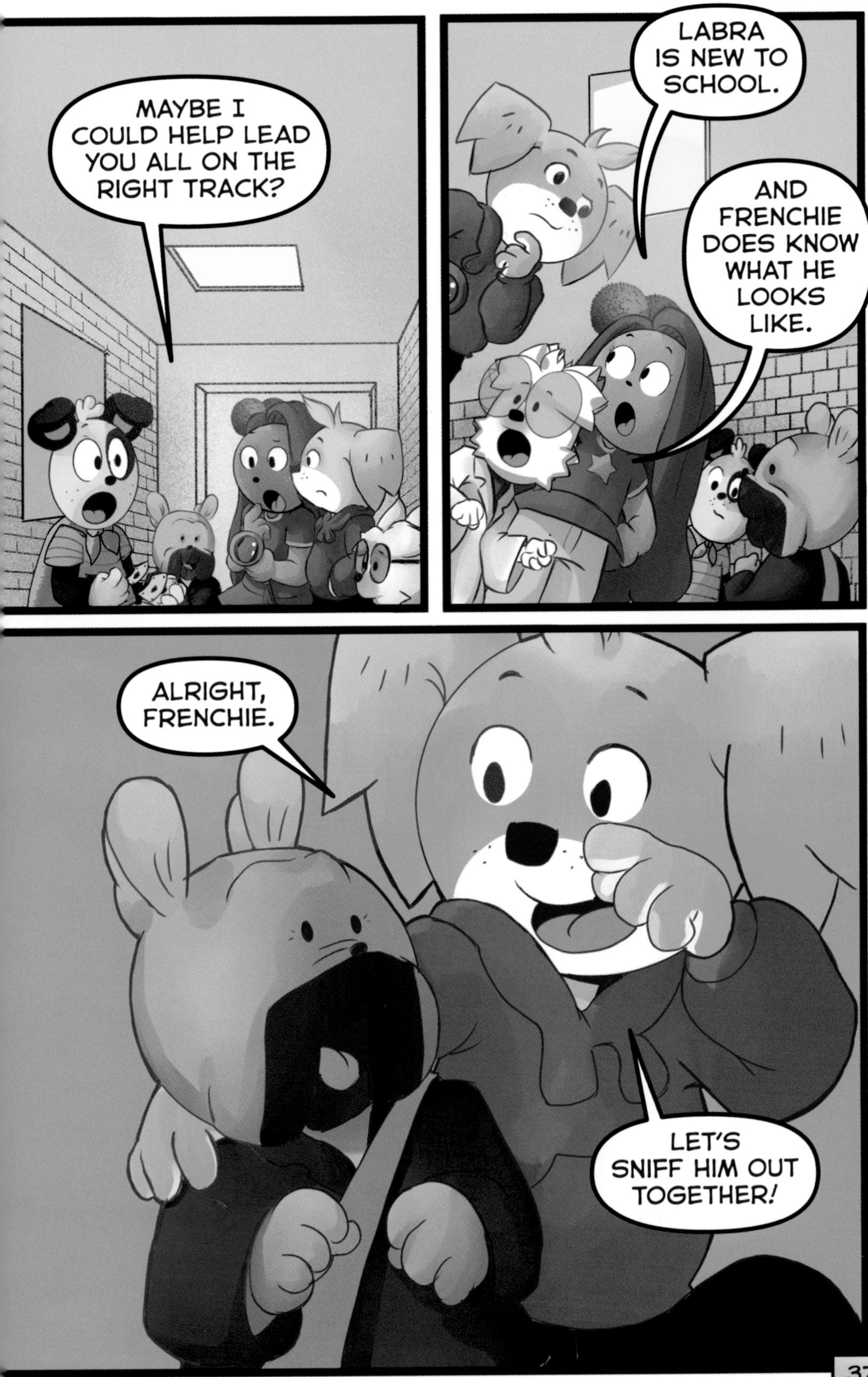

MAYBE I COULD HELP LEAD YOU ALL ON THE RIGHT TRACK?
LABRA IS NEW TO SCHOOL.
AND FRENCHIE DOES KNOW WHAT HE LOOKS LIKE.
ALRIGHT, FRENCHIE.
LET'S SNIFF HIM OUT TOGETHER!

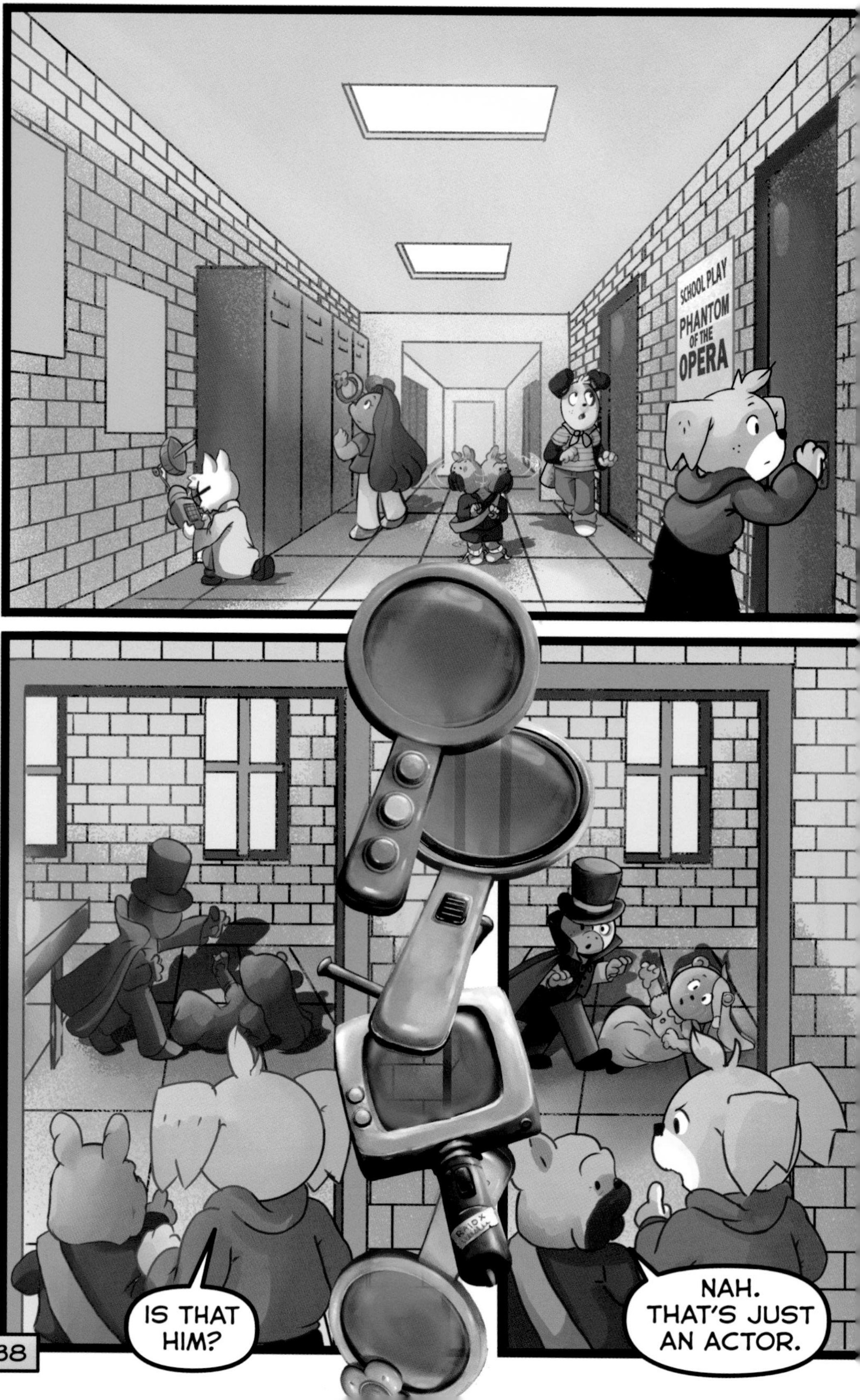
SCHOOL PLAY
PHANTOM OF THE OPERA
IS THAT HIM?
NAH. THAT'S JUST AN ACTOR.

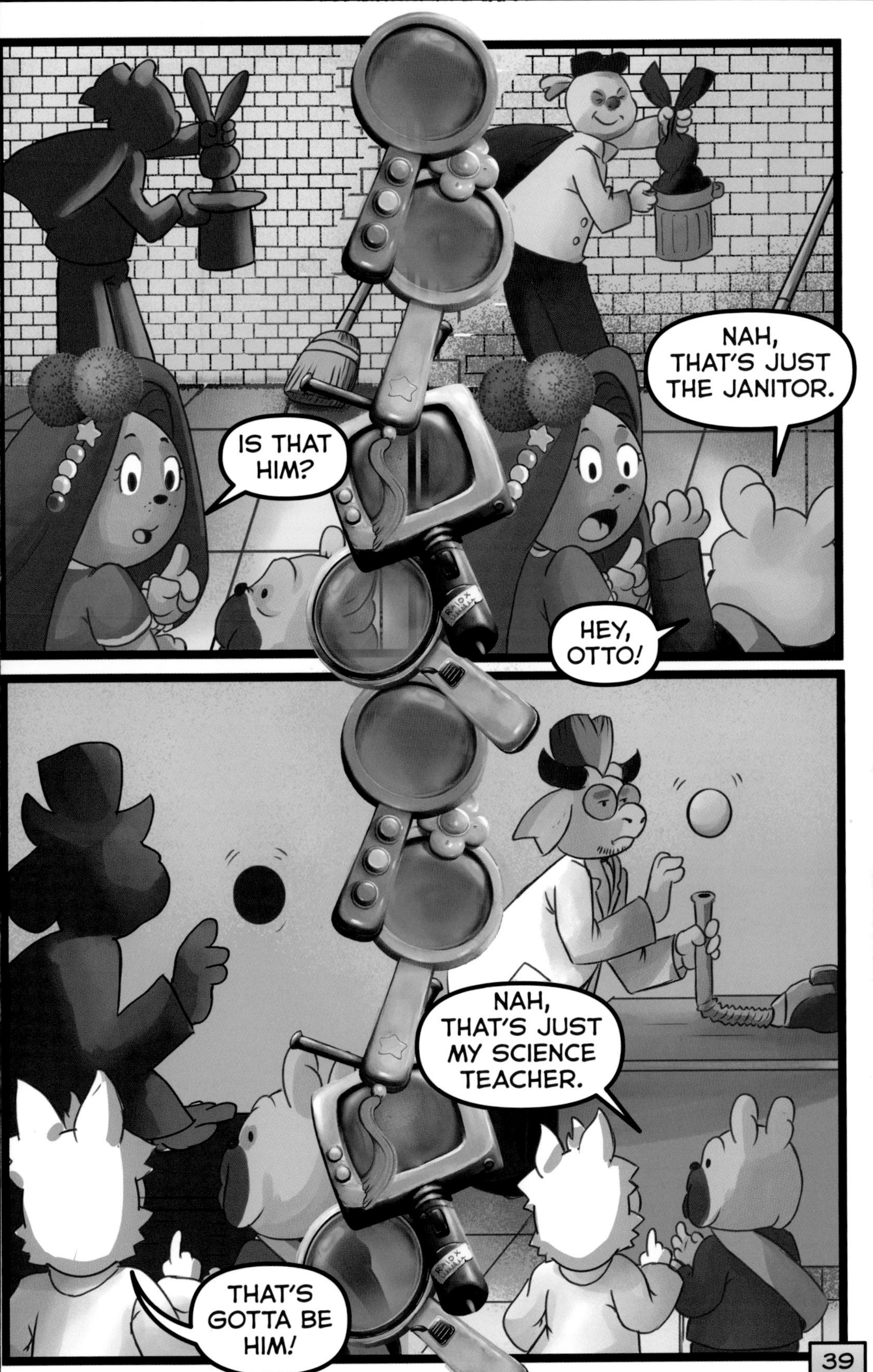
IS THAT HIM?
NAH, THAT'S JUST THE JANITOR.
HEY, OTTO!
NAH, THAT'S JUST MY SCIENCE TEACHER.
THAT'S GOTTA BE HIM!

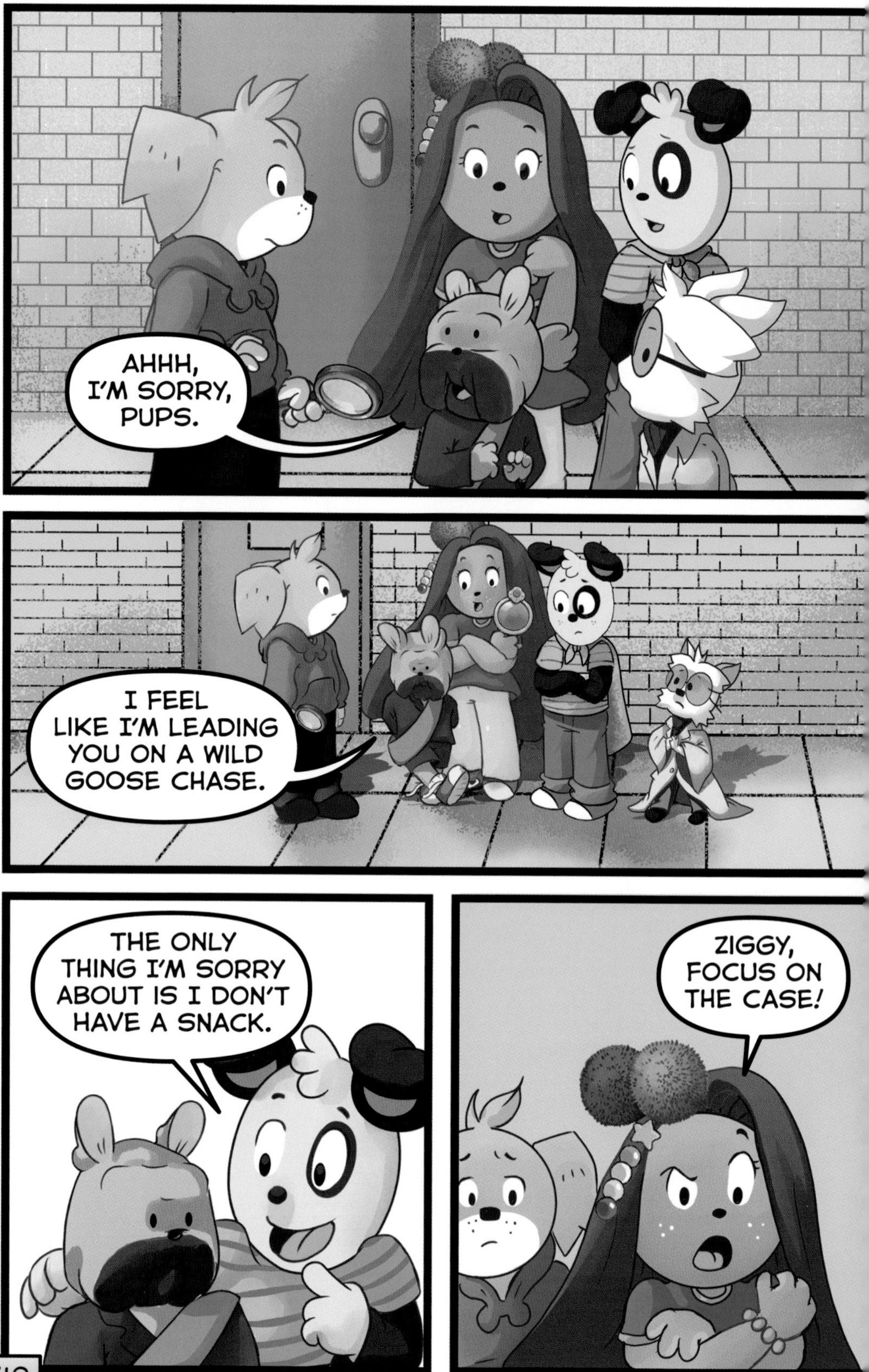
AHHH, I'M SORRY, PUPS.
I FEEL LIKE I'M LEADING YOU ON A WILD GOOSE CHASE.
THE ONLY THING I'M SORRY ABOUT IS I DON'T HAVE A SNACK.
ZIGGY, FOCUS ON THE CASE!

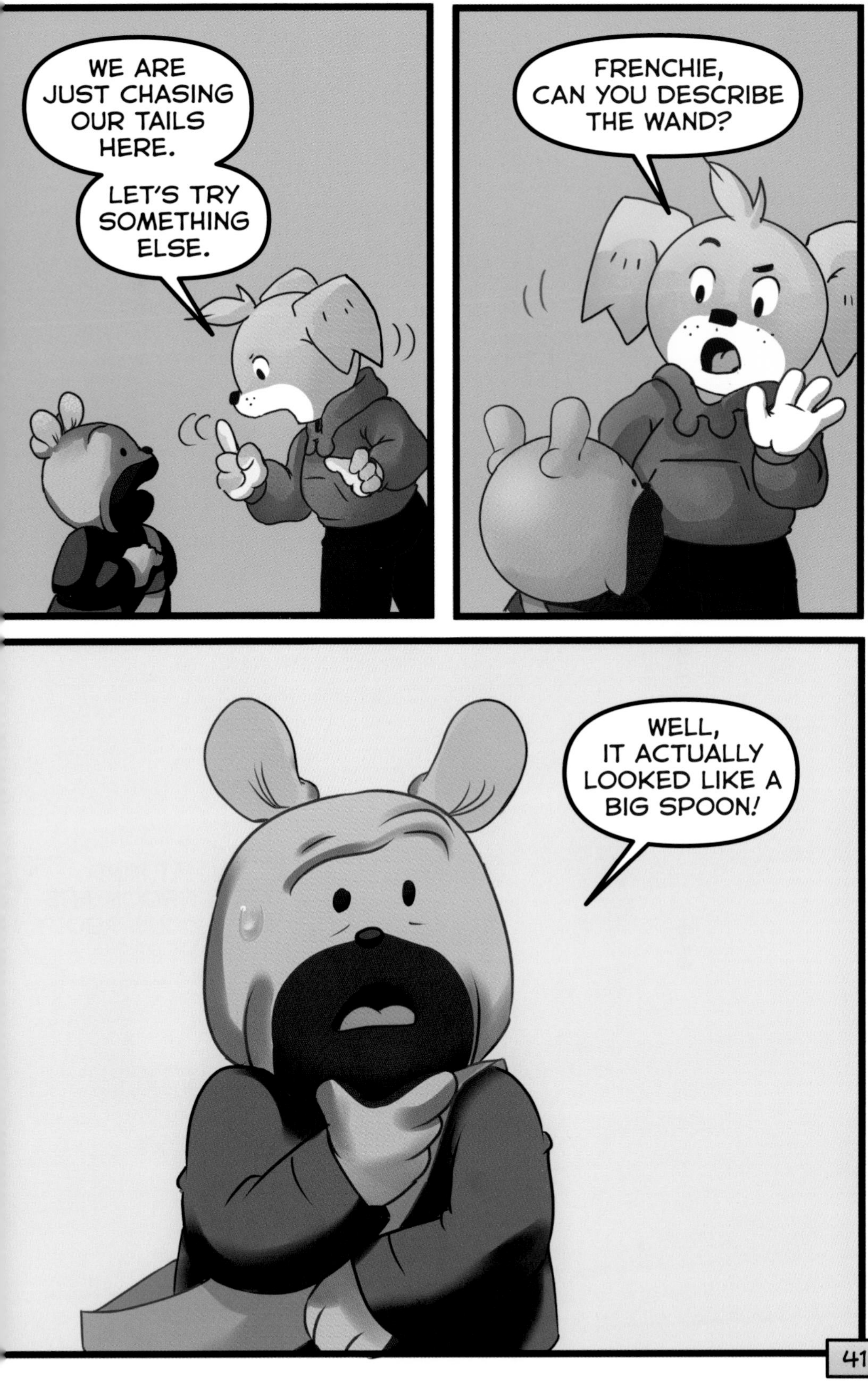
WE ARE JUST CHASING OUR TAILS HERE.
LET'S TRY SOMETHING ELSE.
FRENCHIE, CAN YOU DESCRIBE THE WAND?
WELL, IT ACTUALLY LOOKED LIKE A BIG SPOON!

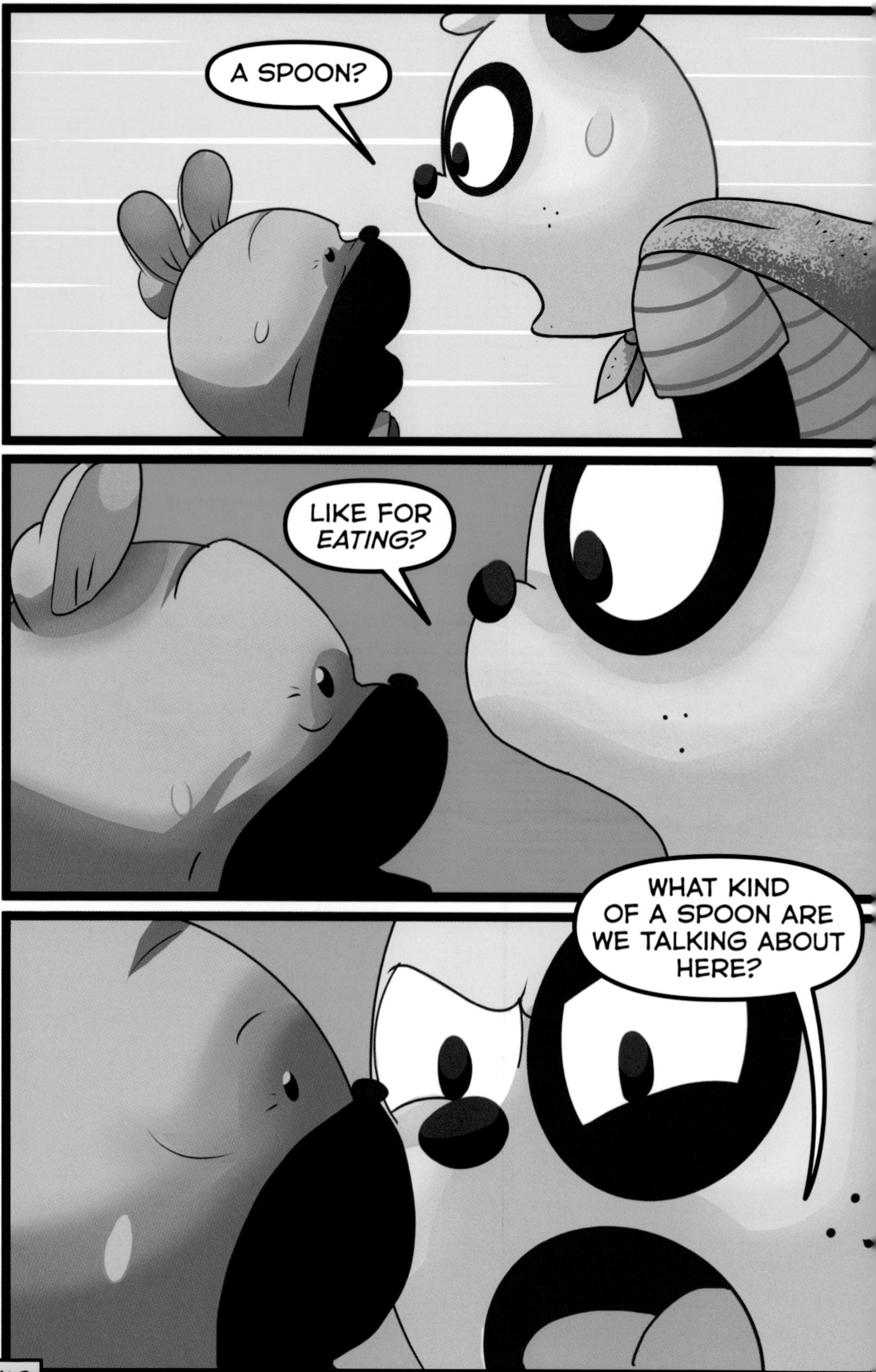
A SPOON?
LIKE FOR EATING?
WHAT KIND OF A SPOON ARE WE TALKING ABOUT HERE?

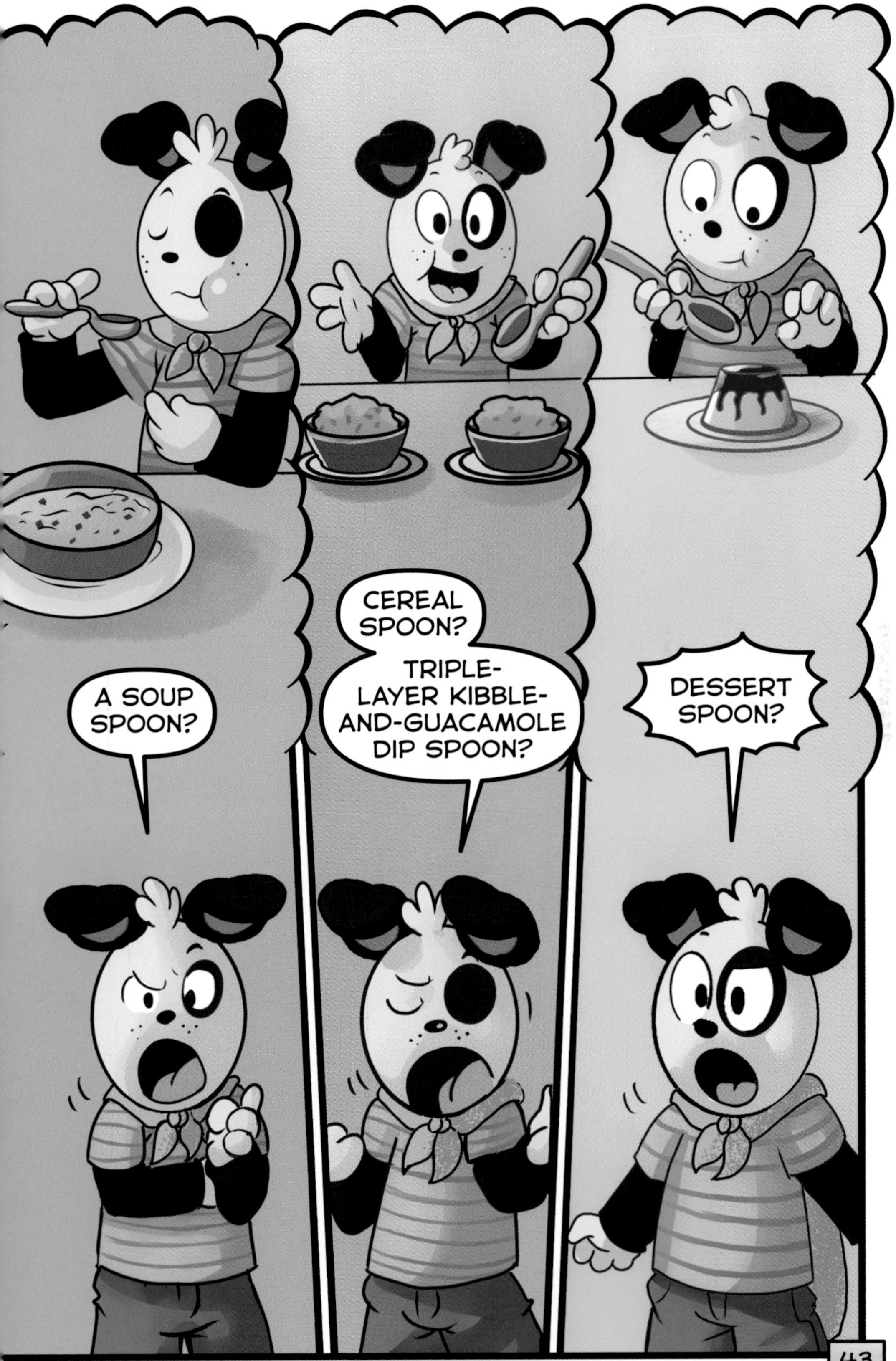
A SOUP SPOON?
CEREAL SPOON?
TRIPLE-LAYER KIBBLE-AND-GUACAMOLE DIP SPOON?
DESSERT SPOON?

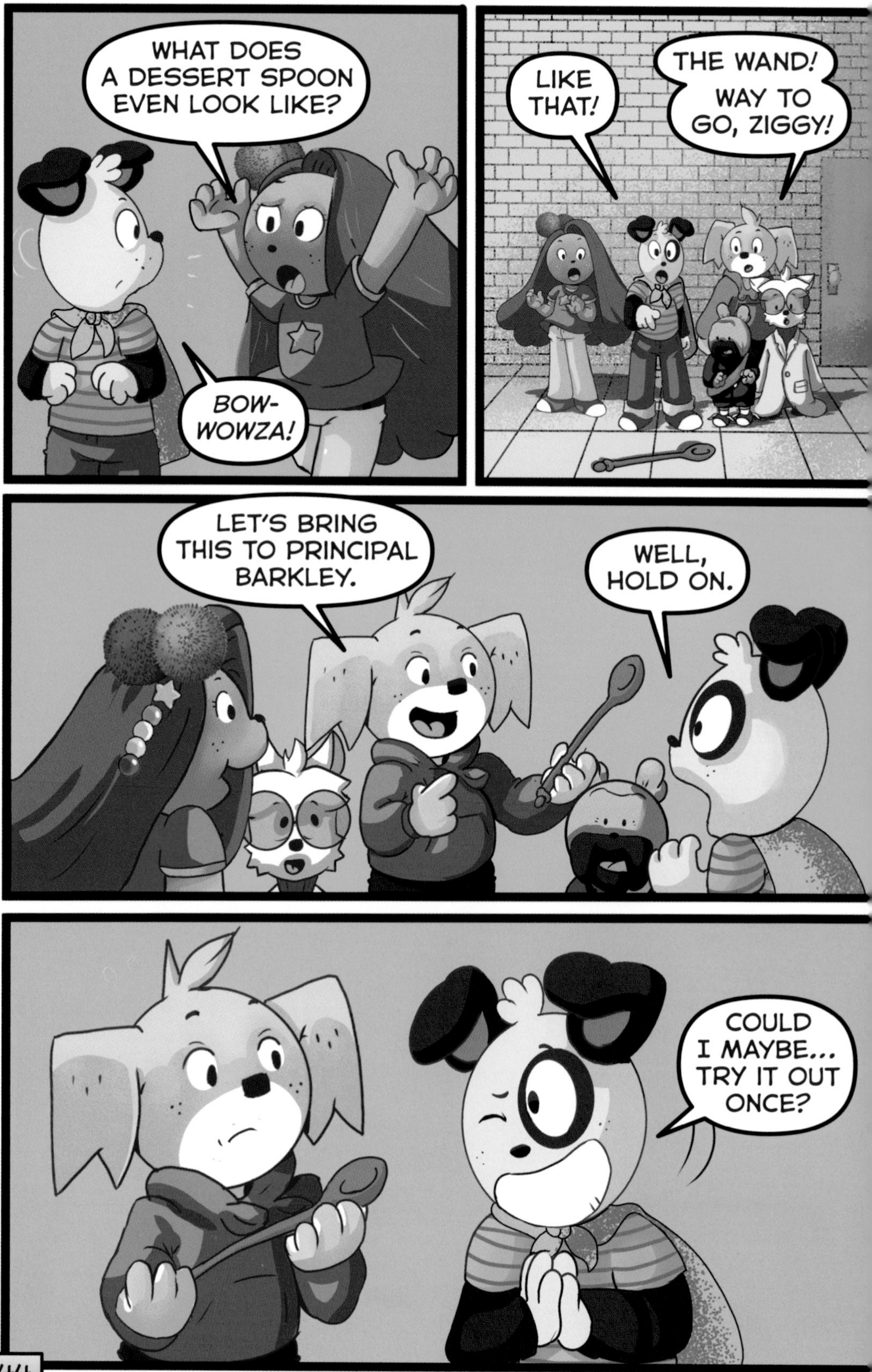
WHAT DOES A DESSERT SPOON EVEN LOOK LIKE?
BOW-WOWZA!
LIKE THAT!
THE WAND!
WAY TO GO, ZIGGY!
LET'S BRING THIS TO PRINCIPAL BARKLEY.
WELL, HOLD ON.
COULD I MAYBE... TRY IT OUT ONCE?

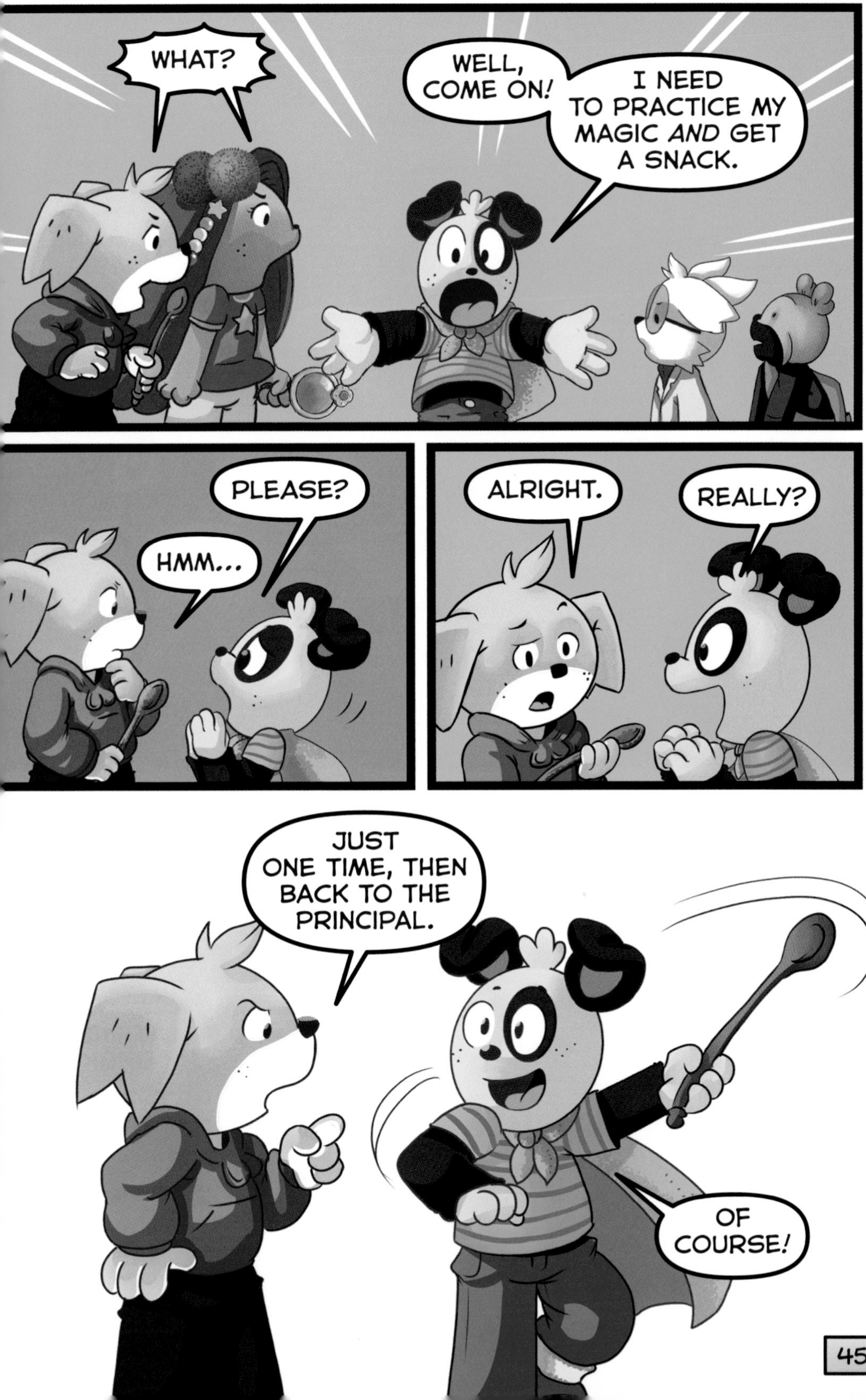
WHAT?
WELL, COME ON!
I NEED TO PRACTICE MY MAGIC *AND* GET A SNACK.
PLEASE?
HMM...
ALRIGHT.
REALLY?
JUST ONE TIME, THEN BACK TO THE PRINCIPAL.
OF COURSE!

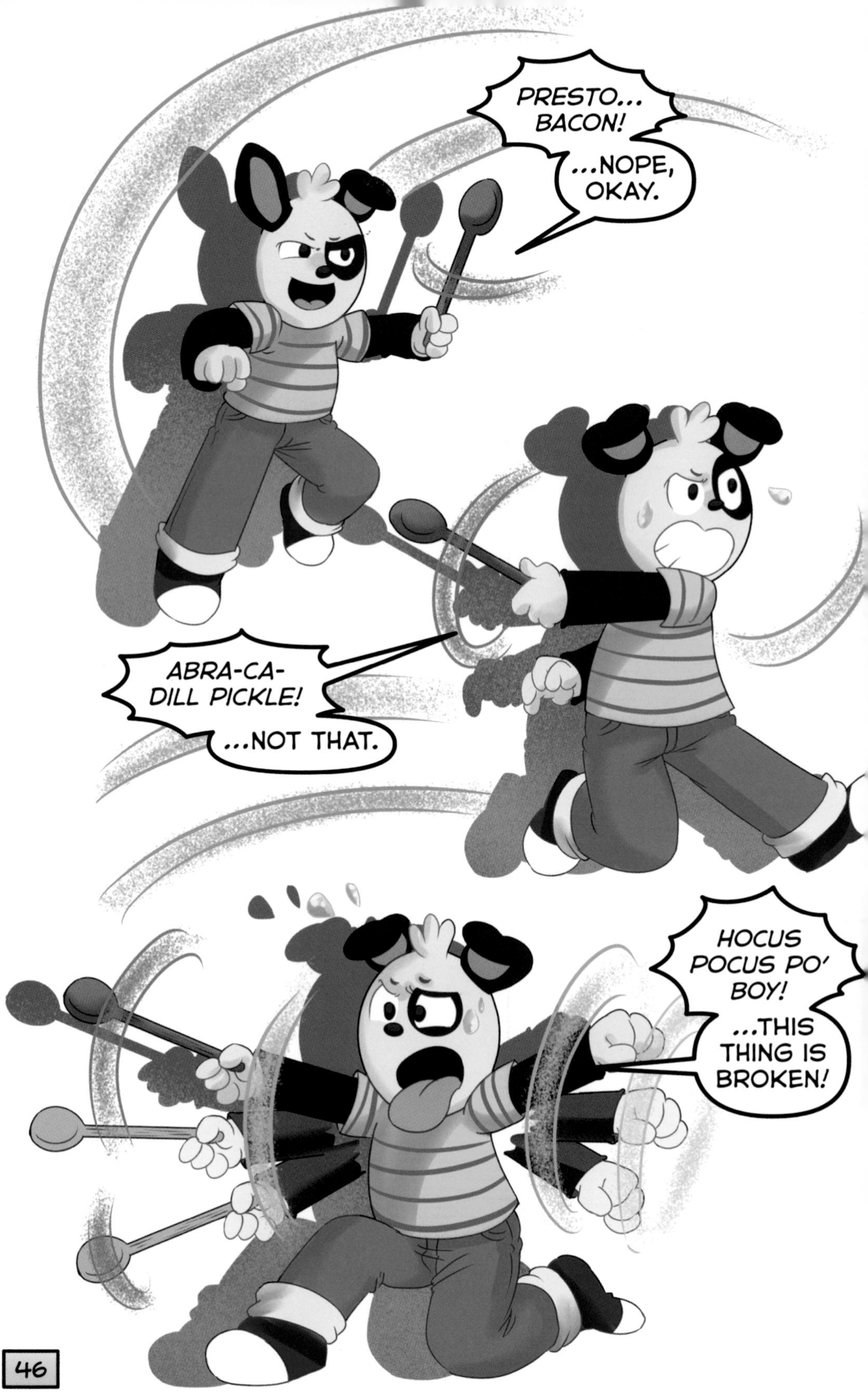
PRESTO... BACON!
...NOPE, OKAY.
ABRA-CA-DILL PICKLE!
...NOT THAT.
HOCUS POCUS PO' BOY!
...THIS THING IS BROKEN!

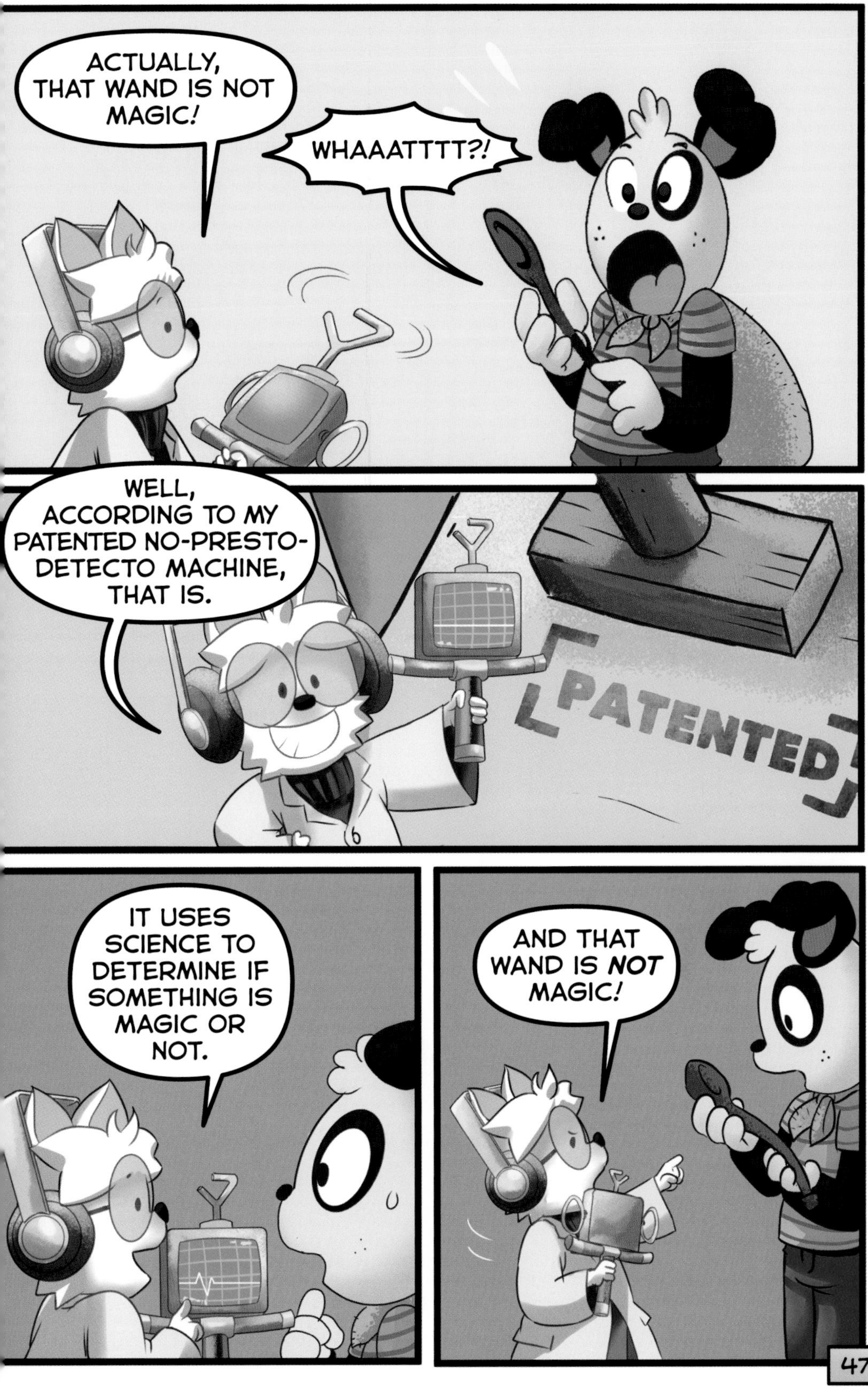
ACTUALLY, THAT WAND IS NOT MAGIC!
WHAAATTTT?!
WELL, ACCORDING TO MY PATENTED NO-PRESTO-DETECTO MACHINE, THAT IS.
PATENTED
IT USES SCIENCE TO DETERMINE IF SOMETHING IS MAGIC OR NOT.
AND THAT WAND IS *NOT* MAGIC!

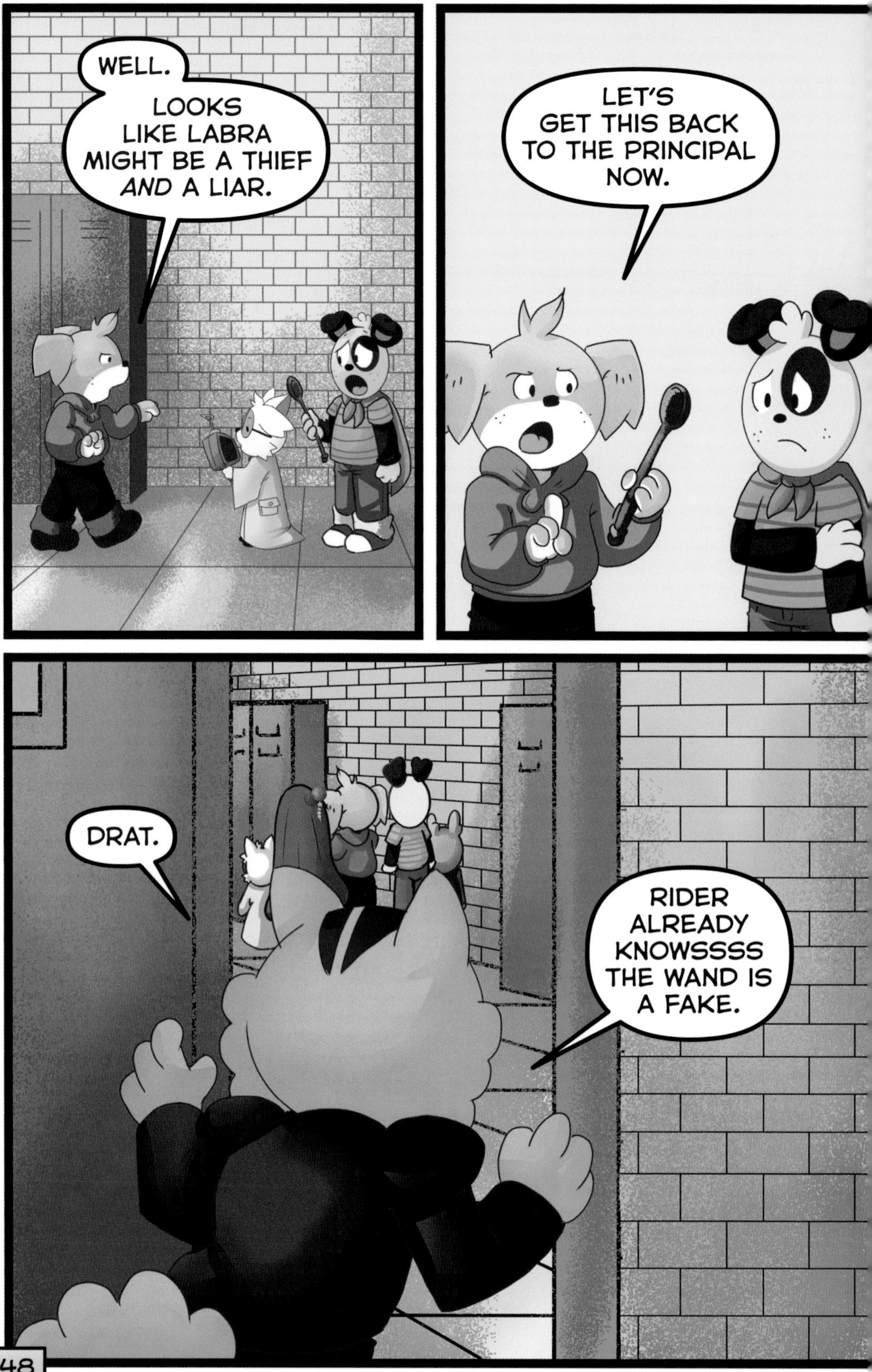
WELL.
LOOKS LIKE LABRA MIGHT BE A THIEF *AND* A LIAR.
LET'S GET THIS BACK TO THE PRINCIPAL NOW.
DRAT.
RIDER ALREADY KNOWSSSS THE WAND IS A FAKE.

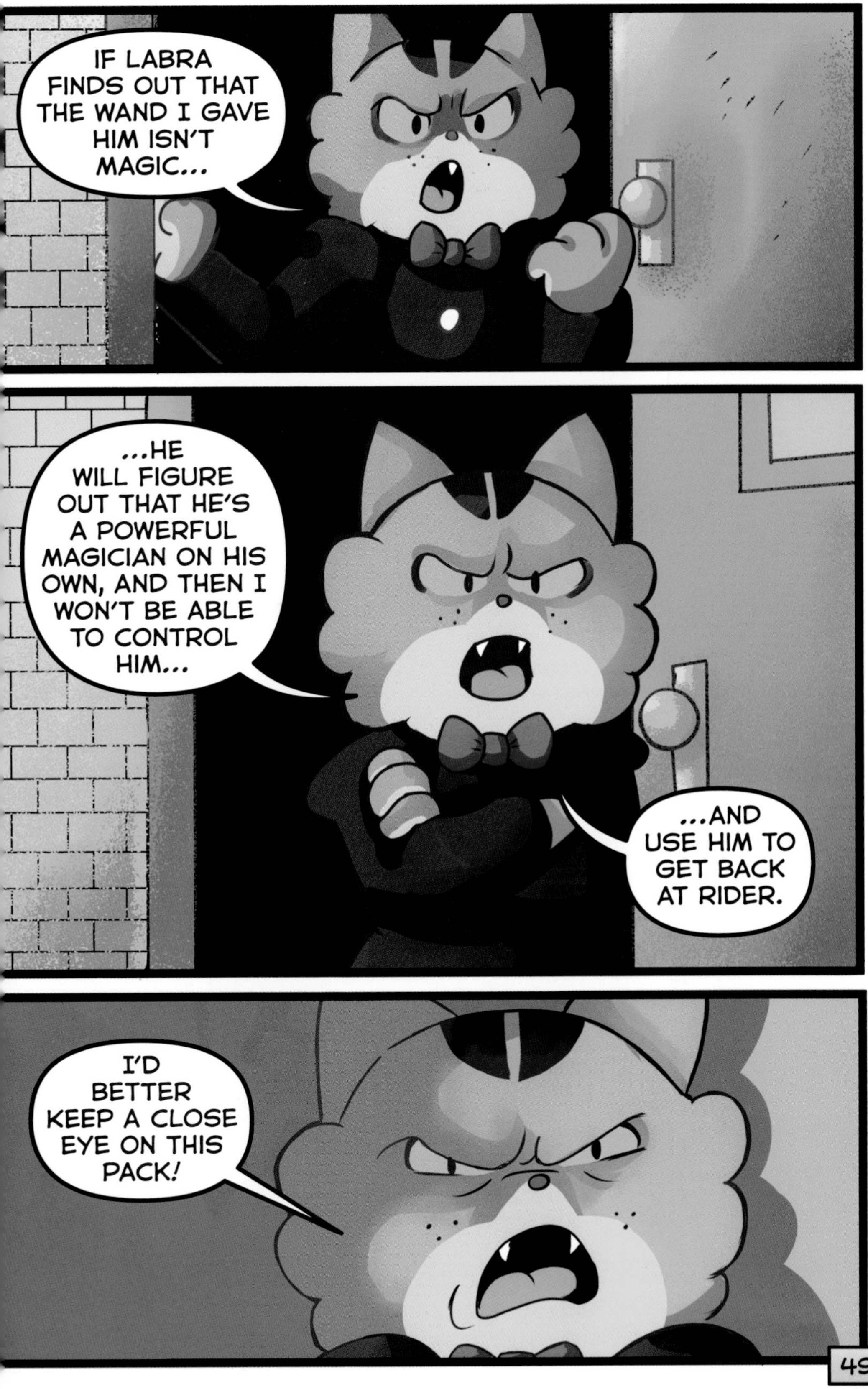
IF LABRA FINDS OUT THAT THE WAND I GAVE HIM ISN'T MAGIC...
...HE WILL FIGURE OUT THAT HE'S A POWERFUL MAGICIAN ON HIS OWN, AND THEN I WON'T BE ABLE TO CONTROL HIM...
...AND USE HIM TO GET BACK AT RIDER.
I'D BETTER KEEP A CLOSE EYE ON THIS PACK!

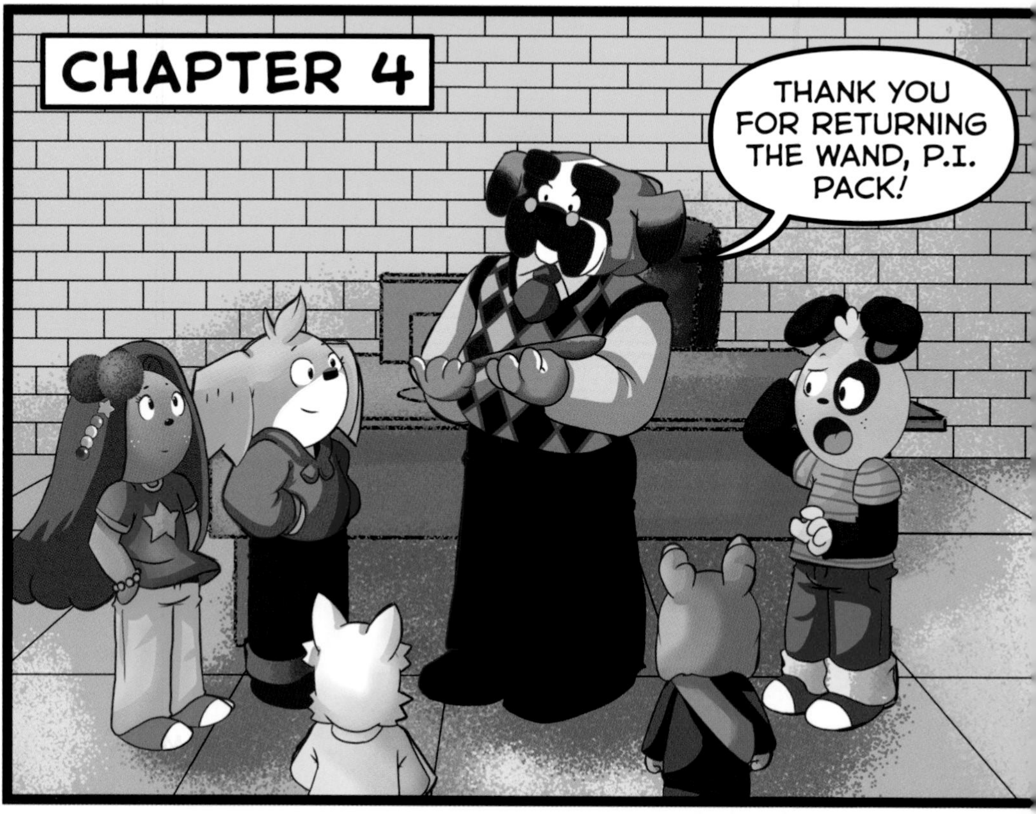
CHAPTER 4
THANK YOU FOR RETURNING THE WAND, P.I. PACK!

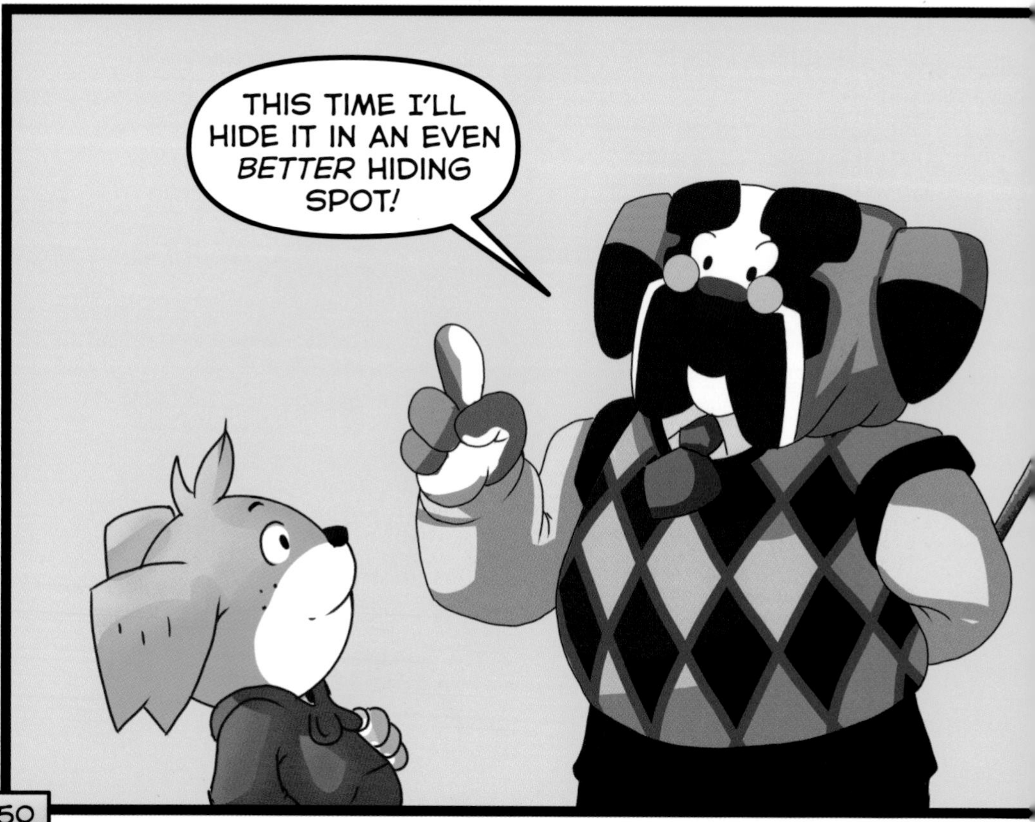
THIS TIME I'LL HIDE IT IN AN EVEN *BETTER* HIDING SPOT!

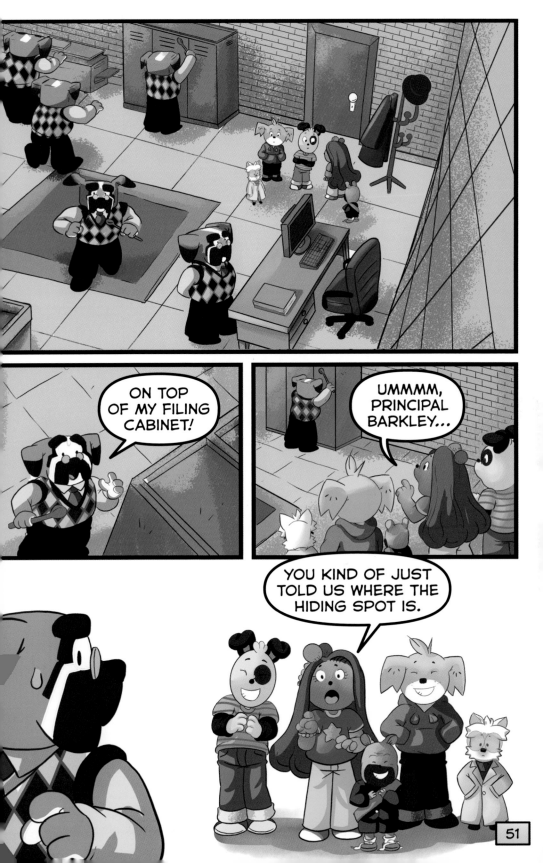

ON TOP OF MY FILING CABINET!

UMMMM, PRINCIPAL BARKLEY...

YOU KIND OF JUST TOLD US WHERE THE HIDING SPOT IS.

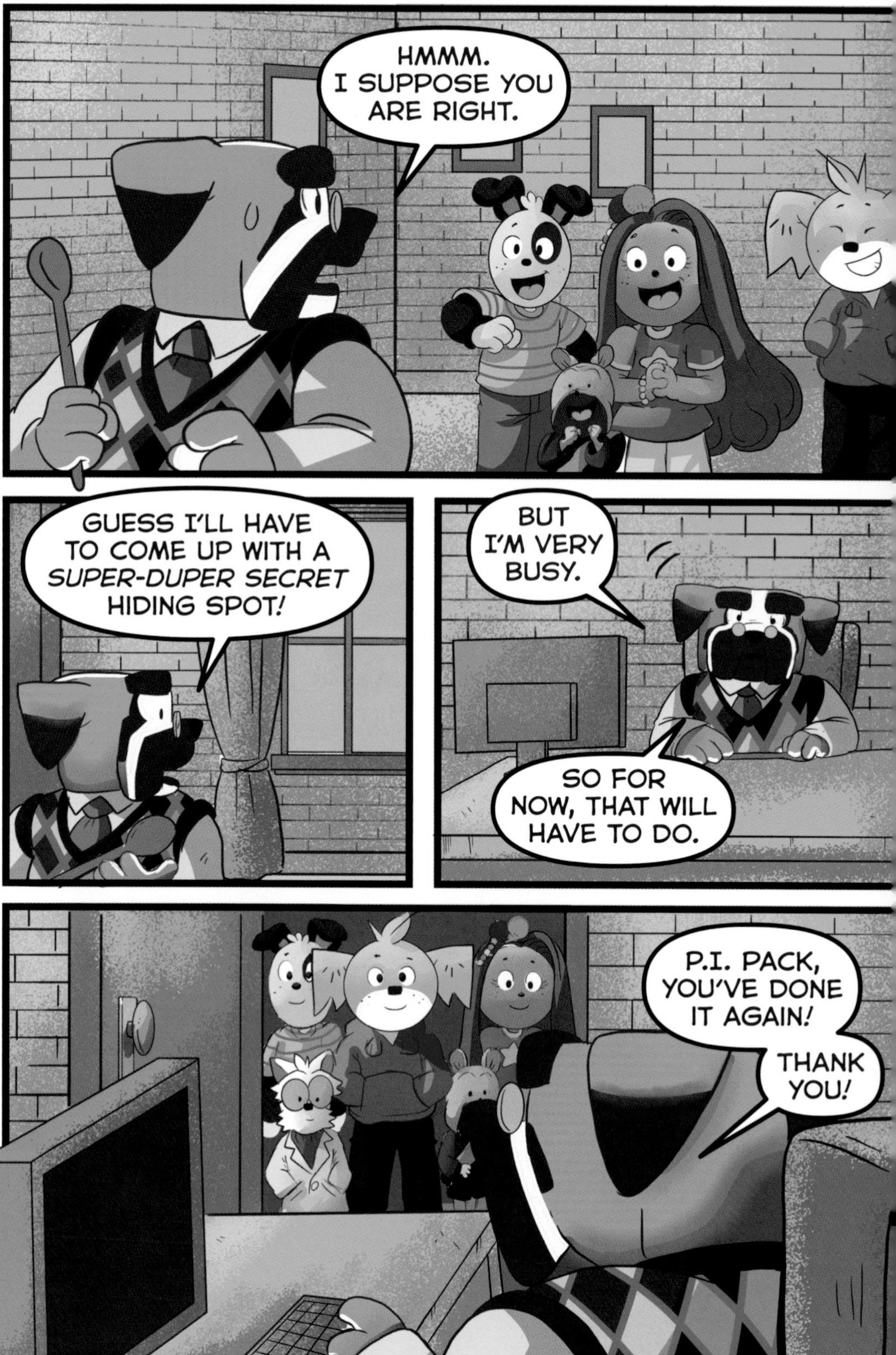
HMMM. I SUPPOSE YOU ARE RIGHT.
GUESS I'LL HAVE TO COME UP WITH A *SUPER-DUPER SECRET* HIDING SPOT!
BUT I'M VERY BUSY.
SO FOR NOW, THAT WILL HAVE TO DO.
P.I. PACK, YOU'VE DONE IT AGAIN!
THANK YOU!

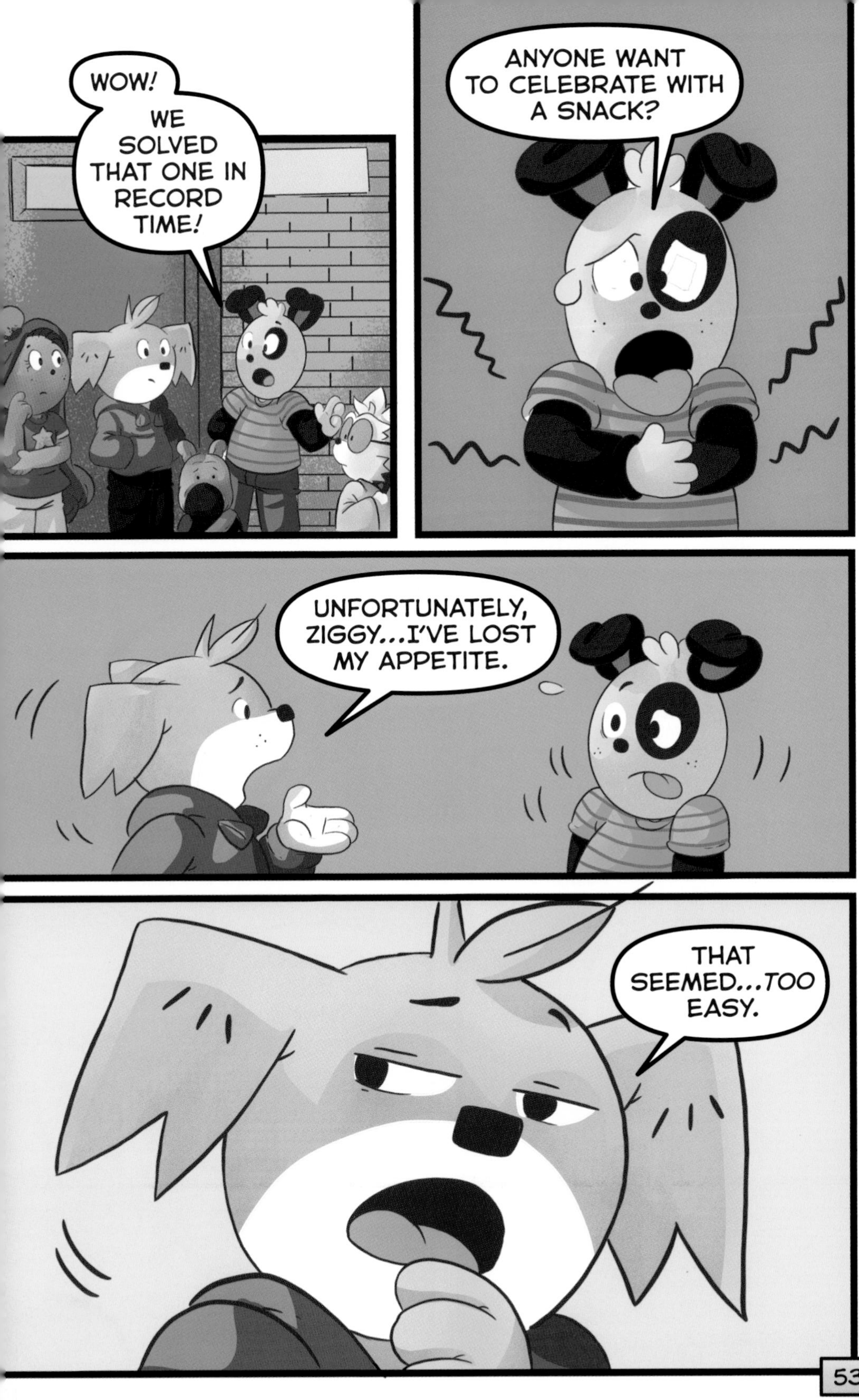
WOW!
WE SOLVED THAT ONE IN RECORD TIME!
ANYONE WANT TO CELEBRATE WITH A SNACK?
UNFORTUNATELY, ZIGGY...I'VE LOST MY APPETITE.
THAT SEEMED...*TOO* EASY.

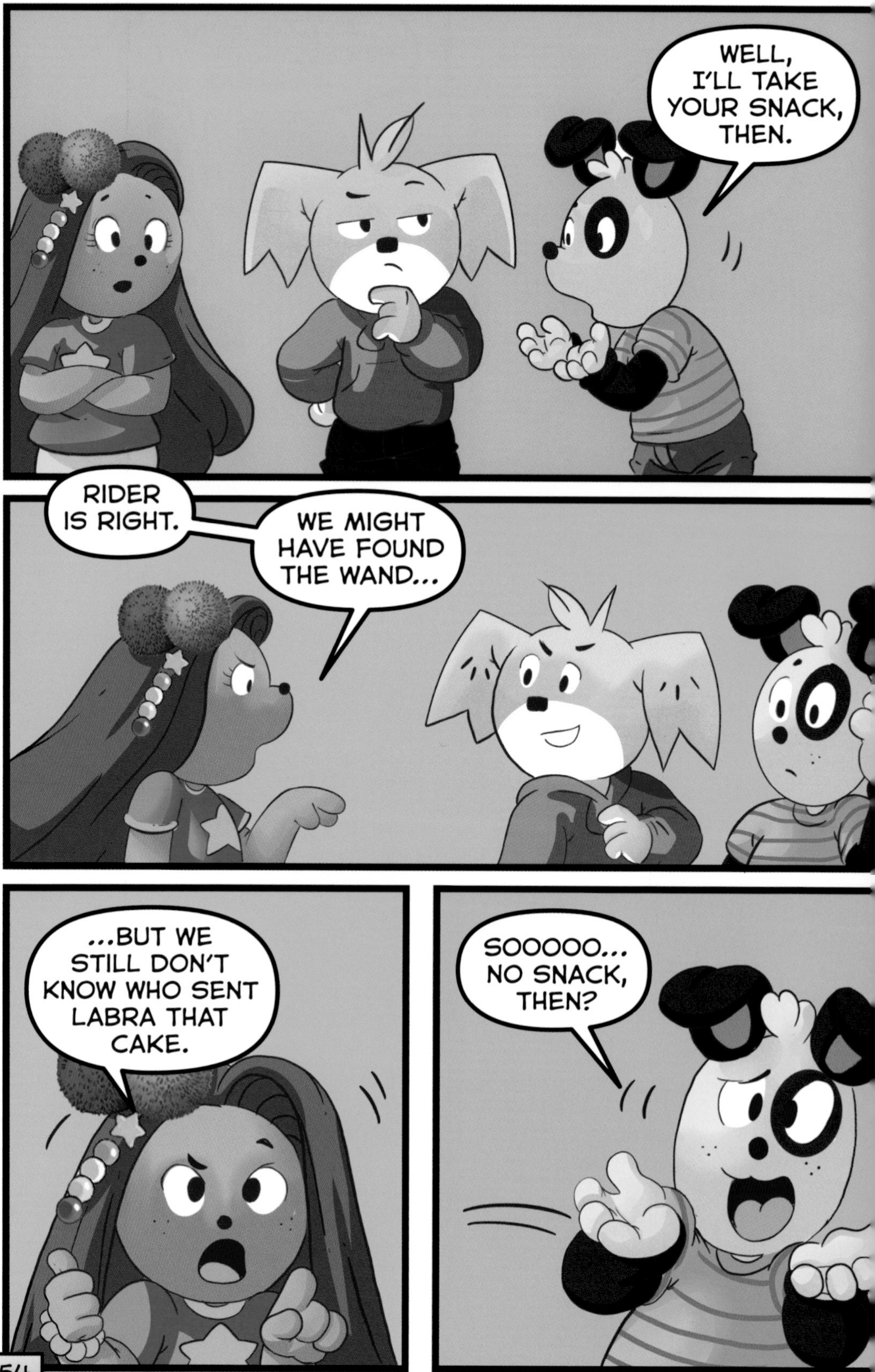

WELL, I'LL TAKE YOUR SNACK, THEN.
RIDER IS RIGHT.
WE MIGHT HAVE FOUND THE WAND...
...BUT WE STILL DON'T KNOW WHO SENT LABRA THAT CAKE.
SOOOOO... NO SNACK, THEN?

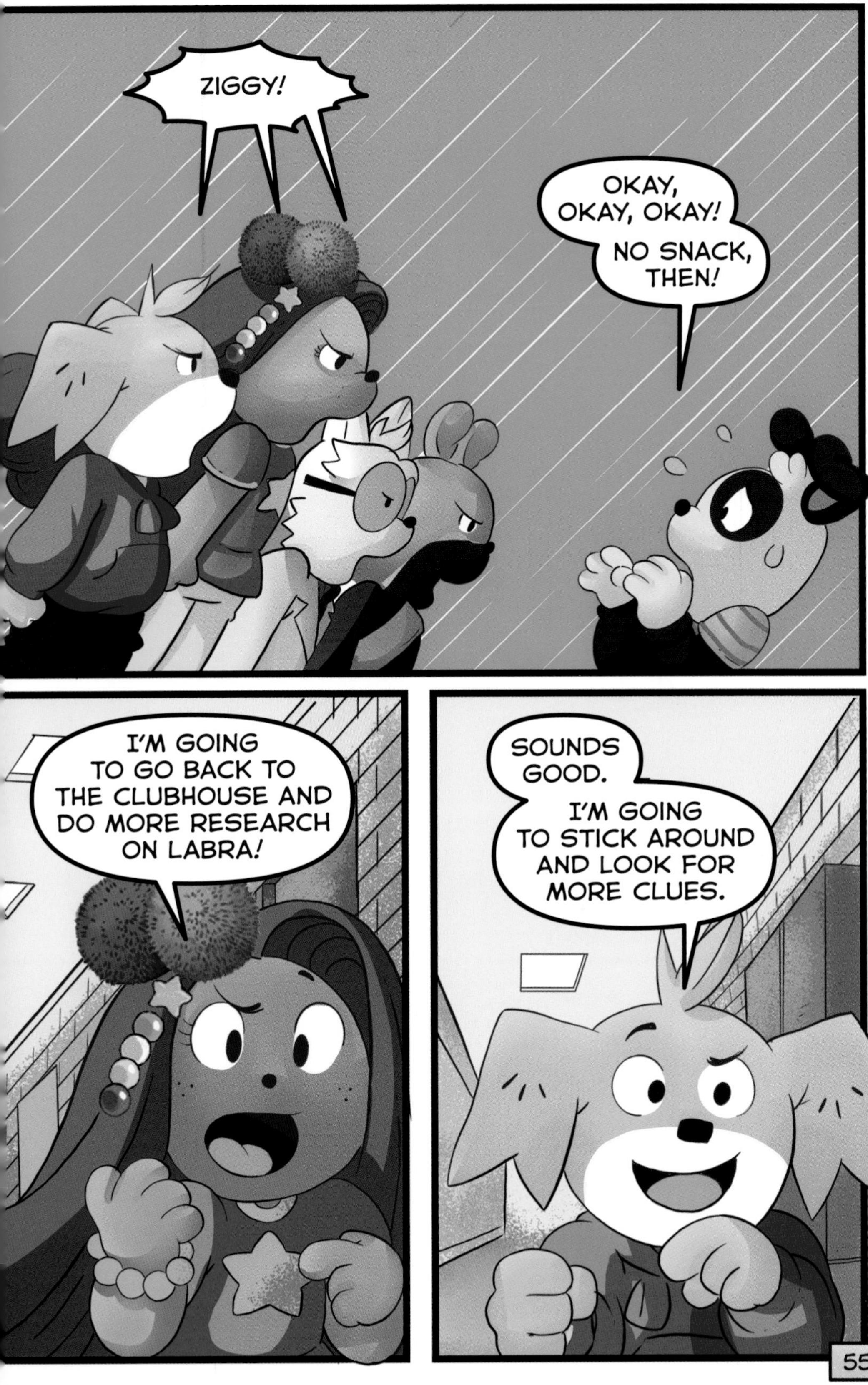
ZIGGY!
OKAY, OKAY, OKAY!
NO SNACK, THEN!
I'M GOING TO GO BACK TO THE CLUBHOUSE AND DO MORE RESEARCH ON LABRA!
SOUNDS GOOD.
I'M GOING TO STICK AROUND AND LOOK FOR MORE CLUES.

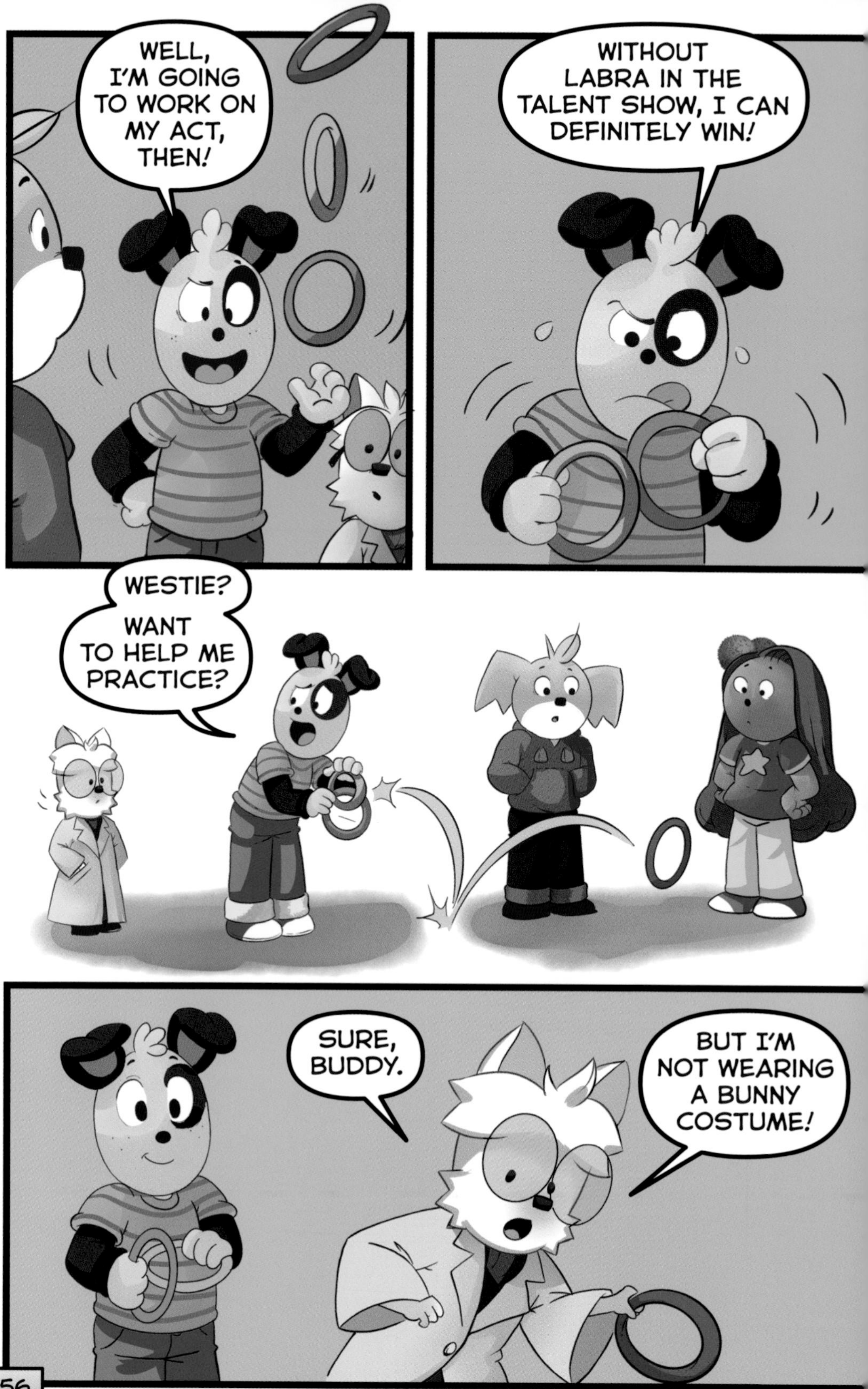
WELL, I'M GOING TO WORK ON MY ACT, THEN!
WITHOUT LABRA IN THE TALENT SHOW, I CAN DEFINITELY WIN!
WESTIE?
WANT TO HELP ME PRACTICE?
SURE, BUDDY.
BUT I'M NOT WEARING A BUNNY COSTUME!

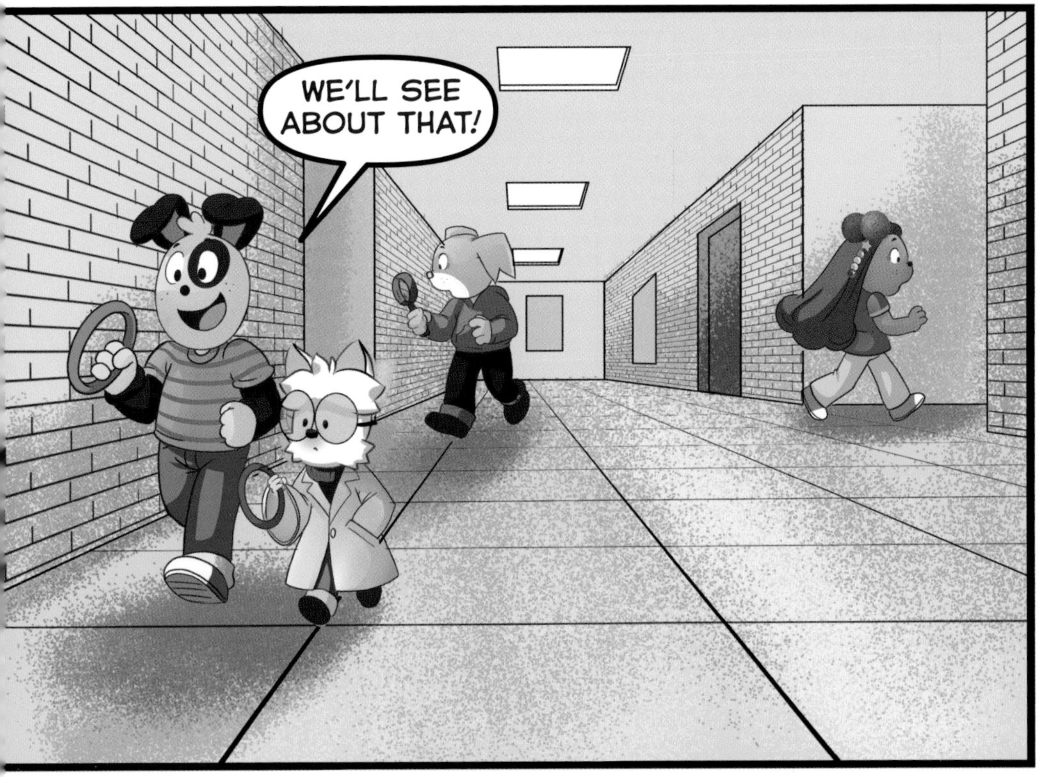
WE'LL SEE ABOUT THAT!

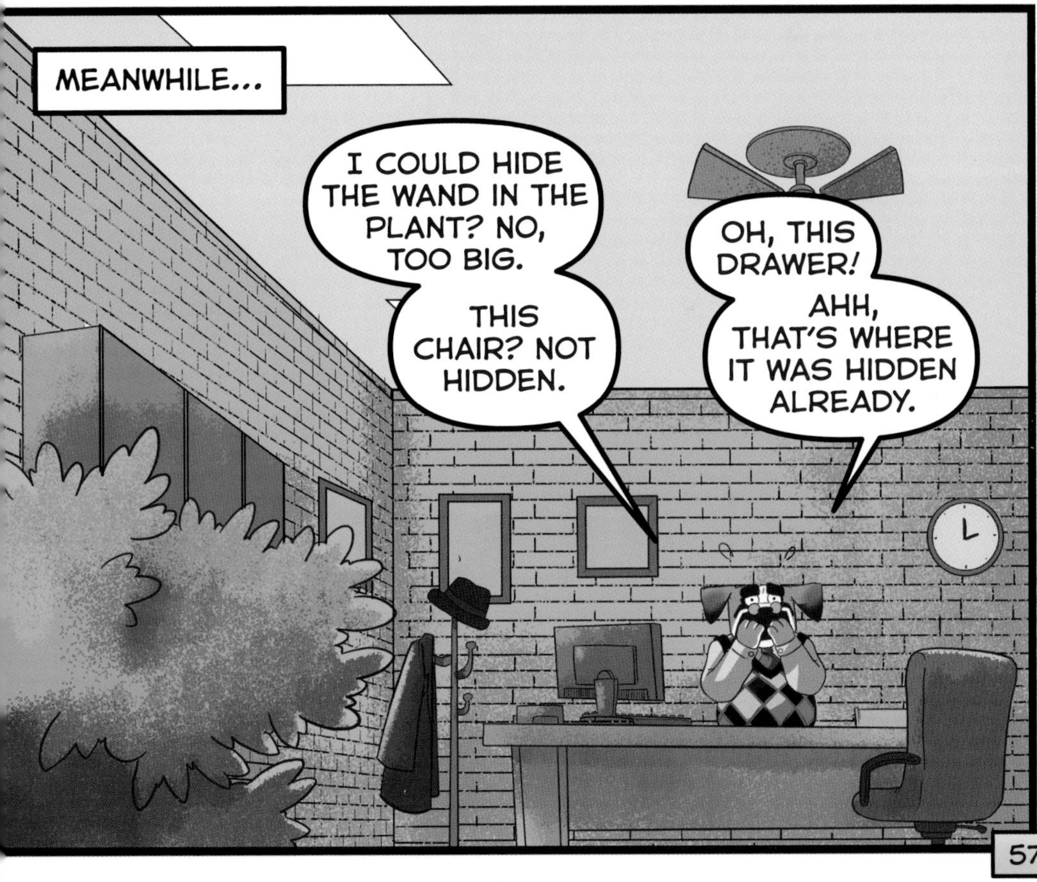
MEANWHILE...
I COULD HIDE THE WAND IN THE PLANT? NO, TOO BIG.
THIS CHAIR? NOT HIDDEN.
OH, THIS DRAWER!
AHH, THAT'S WHERE IT WAS HIDDEN ALREADY.

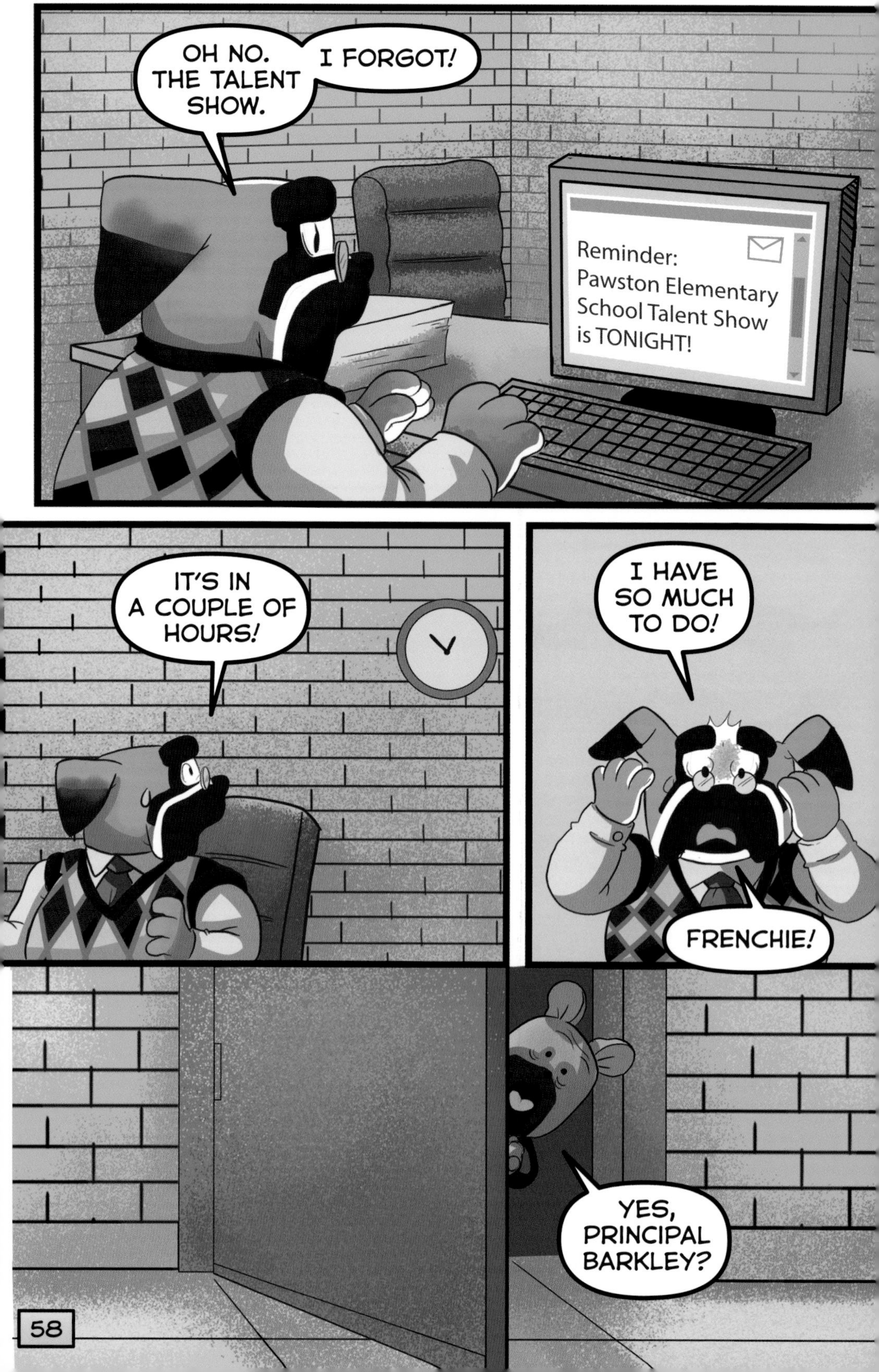

OH NO. THE TALENT SHOW.
I FORGOT!
Reminder: Pawston Elementary School Talent Show is TONIGHT!
IT'S IN A COUPLE OF HOURS!
I HAVE SO MUCH TO DO!
FRENCHIE!
YES, PRINCIPAL BARKLEY?

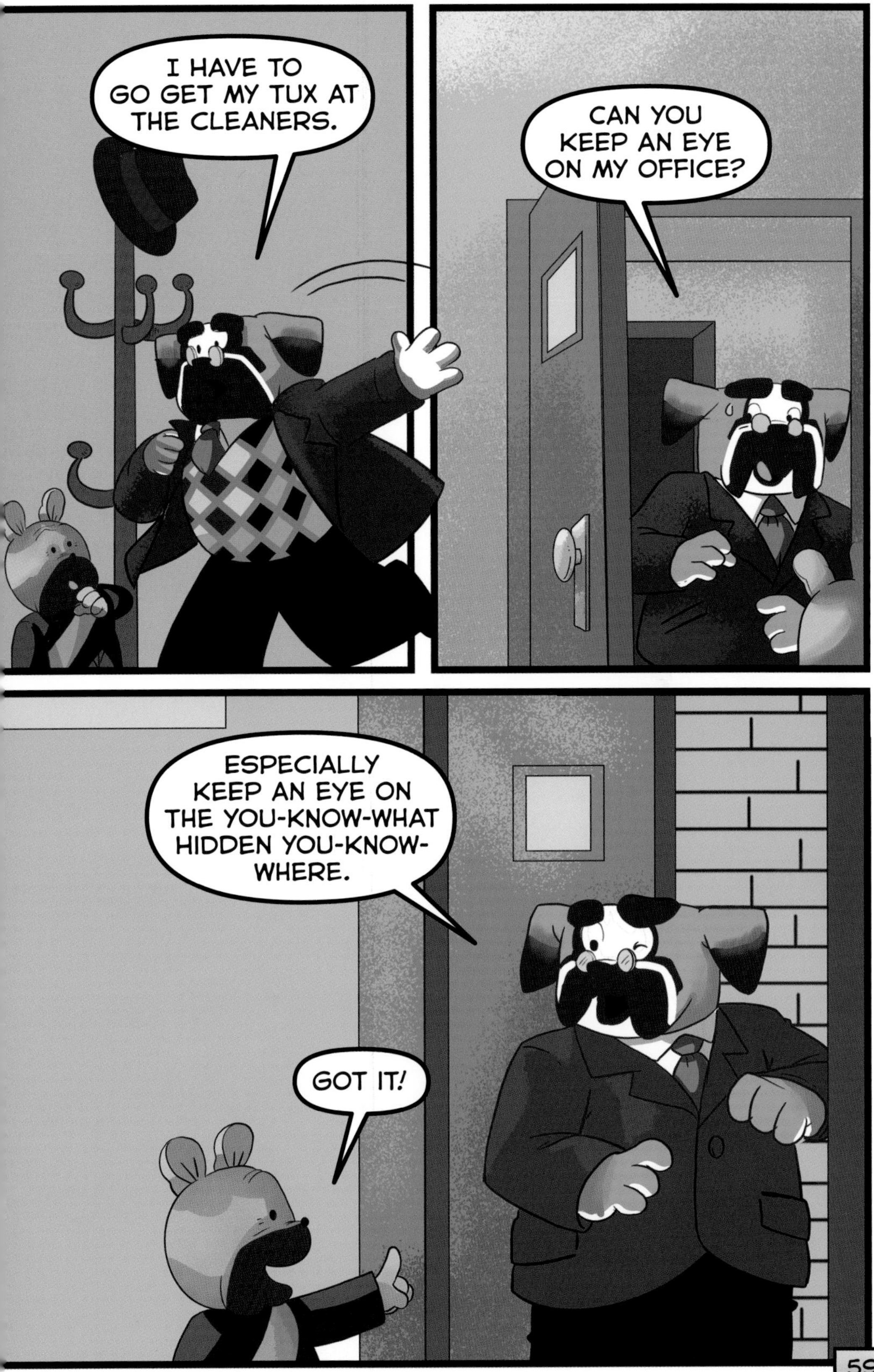
I HAVE TO GO GET MY TUX AT THE CLEANERS.
CAN YOU KEEP AN EYE ON MY OFFICE?
ESPECIALLY KEEP AN EYE ON THE YOU-KNOW-WHAT HIDDEN YOU-KNOW-WHERE.
GOT IT!

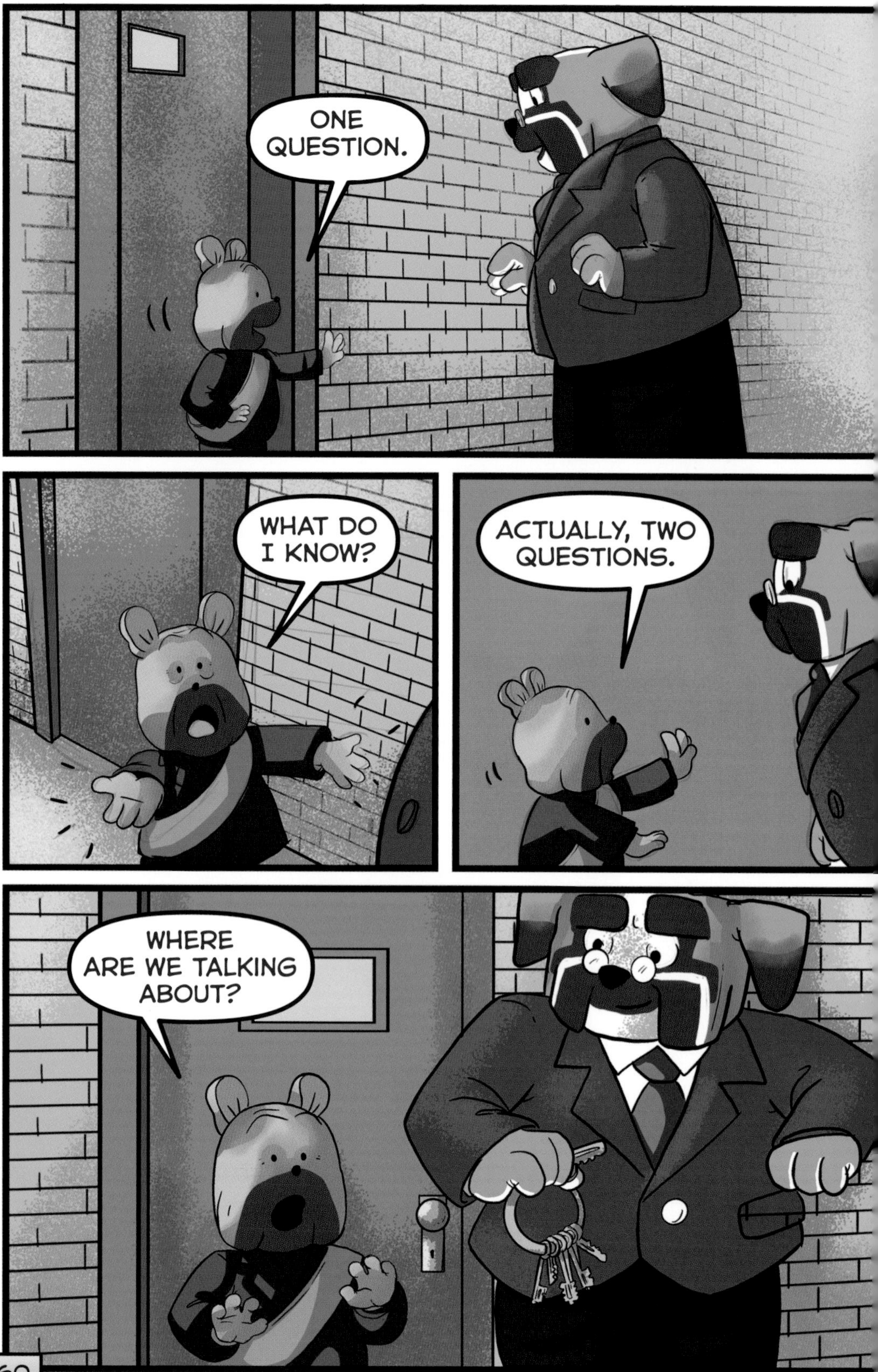
ONE QUESTION.
WHAT DO I KNOW?
ACTUALLY, TWO QUESTIONS.
WHERE ARE WE TALKING ABOUT?

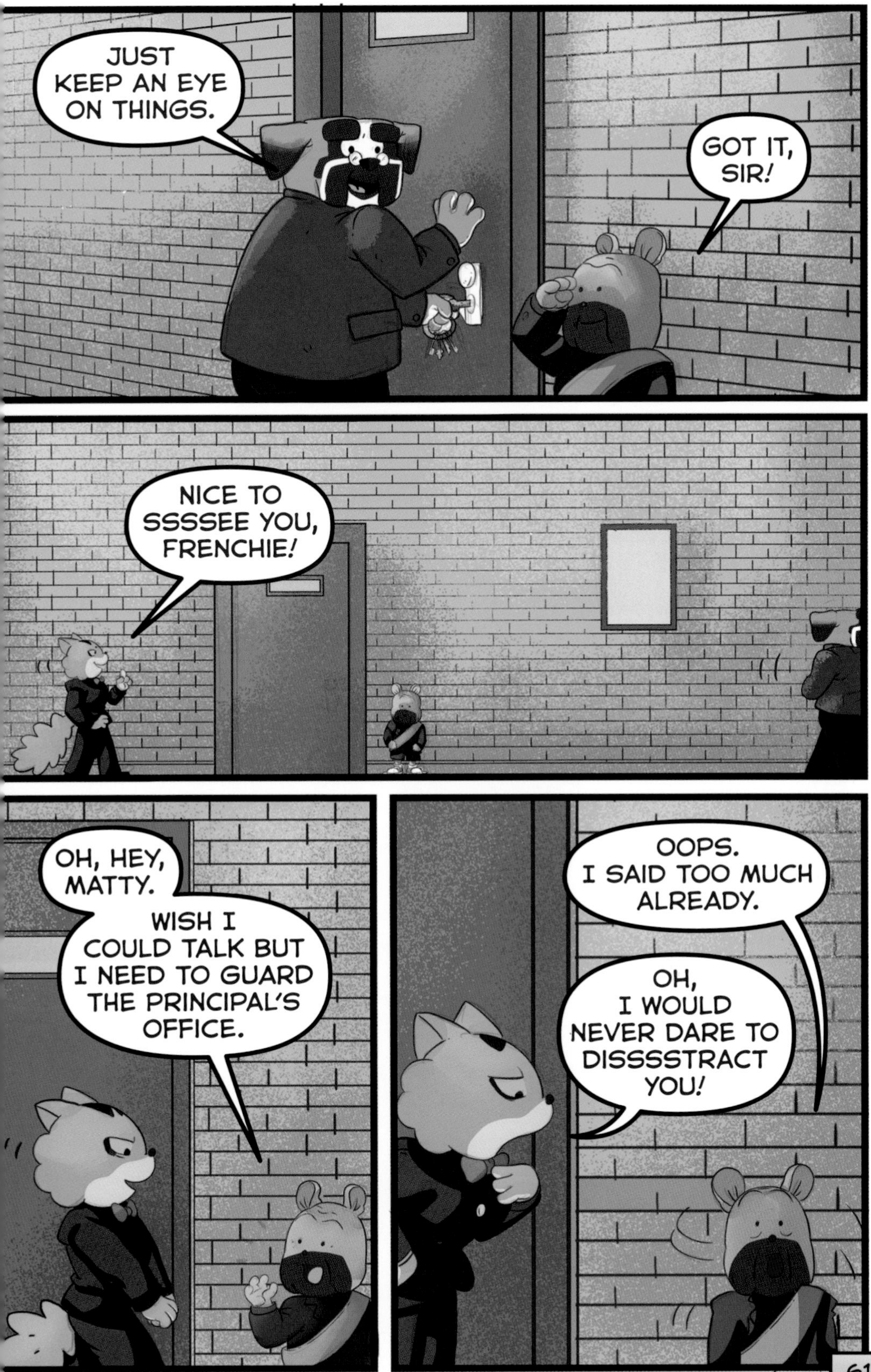
JUST KEEP AN EYE ON THINGS.
GOT IT, SIR!
NICE TO SSSSEE YOU, FRENCHIE!
OH, HEY, MATTY.
WISH I COULD TALK BUT I NEED TO GUARD THE PRINCIPAL'S OFFICE.
OOPS. I SAID TOO MUCH ALREADY.
OH, I WOULD NEVER DARE TO DISSSSTRACT YOU!

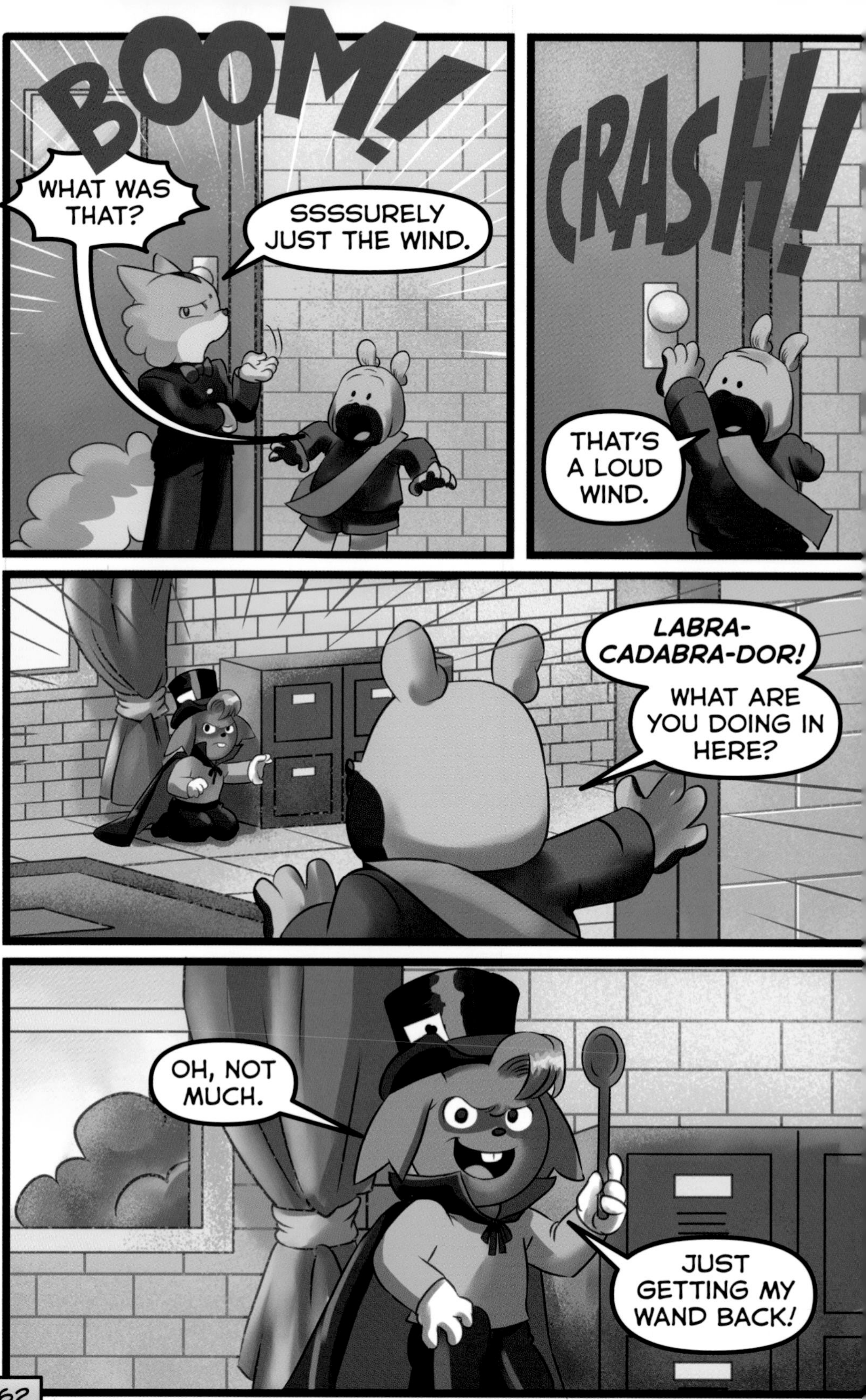
BOOM!
WHAT WAS THAT?
SSSSURELY JUST THE WIND.
CRASH!
THAT'S A LOUD WIND.
LABRA-CADABRA-DOR!
WHAT ARE YOU DOING IN HERE?
OH, NOT MUCH.
JUST GETTING MY WAND BACK!

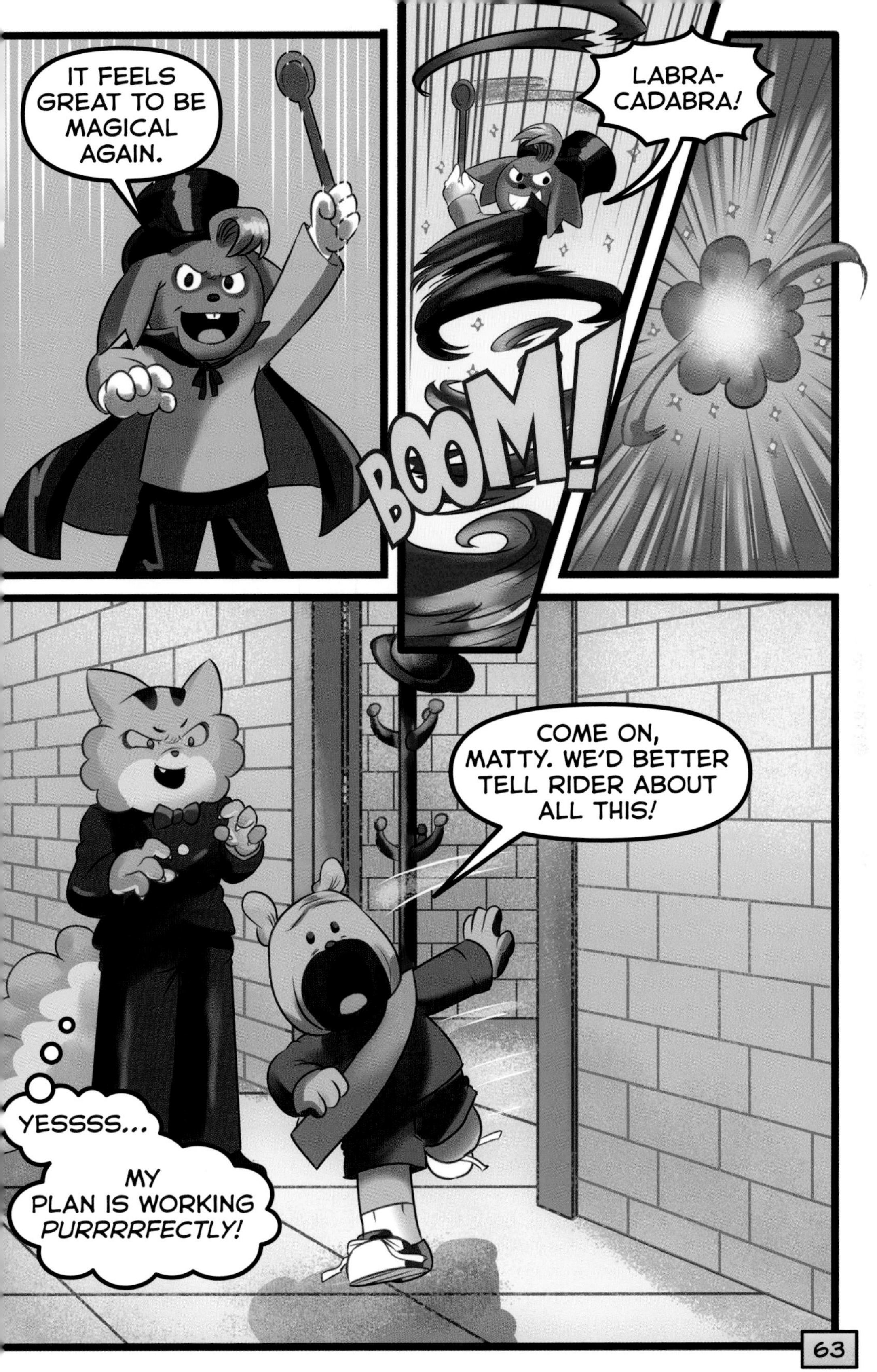
IT FEELS GREAT TO BE MAGICAL AGAIN.
LABRA-CADABRA!
BOOM!
COME ON, MATTY. WE'D BETTER TELL RIDER ABOUT ALL THIS!
YESSSS...
MY PLAN IS WORKING *PURRRRFECTLY!*

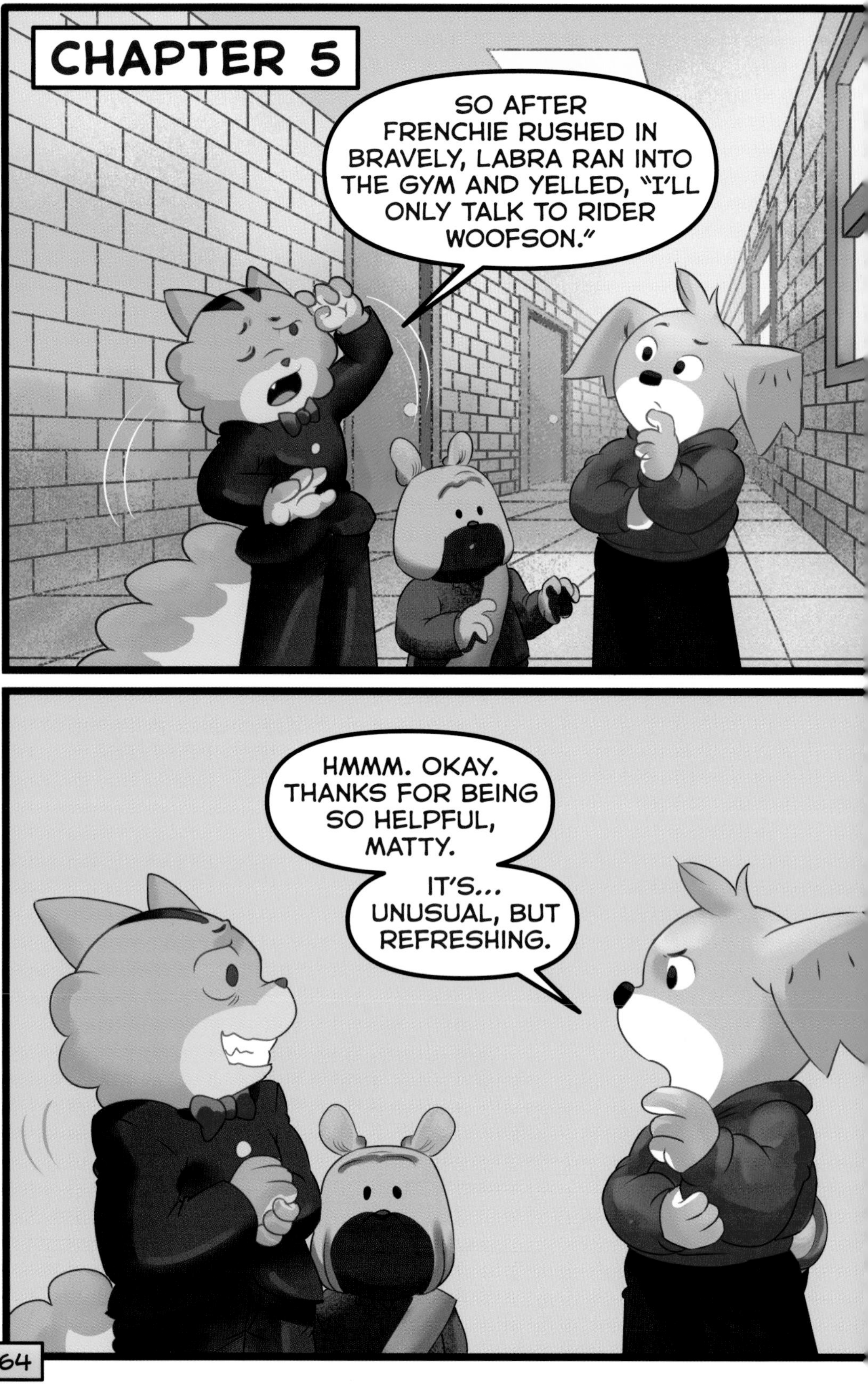
CHAPTER 5
SO AFTER FRENCHIE RUSHED IN BRAVELY, LABRA RAN INTO THE GYM AND YELLED, "I'LL ONLY TALK TO RIDER WOOFSON."
HMMM. OKAY. THANKS FOR BEING SO HELPFUL, MATTY.
IT'S... UNUSUAL, BUT REFRESHING.

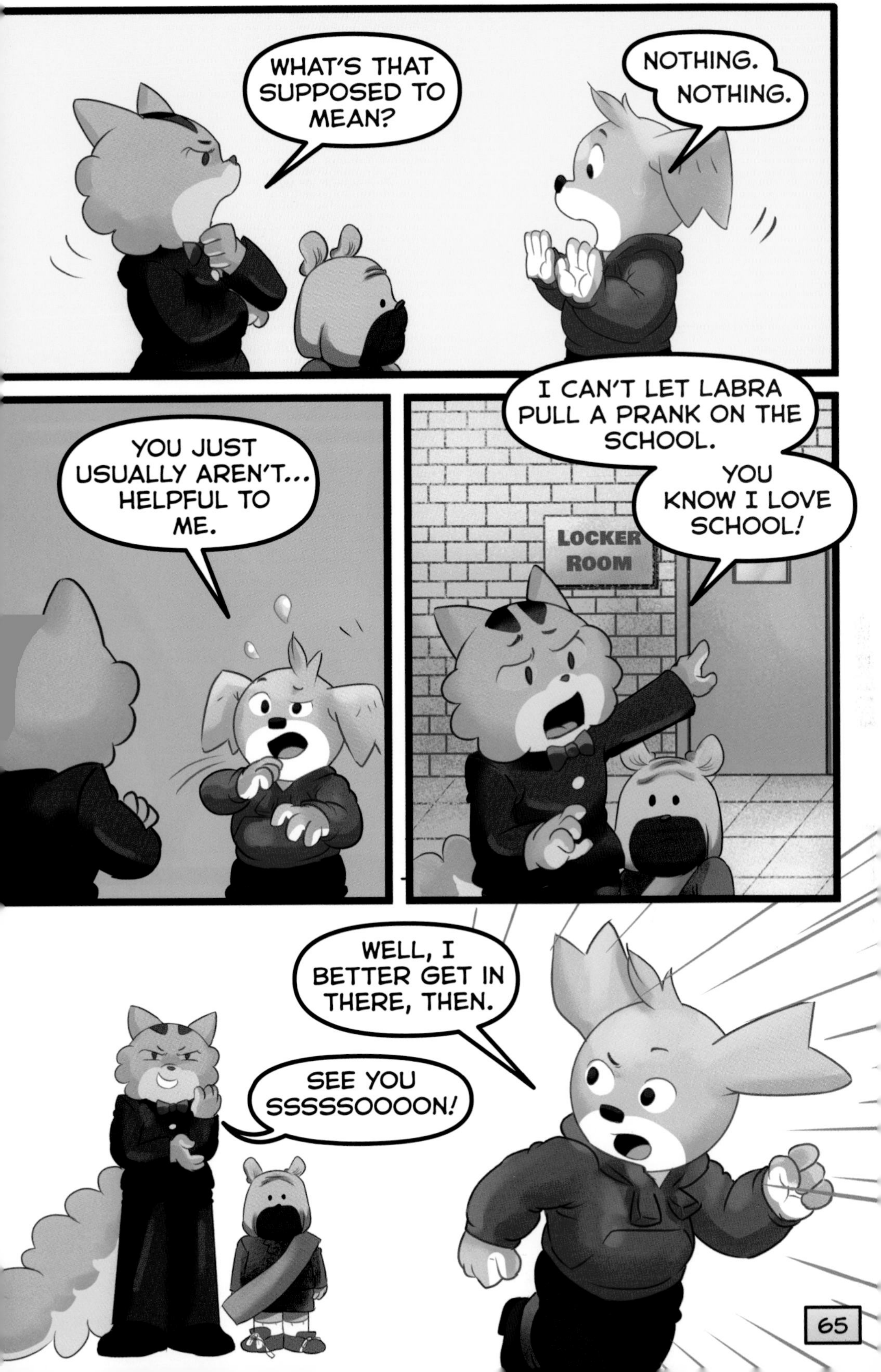

WHAT'S THAT SUPPOSED TO MEAN?
NOTHING. NOTHING.
YOU JUST USUALLY AREN'T... HELPFUL TO ME.
I CAN'T LET LABRA PULL A PRANK ON THE SCHOOL.
YOU KNOW I LOVE SCHOOL!
LOCKER ROOM
WELL, I BETTER GET IN THERE, THEN.
SEE YOU SSSSSOOOON!

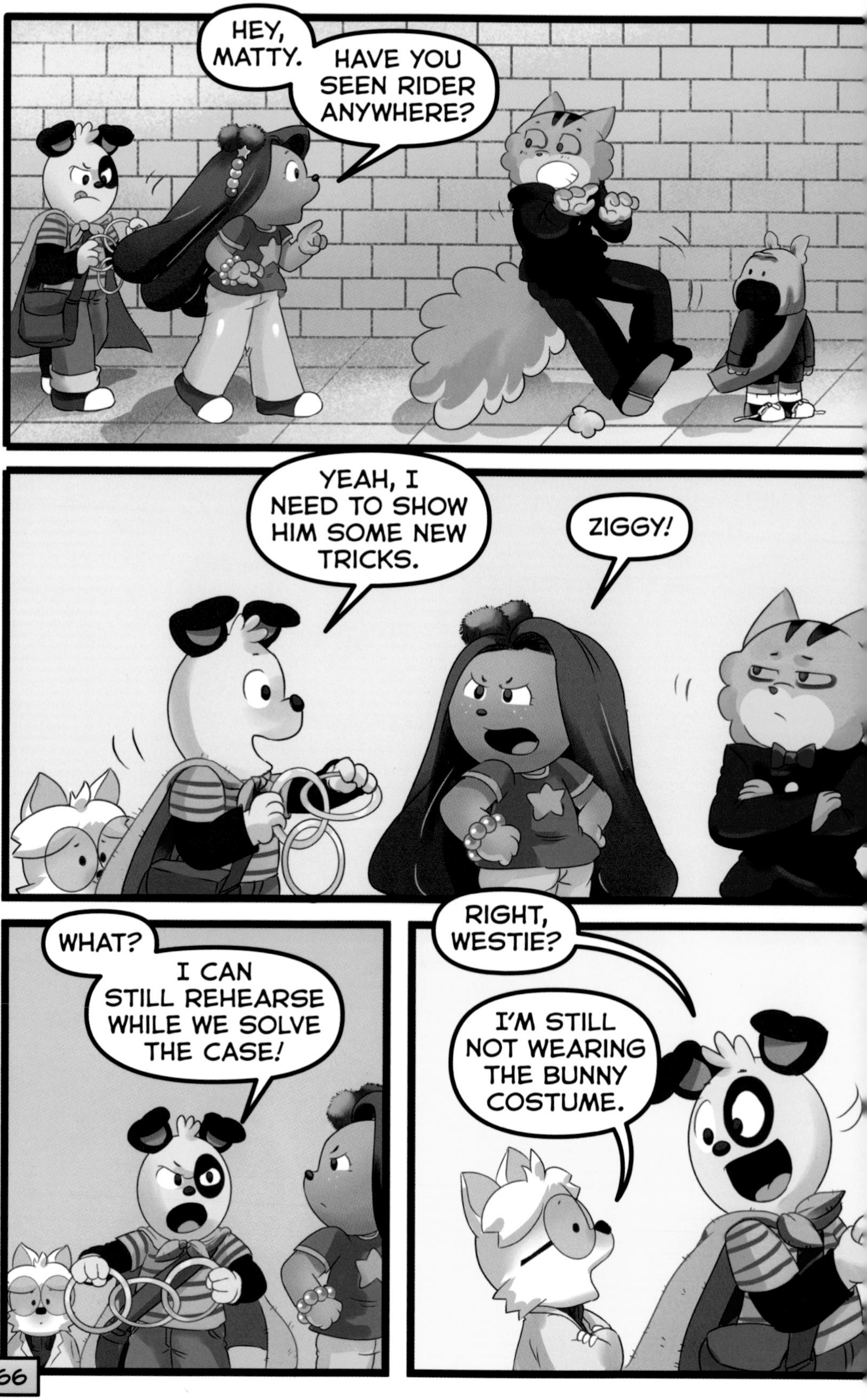
HEY, MATTY.
HAVE YOU SEEN RIDER ANYWHERE?
YEAH, I NEED TO SHOW HIM SOME NEW TRICKS.
ZIGGY!
WHAT?
I CAN STILL REHEARSE WHILE WE SOLVE THE CASE!
RIGHT, WESTIE?
I'M STILL NOT WEARING THE BUNNY COSTUME.

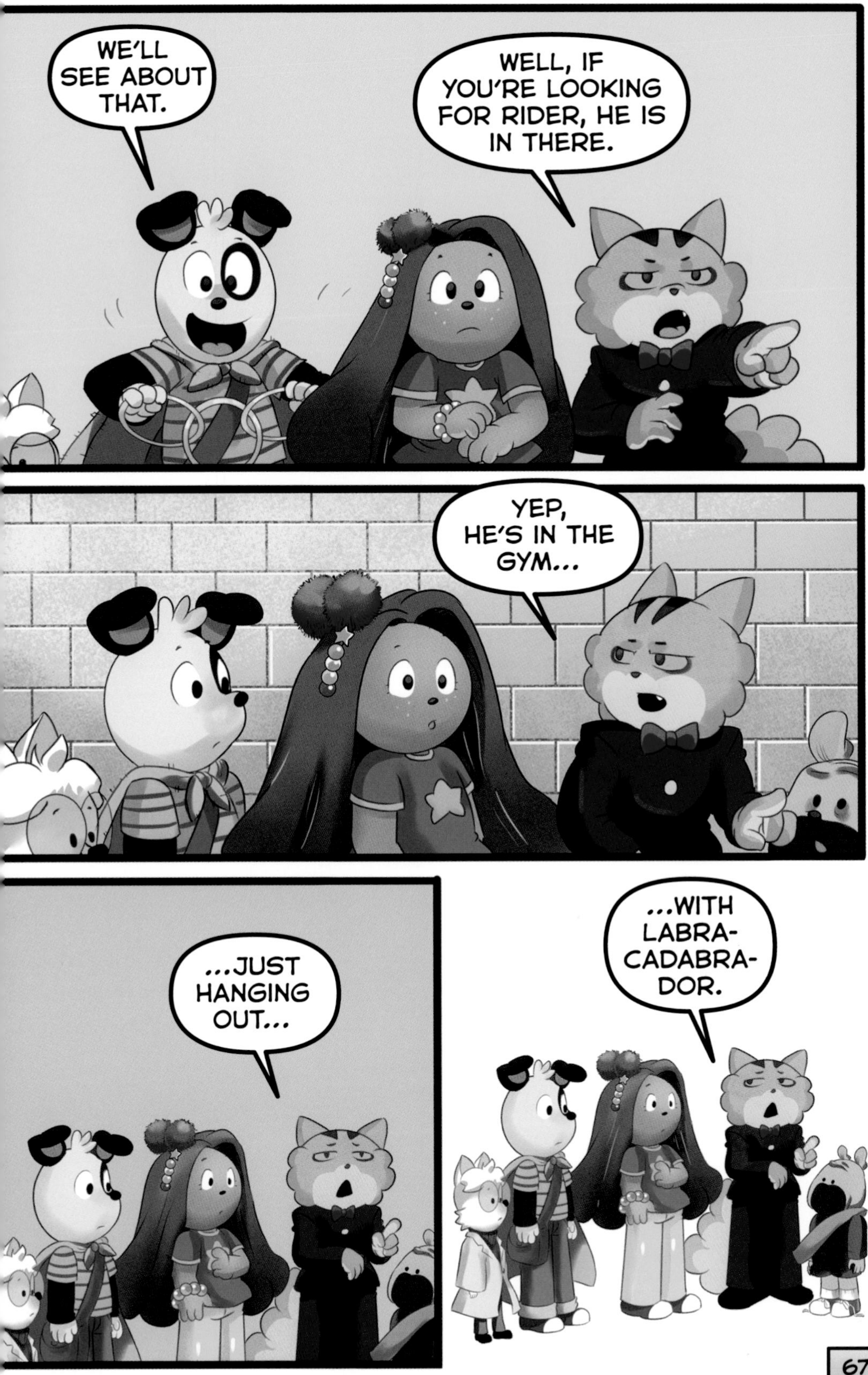
WE'LL SEE ABOUT THAT.
WELL, IF YOU'RE LOOKING FOR RIDER, HE IS IN THERE.
YEP, HE'S IN THE GYM...
...JUST HANGING OUT...
...WITH LABRA-CADABRA-DOR.

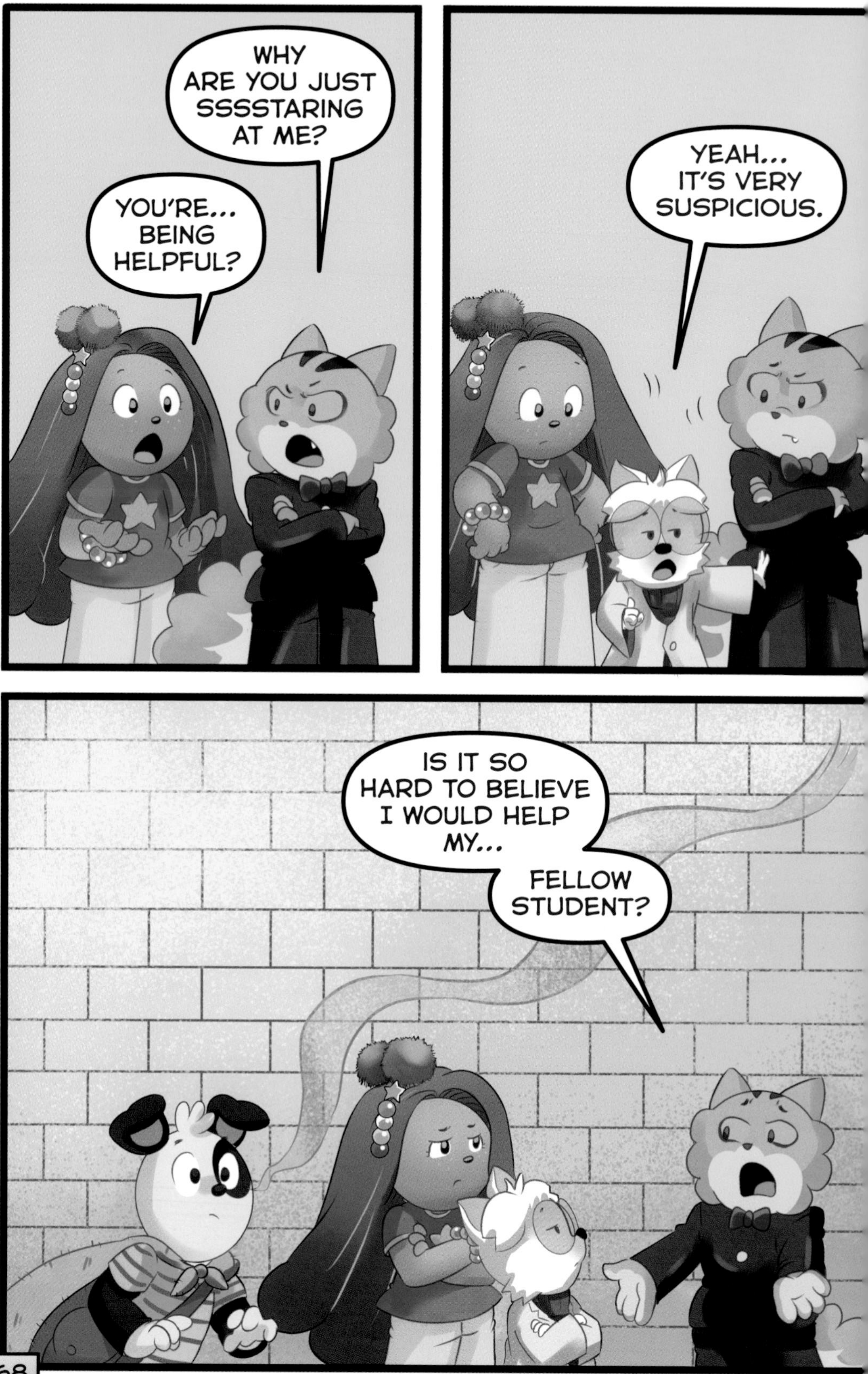

WHY ARE YOU JUST SSSSTARING AT ME?
YOU'RE... BEING HELPFUL?
YEAH... IT'S VERY SUSPICIOUS.
IS IT SO HARD TO BELIEVE I WOULD HELP MY...
FELLOW STUDENT?

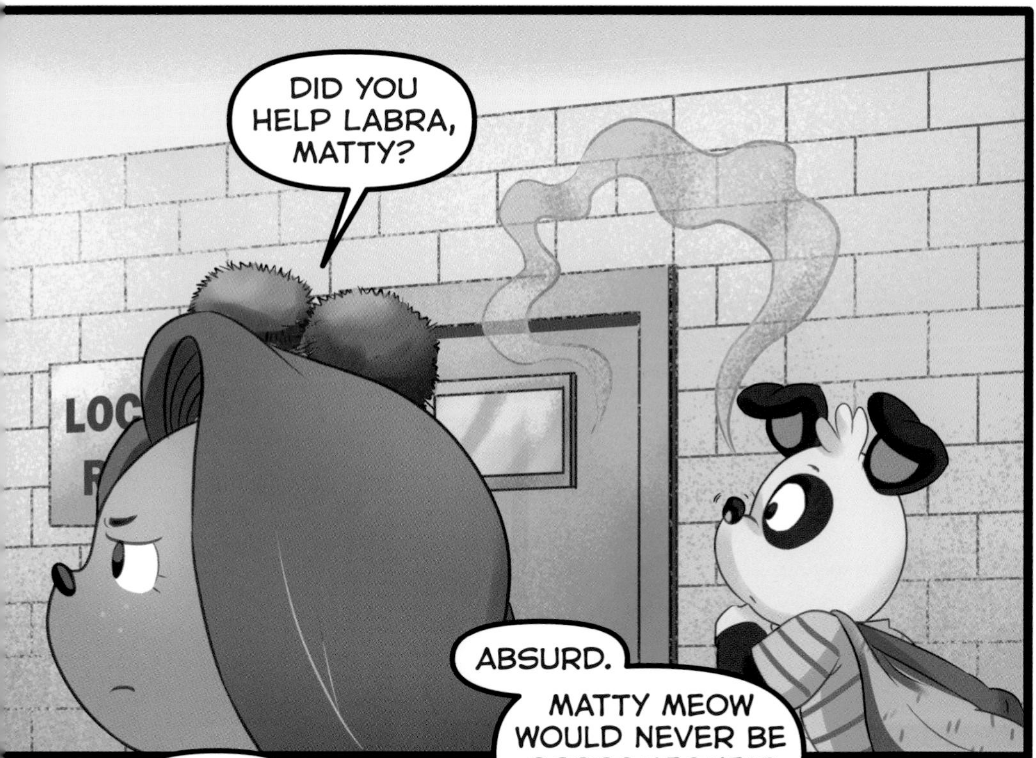
DID YOU HELP LABRA, MATTY?
LOC
ABSURD.
MATTY MEOW WOULD NEVER BE SSSSOMEONE'S ASSISTANT!
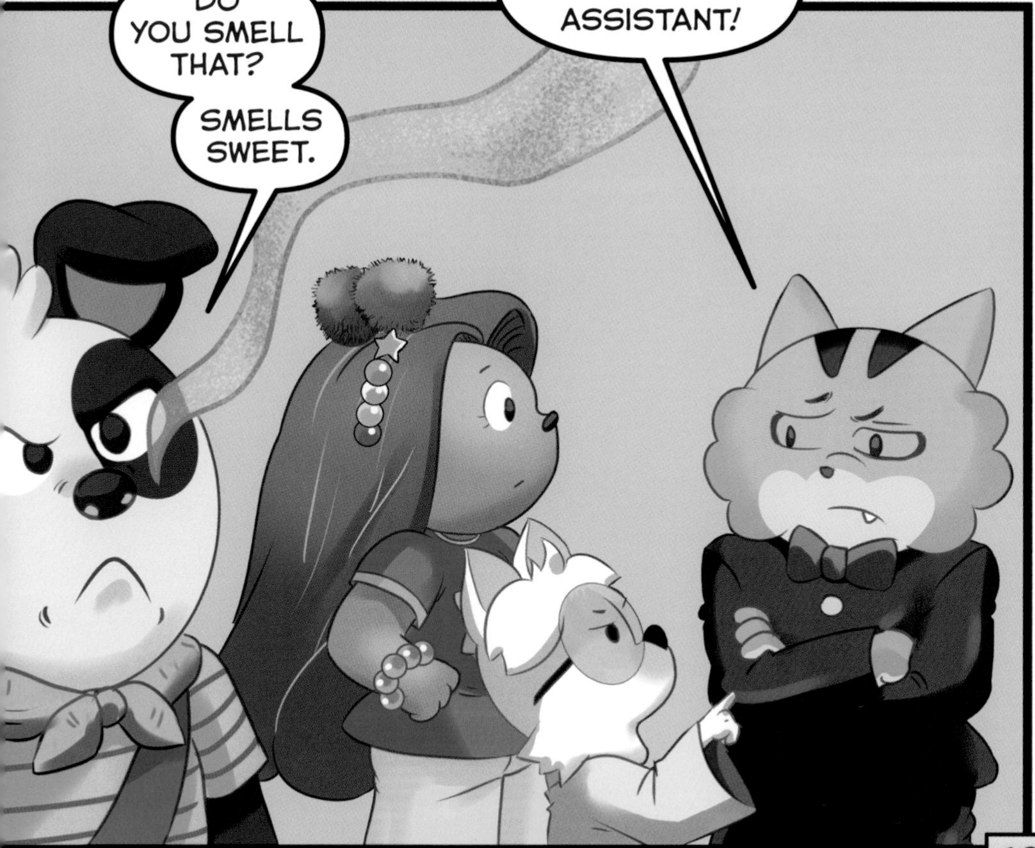
DO YOU SMELL THAT?
SMELLS SWEET.

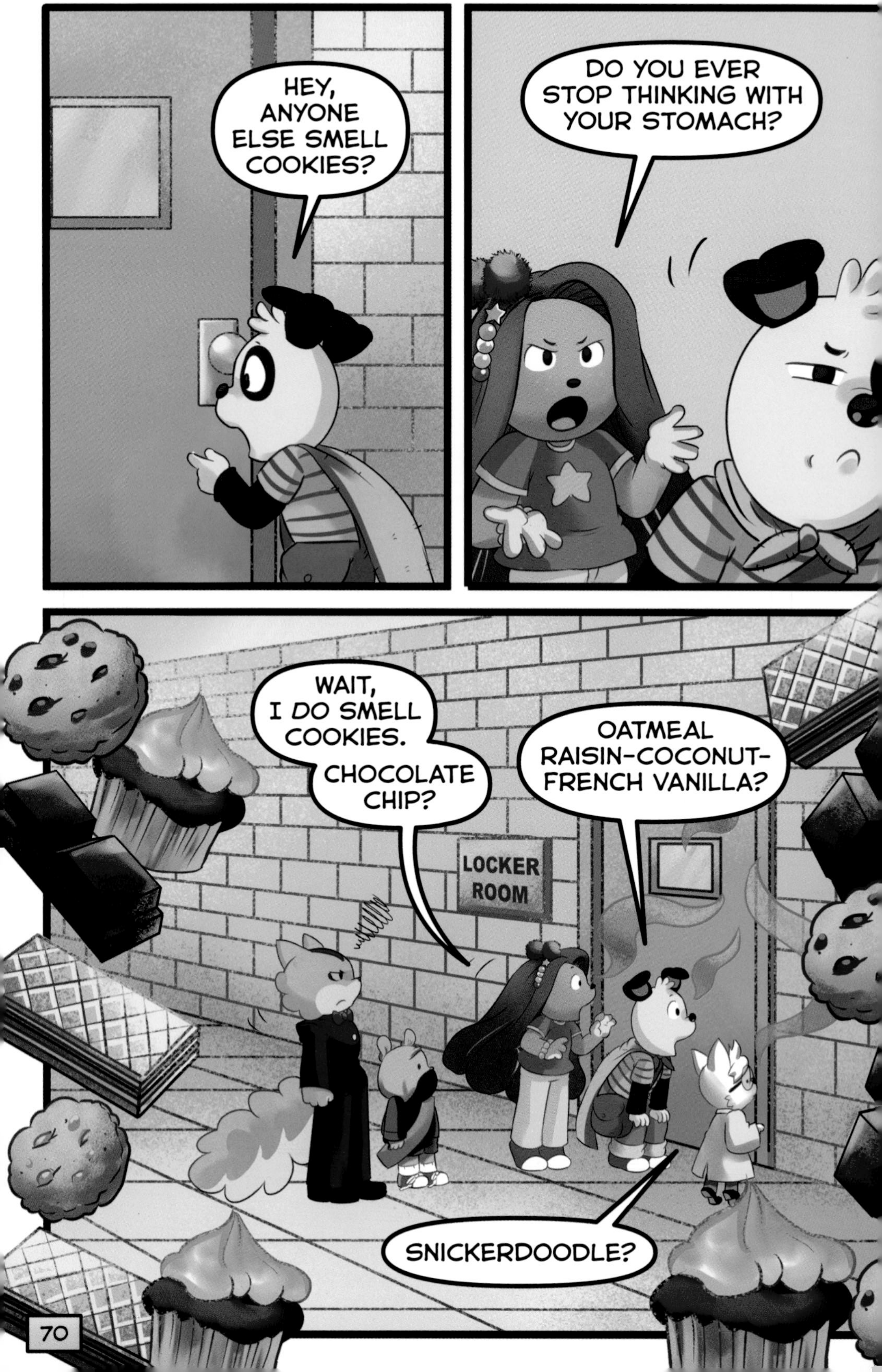
HEY, ANYONE ELSE SMELL COOKIES?
DO YOU EVER STOP THINKING WITH YOUR STOMACH?
WAIT, I *DO* SMELL COOKIES.
CHOCOLATE CHIP?
OATMEAL RAISIN-COCONUT-FRENCH VANILLA?
LOCKER ROOM
SNICKERDOODLE?

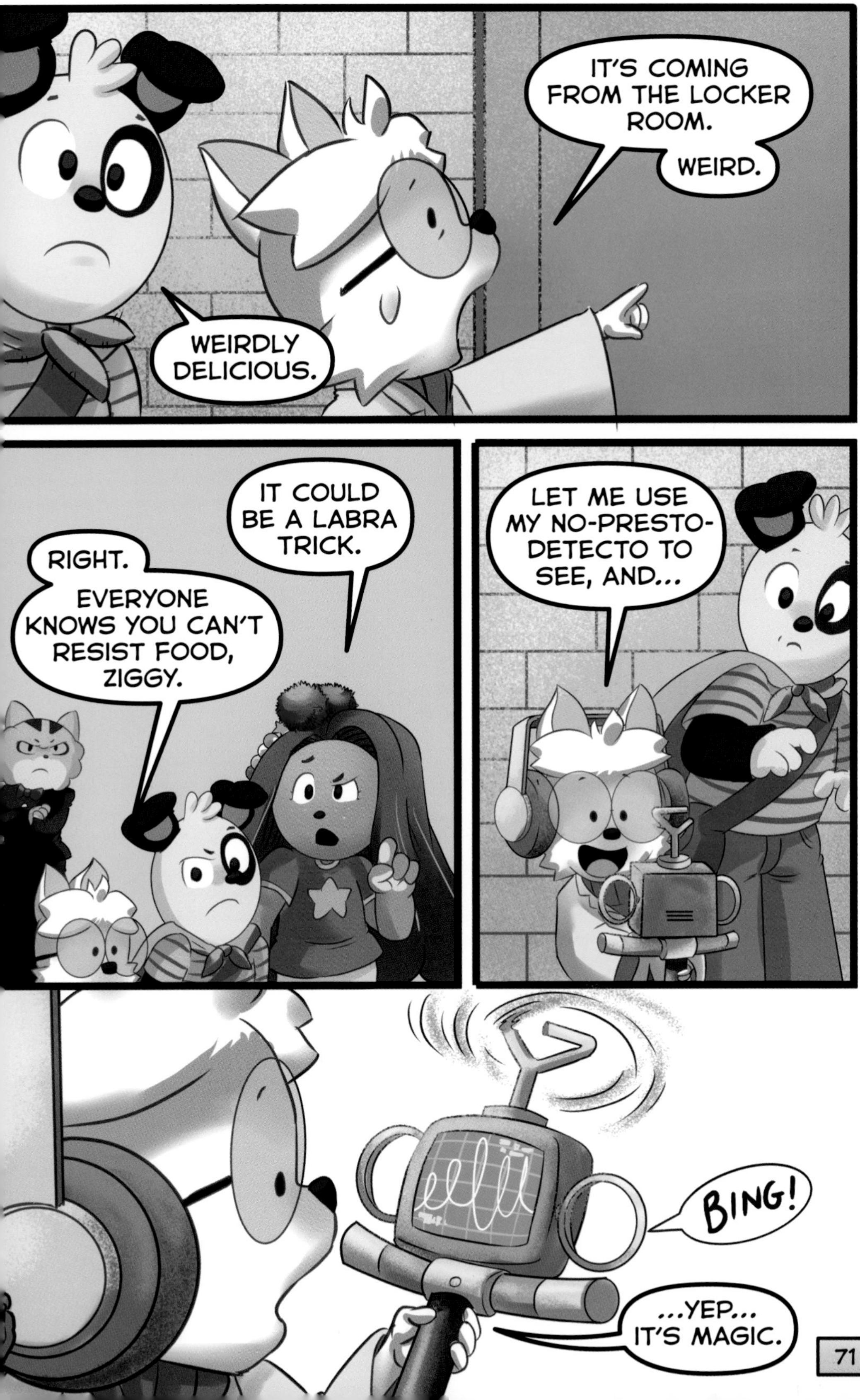
IT'S COMING FROM THE LOCKER ROOM.
WEIRD.
WEIRDLY DELICIOUS.
IT COULD BE A LABRA TRICK.
RIGHT.
EVERYONE KNOWS YOU CAN'T RESIST FOOD, ZIGGY.
LET ME USE MY NO-PRESTO-DETECTO TO SEE, AND...
BING!
...YEP... IT'S MAGIC.

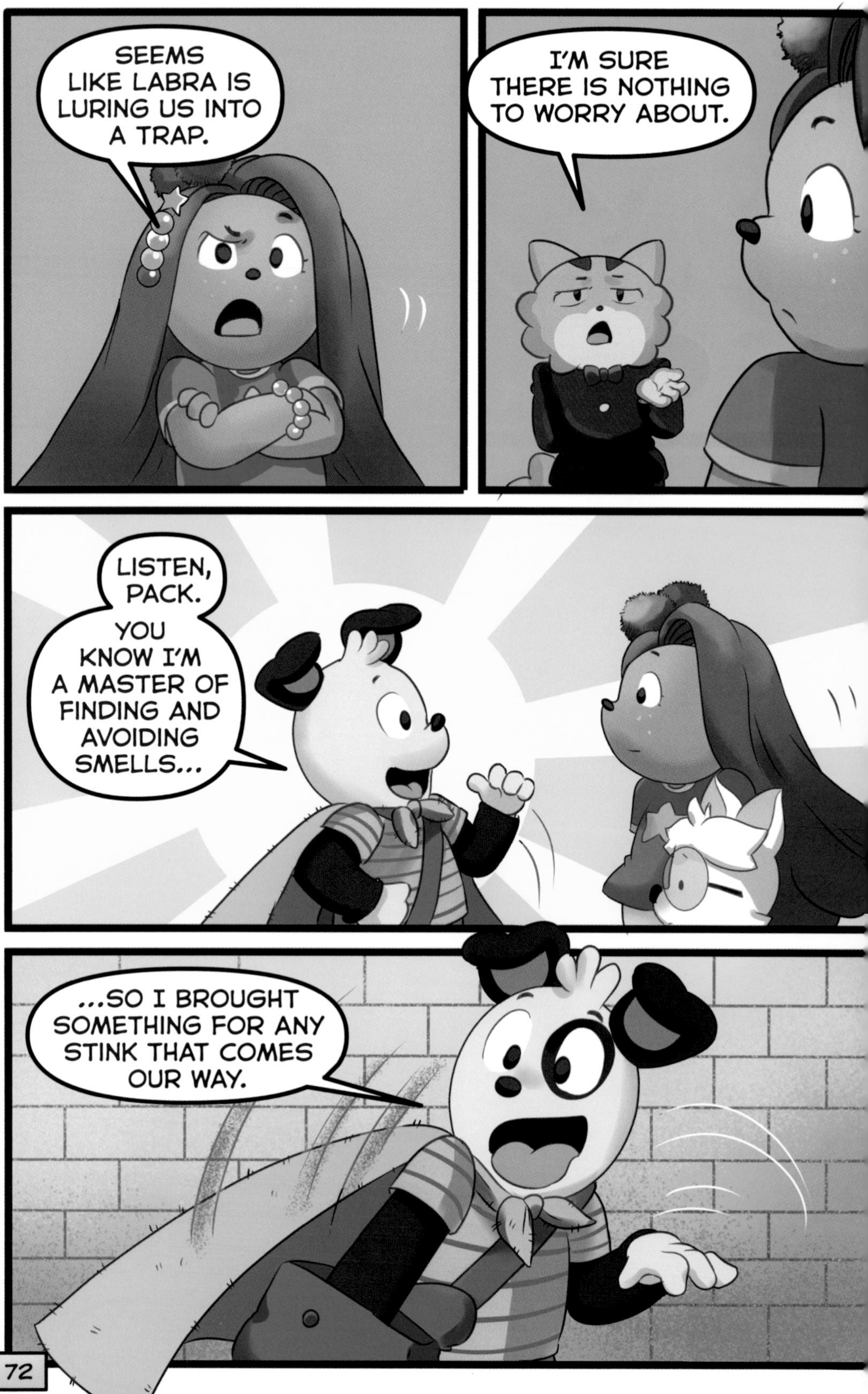
SEEMS LIKE LABRA IS LURING US INTO A TRAP.
I'M SURE THERE IS NOTHING TO WORRY ABOUT.
LISTEN, PACK.
YOU KNOW I'M A MASTER OF FINDING AND AVOIDING SMELLS...
...SO I BROUGHT SOMETHING FOR ANY STINK THAT COMES OUR WAY.

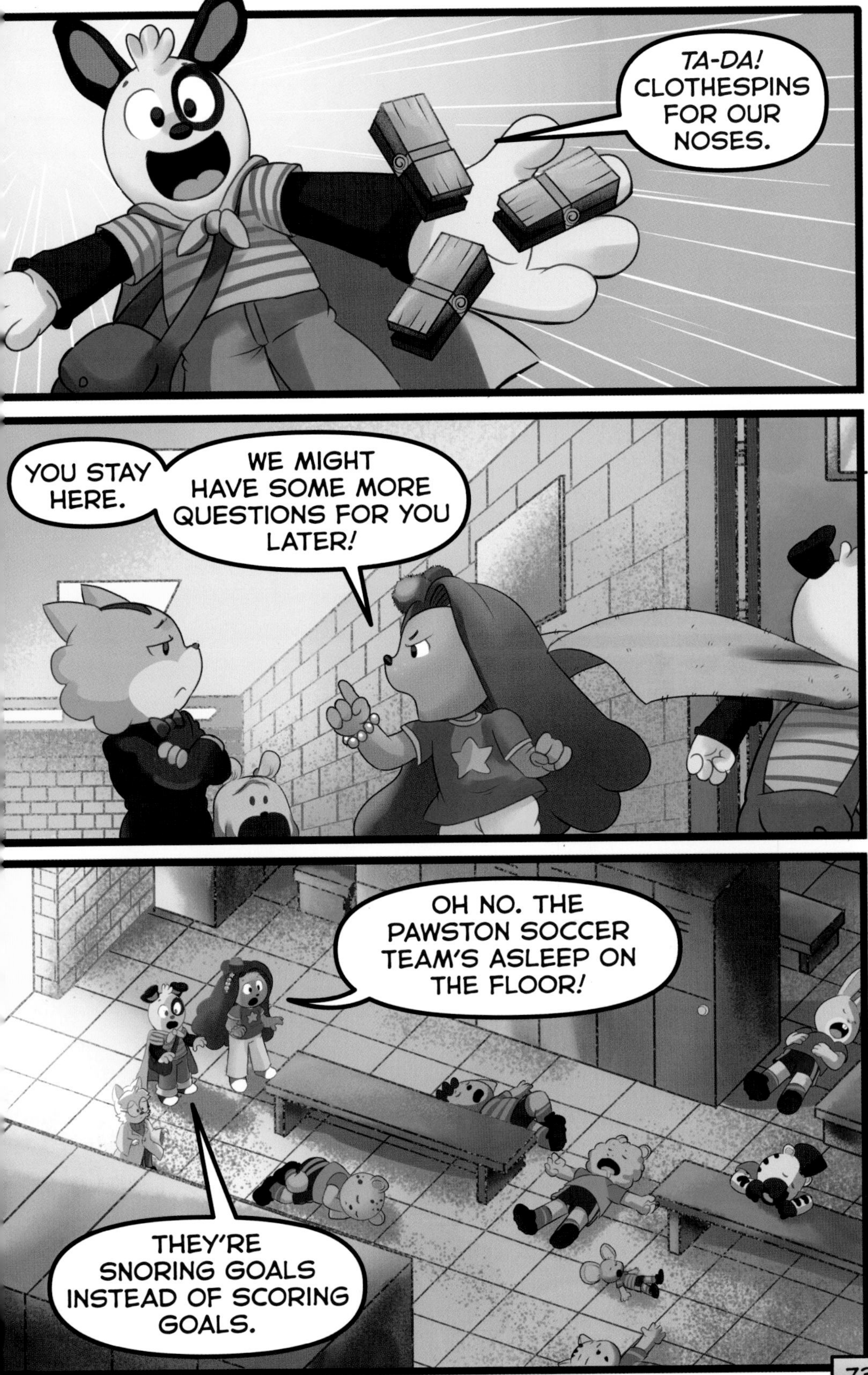
TA-DA! CLOTHESPINS FOR OUR NOSES.
YOU STAY HERE.
WE MIGHT HAVE SOME MORE QUESTIONS FOR YOU LATER!
OH NO. THE PAWSTON SOCCER TEAM'S ASLEEP ON THE FLOOR!
THEY'RE SNORING GOALS INSTEAD OF SCORING GOALS.

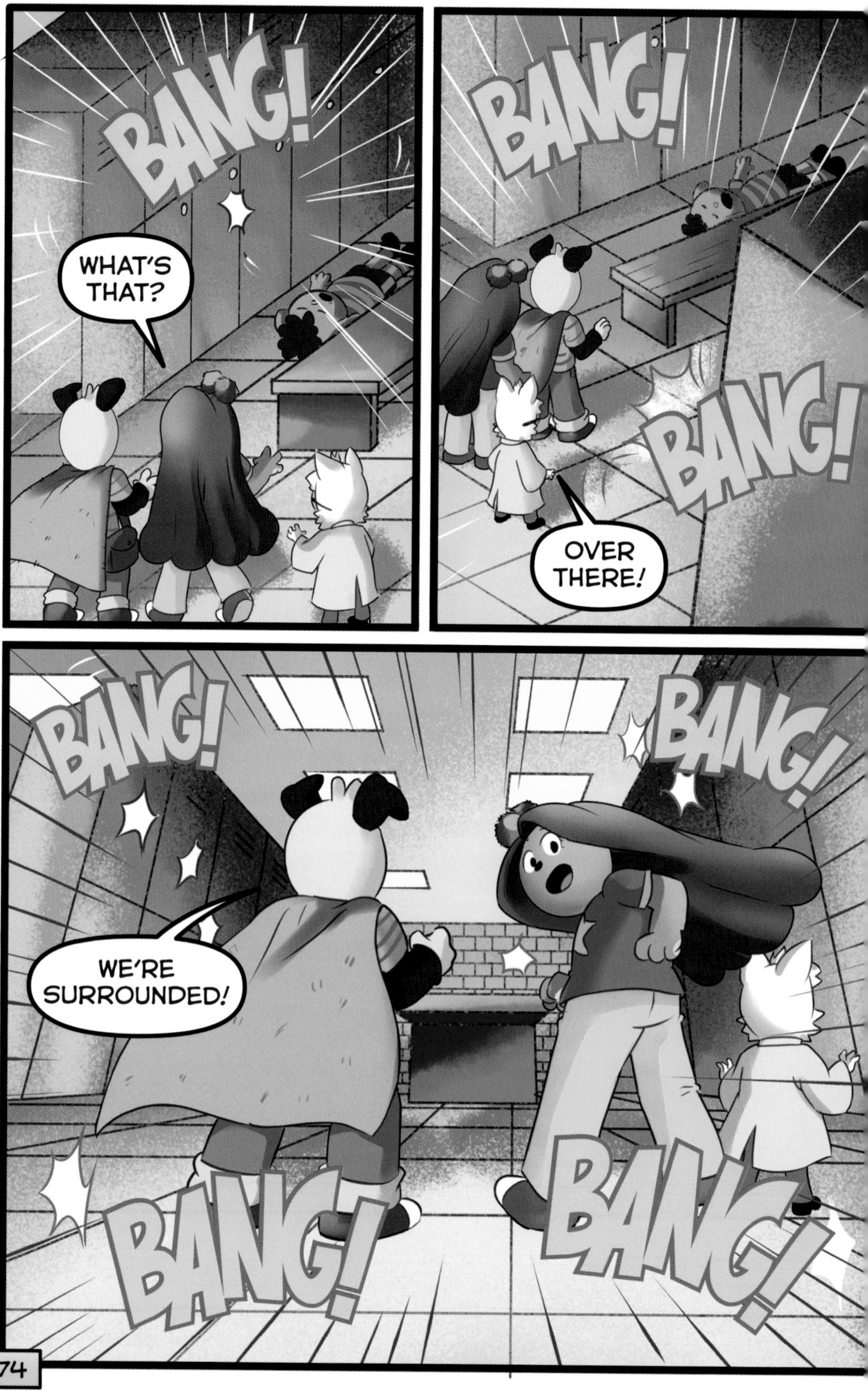
BANG!
WHAT'S THAT?
BANG!
BANG!
OVER THERE!
BANG!
BANG!
WE'RE SURROUNDED!
BANG!
BANG!

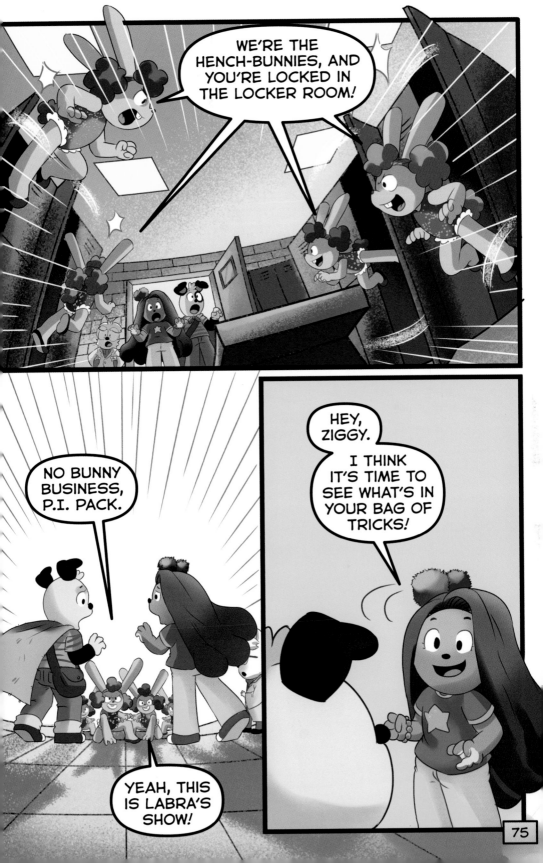

WE'RE THE HENCH-BUNNIES, AND YOU'RE LOCKED IN THE LOCKER ROOM!

NO BUNNY BUSINESS, P.I. PACK.

YEAH, THIS IS LABRA'S SHOW!

HEY, ZIGGY.

I THINK IT'S TIME TO SEE WHAT'S IN YOUR BAG OF TRICKS!

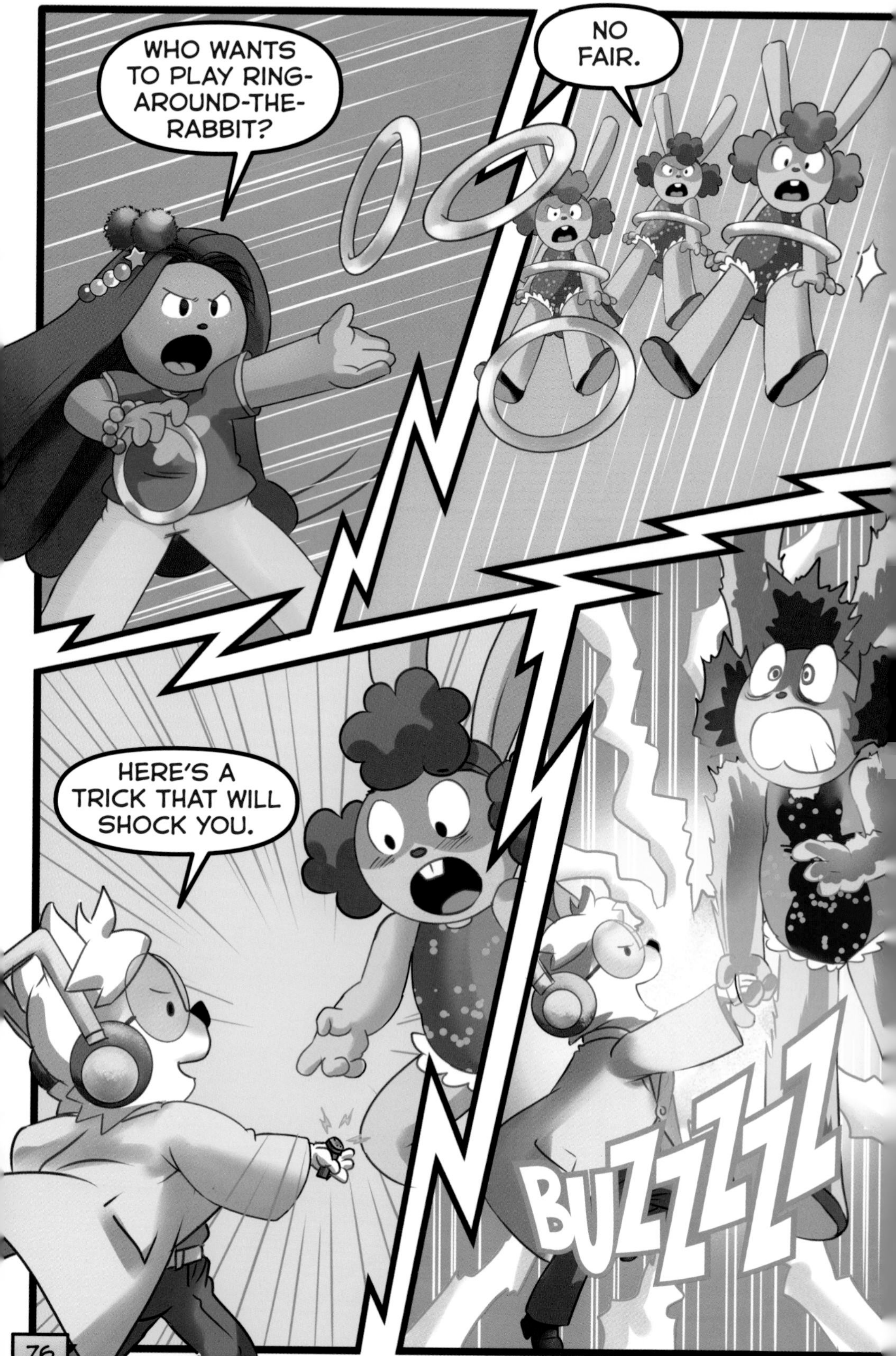
WHO WANTS TO PLAY RING-AROUND-THE-RABBIT?
NO FAIR.
HERE'S A TRICK THAT WILL SHOCK YOU.
BUZZZZZ

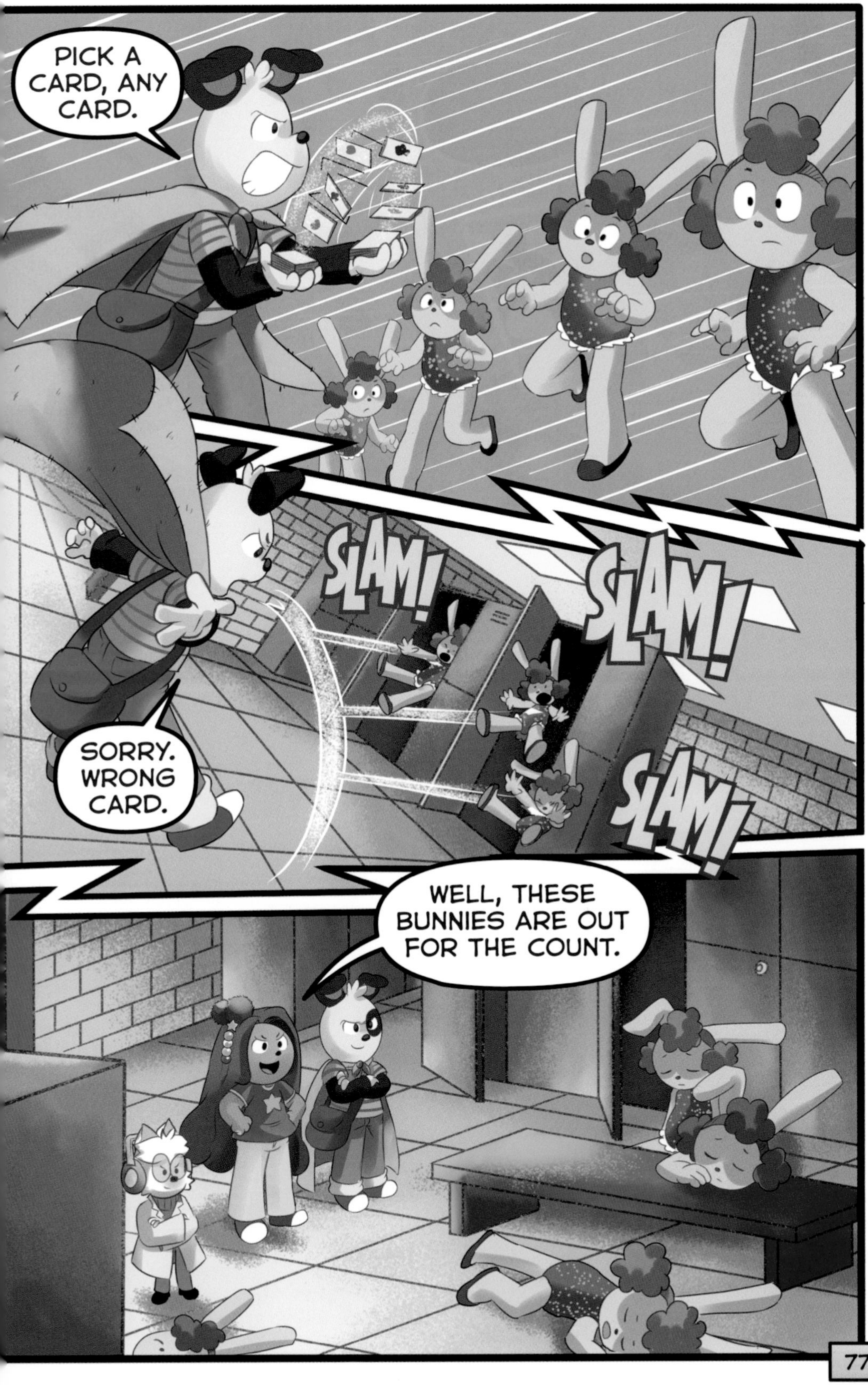
PICK A CARD, ANY CARD.
SLAM!
SLAM!
SORRY. WRONG CARD.
SLAM!
WELL, THESE BUNNIES ARE OUT FOR THE COUNT.

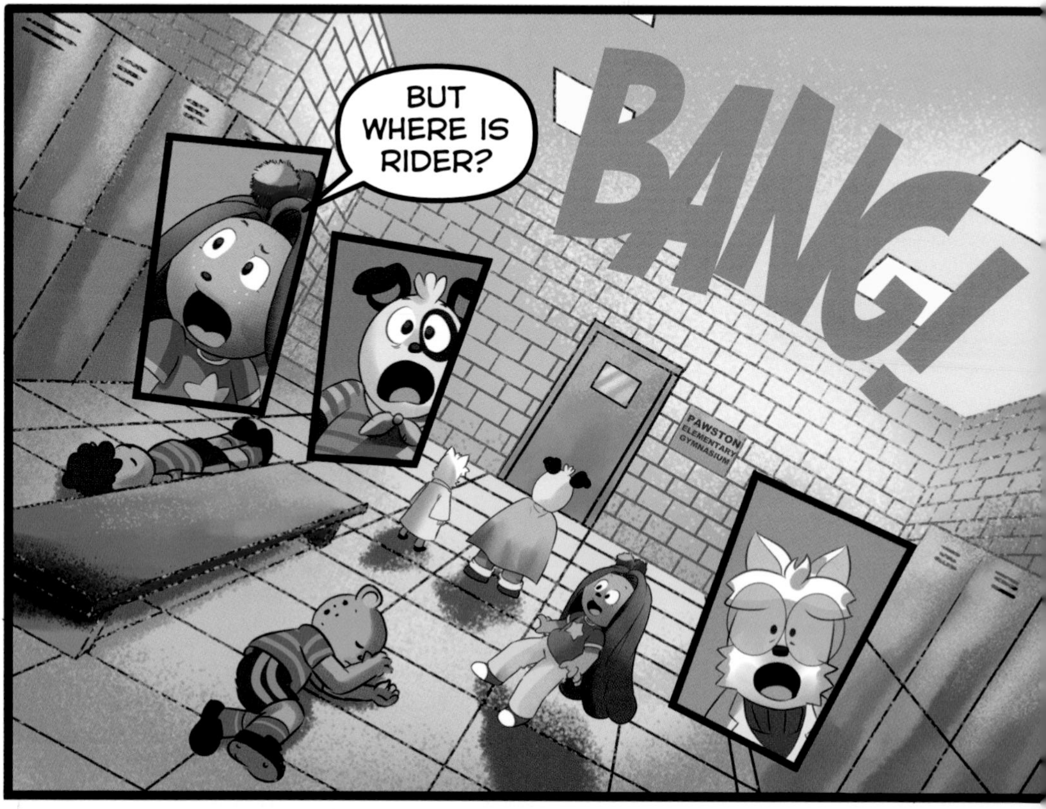
BUT WHERE IS RIDER?
BANG!
PAWSTON ELEMENTARY GYMNASIUM

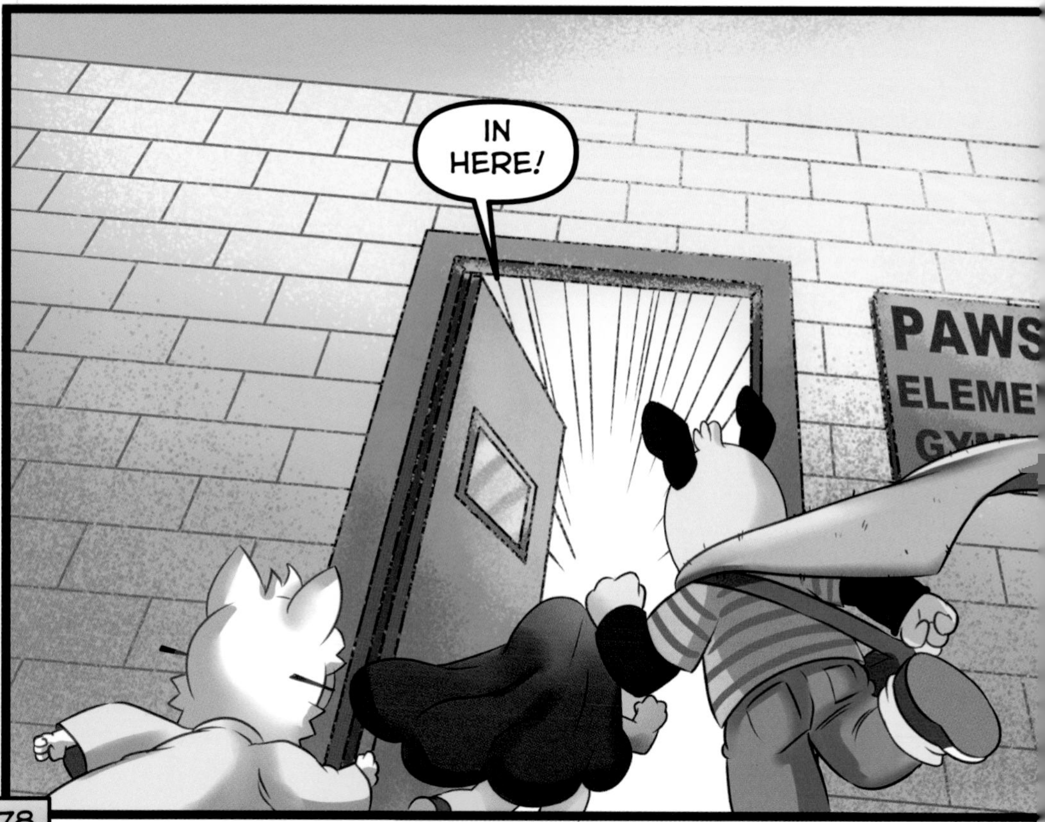
IN HERE!

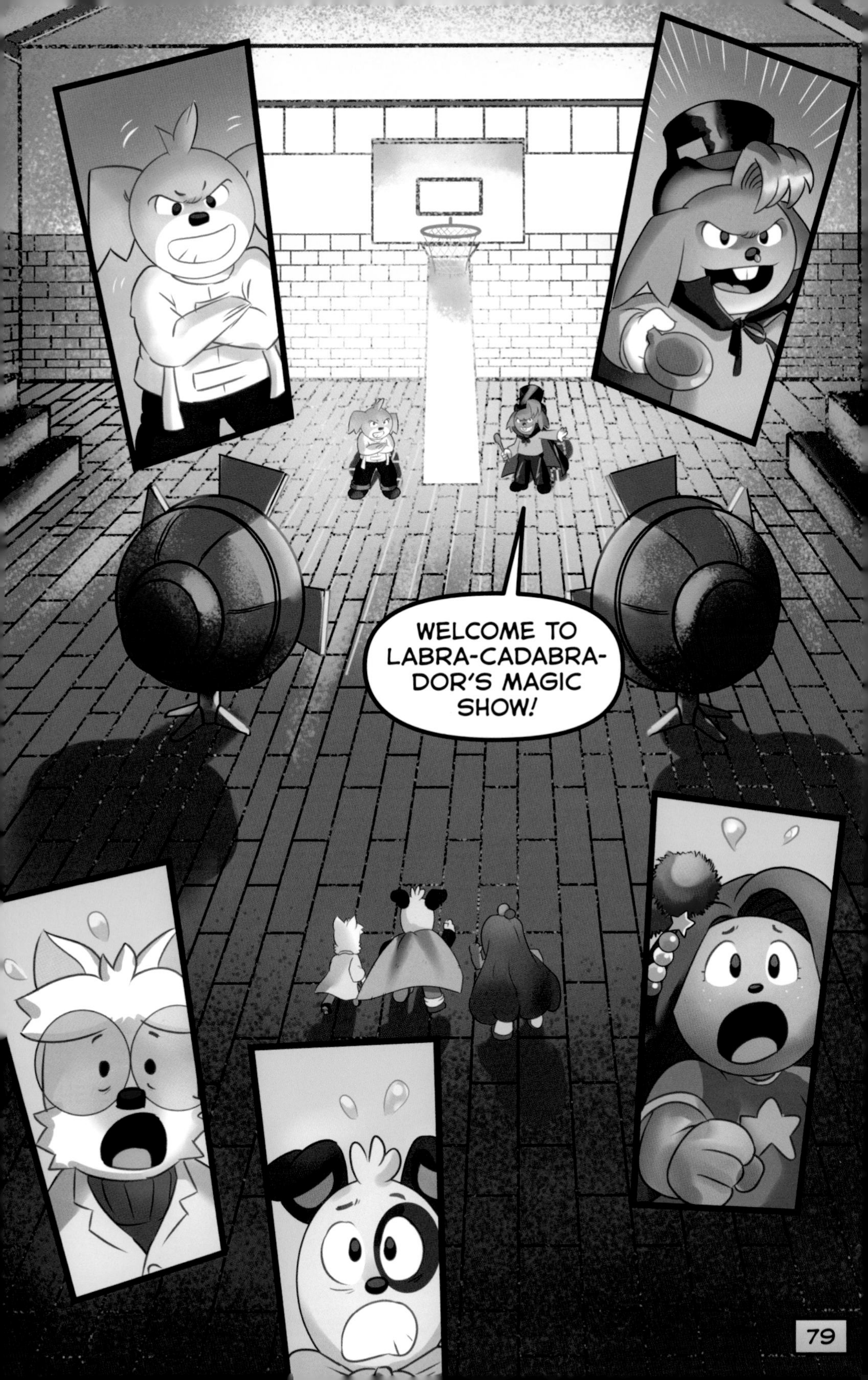
WELCOME TO LABRA-CADABRADOR'S MAGIC SHOW!

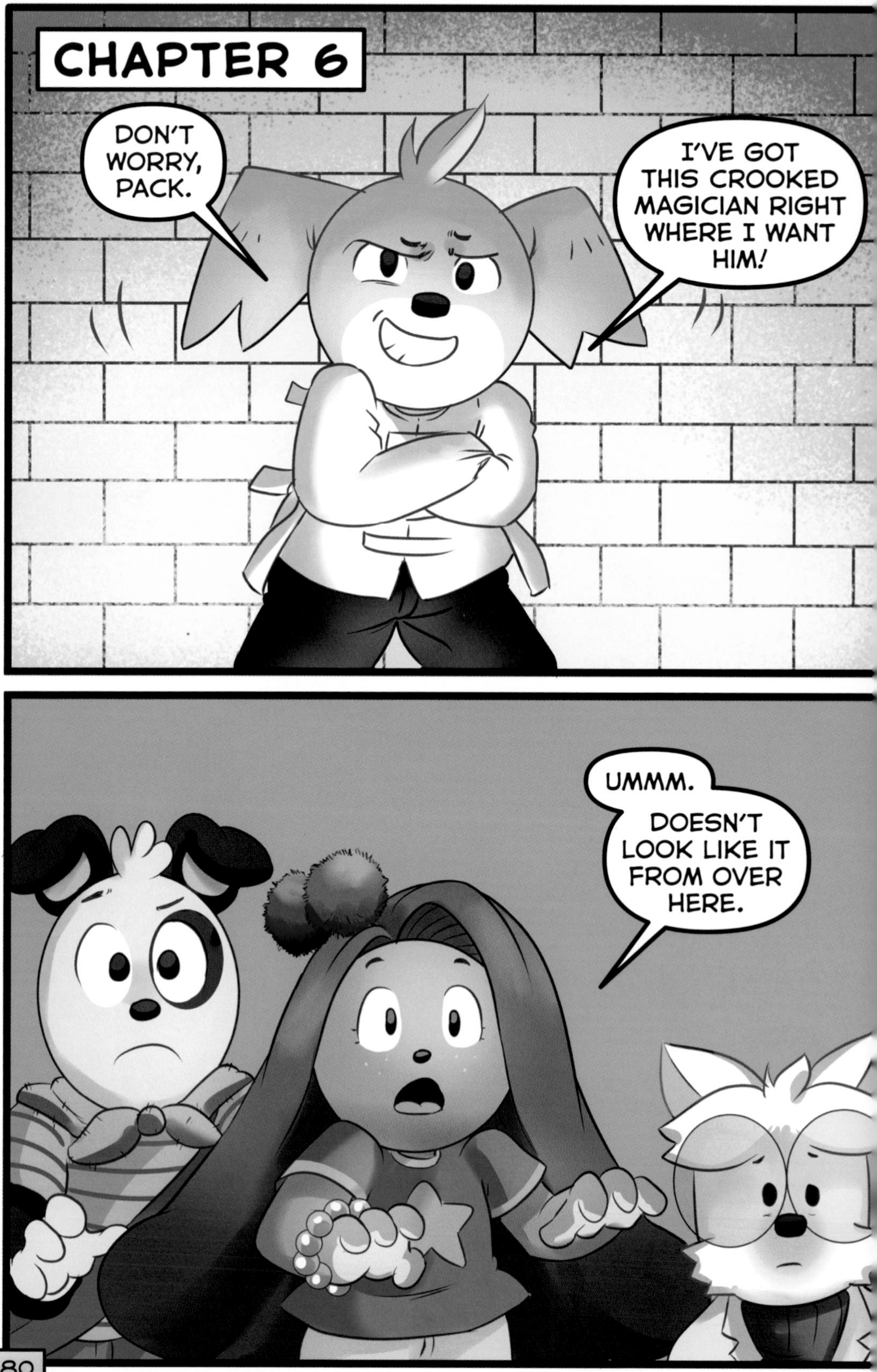
CHAPTER 6
DON'T WORRY, PACK.
I'VE GOT THIS CROOKED MAGICIAN RIGHT WHERE I WANT HIM!
UMMM.
DOESN'T LOOK LIKE IT FROM OVER HERE.

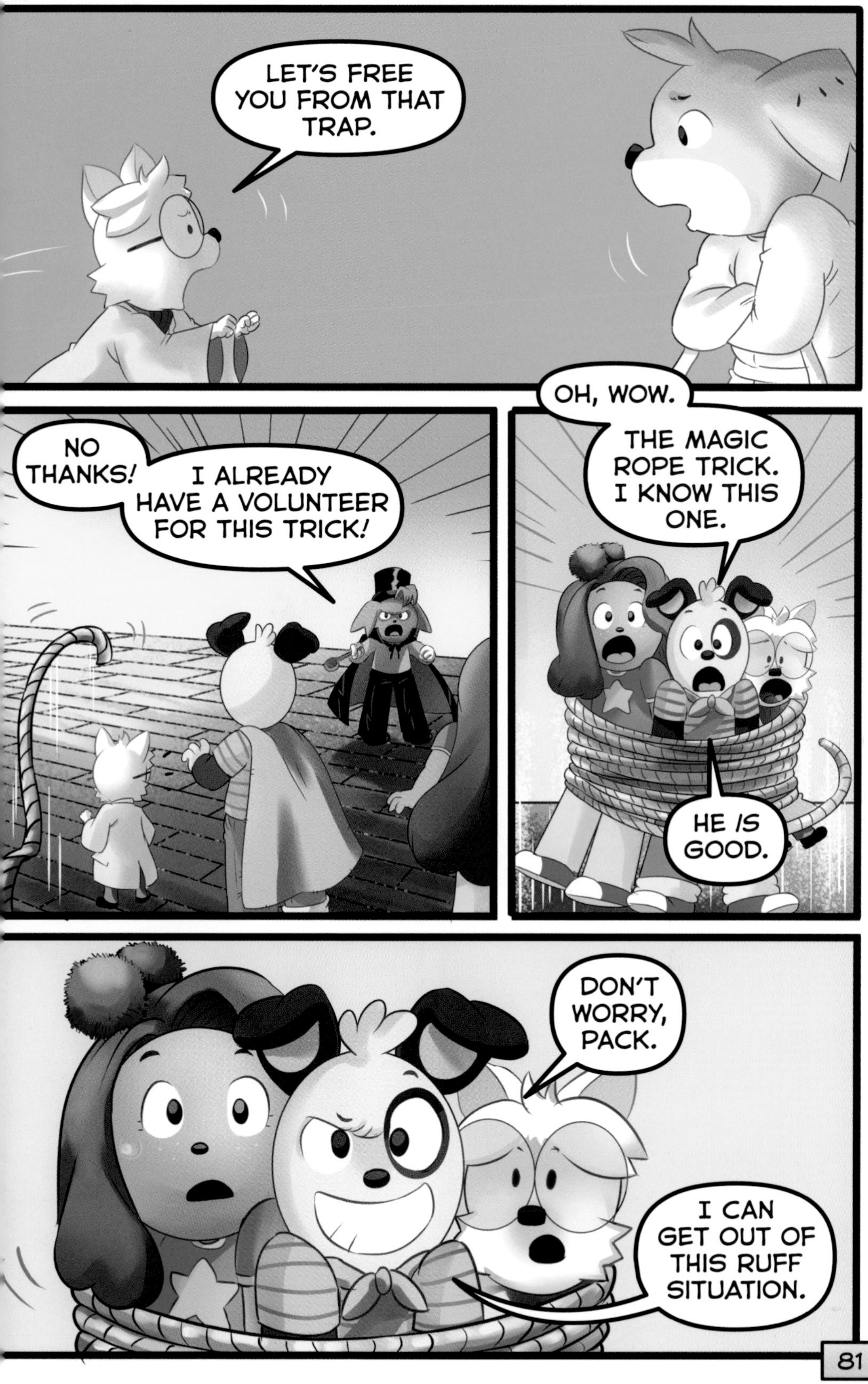
LET'S FREE YOU FROM THAT TRAP.
NO THANKS!
I ALREADY HAVE A VOLUNTEER FOR THIS TRICK!
OH, WOW.
THE MAGIC ROPE TRICK. I KNOW THIS ONE.
HE *IS* GOOD.
DON'T WORRY, PACK.
I CAN GET OUT OF THIS RUFF SITUATION.

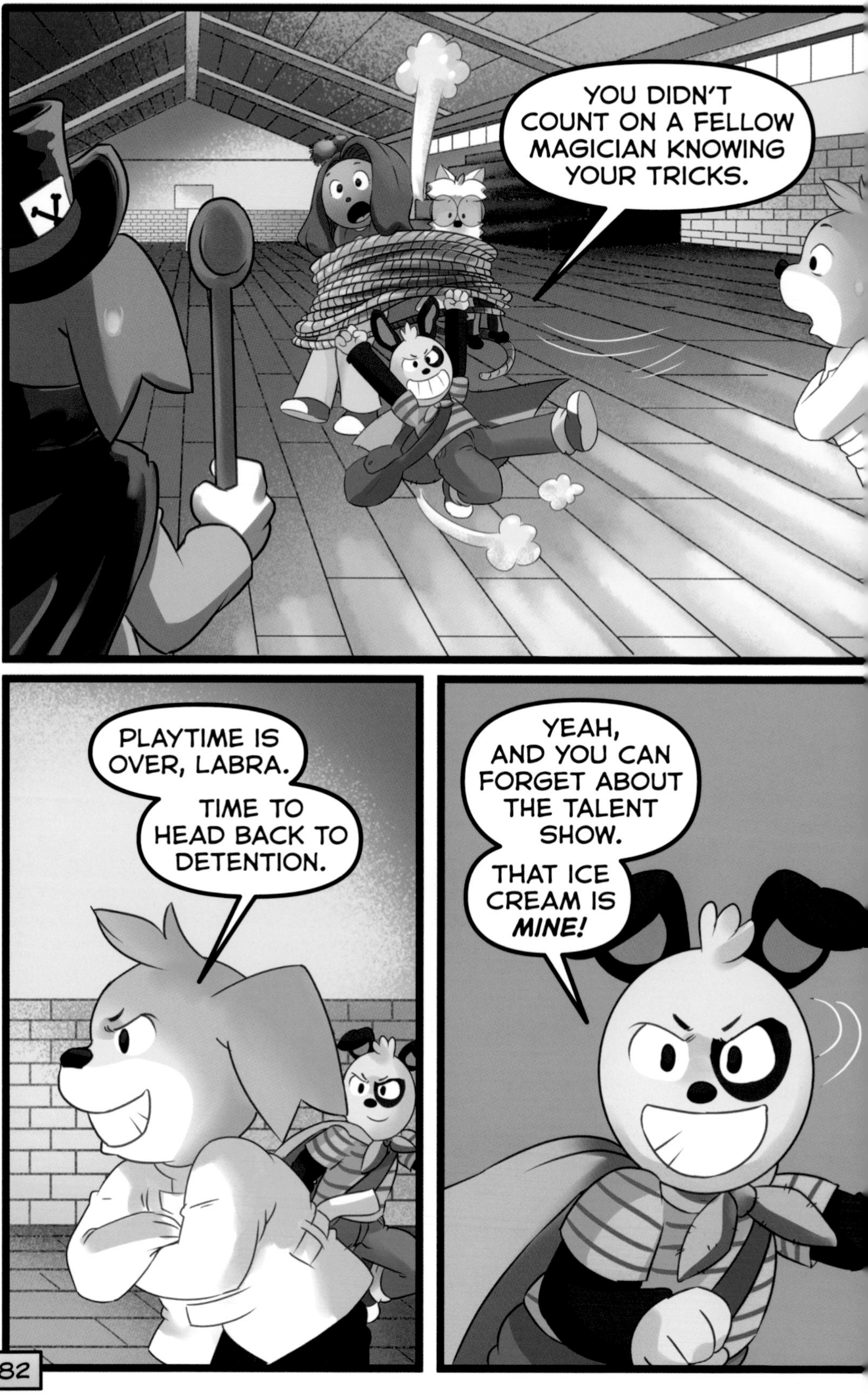
YOU DIDN'T COUNT ON A FELLOW MAGICIAN KNOWING YOUR TRICKS.
PLAYTIME IS OVER, LABRA.
TIME TO HEAD BACK TO DETENTION.
YEAH, AND YOU CAN FORGET ABOUT THE TALENT SHOW.
THAT ICE CREAM IS *MINE!*

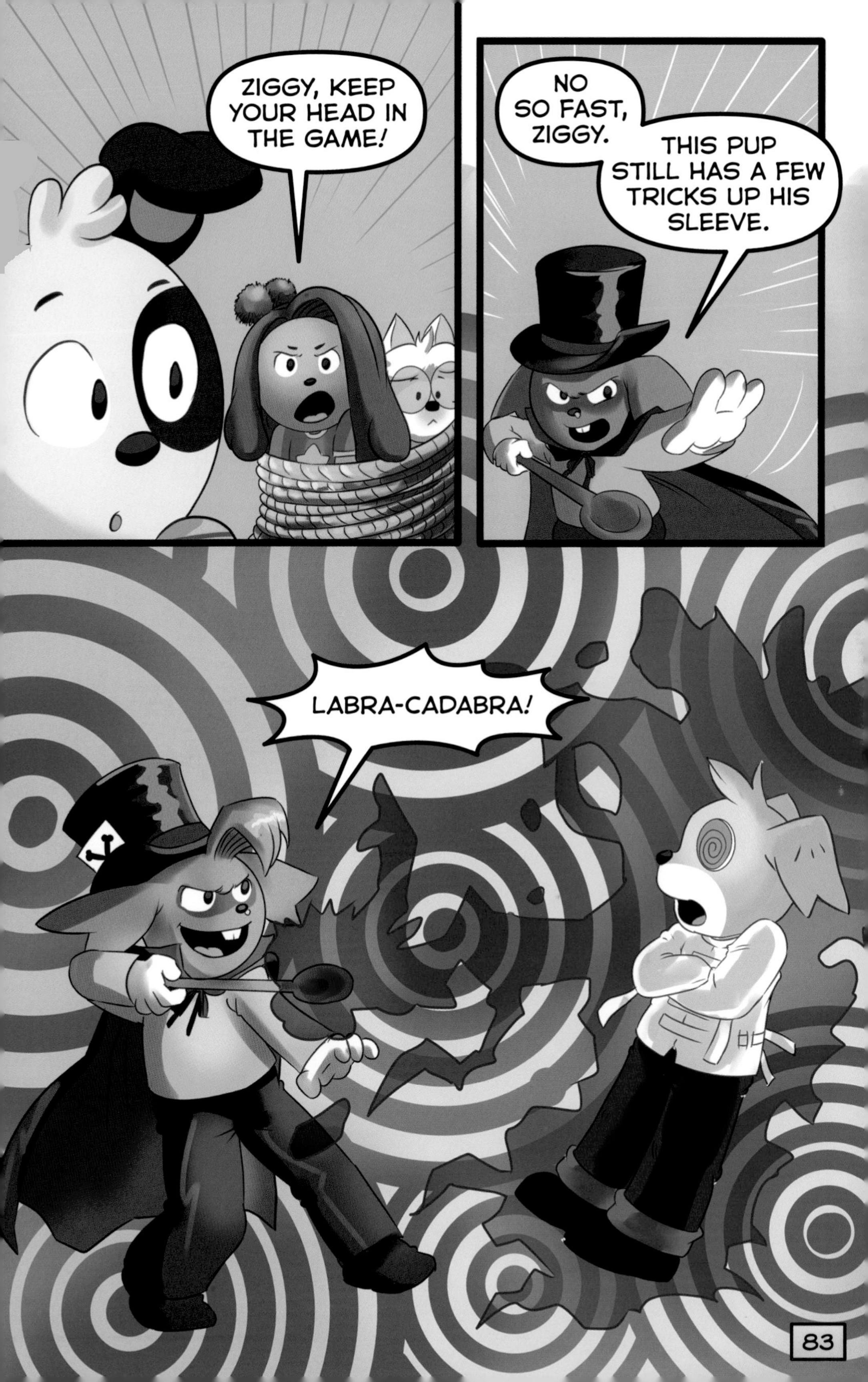
ZIGGY, KEEP YOUR HEAD IN THE GAME!
NO SO FAST, ZIGGY.
THIS PUP STILL HAS A FEW TRICKS UP HIS SLEEVE.
LABRA-CADABRA!

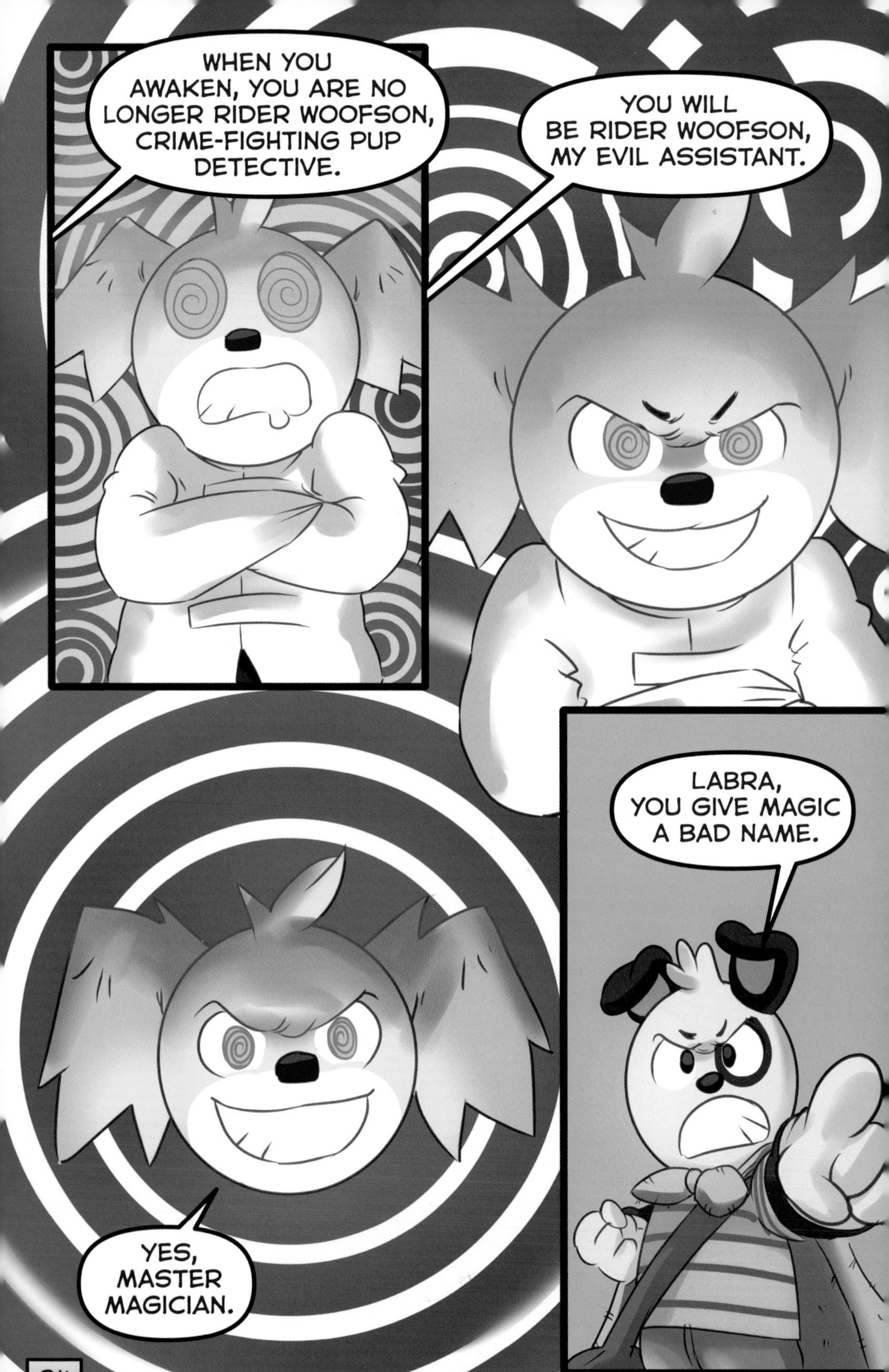
WHEN YOU AWAKEN, YOU ARE NO LONGER RIDER WOOFSON, CRIME-FIGHTING PUP DETECTIVE.
YOU WILL BE RIDER WOOFSON, MY EVIL ASSISTANT.
YES, MASTER MAGICIAN.
LABRA, YOU GIVE MAGIC A BAD NAME.

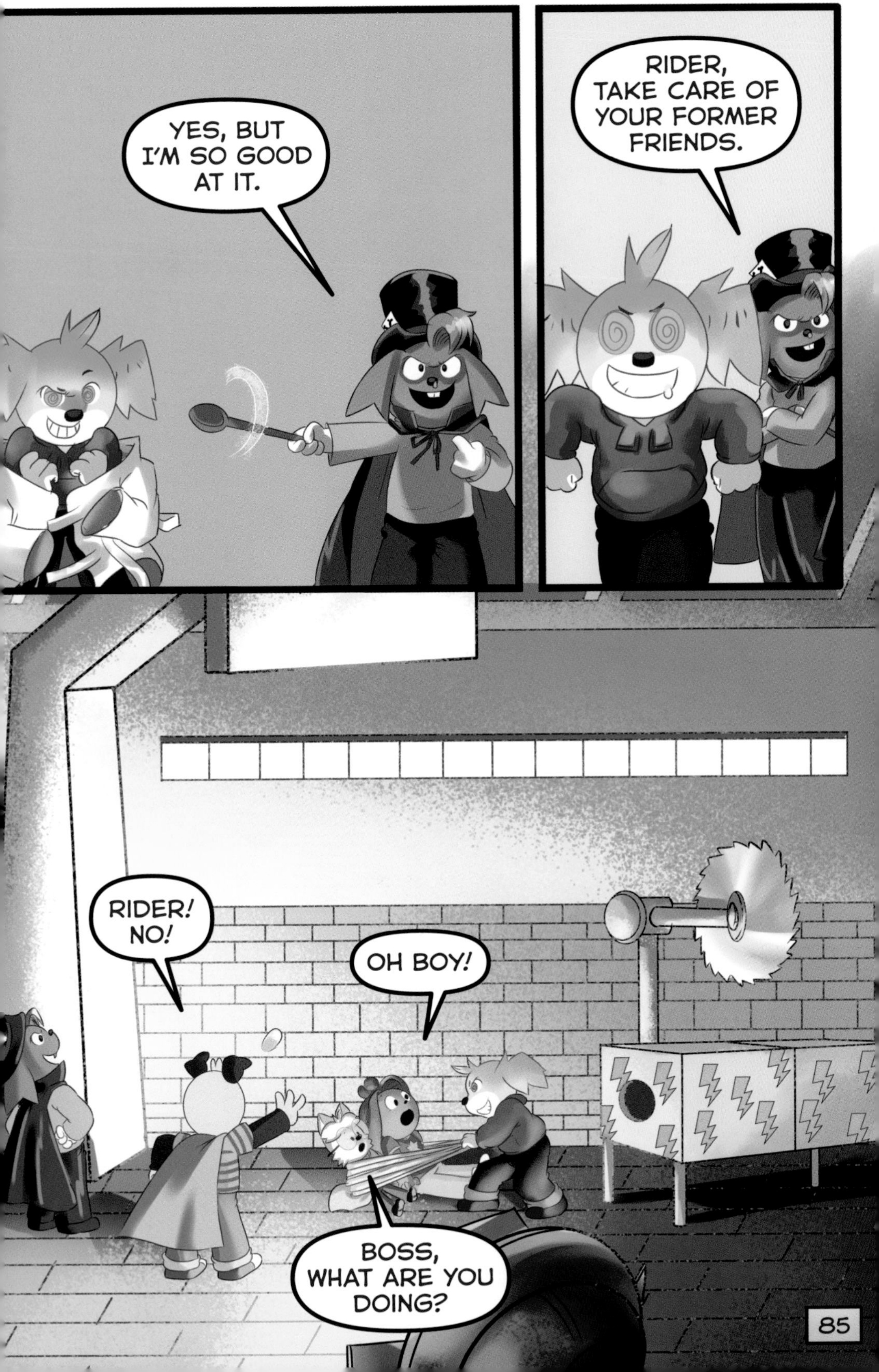
YES, BUT I'M SO GOOD AT IT.
RIDER, TAKE CARE OF YOUR FORMER FRIENDS.
RIDER! NO!
OH BOY!
BOSS, WHAT ARE YOU DOING?

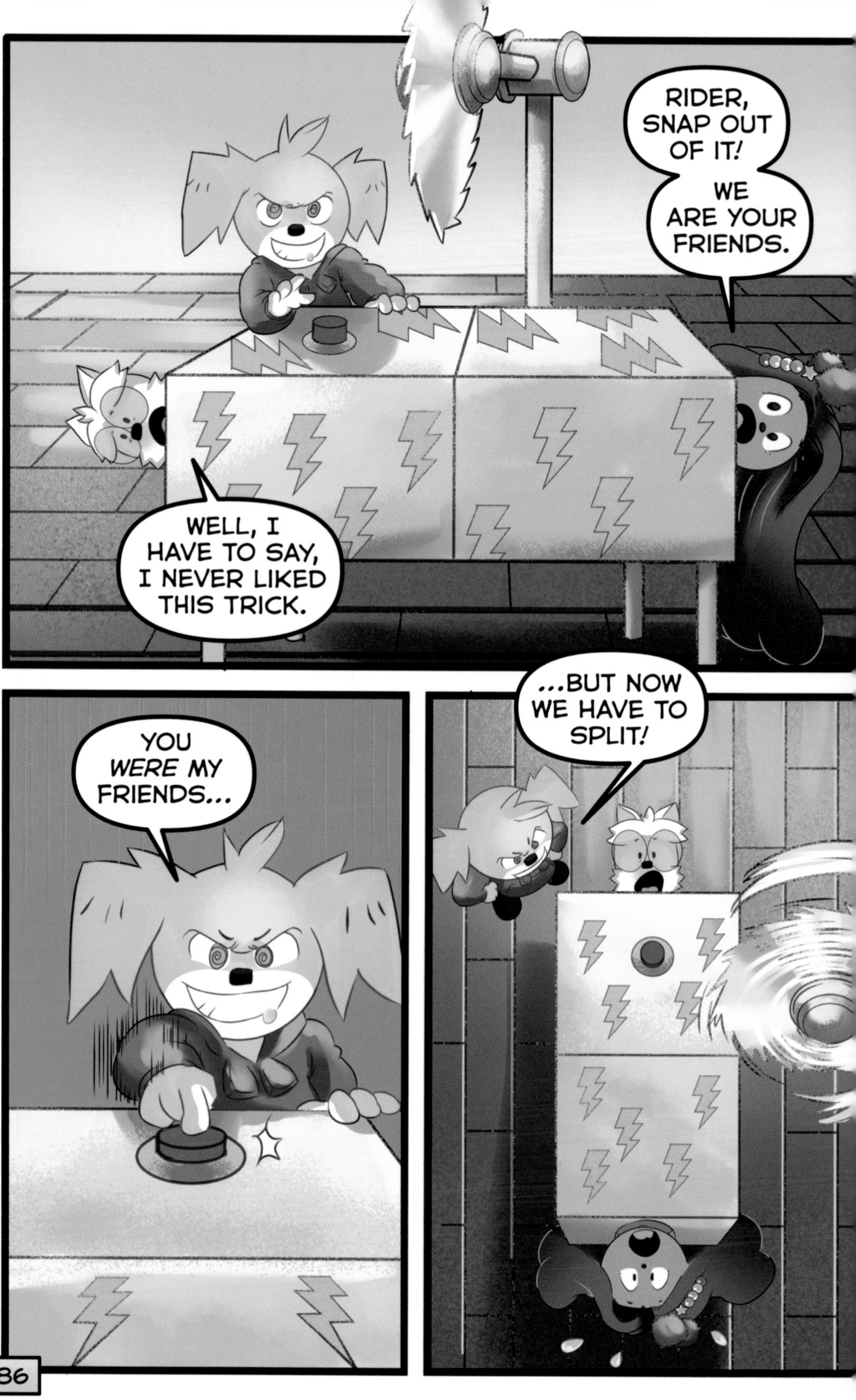
RIDER, SNAP OUT OF IT!
WE ARE YOUR FRIENDS.
WELL, I HAVE TO SAY, I NEVER LIKED THIS TRICK.
YOU *WERE* MY FRIENDS...
...BUT NOW WE HAVE TO SPLIT!

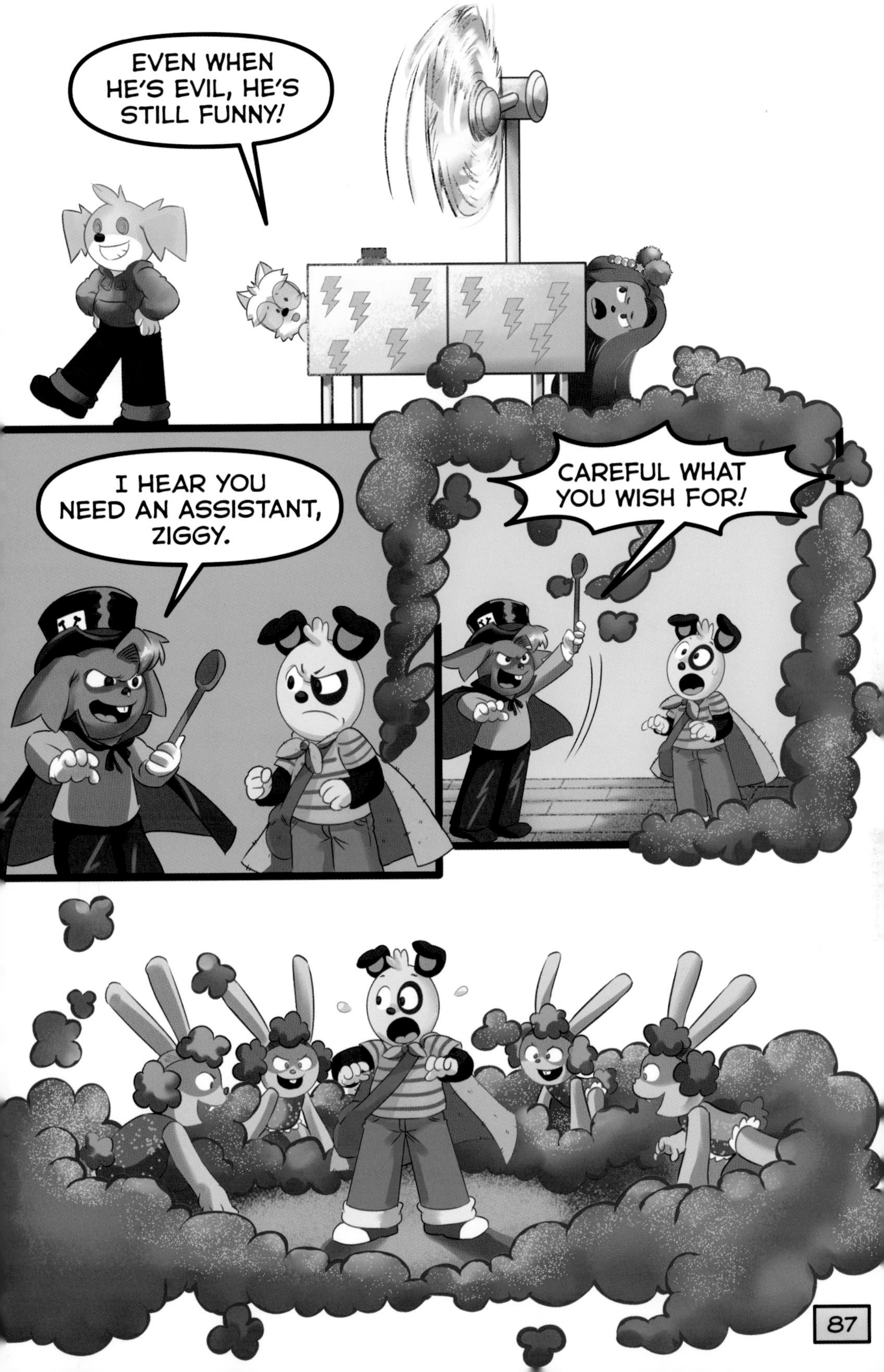
EVEN WHEN HE'S EVIL, HE'S STILL FUNNY!
I HEAR YOU NEED AN ASSISTANT, ZIGGY.
CAREFUL WHAT YOU WISH FOR!

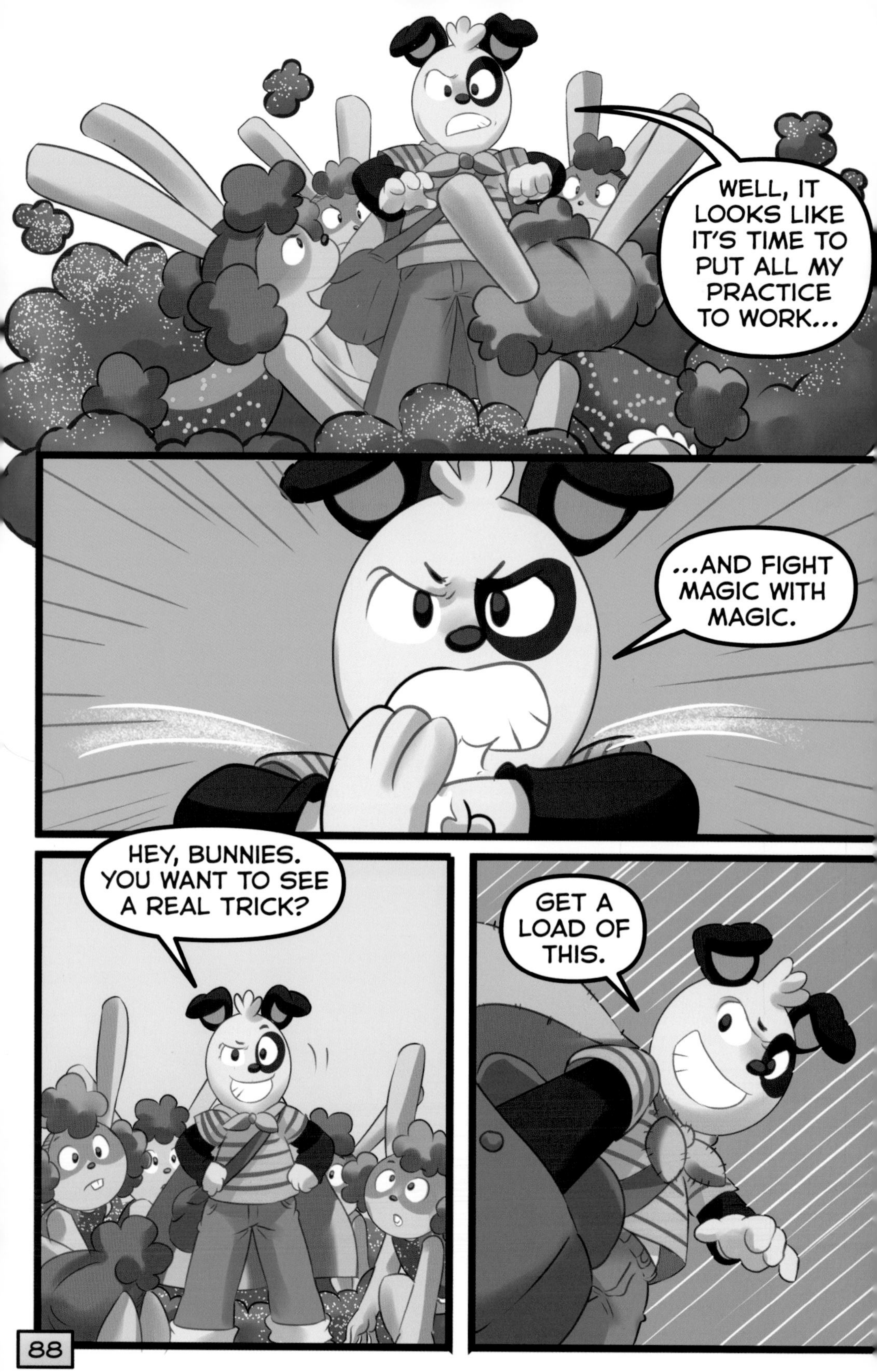
WELL, IT LOOKS LIKE IT'S TIME TO PUT ALL MY PRACTICE TO WORK...
...AND FIGHT MAGIC WITH MAGIC.
HEY, BUNNIES. YOU WANT TO SEE A REAL TRICK?
GET A LOAD OF THIS.

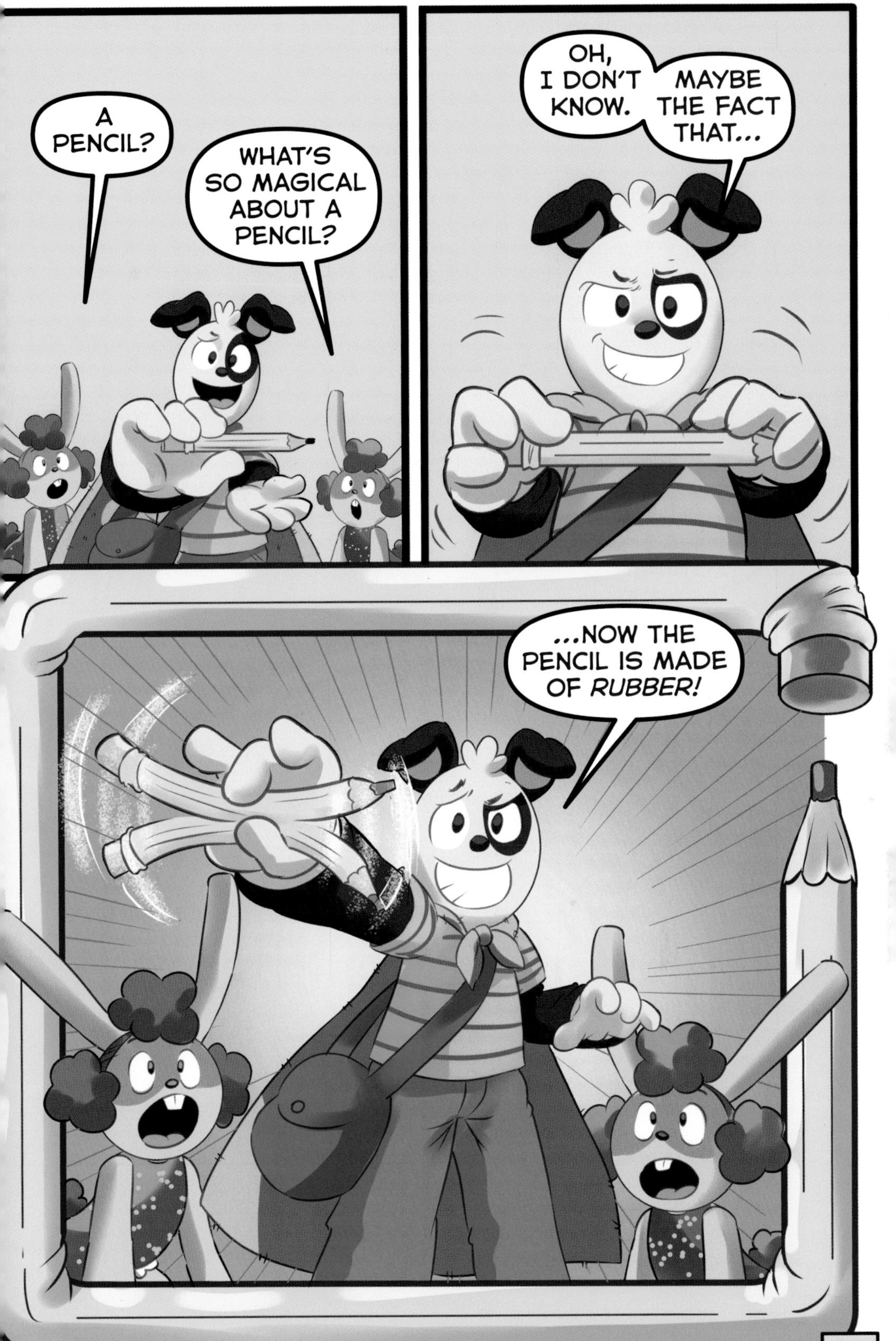
A PENCIL?
WHAT'S SO MAGICAL ABOUT A PENCIL?
OH, I DON'T KNOW.
MAYBE THE FACT THAT...
...NOW THE PENCIL IS MADE OF *RUBBER!*

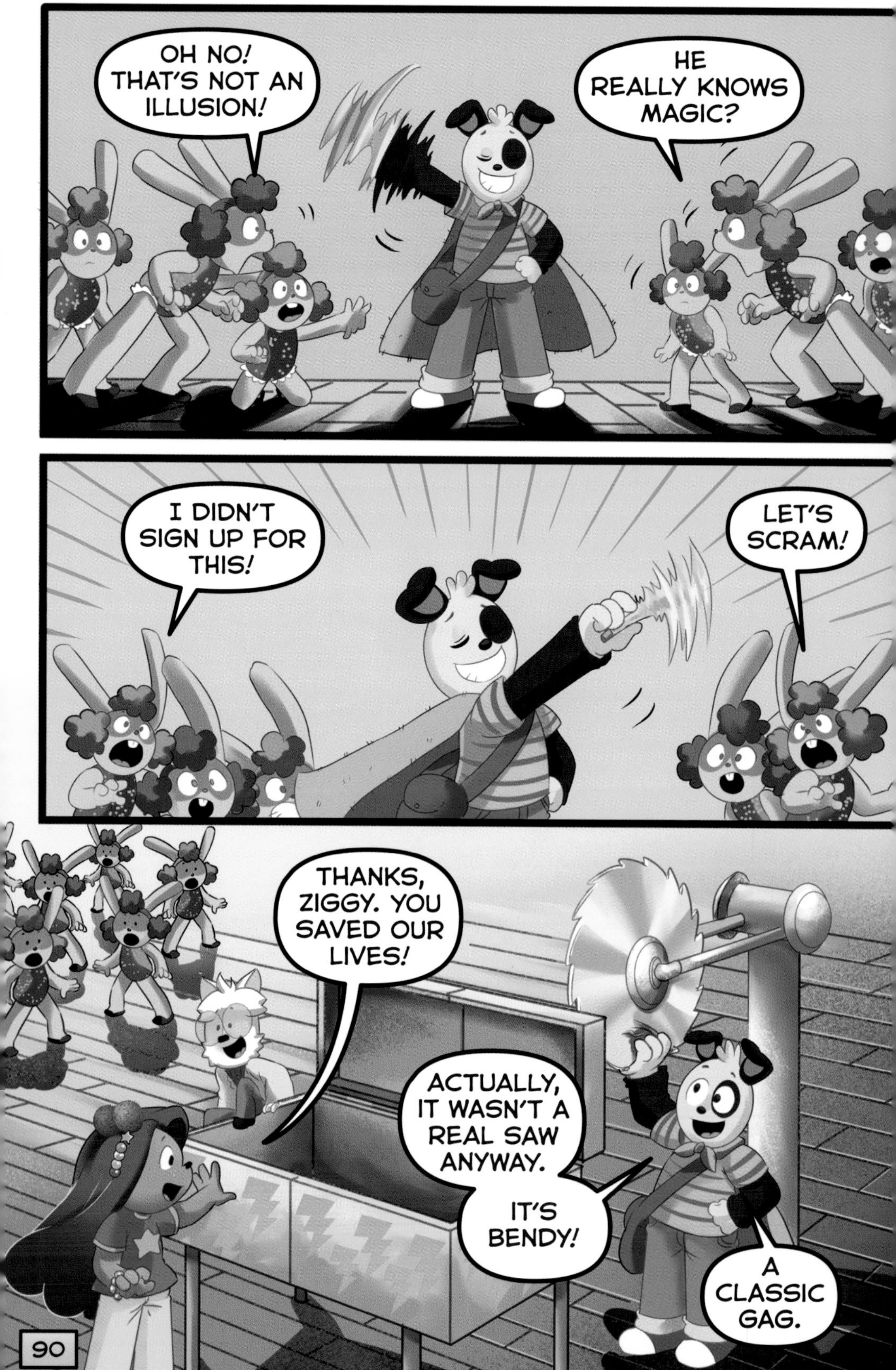
OH NO! THAT'S NOT AN ILLUSION!
HE REALLY KNOWS MAGIC?
I DIDN'T SIGN UP FOR THIS!
LET'S SCRAM!
THANKS, ZIGGY. YOU SAVED OUR LIVES!
ACTUALLY, IT WASN'T A REAL SAW ANYWAY.
IT'S BENDY!
A CLASSIC GAG.

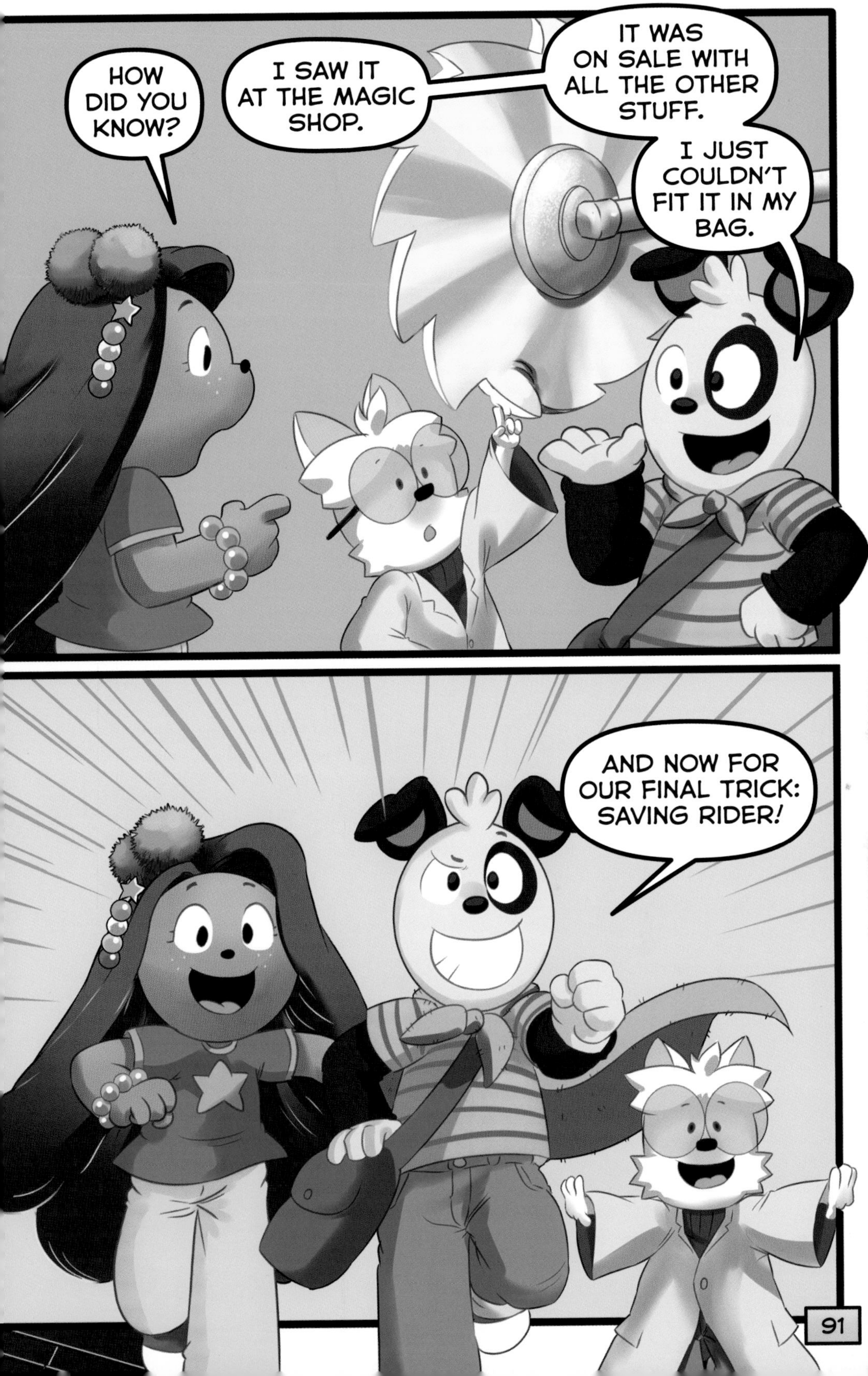
HOW DID YOU KNOW?
I SAW IT AT THE MAGIC SHOP.
IT WAS ON SALE WITH ALL THE OTHER STUFF.
I JUST COULDN'T FIT IT IN MY BAG.
AND NOW FOR OUR FINAL TRICK: SAVING RIDER!

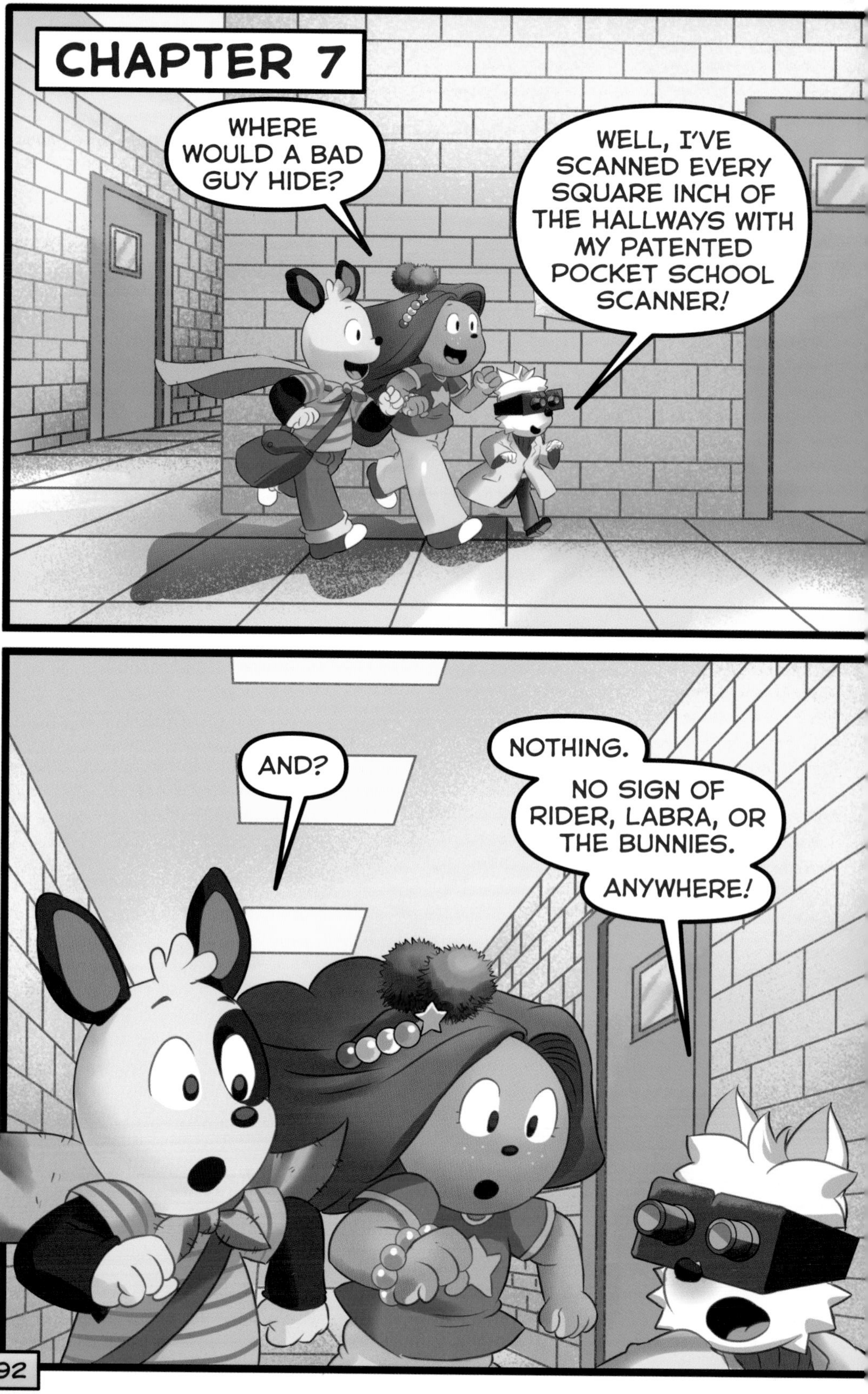
CHAPTER 7
WHERE WOULD A BAD GUY HIDE?
WELL, I'VE SCANNED EVERY SQUARE INCH OF THE HALLWAYS WITH MY PATENTED POCKET SCHOOL SCANNER!
AND?
NOTHING.
NO SIGN OF RIDER, LABRA, OR THE BUNNIES.
ANYWHERE!

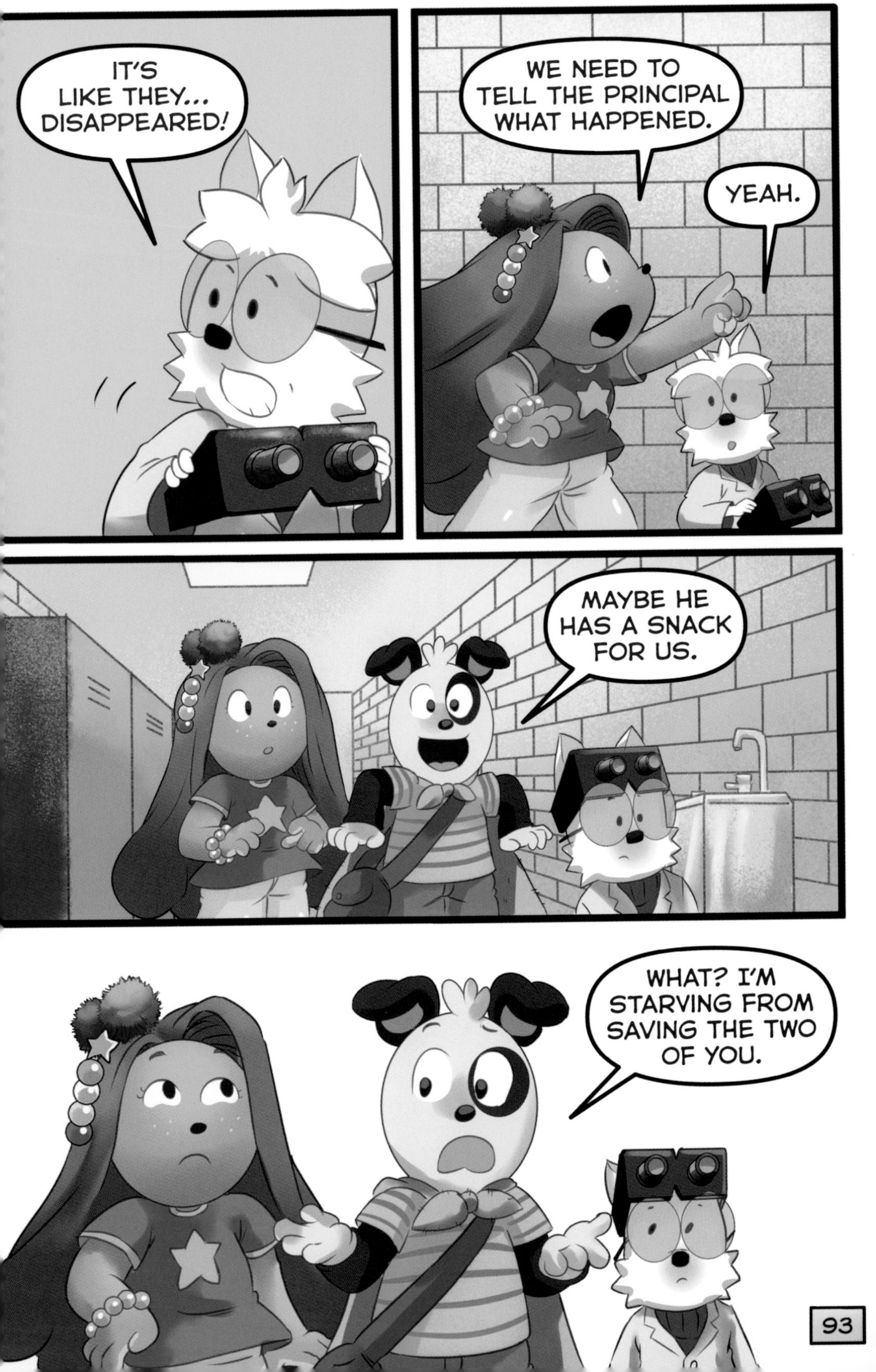

IT'S LIKE THEY... DISAPPEARED!
WE NEED TO TELL THE PRINCIPAL WHAT HAPPENED.
YEAH.
MAYBE HE HAS A SNACK FOR US.
WHAT? I'M STARVING FROM SAVING THE TWO OF YOU.

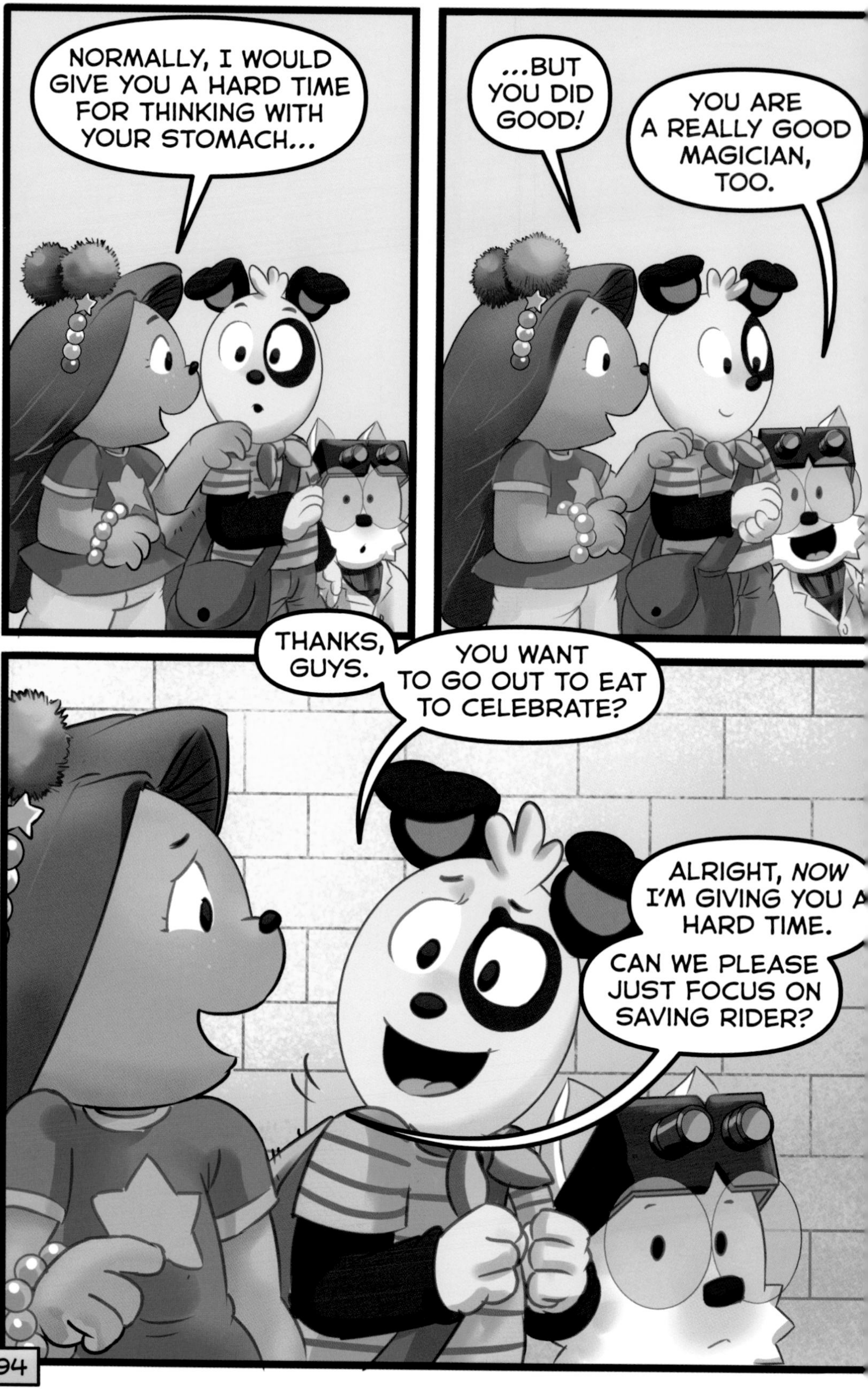
NORMALLY, I WOULD GIVE YOU A HARD TIME FOR THINKING WITH YOUR STOMACH...
...BUT YOU DID GOOD!
YOU ARE A REALLY GOOD MAGICIAN, TOO.
THANKS, GUYS.
YOU WANT TO GO OUT TO EAT TO CELEBRATE?
ALRIGHT, *NOW* I'M GIVING YOU A HARD TIME.
CAN WE PLEASE JUST FOCUS ON SAVING RIDER?

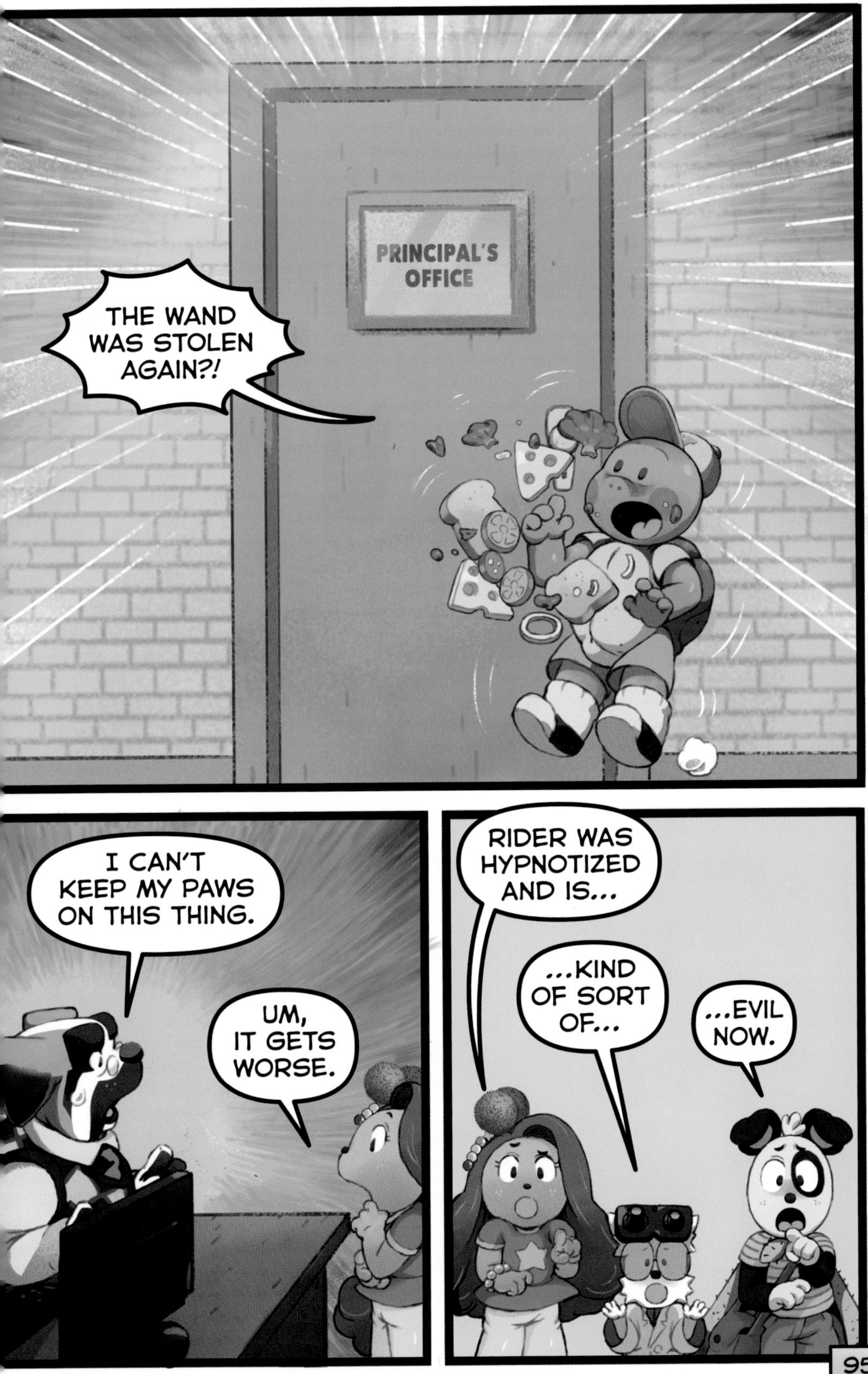
PRINCIPAL'S OFFICE
THE WAND WAS STOLEN AGAIN?!
I CAN'T KEEP MY PAWS ON THIS THING.
UM, IT GETS WORSE.
RIDER WAS HYPNOTIZED AND IS...
...KIND OF SORT OF...
...EVIL NOW.

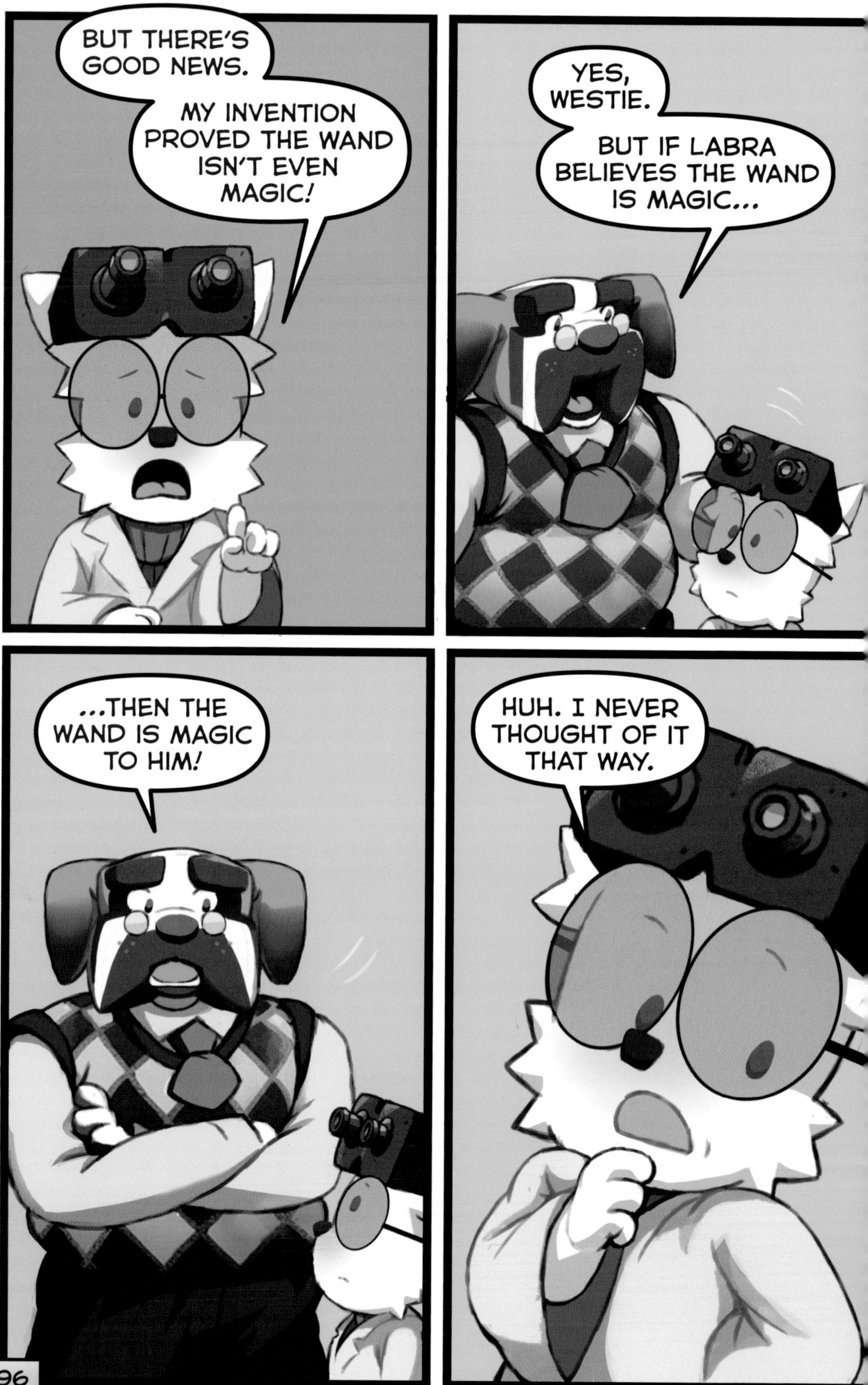
BUT THERE'S GOOD NEWS.
MY INVENTION PROVED THE WAND ISN'T EVEN MAGIC!
YES, WESTIE.
BUT IF LABRA BELIEVES THE WAND IS MAGIC...
...THEN THE WAND IS MAGIC TO HIM!
HUH. I NEVER THOUGHT OF IT THAT WAY.

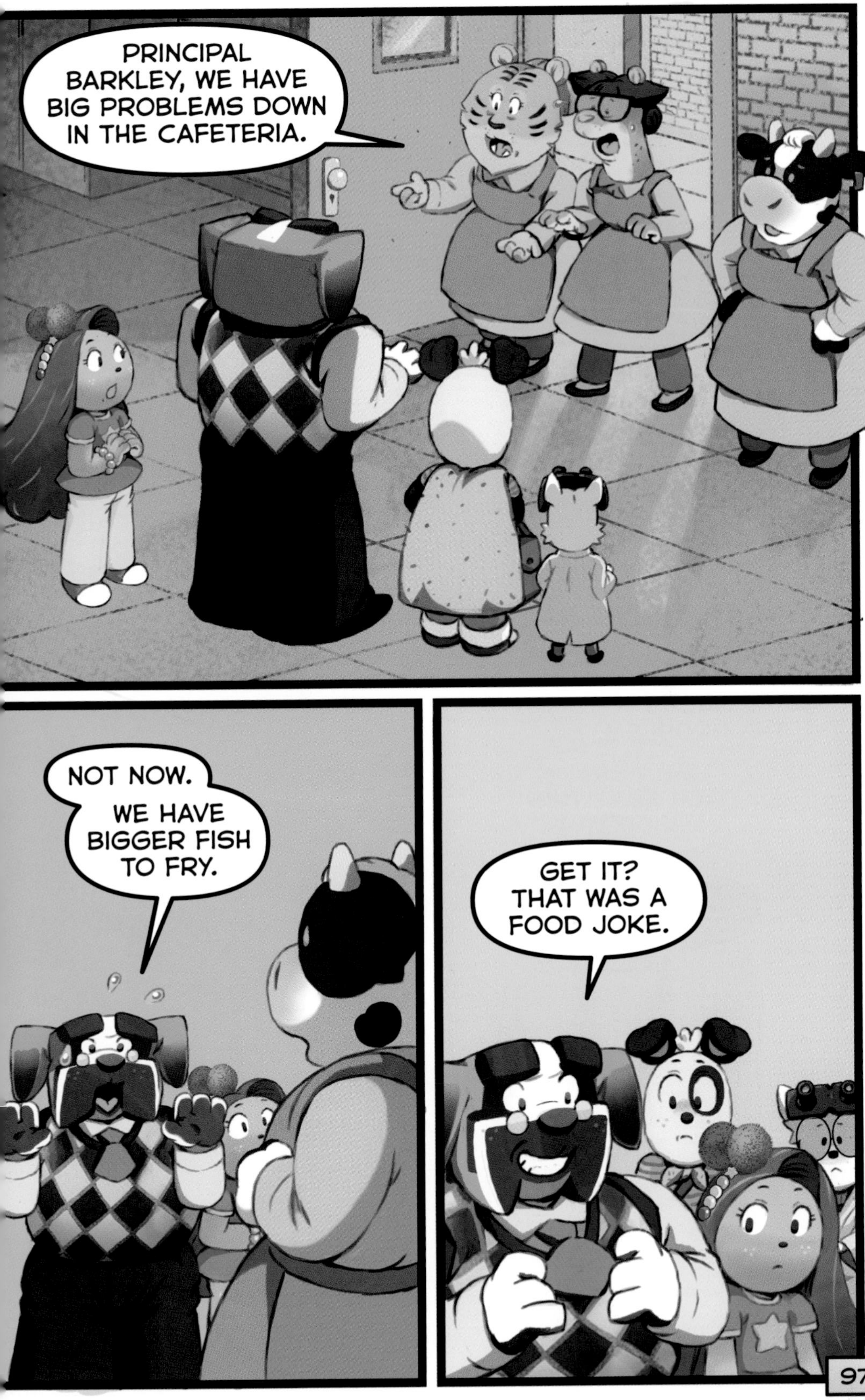
PRINCIPAL BARKLEY, WE HAVE BIG PROBLEMS DOWN IN THE CAFETERIA.
NOT NOW.
WE HAVE BIGGER FISH TO FRY.
GET IT? THAT WAS A FOOD JOKE.

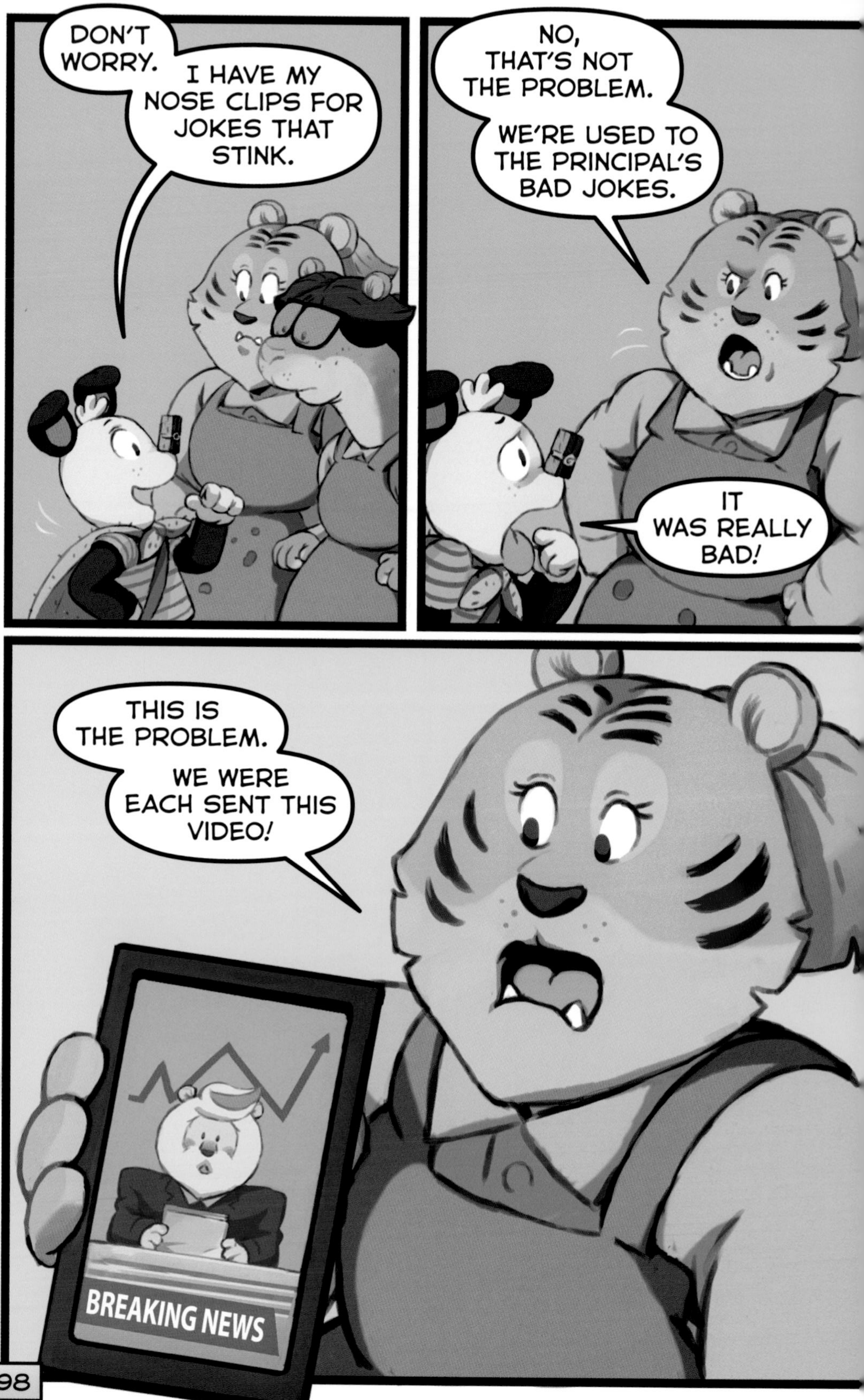
DON'T WORRY.
I HAVE MY NOSE CLIPS FOR JOKES THAT STINK.
NO, THAT'S NOT THE PROBLEM.
WE'RE USED TO THE PRINCIPAL'S BAD JOKES.
IT WAS REALLY BAD!
THIS IS THE PROBLEM.
WE WERE EACH SENT THIS VIDEO!
BREAKING NEWS

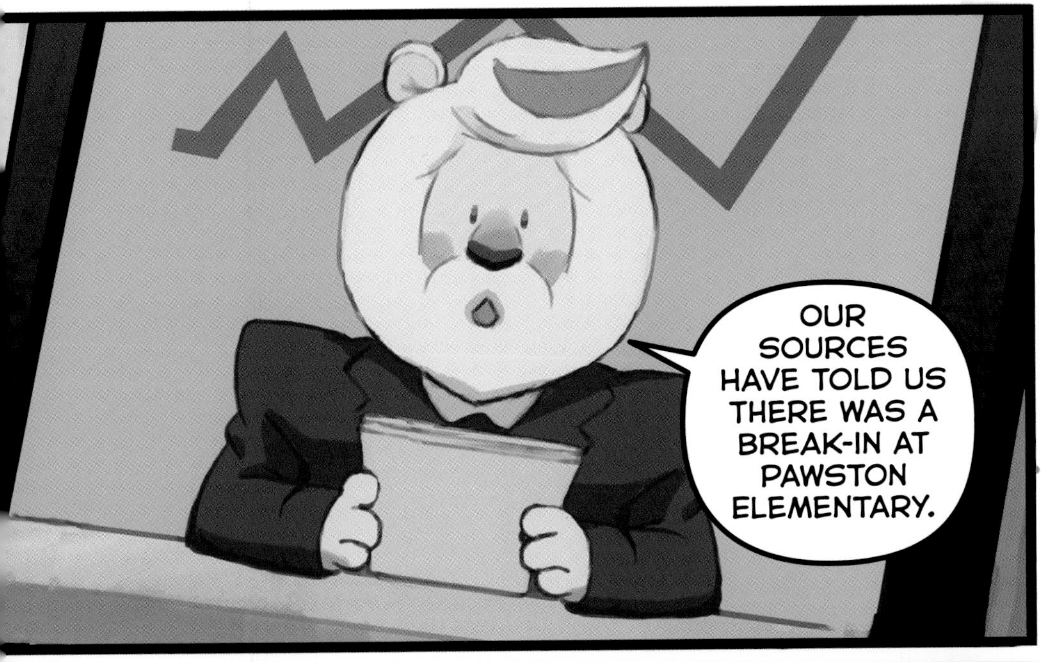
OUR SOURCES HAVE TOLD US THERE WAS A BREAK-IN AT PAWSTON ELEMENTARY.

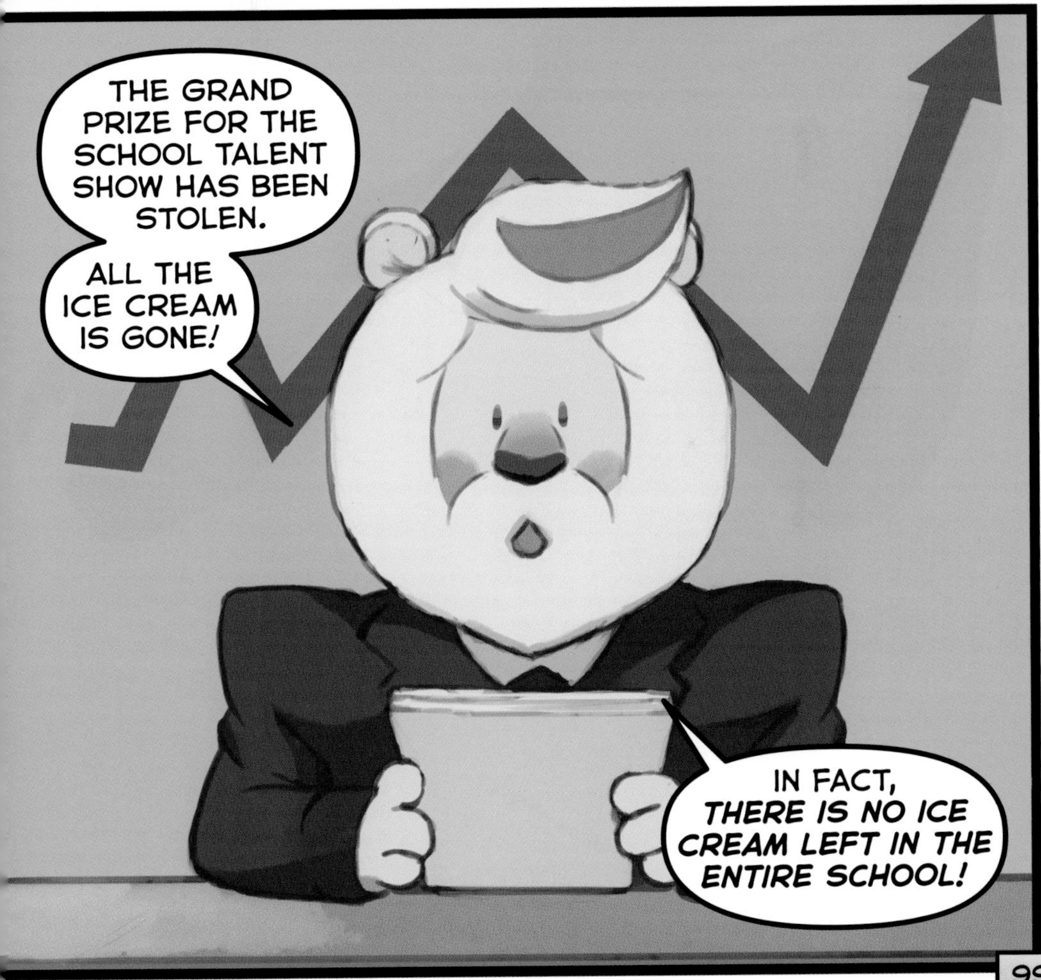
THE GRAND PRIZE FOR THE SCHOOL TALENT SHOW HAS BEEN STOLEN.
ALL THE ICE CREAM IS GONE!
IN FACT, *THERE IS NO ICE CREAM LEFT IN THE ENTIRE SCHOOL!*

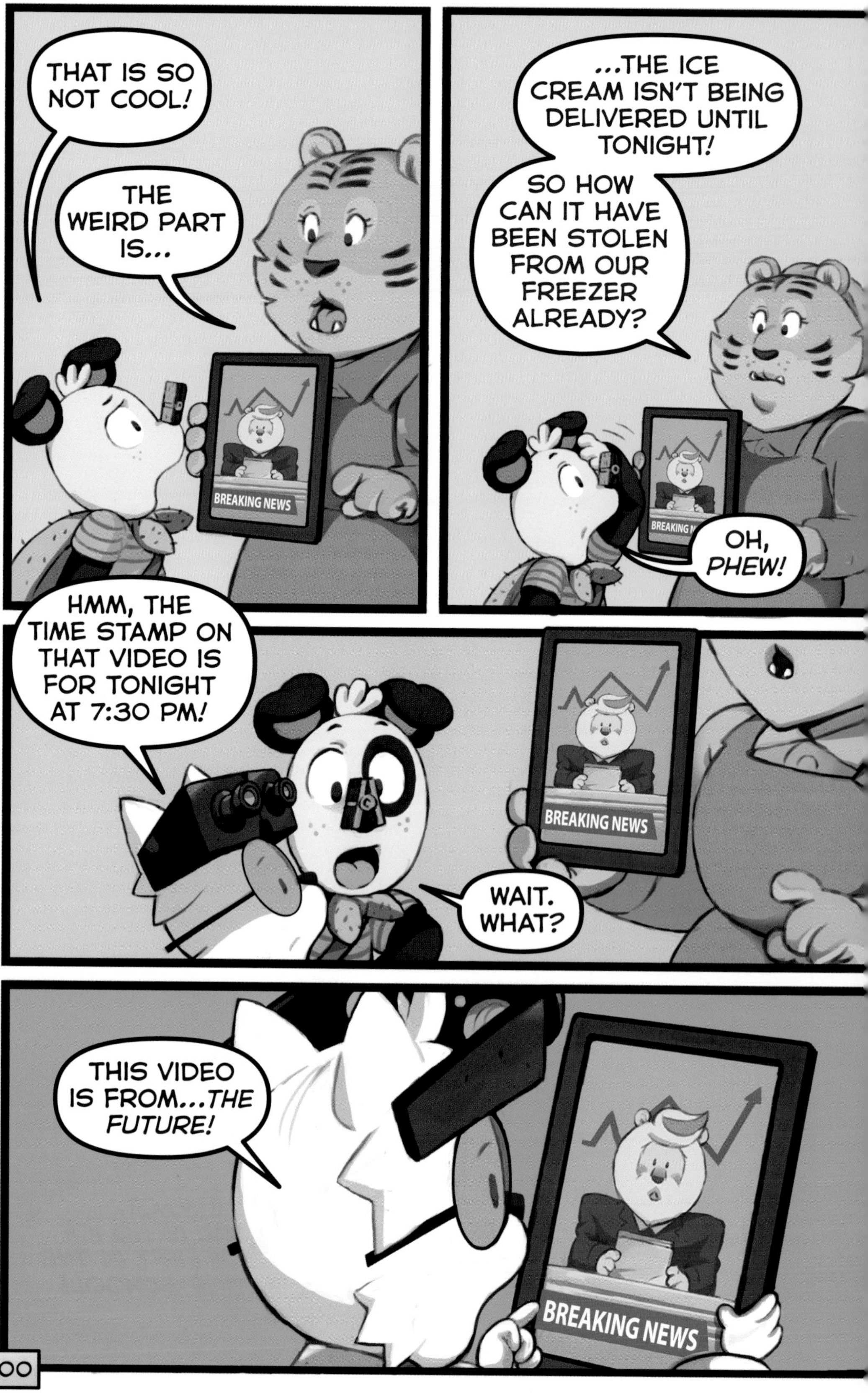
THAT IS SO NOT COOL!
THE WEIRD PART IS...
...THE ICE CREAM ISN'T BEING DELIVERED UNTIL TONIGHT!
SO HOW CAN IT HAVE BEEN STOLEN FROM OUR FREEZER ALREADY?
BREAKING NEWS
OH, *PHEW!*
HMM, THE TIME STAMP ON THAT VIDEO IS FOR TONIGHT AT 7:30 PM!
BREAKING NEWS
WAIT. WHAT?
THIS VIDEO IS FROM...*THE FUTURE!*
BREAKING NEWS

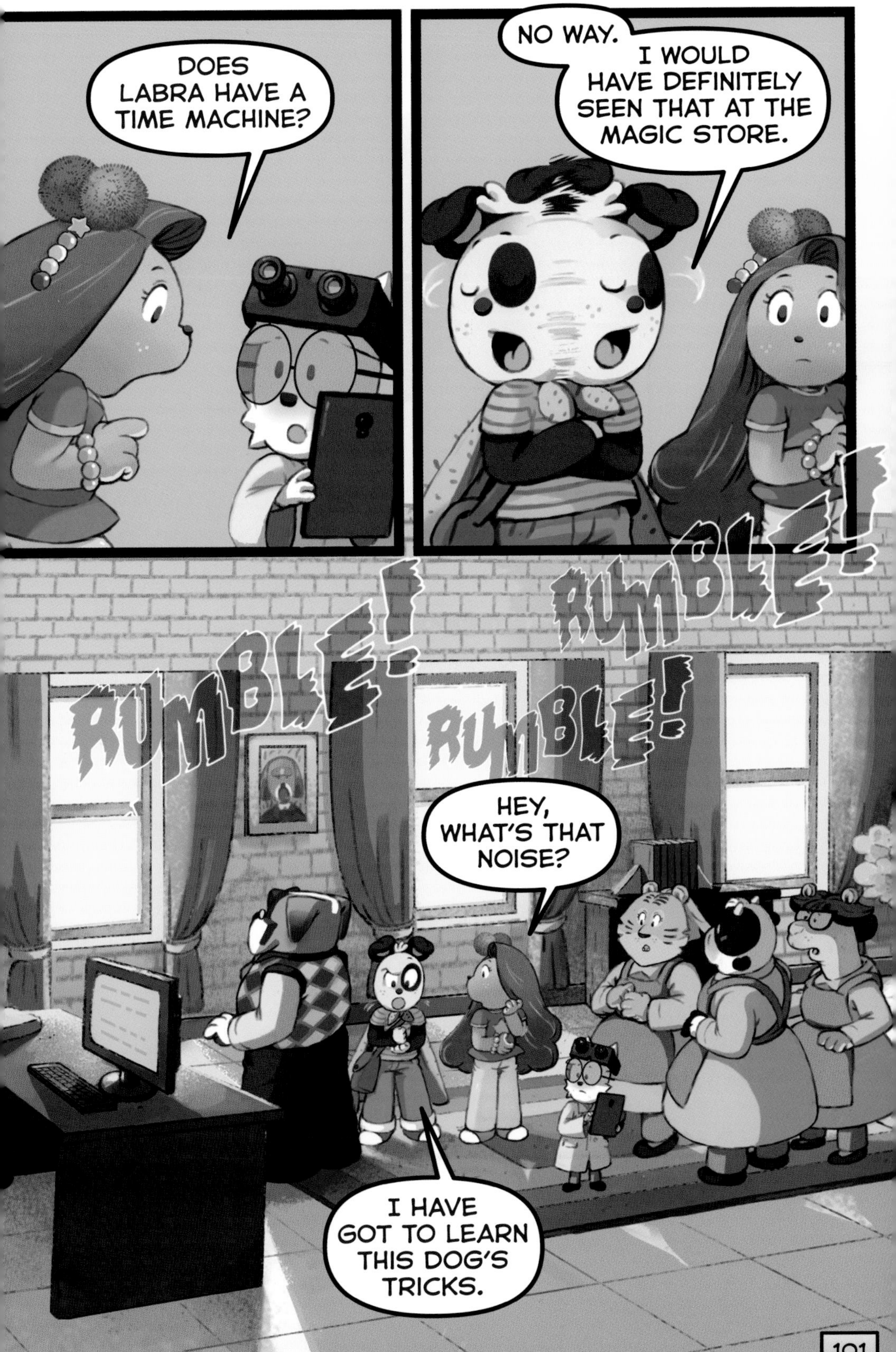

DOES LABRA HAVE A TIME MACHINE?
NO WAY.
I WOULD HAVE DEFINITELY SEEN THAT AT THE MAGIC STORE.
RUMBLE!
RUMBLE!
RUMBLE!
HEY, WHAT'S THAT NOISE?
I HAVE GOT TO LEARN THIS DOG'S TRICKS.

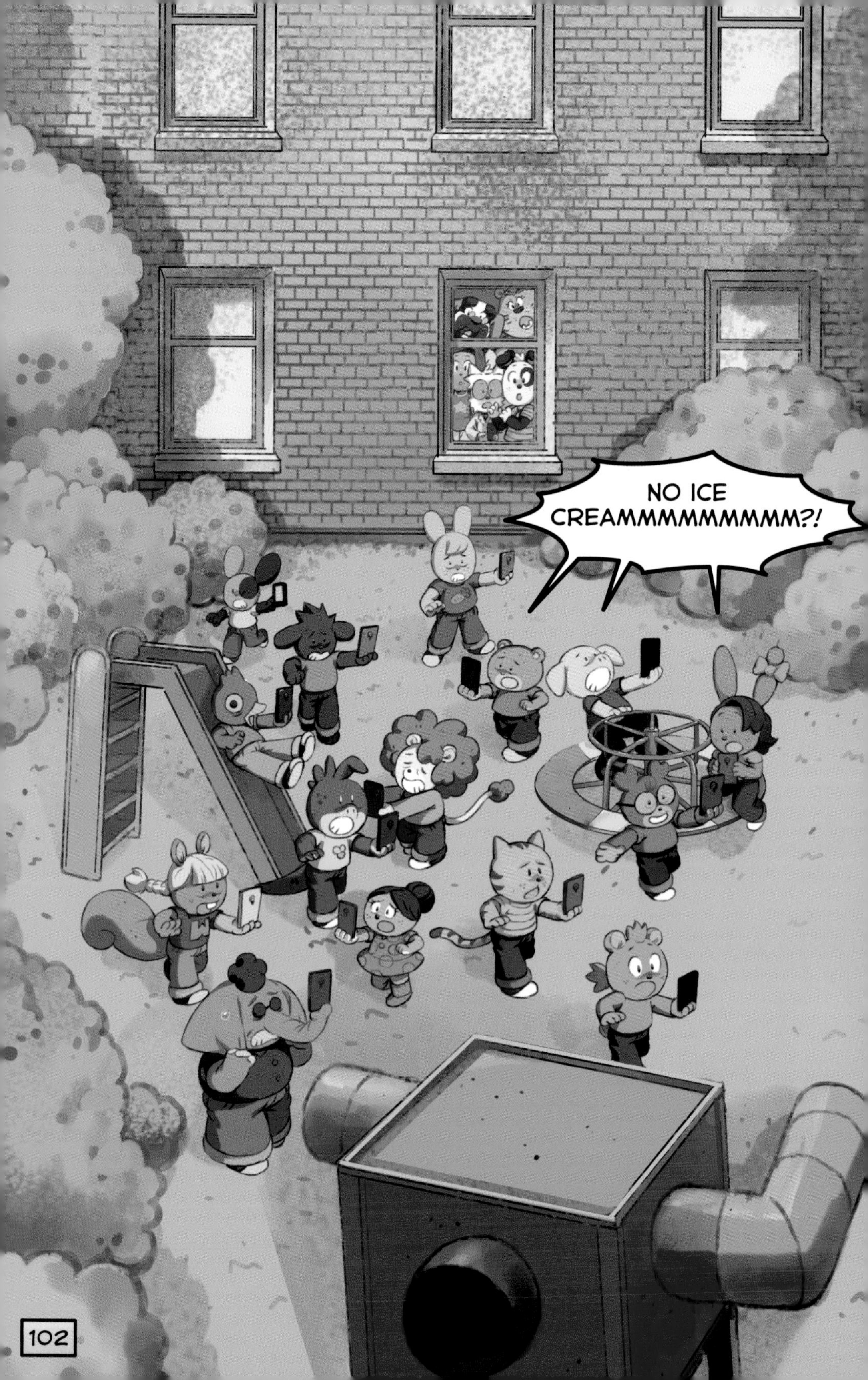
NO ICE CREAMMMMMMMMM?!

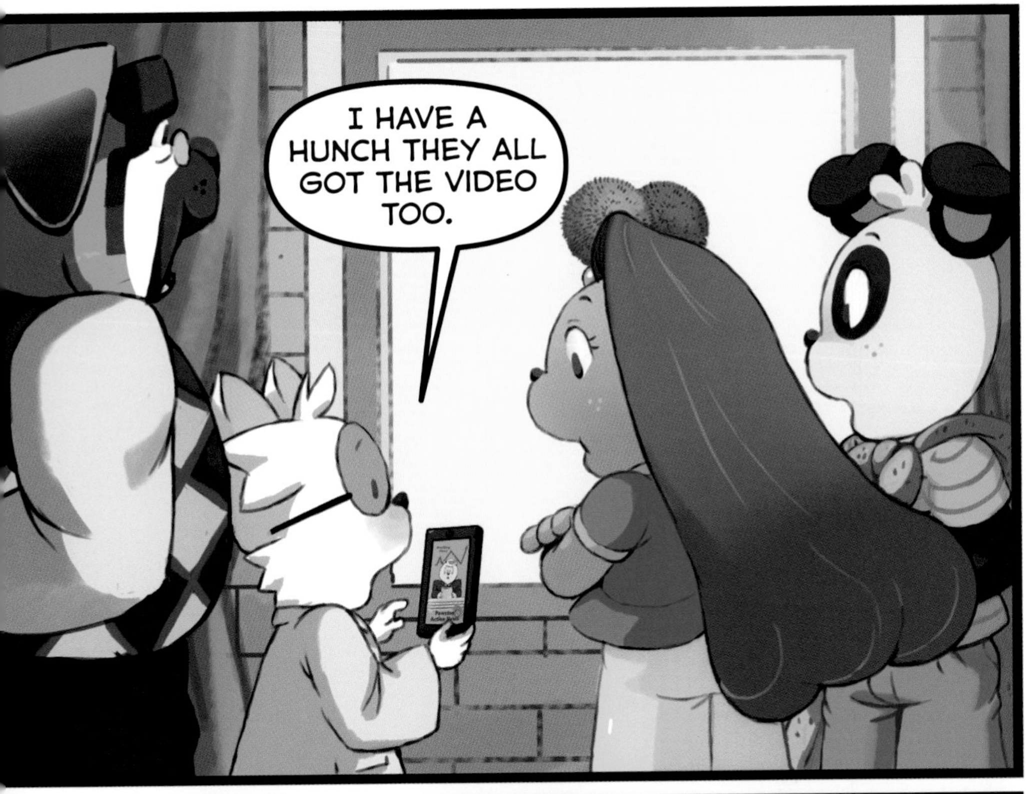
I HAVE A HUNCH THEY ALL GOT THE VIDEO TOO.

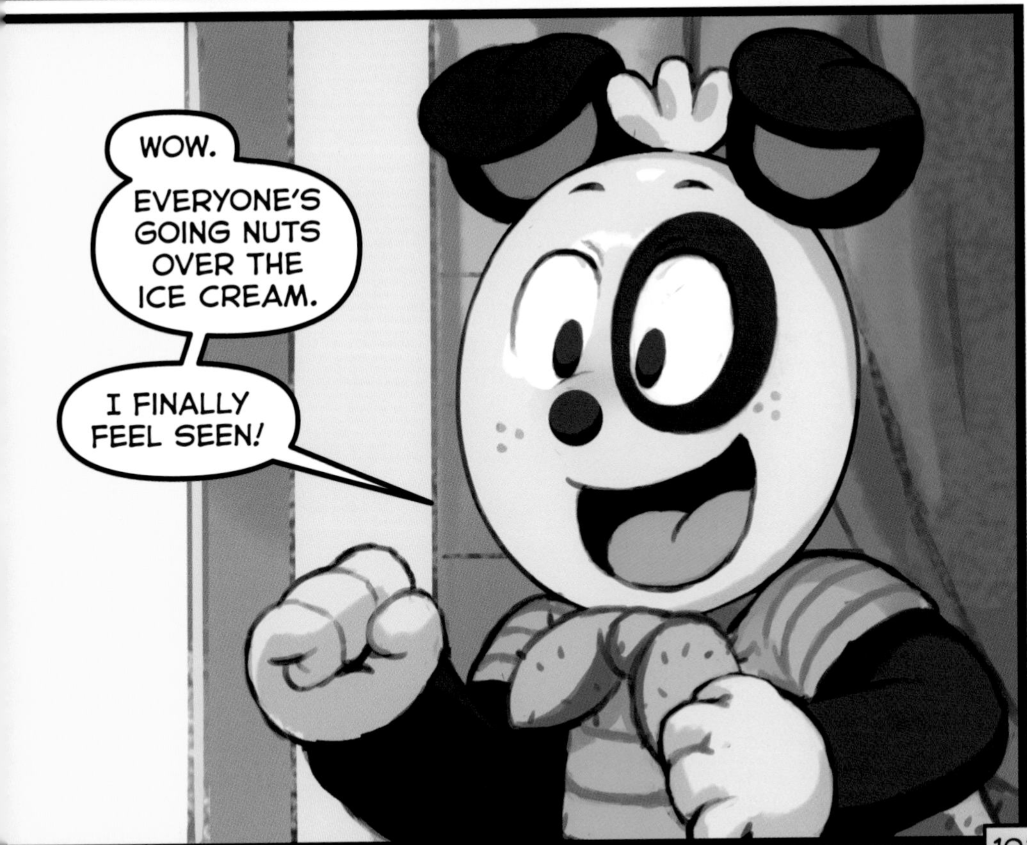
WOW.
EVERYONE'S GOING NUTS OVER THE ICE CREAM.
I FINALLY FEEL SEEN!

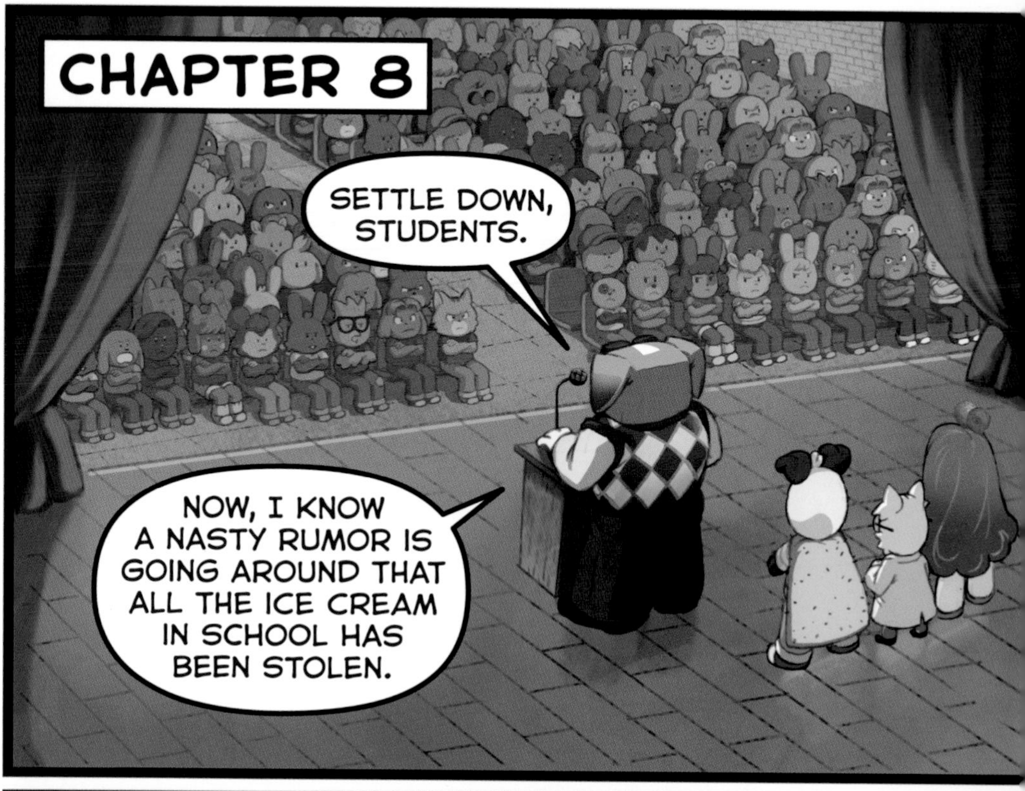
CHAPTER 8
SETTLE DOWN, STUDENTS.
NOW, I KNOW A NASTY RUMOR IS GOING AROUND THAT ALL THE ICE CREAM IN SCHOOL HAS BEEN STOLEN.

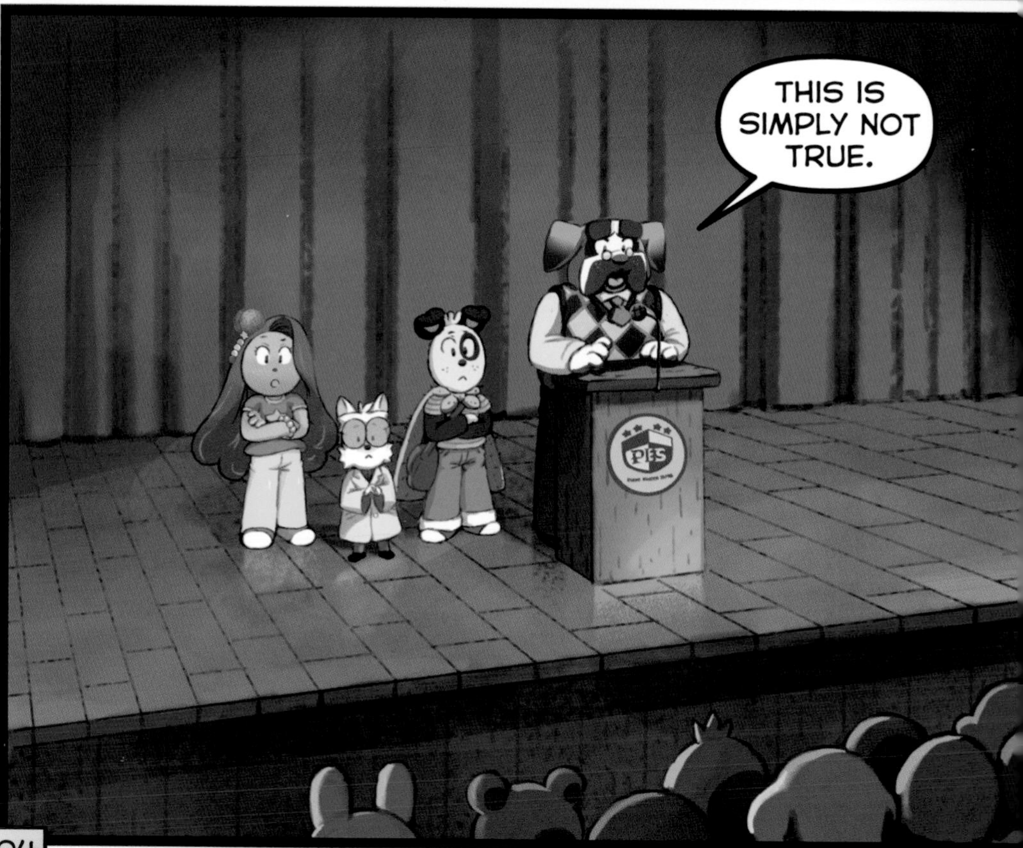
THIS IS SIMPLY NOT TRUE.
PES

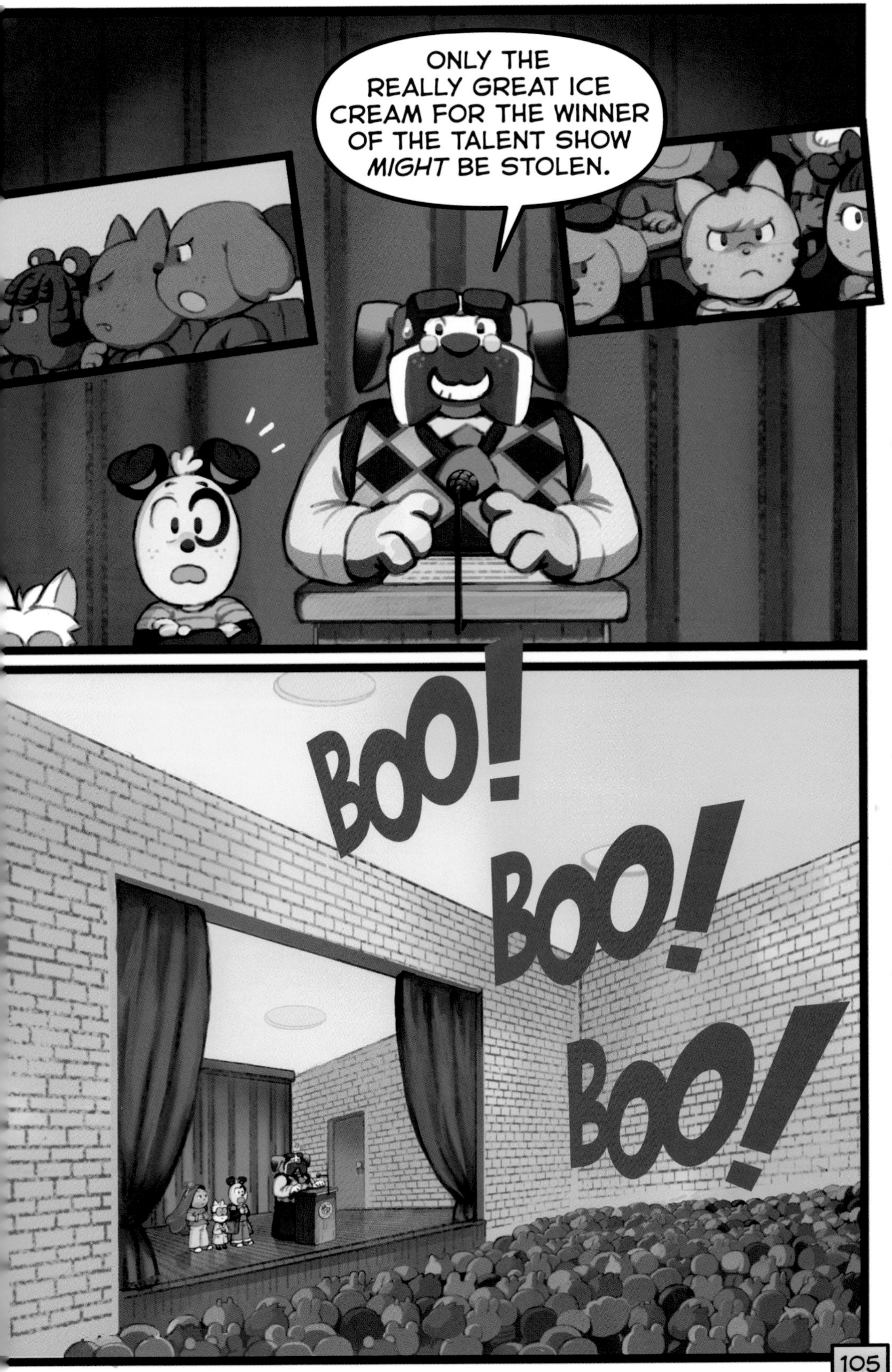

ONLY THE REALLY GREAT ICE CREAM FOR THE WINNER OF THE TALENT SHOW *MIGHT* BE STOLEN.
BOO!
BOO!
BOO!

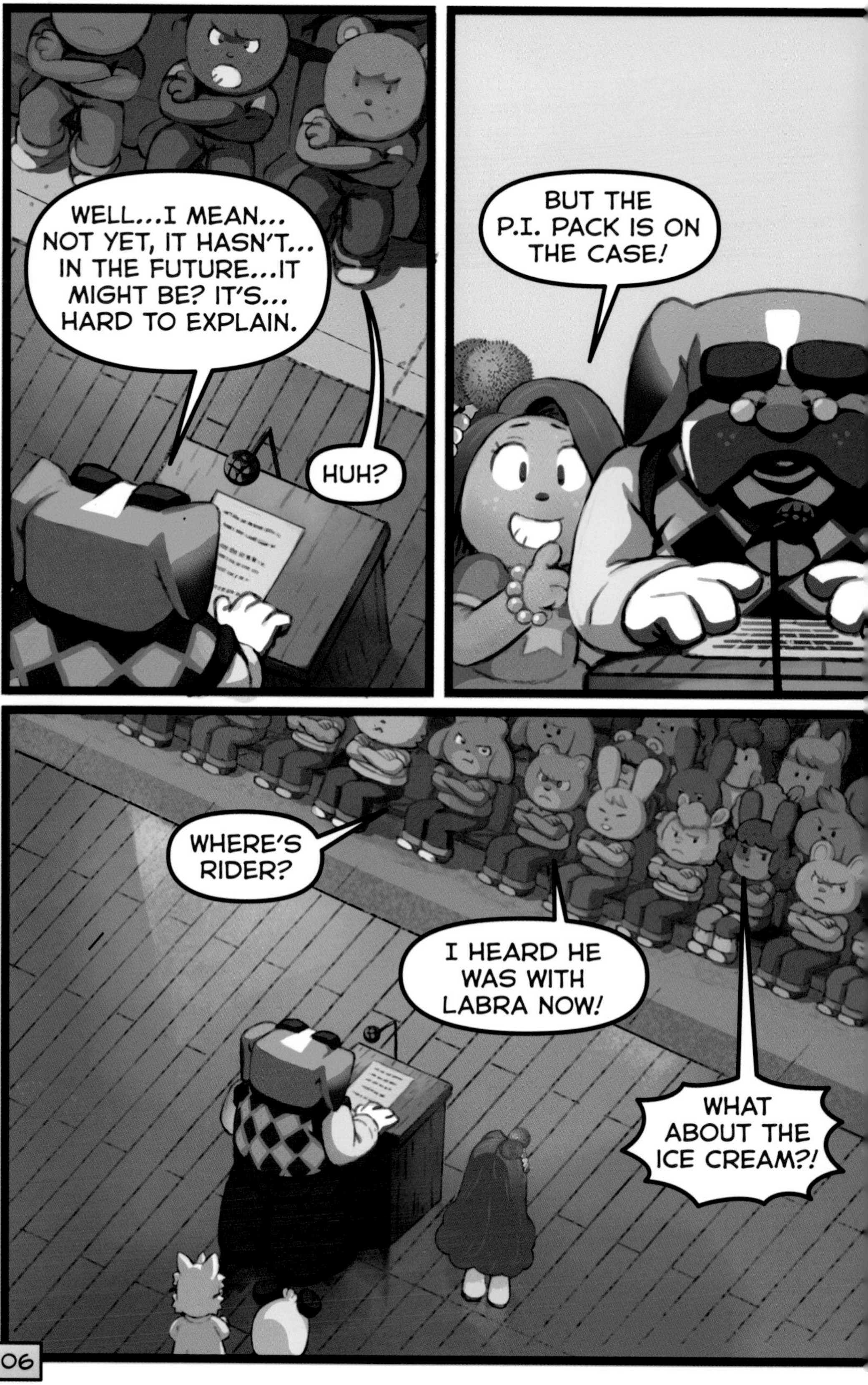
WELL...I MEAN... NOT YET, IT HASN'T... IN THE FUTURE...IT MIGHT BE? IT'S... HARD TO EXPLAIN.
HUH?
BUT THE P.I. PACK IS ON THE CASE!
WHERE'S RIDER?
I HEARD HE WAS WITH LABRA NOW!
WHAT ABOUT THE ICE CREAM?!

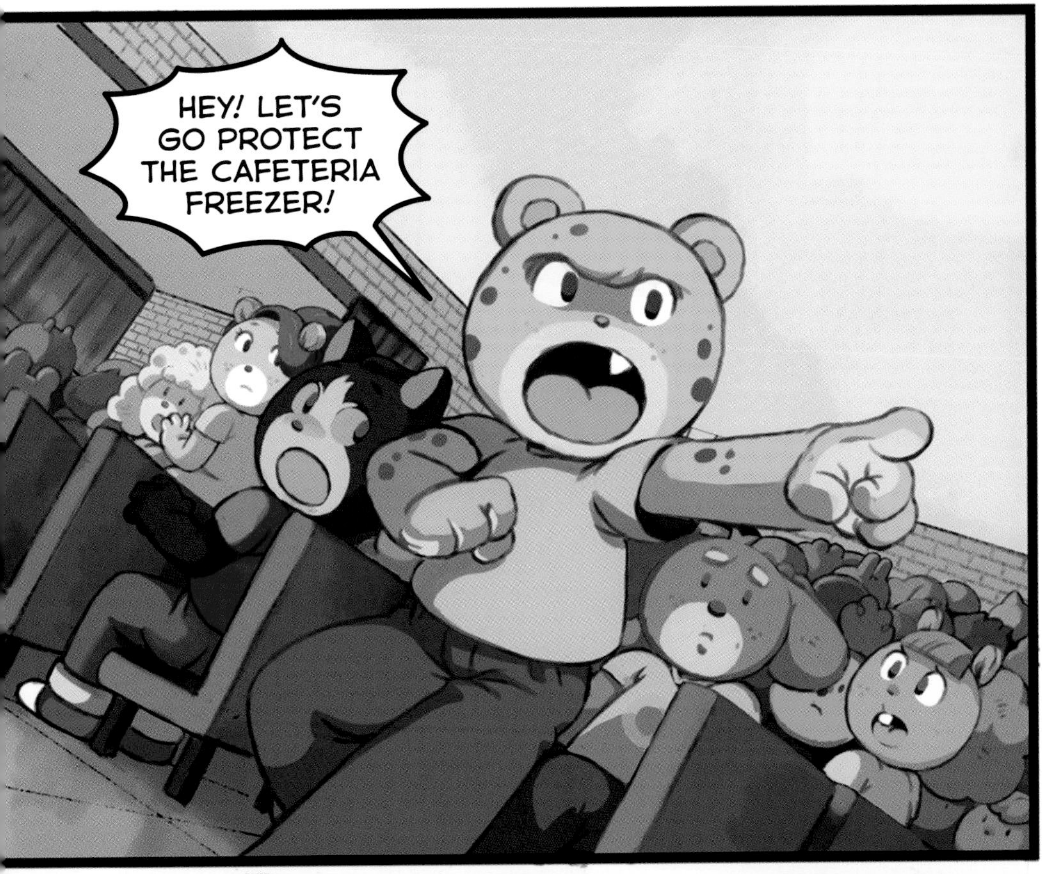
HEY! LET'S GO PROTECT THE CAFETERIA FREEZER!

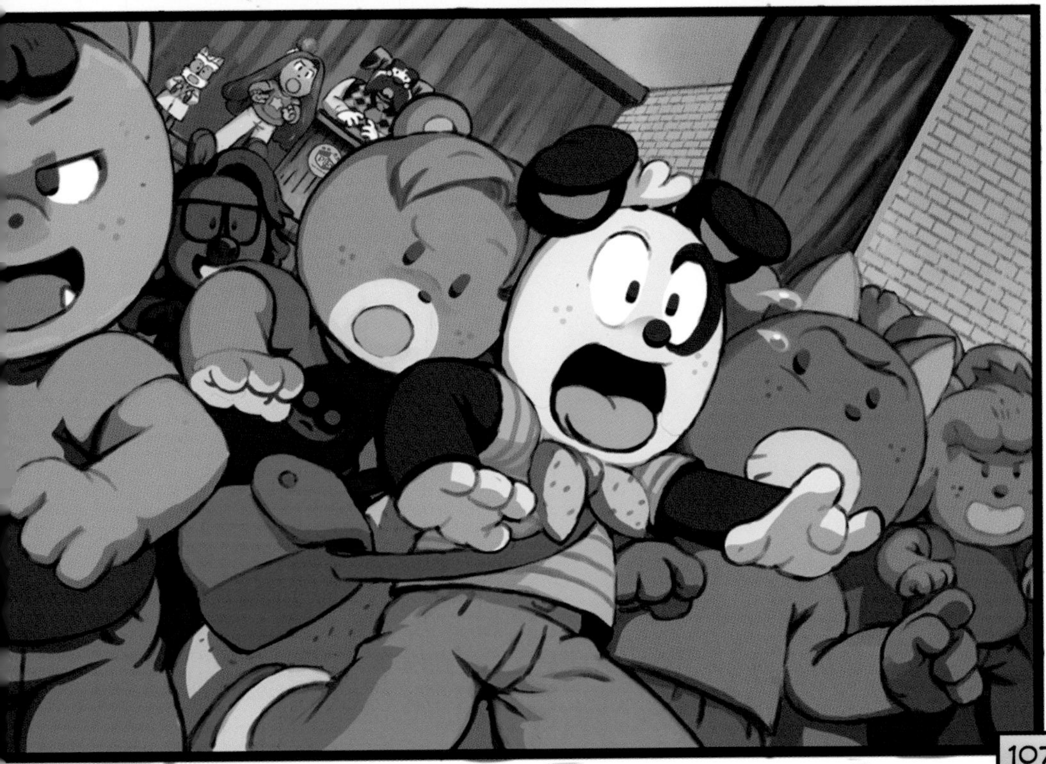

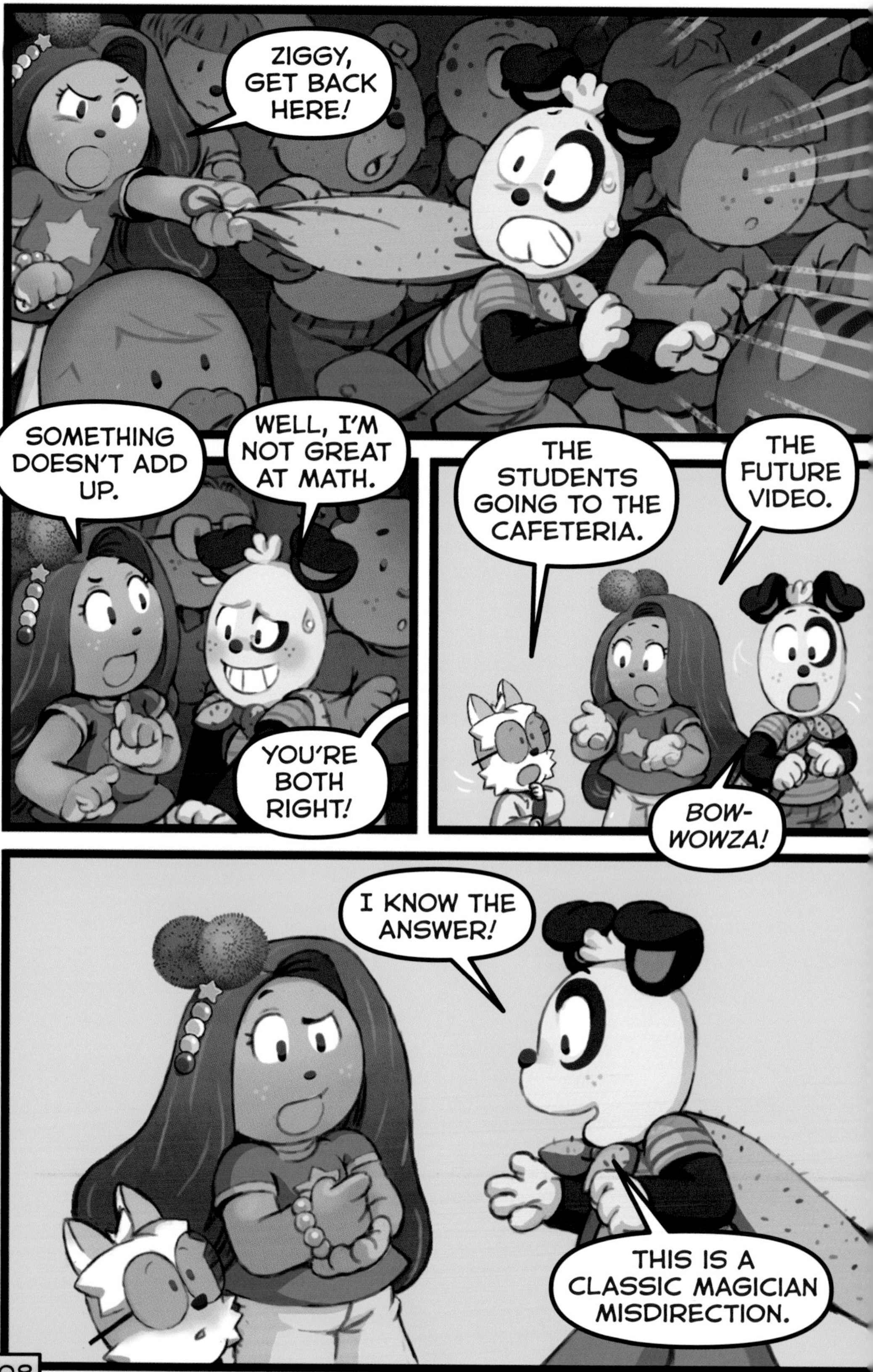

ZIGGY, GET BACK HERE!
SOMETHING DOESN'T ADD UP.
WELL, I'M NOT GREAT AT MATH.
YOU'RE BOTH RIGHT!
THE STUDENTS GOING TO THE CAFETERIA.
THE FUTURE VIDEO.
BOW-WOWZA!
I KNOW THE ANSWER!
THIS IS A CLASSIC MAGICIAN MISDIRECTION.

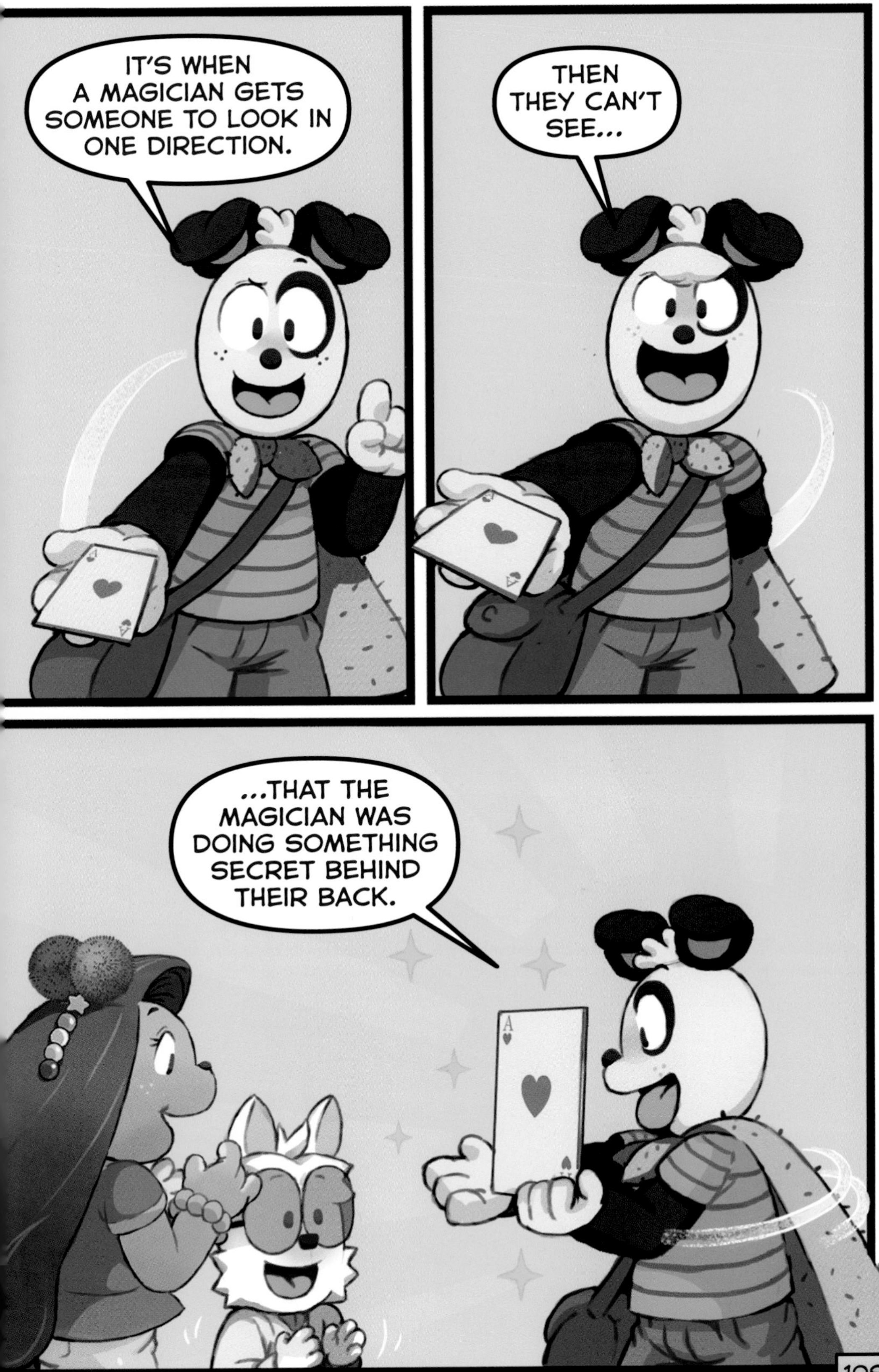
IT'S WHEN A MAGICIAN GETS SOMEONE TO LOOK IN ONE DIRECTION.
THEN THEY CAN'T SEE...
...THAT THE MAGICIAN WAS DOING SOMETHING SECRET BEHIND THEIR BACK.

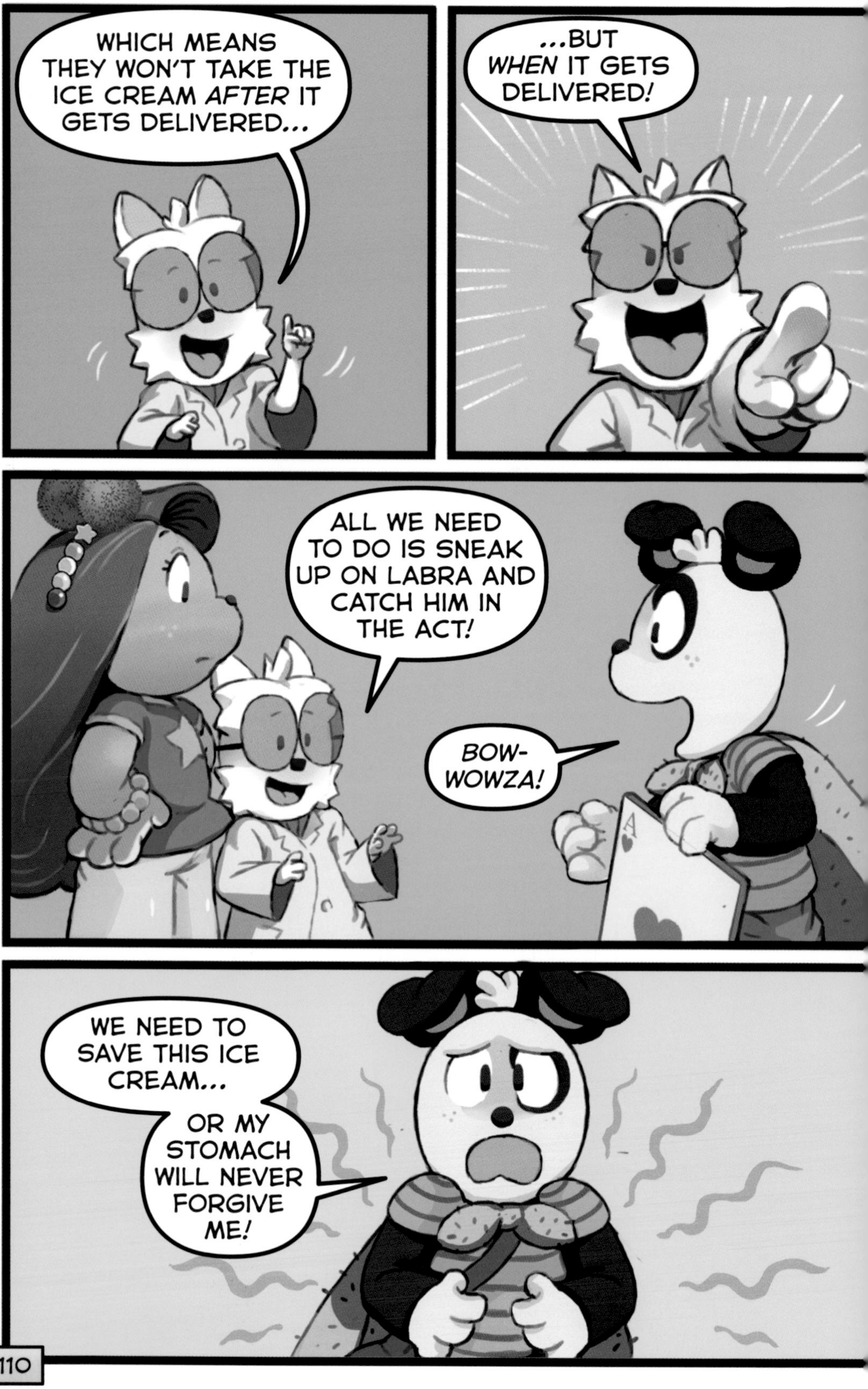
WHICH MEANS THEY WON'T TAKE THE ICE CREAM *AFTER* IT GETS DELIVERED...
...BUT *WHEN* IT GETS DELIVERED!
ALL WE NEED TO DO IS SNEAK UP ON LABRA AND CATCH HIM IN THE ACT!
BOW-WOWZA!
WE NEED TO SAVE THIS ICE CREAM...
OR MY STOMACH WILL NEVER FORGIVE ME!

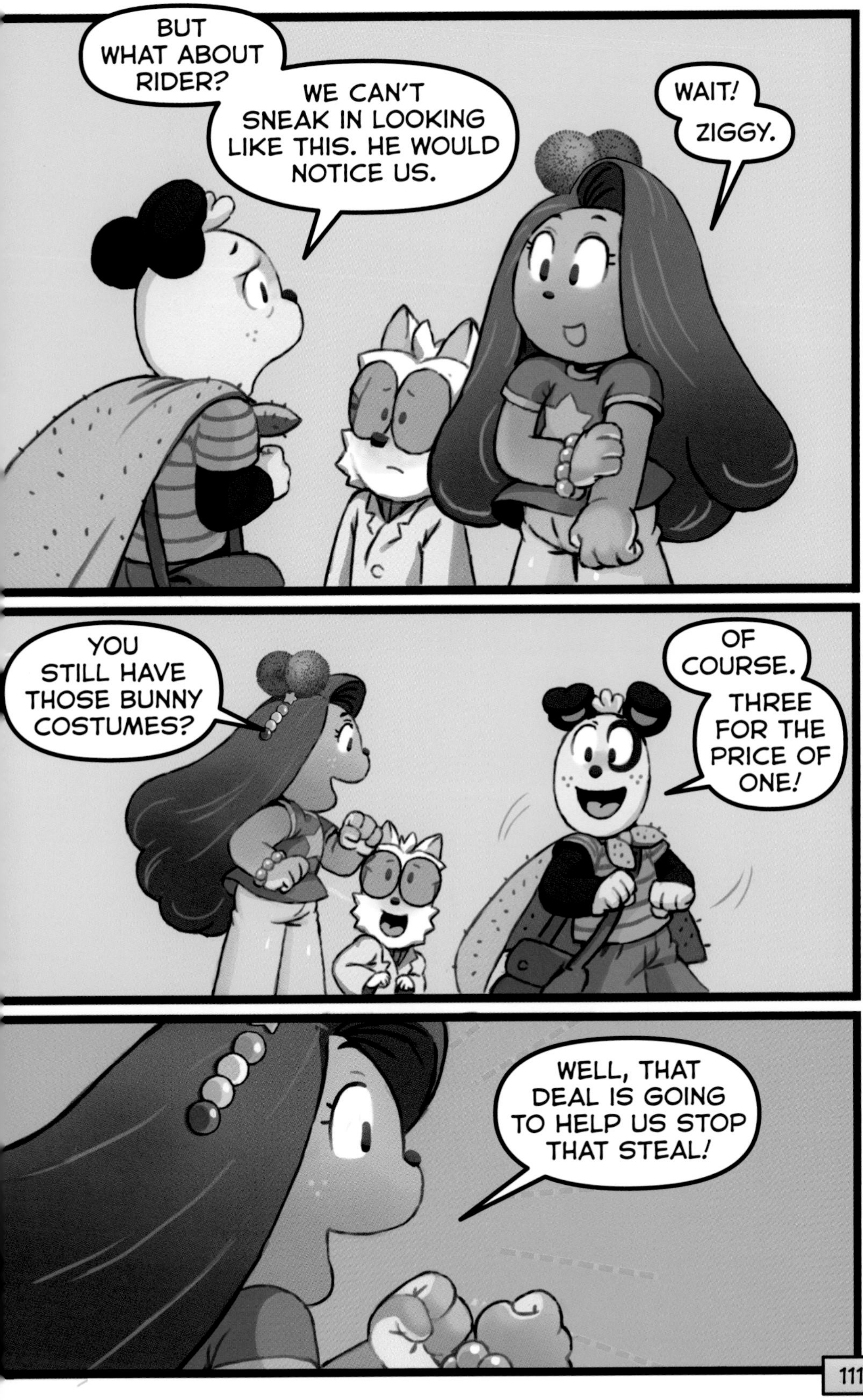
BUT WHAT ABOUT RIDER?
WE CAN'T SNEAK IN LOOKING LIKE THIS. HE WOULD NOTICE US.
WAIT!
ZIGGY.
YOU STILL HAVE THOSE BUNNY COSTUMES?
OF COURSE.
THREE FOR THE PRICE OF ONE!
WELL, THAT DEAL IS GOING TO HELP US STOP THAT STEAL!

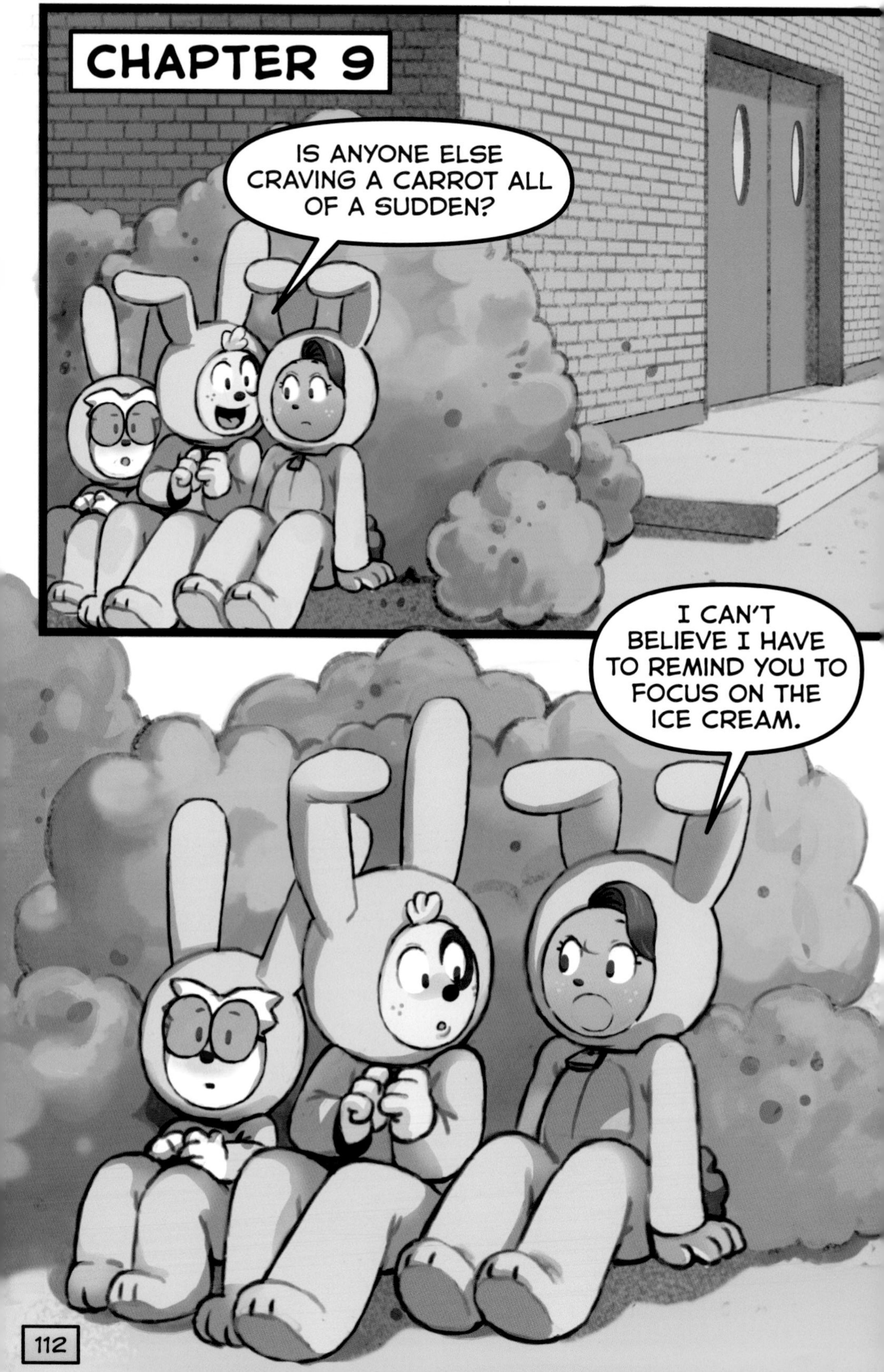
CHAPTER 9
IS ANYONE ELSE CRAVING A CARROT ALL OF A SUDDEN?
I CAN'T BELIEVE I HAVE TO REMIND YOU TO FOCUS ON THE ICE CREAM.

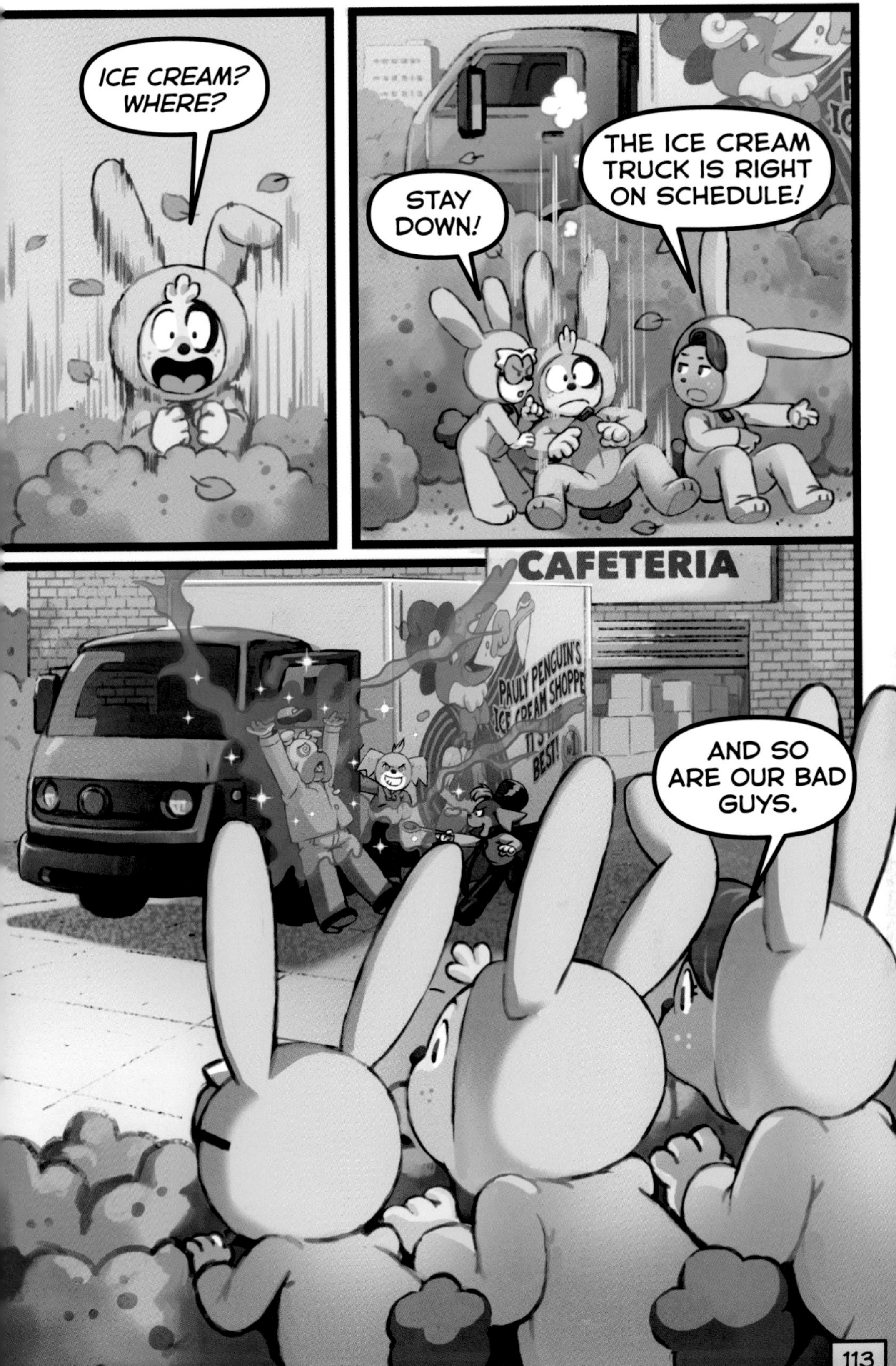
ICE CREAM? WHERE?
STAY DOWN!
THE ICE CREAM TRUCK IS RIGHT ON SCHEDULE!
CAFETERIA
PAULY PENGUIN'S ICE CREAM SHOPPE
BEST!
AND SO ARE OUR BAD GUYS.

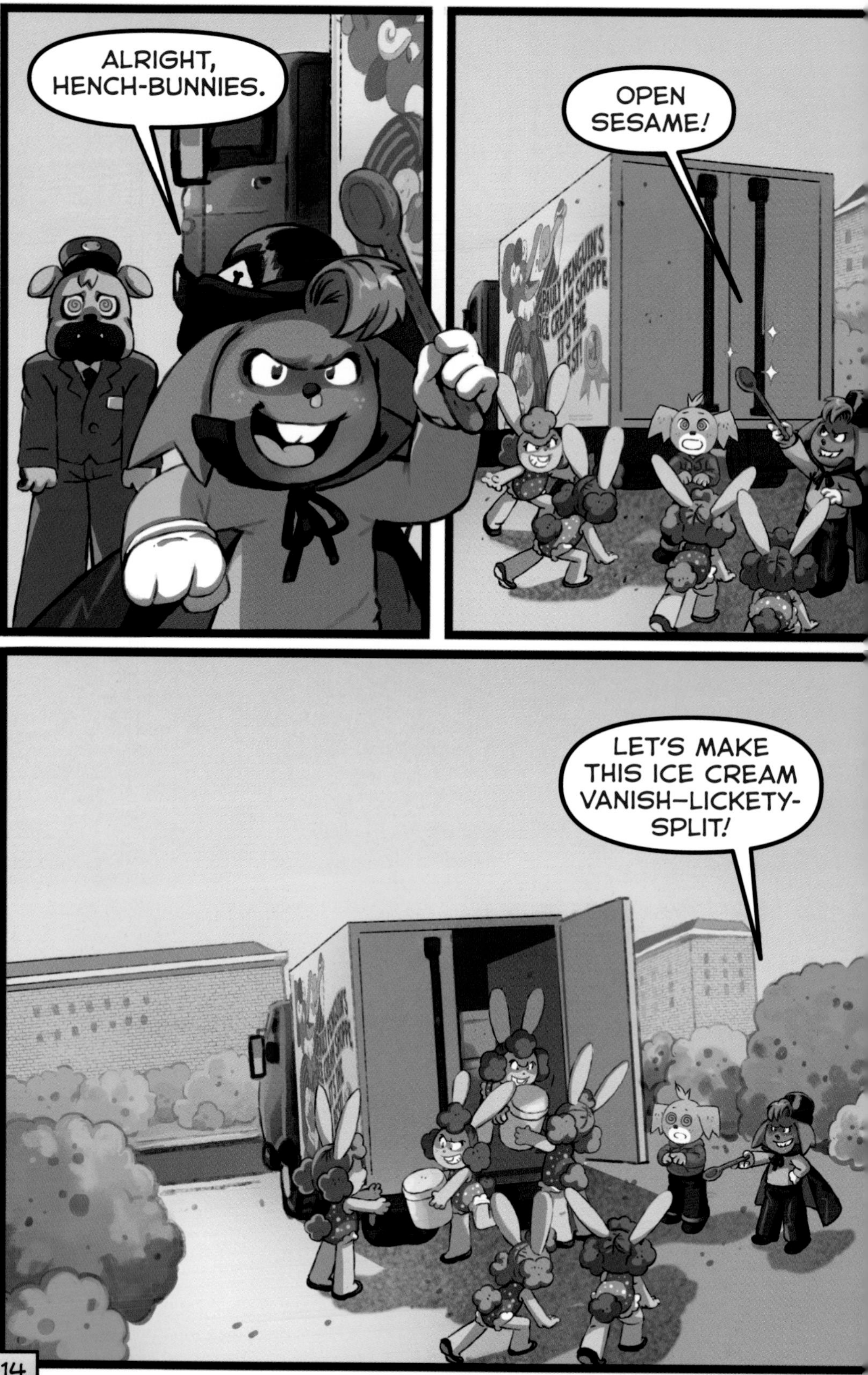
ALRIGHT, HENCH-BUNNIES.
OPEN SESAME!
PAULY PENGUIN'S ICE CREAM SHOPPE
LET'S MAKE THIS ICE CREAM VANISH–LICKETY-SPLIT!

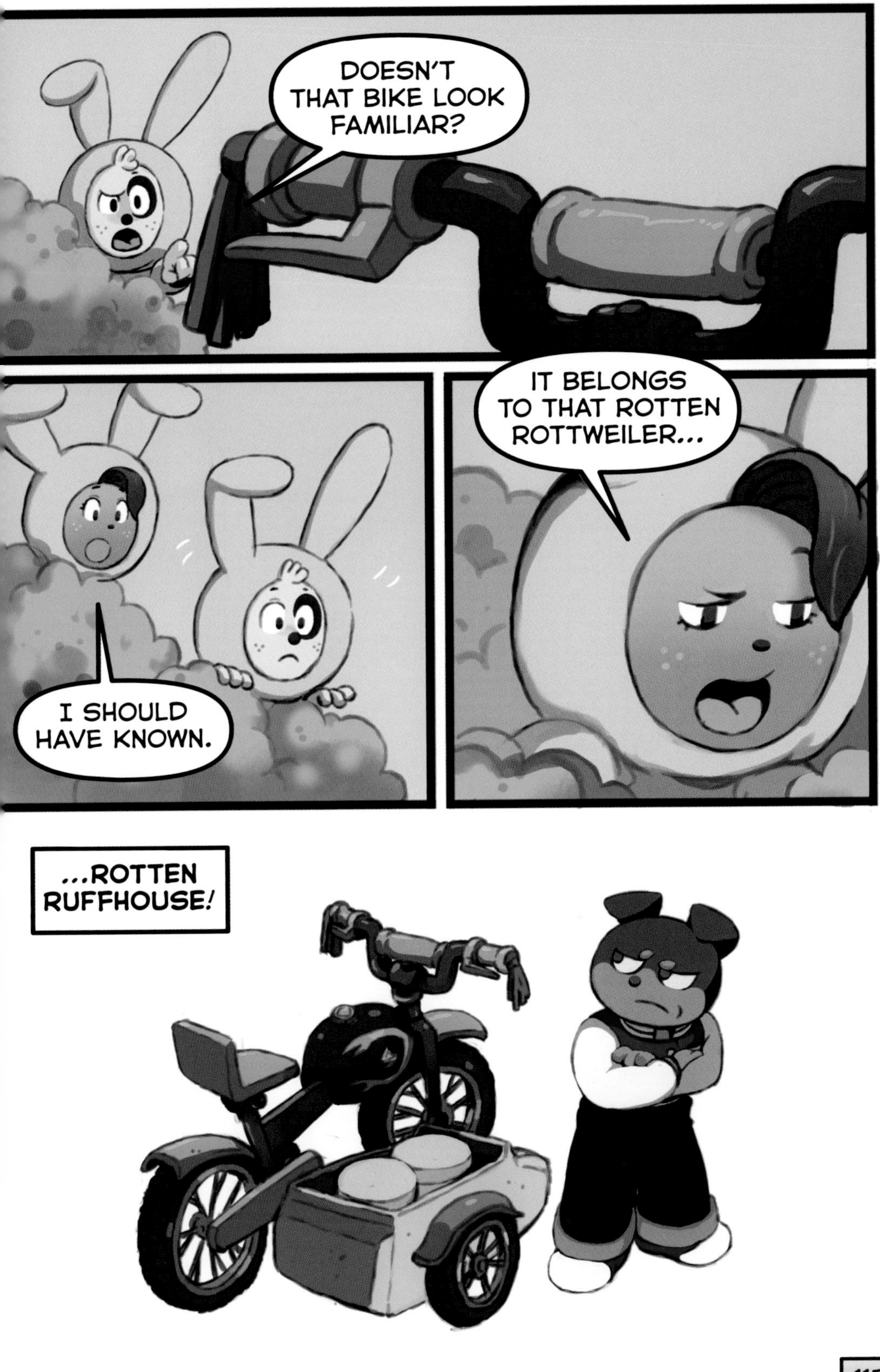
DOESN'T THAT BIKE LOOK FAMILIAR?
I SHOULD HAVE KNOWN.
IT BELONGS TO THAT ROTTEN ROTTWEILER...
...ROTTEN RUFFHOUSE!

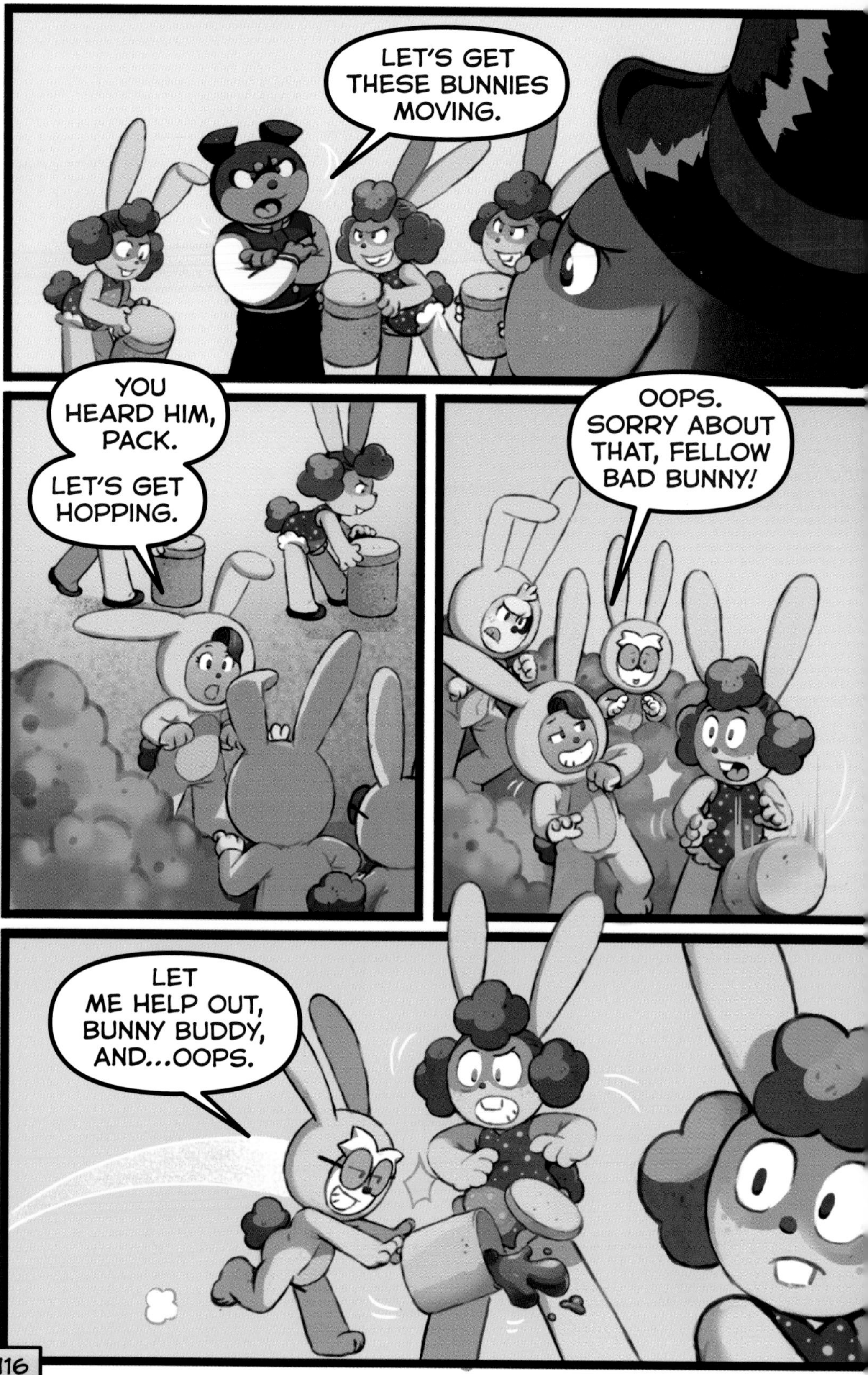
LET'S GET THESE BUNNIES MOVING.
YOU HEARD HIM, PACK.
LET'S GET HOPPING.
OOPS. SORRY ABOUT THAT, FELLOW BAD BUNNY!
LET ME HELP OUT, BUNNY BUDDY, AND...OOPS.

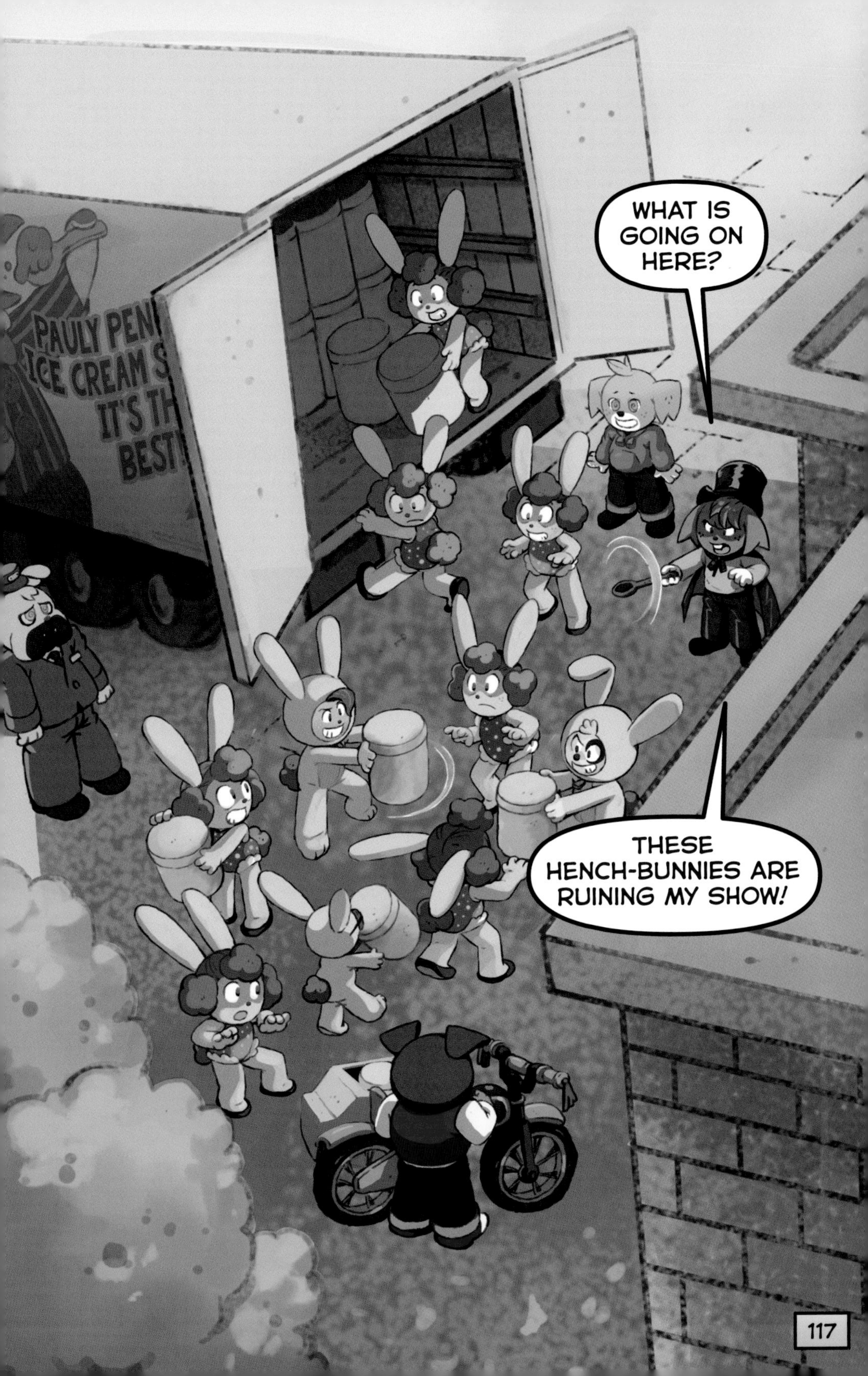
PAULY PEN
ICE CREAM S
IT'S TH
BEST!
WHAT IS GOING ON HERE?
THESE HENCH-BUNNIES ARE RUINING MY SHOW!

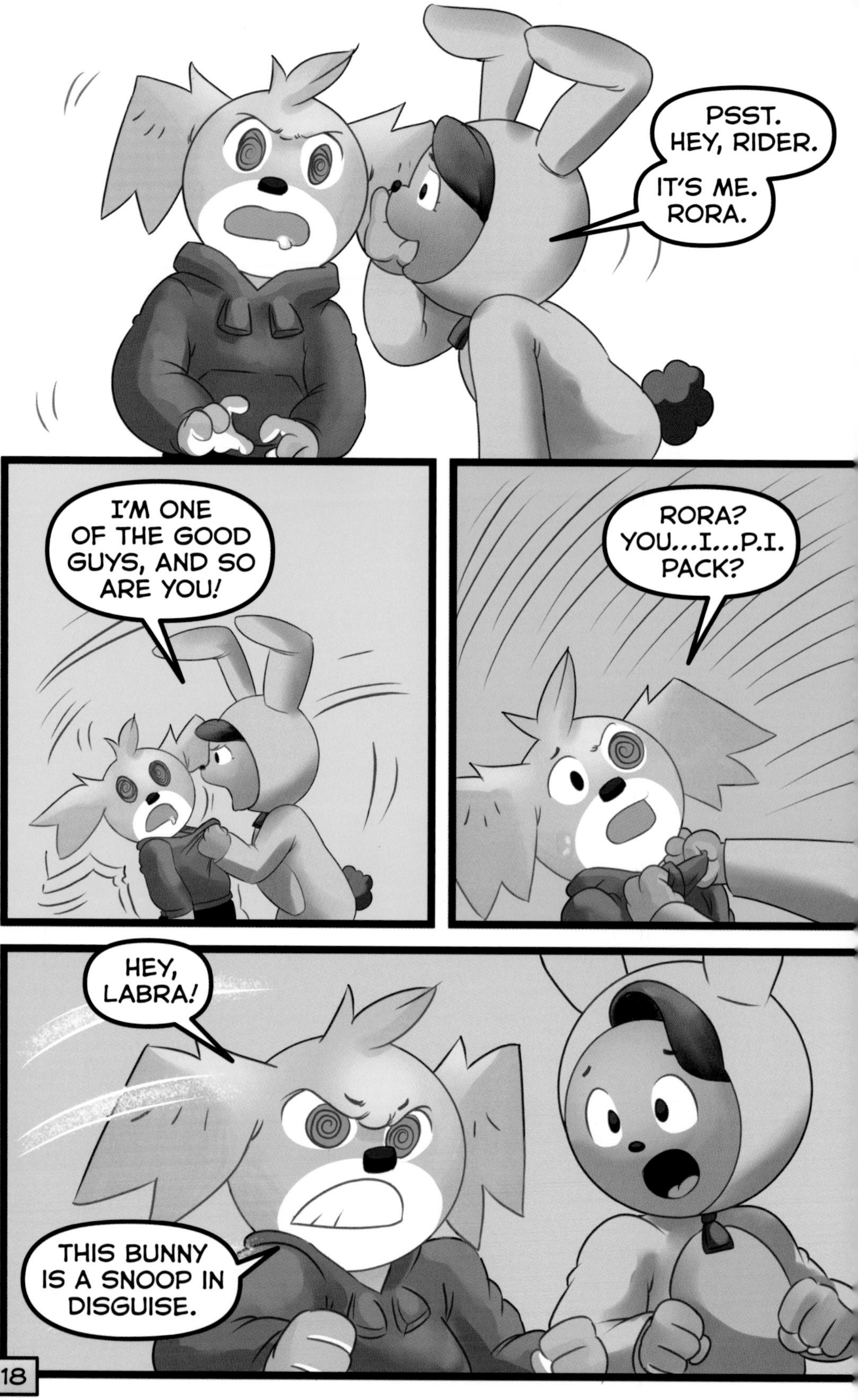
PSST. HEY, RIDER.
IT'S ME. RORA.
I'M ONE OF THE GOOD GUYS, AND SO ARE YOU!
RORA? YOU...I...P.I. PACK?
HEY, LABRA!
THIS BUNNY IS A SNOOP IN DISGUISE.

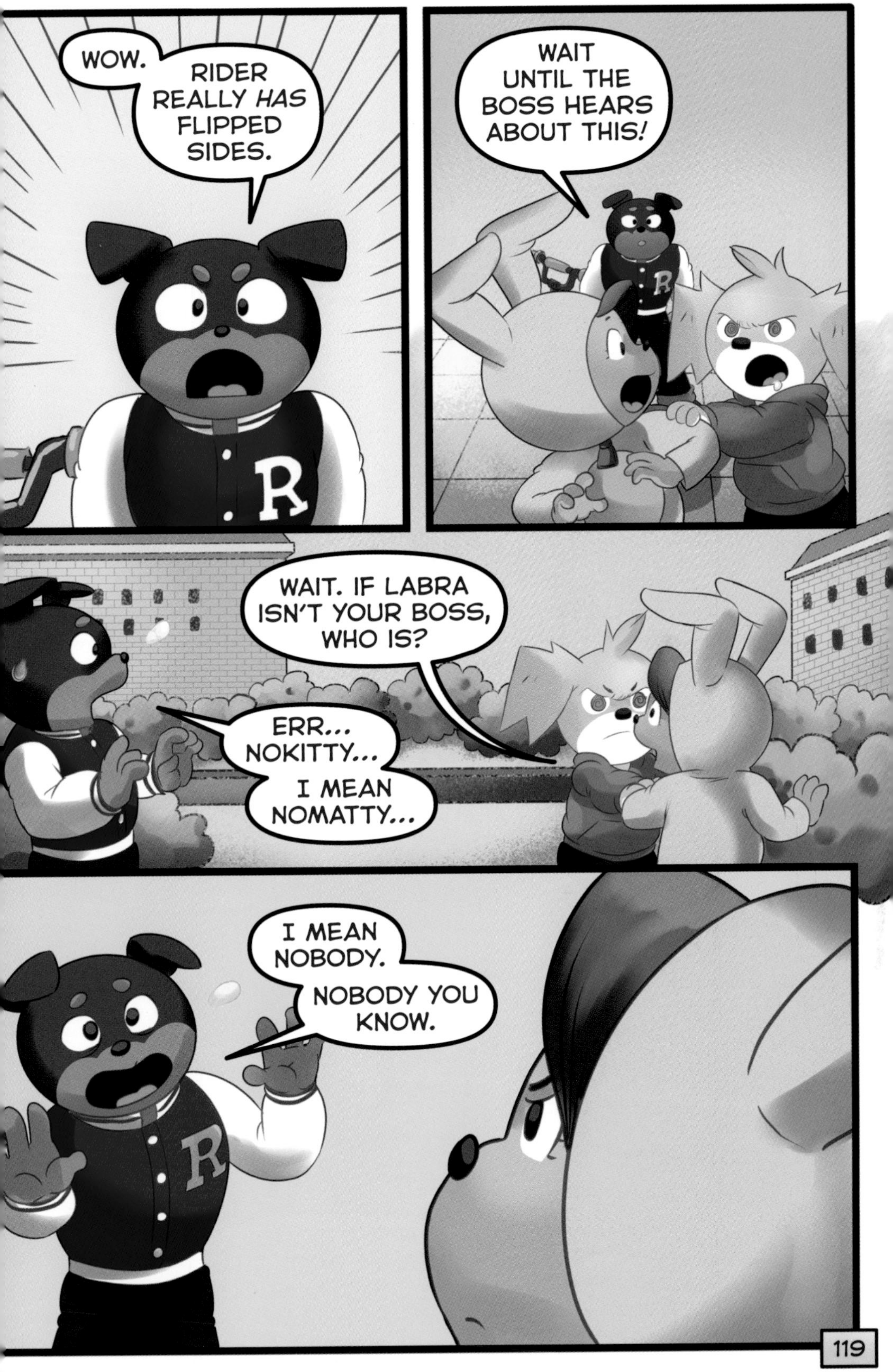
WOW.
RIDER REALLY *HAS* FLIPPED SIDES.
WAIT UNTIL THE BOSS HEARS ABOUT THIS!
WAIT. IF LABRA ISN'T YOUR BOSS, WHO IS?
ERR... NOKITTY...
I MEAN NOMATTY...
I MEAN NOBODY.
NOBODY YOU KNOW.

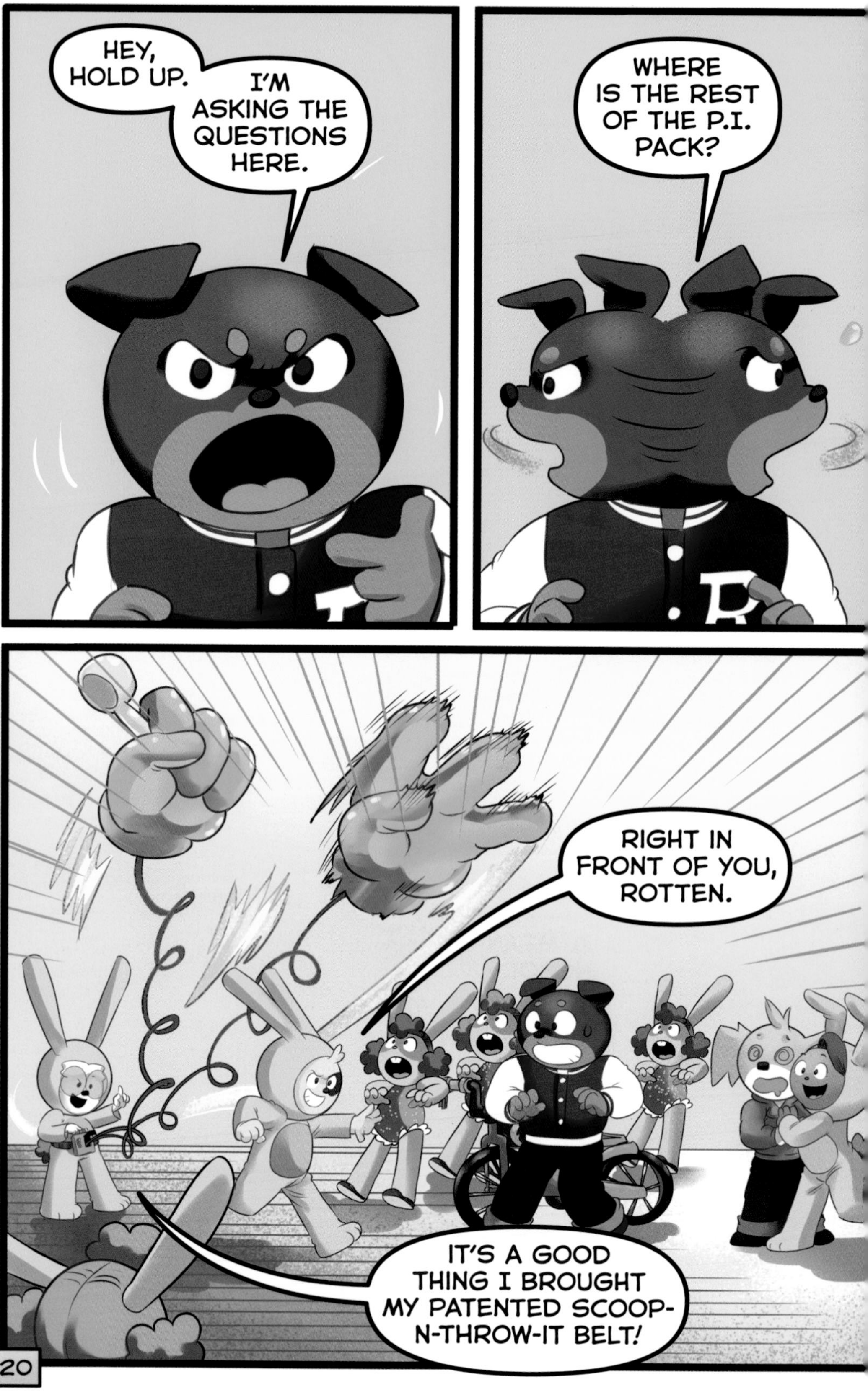

HEY, HOLD UP.
I'M ASKING THE QUESTIONS HERE.
WHERE IS THE REST OF THE P.I. PACK?
RIGHT IN FRONT OF YOU, ROTTEN.
IT'S A GOOD THING I BROUGHT MY PATENTED SCOOP-N-THROW-IT BELT!

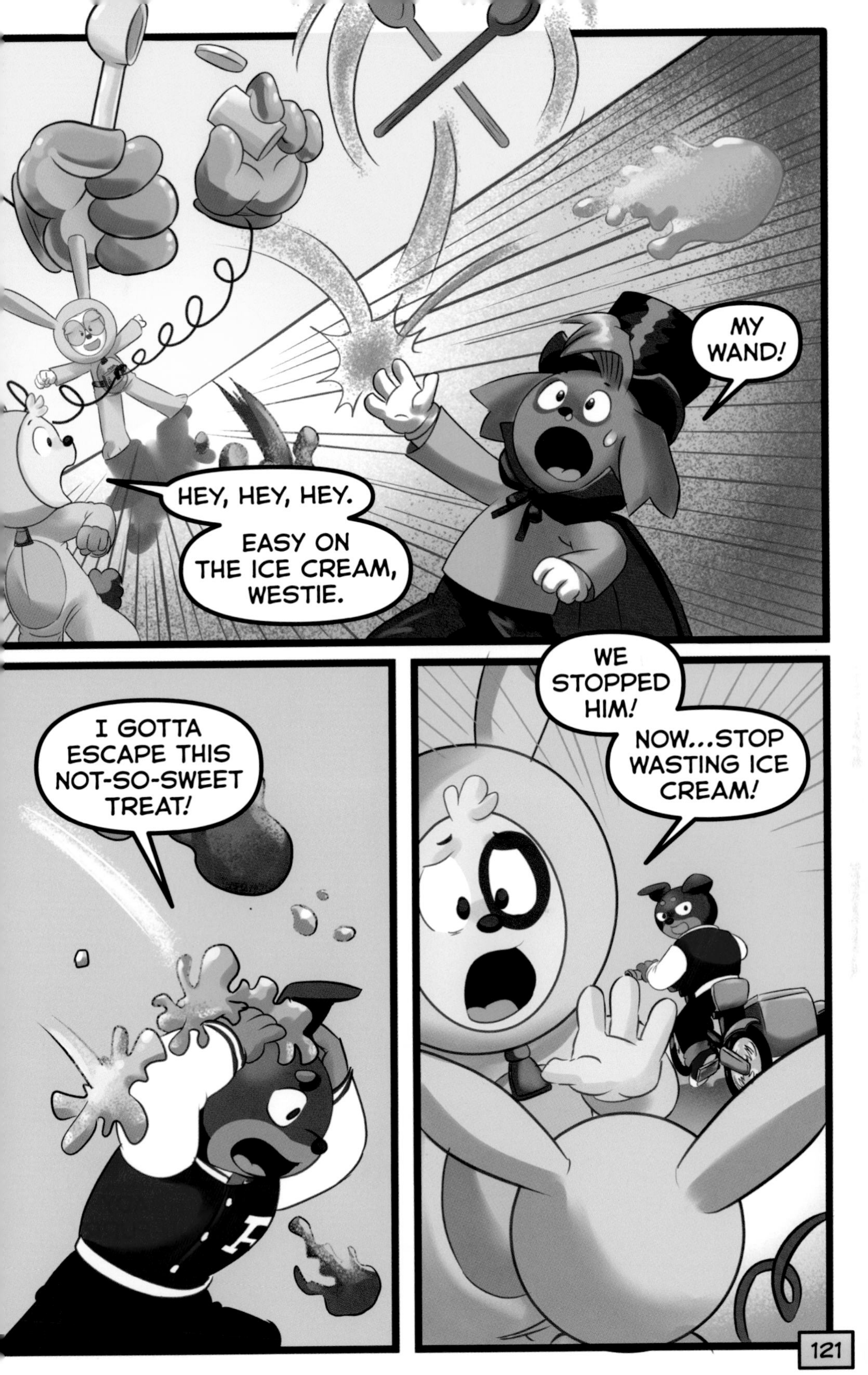
MY WAND!
HEY, HEY, HEY.
EASY ON THE ICE CREAM, WESTIE.
I GOTTA ESCAPE THIS NOT-SO-SWEET TREAT!
WE STOPPED HIM!
NOW...STOP WASTING ICE CREAM!

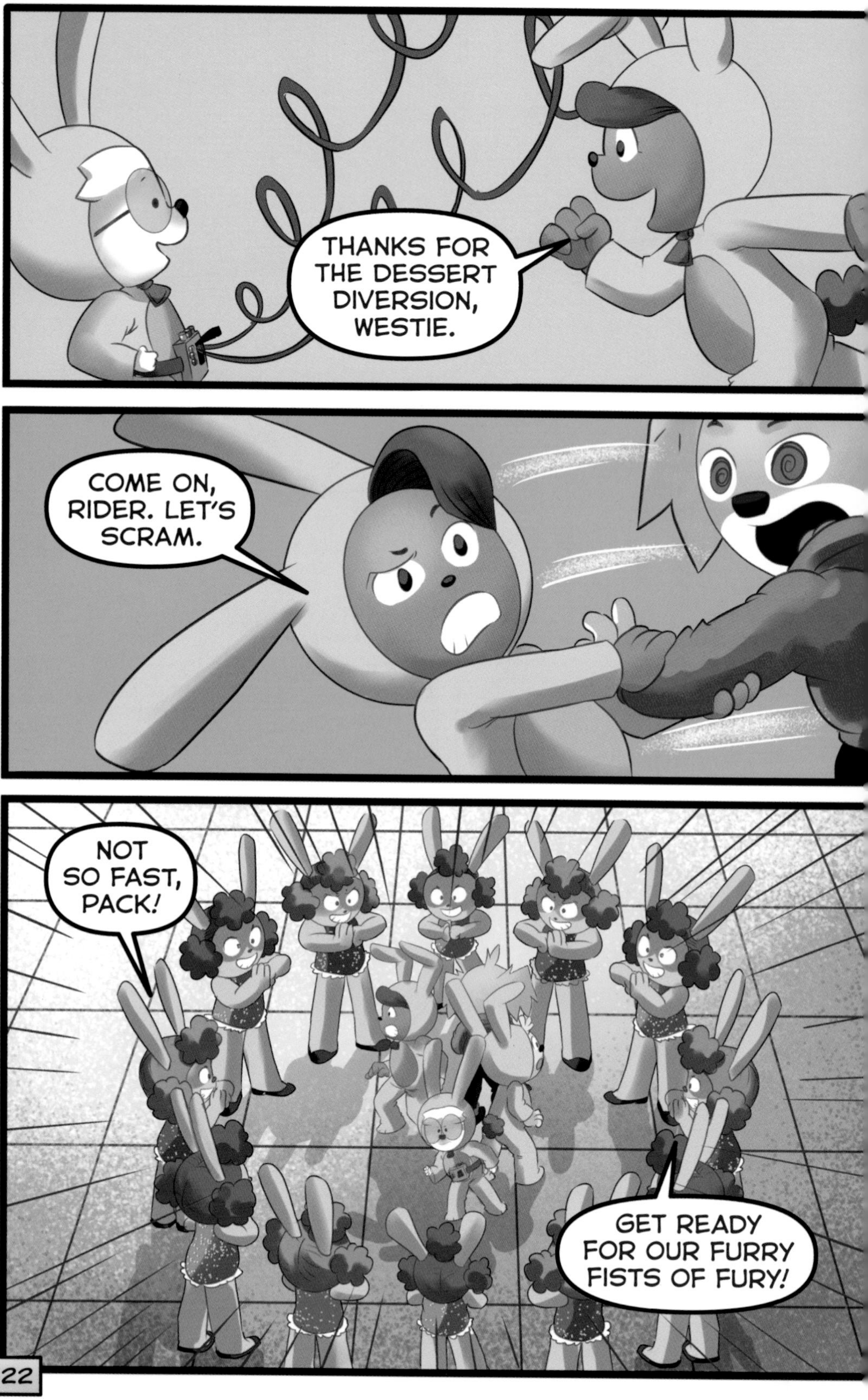
THANKS FOR THE DESSERT DIVERSION, WESTIE.
COME ON, RIDER. LET'S SCRAM.
NOT SO FAST, PACK!
GET READY FOR OUR FURRY FISTS OF FURY!

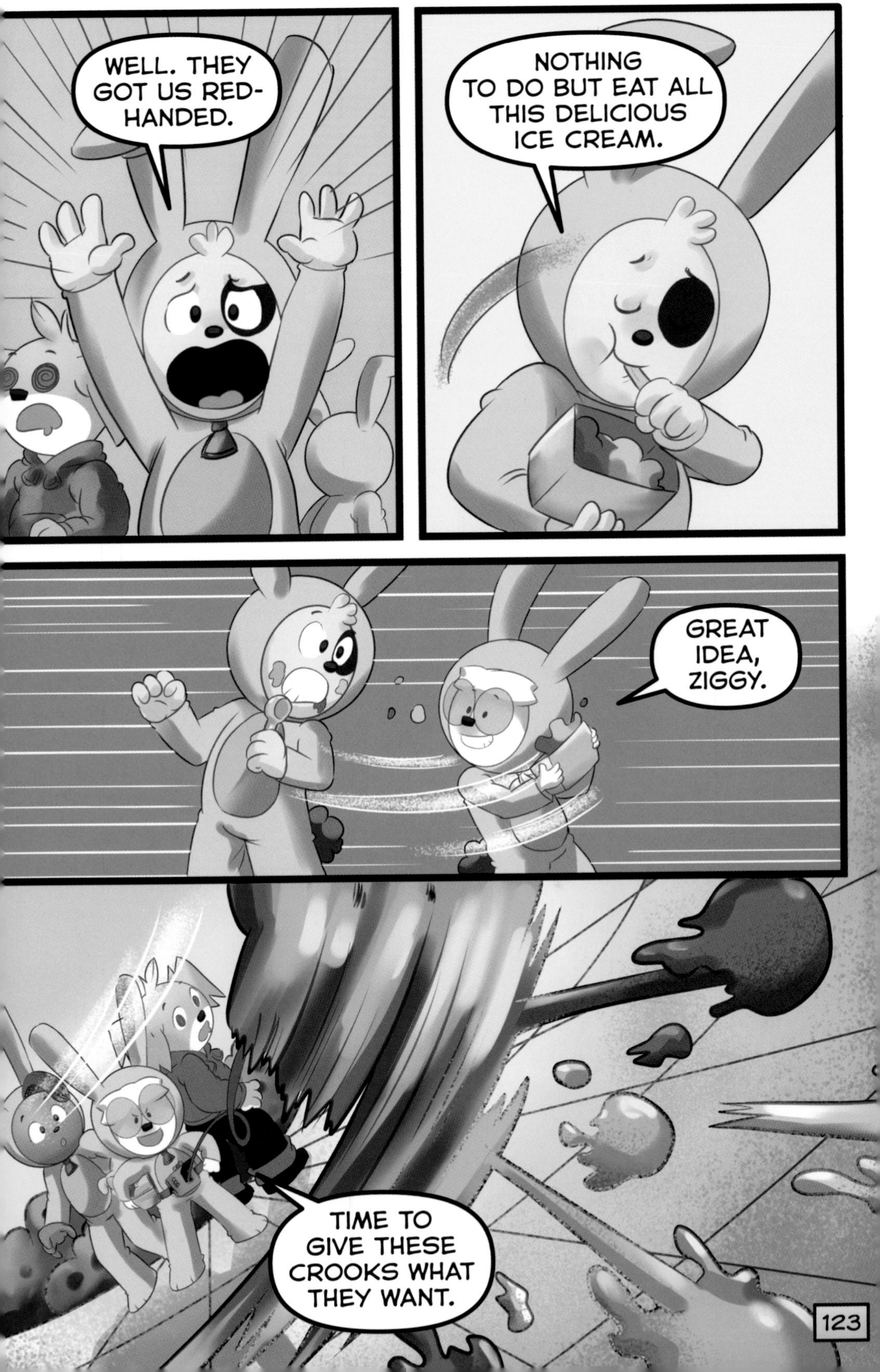
WELL. THEY GOT US RED-HANDED.
NOTHING TO DO BUT EAT ALL THIS DELICIOUS ICE CREAM.
GREAT IDEA, ZIGGY.
TIME TO GIVE THESE CROOKS WHAT THEY WANT.

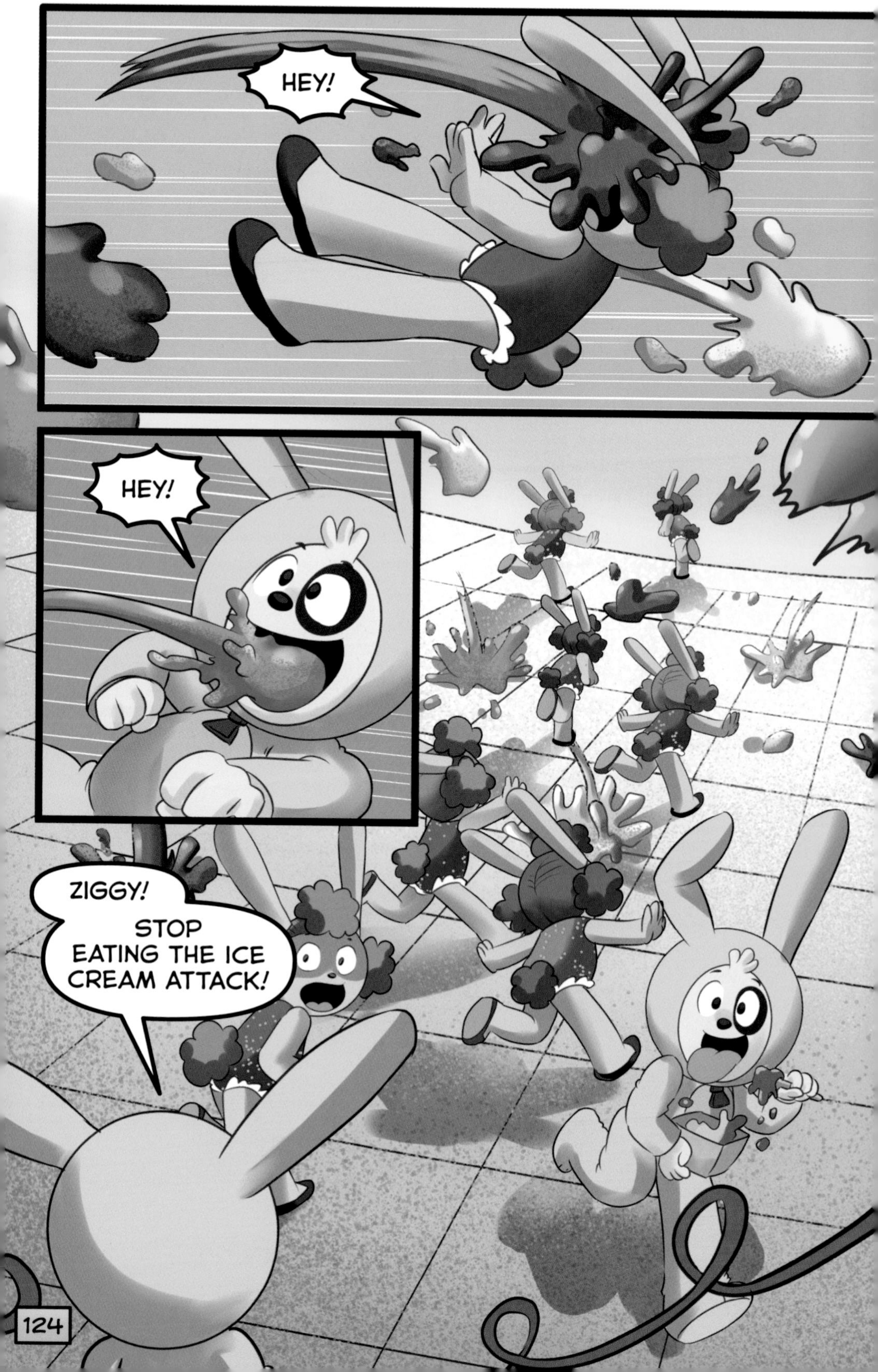
HEY!
HEY!
ZIGGY! STOP EATING THE ICE CREAM ATTACK!

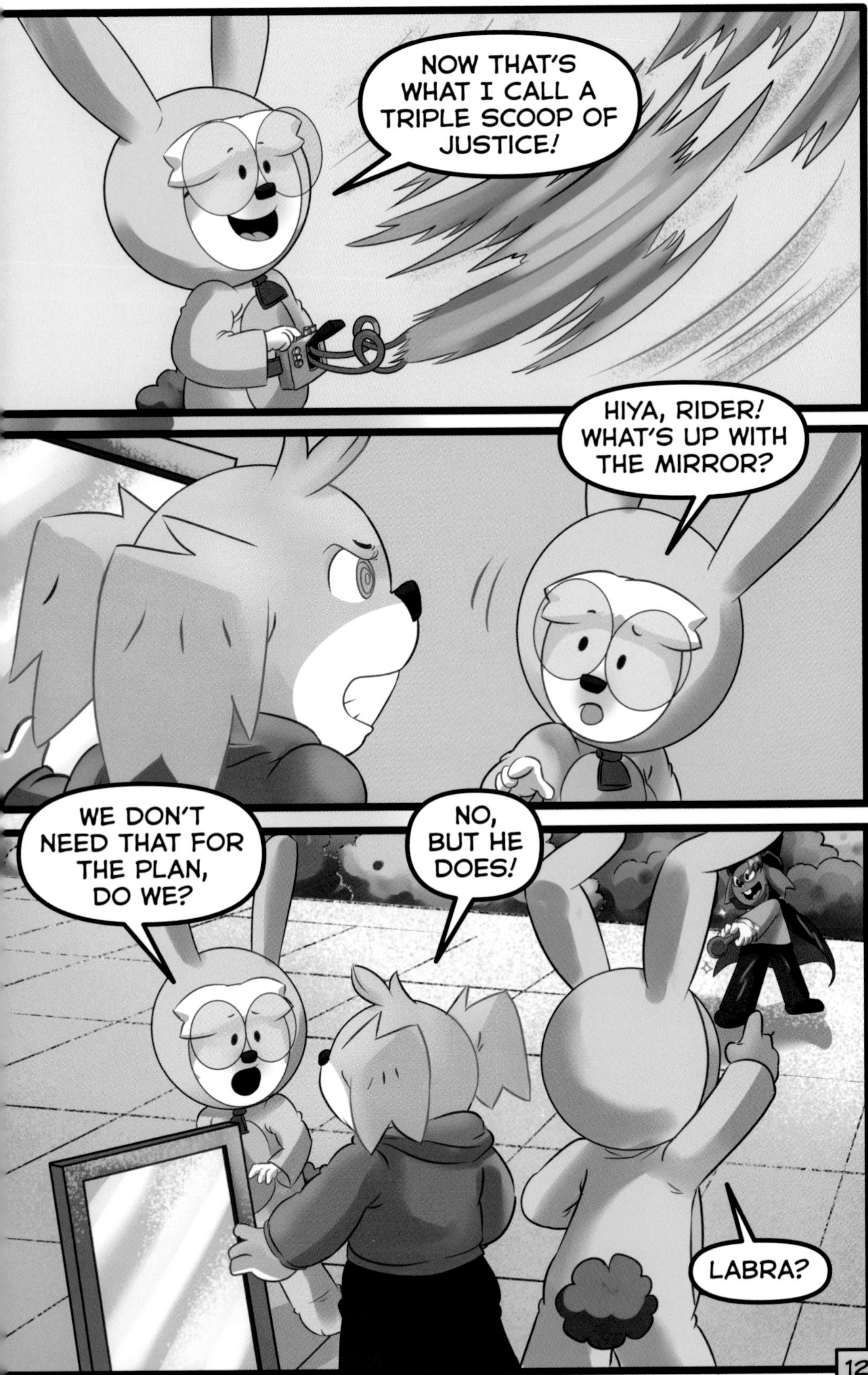
NOW THAT'S WHAT I CALL A TRIPLE SCOOP OF JUSTICE!
HIYA, RIDER! WHAT'S UP WITH THE MIRROR?
WE DON'T NEED THAT FOR THE PLAN, DO WE?
NO, BUT HE DOES!
LABRA?

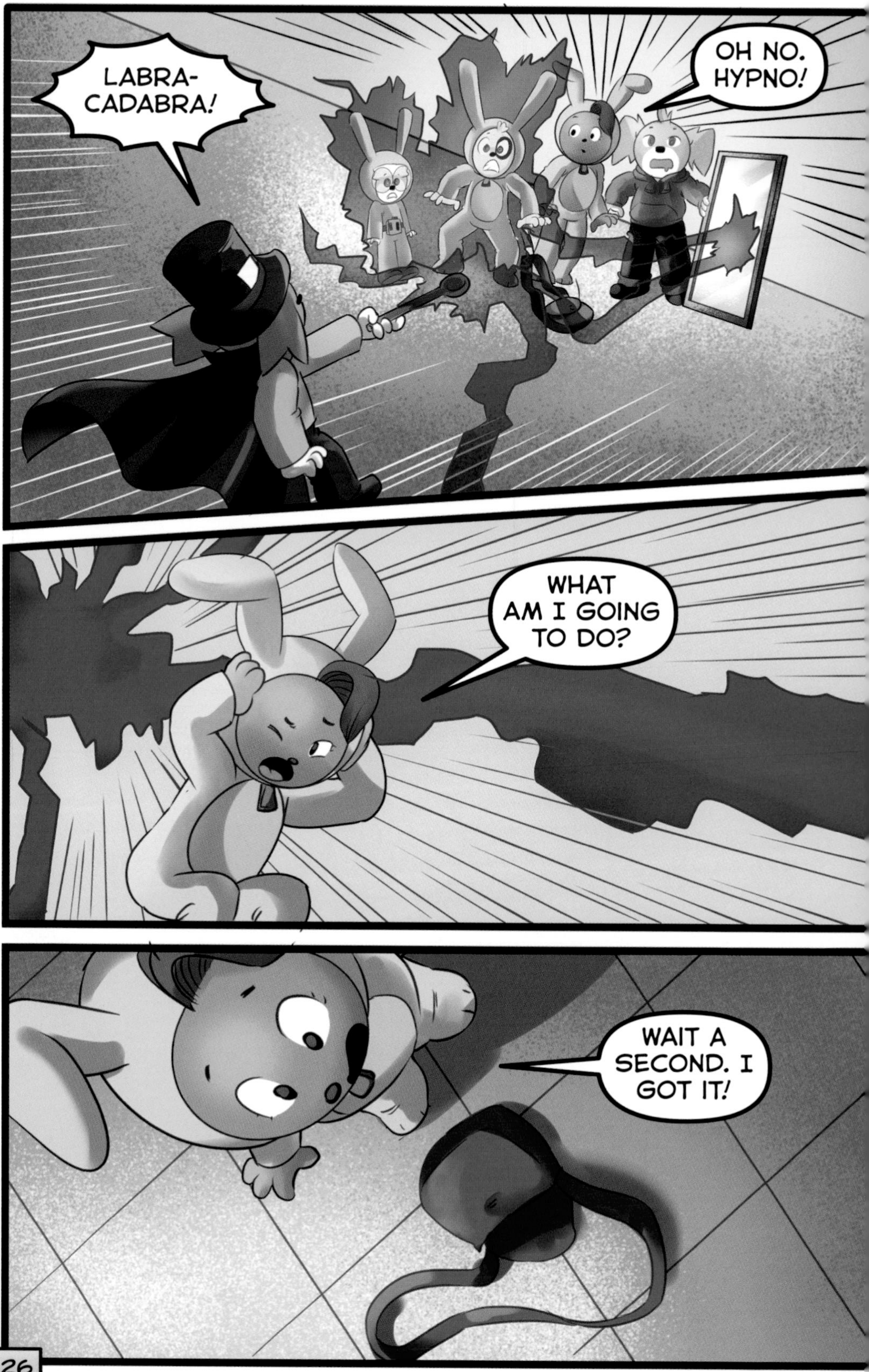
LABRA-CADABRA!
OH NO. HYPNO!
WHAT AM I GOING TO DO?
WAIT A SECOND. I GOT IT!

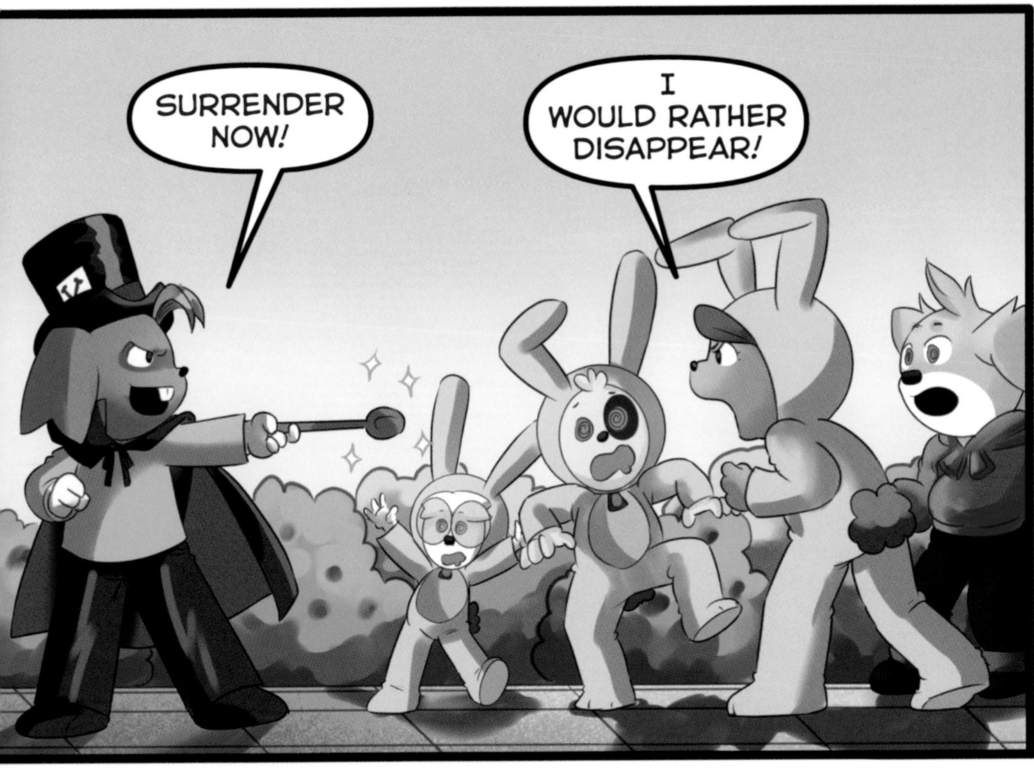
SURRENDER NOW!
I WOULD RATHER DISAPPEAR!

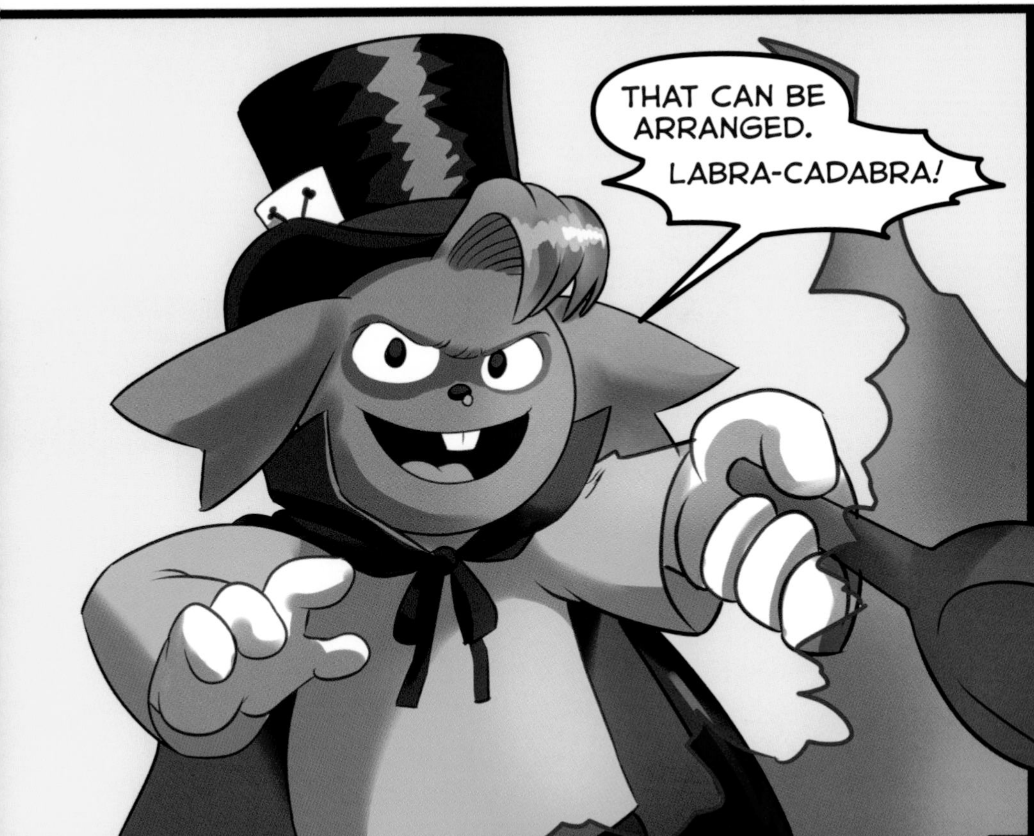
THAT CAN BE ARRANGED.
LABRA-CADABRA!

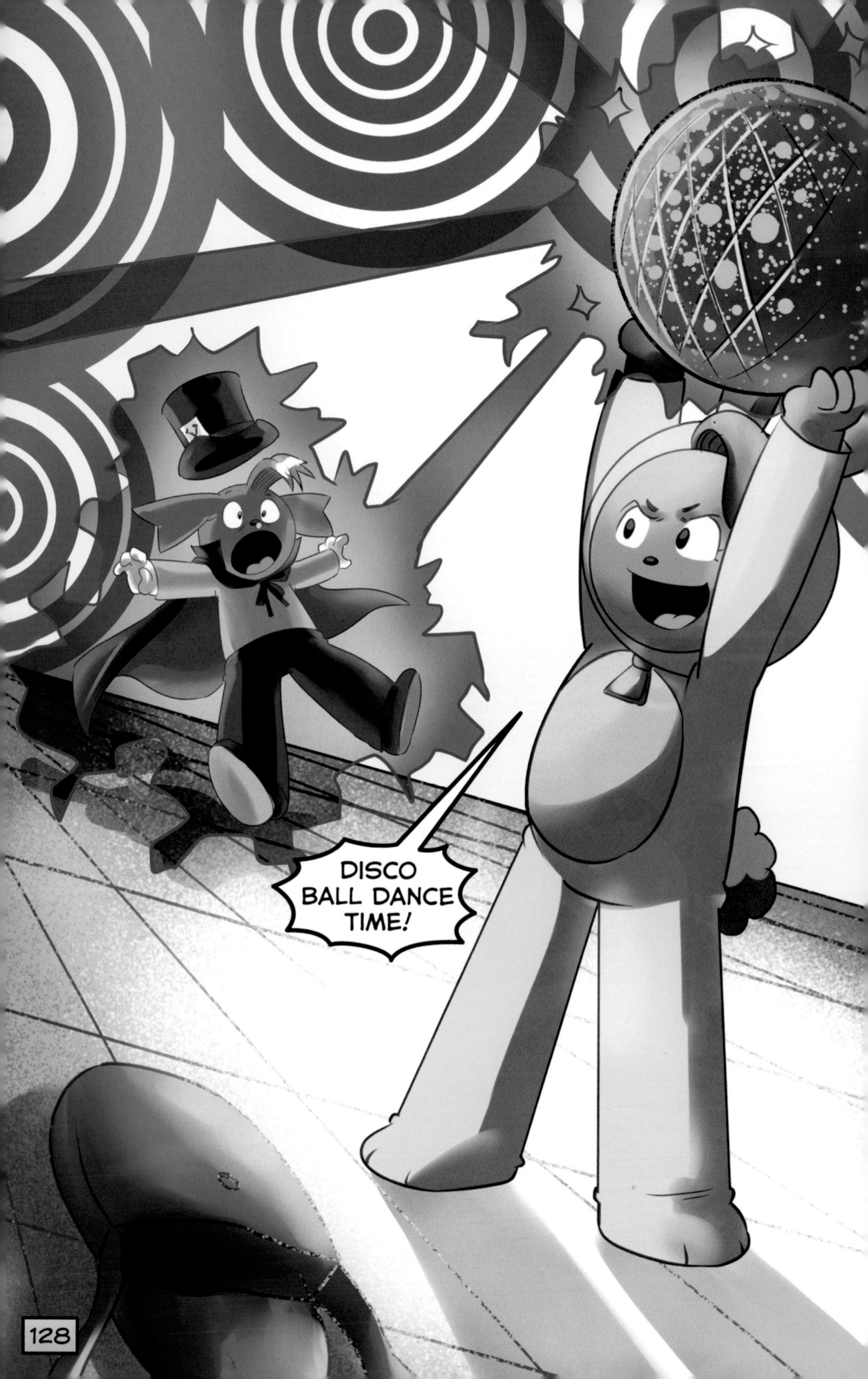
DISCO BALL DANCE TIME!

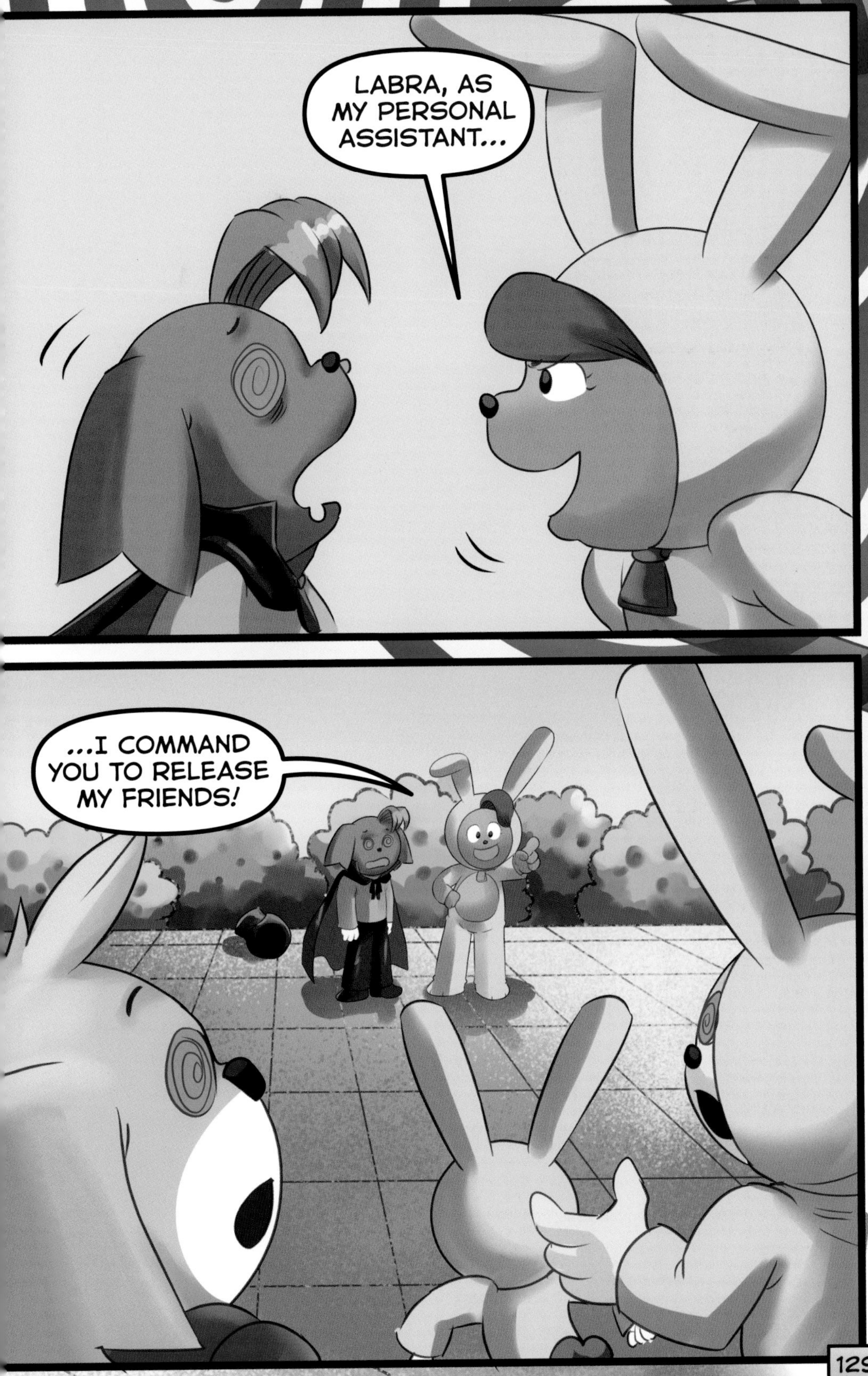
LABRA, AS MY PERSONAL ASSISTANT...
...I COMMAND YOU TO RELEASE MY FRIENDS!

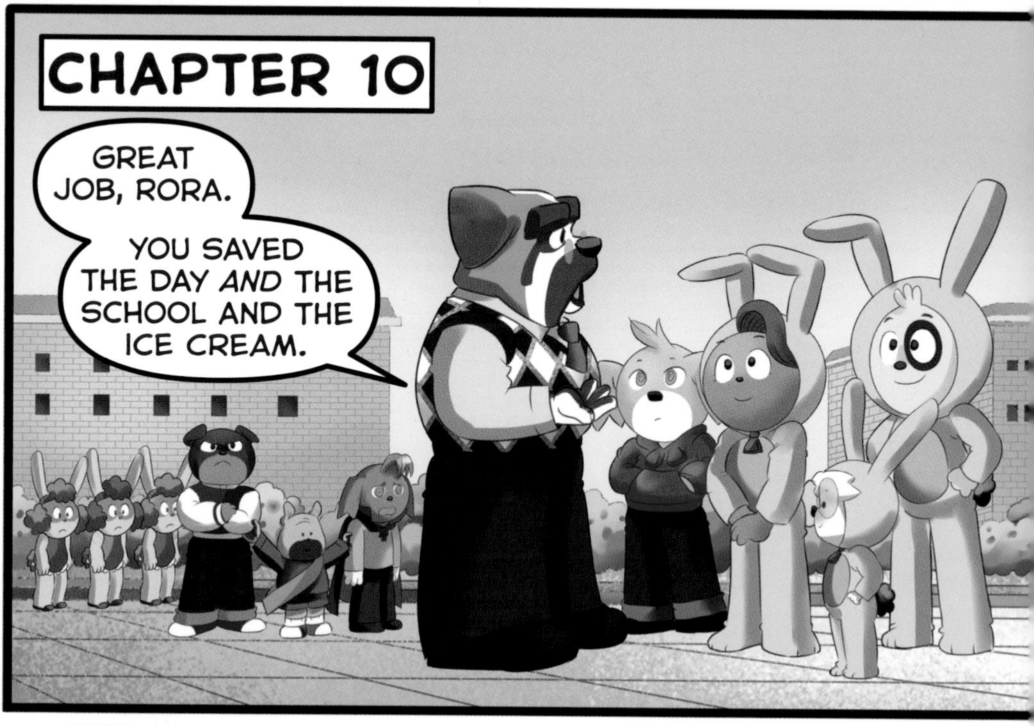
CHAPTER 10
GREAT JOB, RORA.
YOU SAVED THE DAY *AND* THE SCHOOL AND THE ICE CREAM.

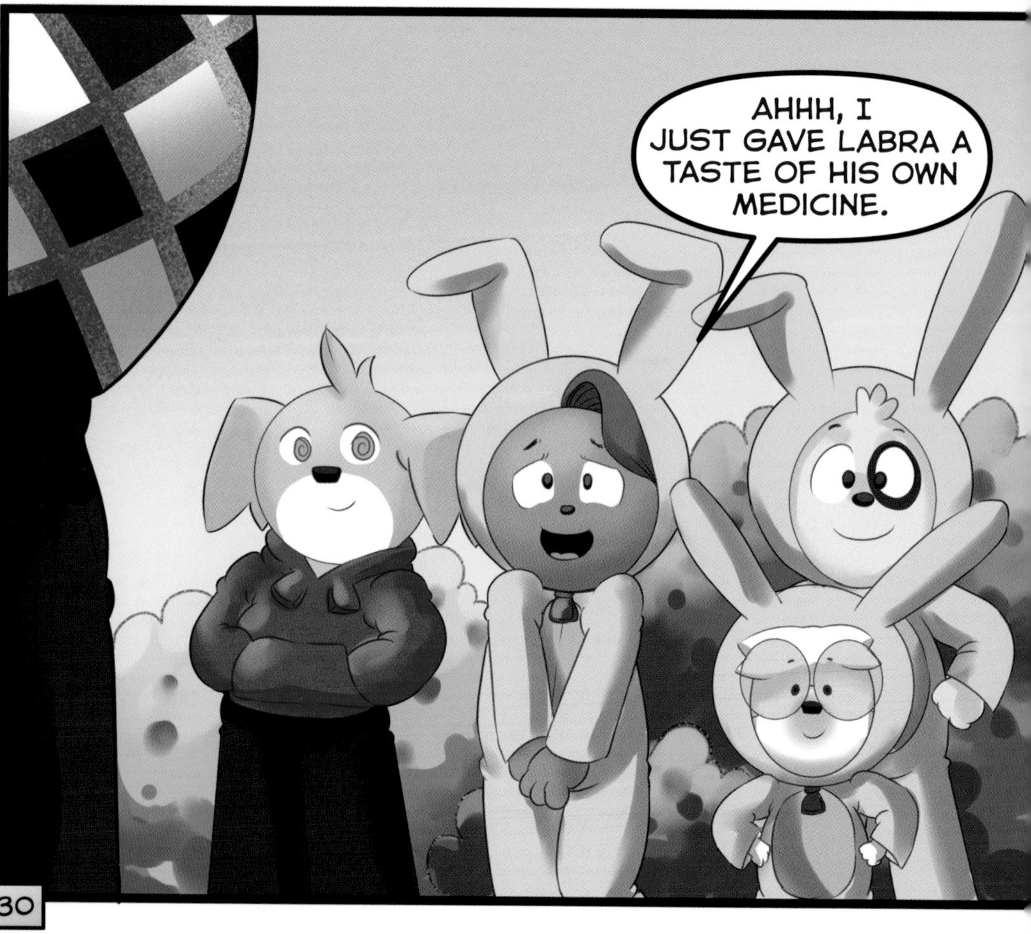
AHHH, I JUST GAVE LABRA A TASTE OF HIS OWN MEDICINE.

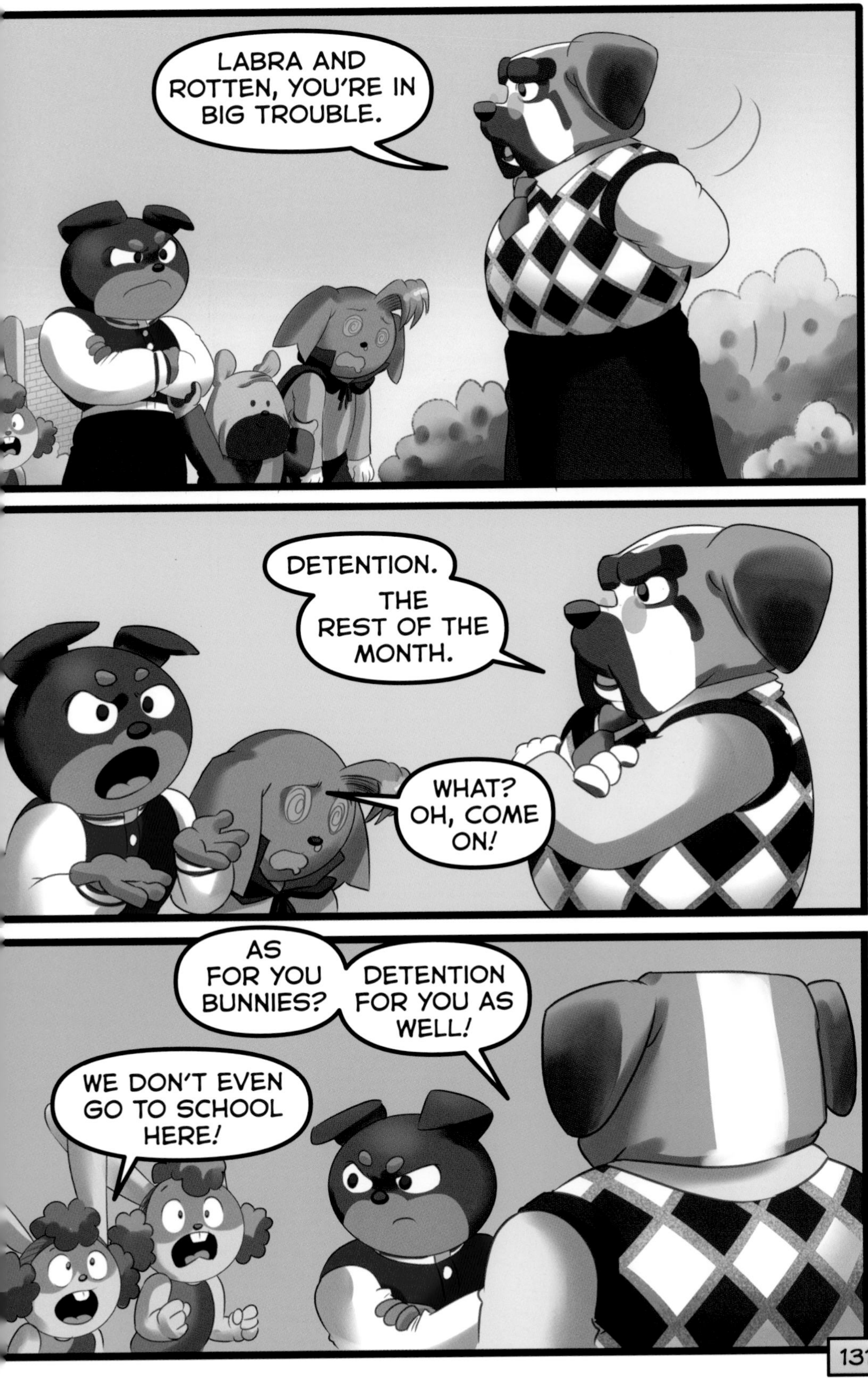
LABRA AND ROTTEN, YOU'RE IN BIG TROUBLE.
DETENTION.
THE REST OF THE MONTH.
WHAT? OH, COME ON!
AS FOR YOU BUNNIES?
DETENTION FOR YOU AS WELL!
WE DON'T EVEN GO TO SCHOOL HERE!

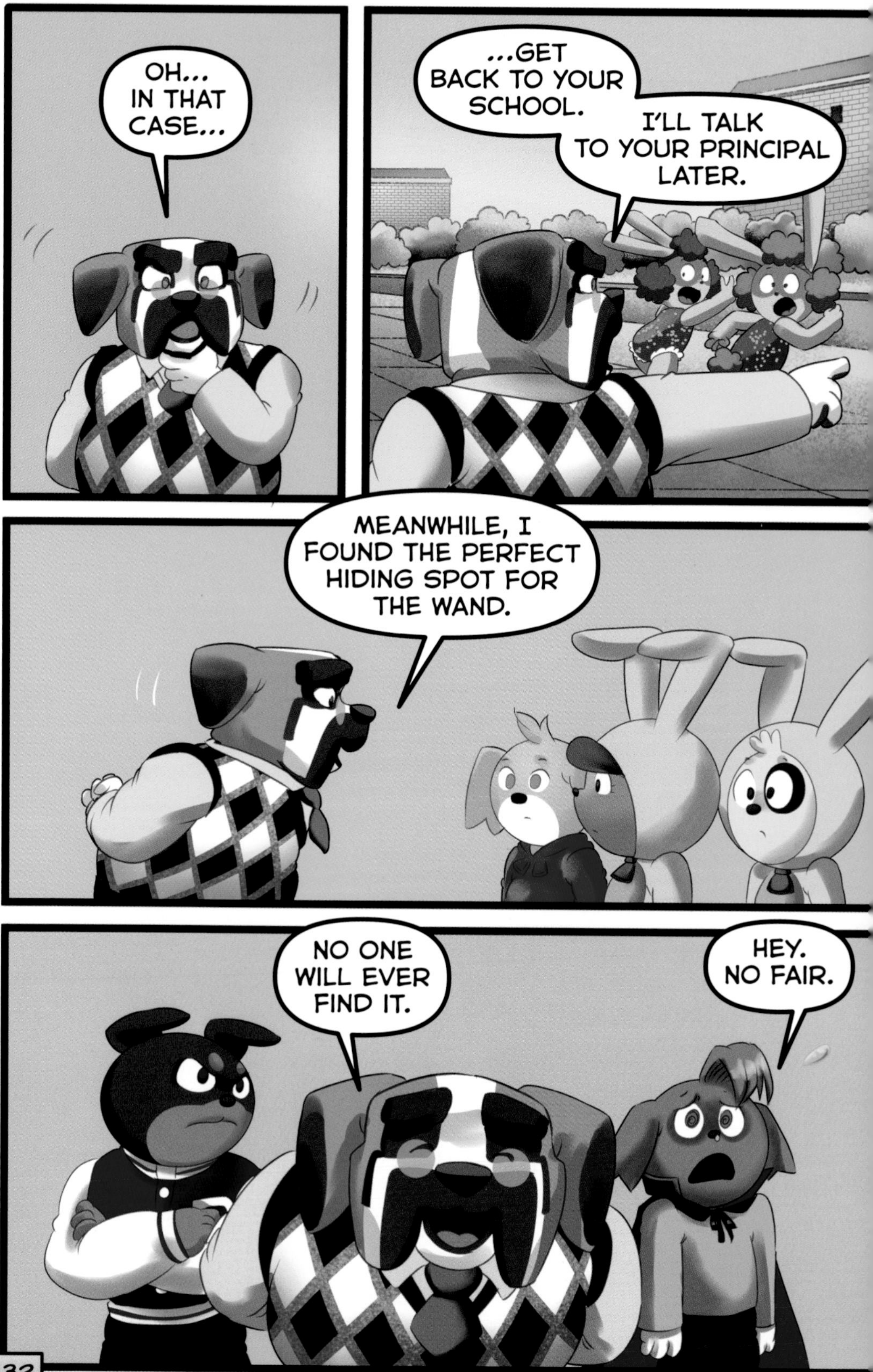
OH... IN THAT CASE...
...GET BACK TO YOUR SCHOOL.
I'LL TALK TO YOUR PRINCIPAL LATER.
MEANWHILE, I FOUND THE PERFECT HIDING SPOT FOR THE WAND.
NO ONE WILL EVER FIND IT.
HEY. NO FAIR.

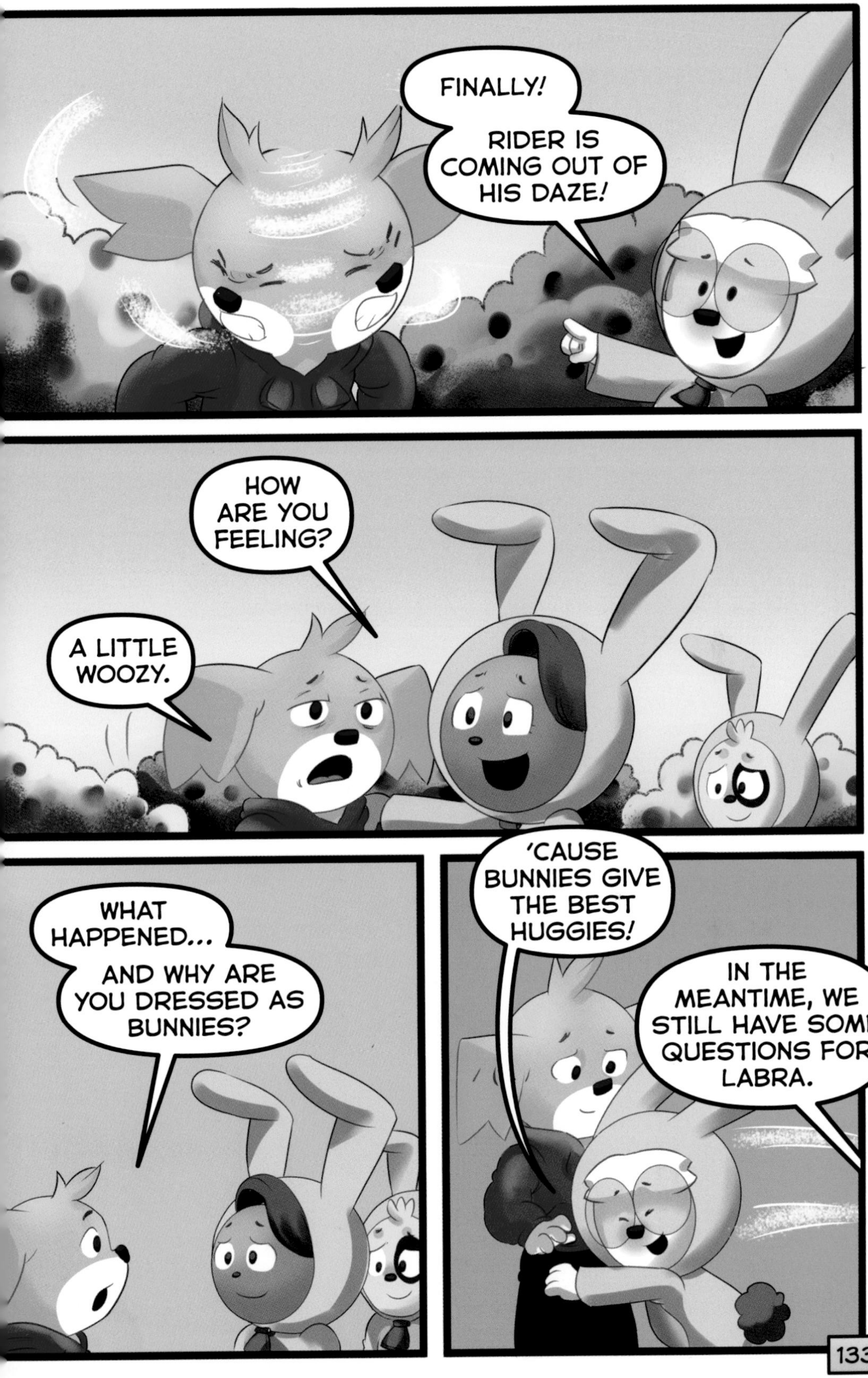
FINALLY!
RIDER IS COMING OUT OF HIS DAZE!
HOW ARE YOU FEELING?
A LITTLE WOOZY.
WHAT HAPPENED...
AND WHY ARE YOU DRESSED AS BUNNIES?
'CAUSE BUNNIES GIVE THE BEST HUGGIES!
IN THE MEANTIME, WE STILL HAVE SOME QUESTIONS FOR LABRA.

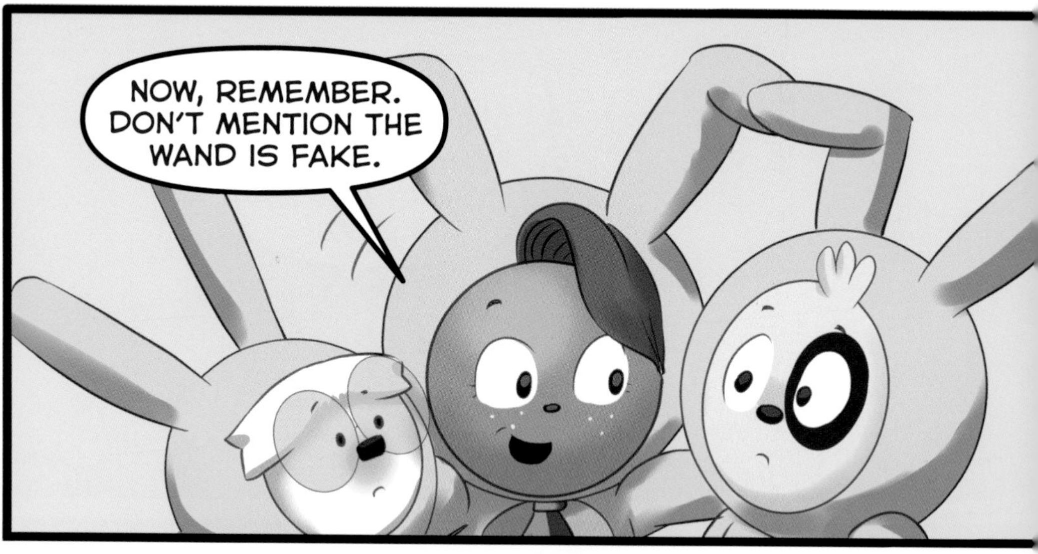
NOW, REMEMBER. DON'T MENTION THE WAND IS FAKE.

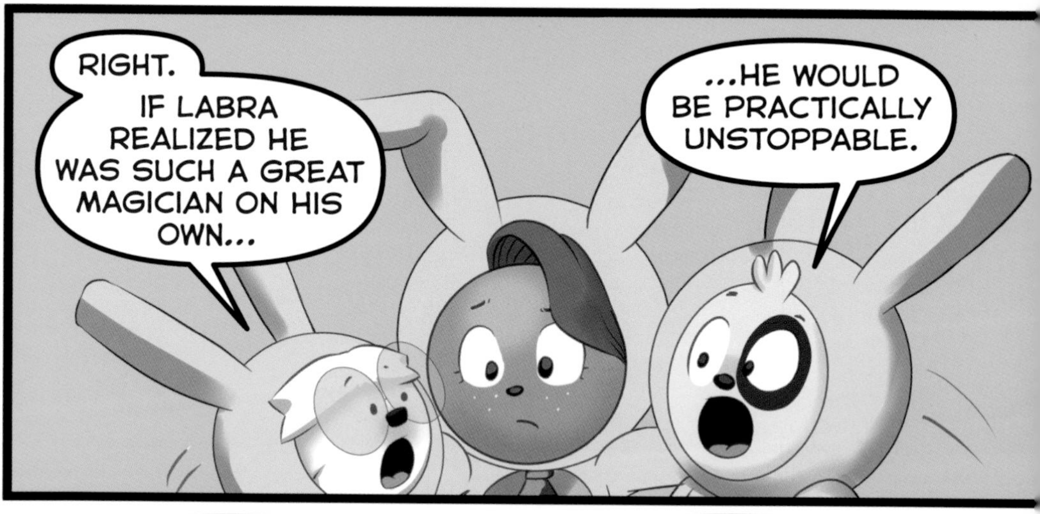
RIGHT.
IF LABRA REALIZED HE WAS SUCH A GREAT MAGICIAN ON HIS OWN...
...HE WOULD BE PRACTICALLY UNSTOPPABLE.

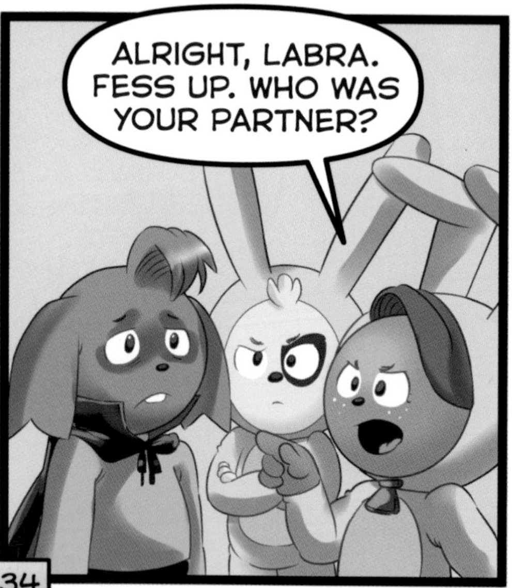
ALRIGHT, LABRA. FESS UP. WHO WAS YOUR PARTNER?

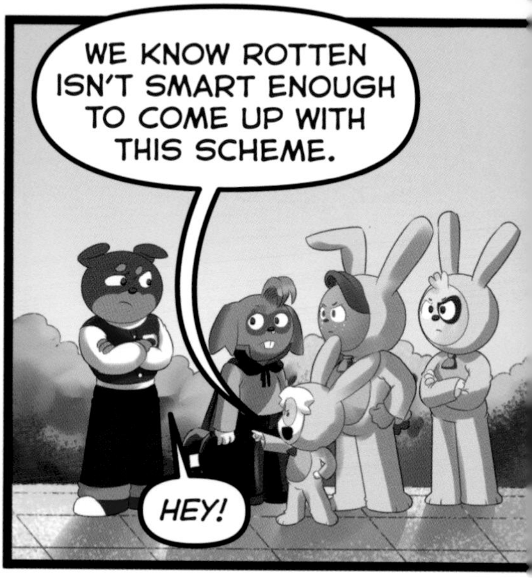
WE KNOW ROTTEN ISN'T SMART ENOUGH TO COME UP WITH THIS SCHEME.
HEY!

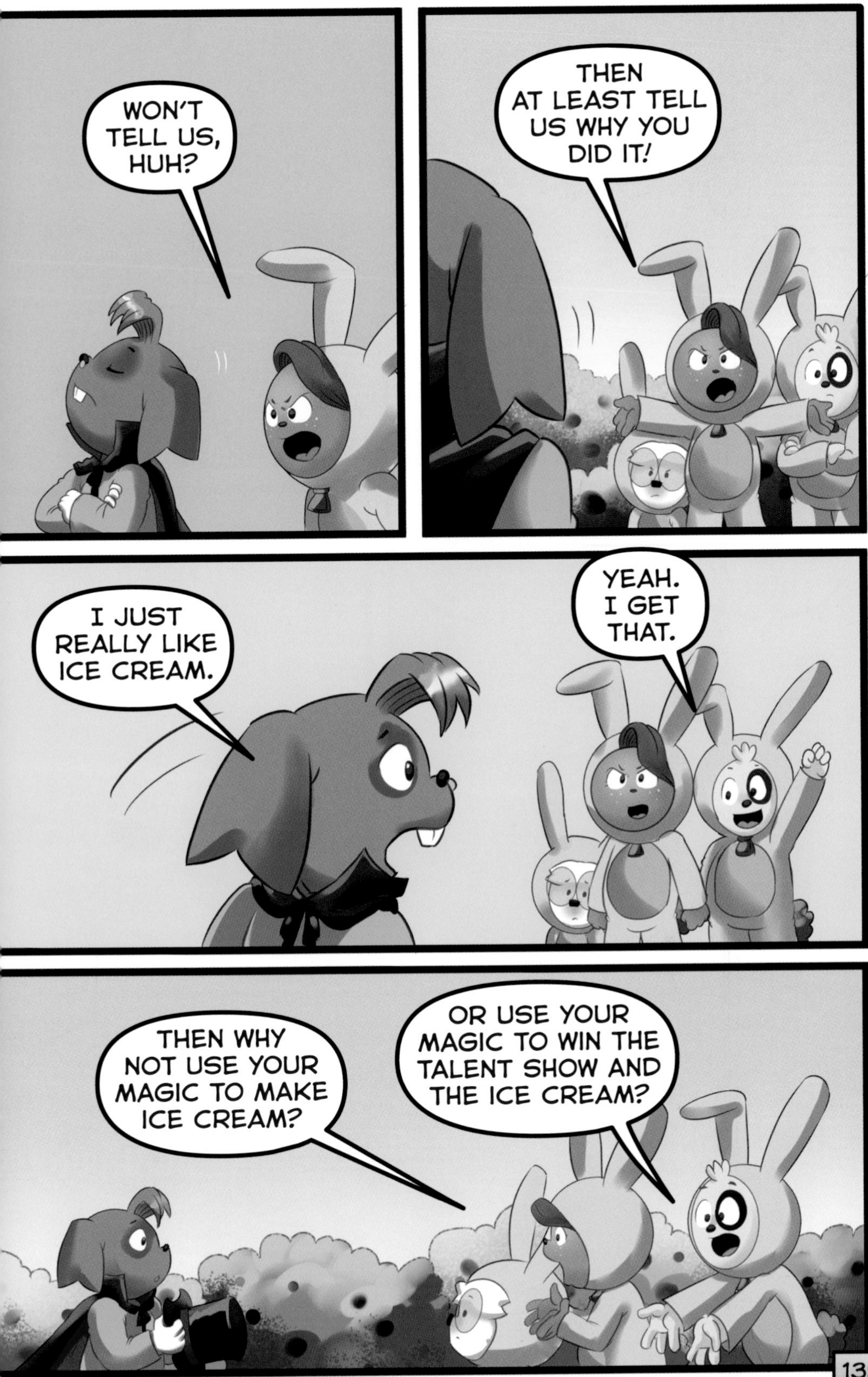
WON'T TELL US, HUH?
THEN AT LEAST TELL US WHY YOU DID IT!
I JUST REALLY LIKE ICE CREAM.
YEAH. I GET THAT.
THEN WHY NOT USE YOUR MAGIC TO MAKE ICE CREAM?
OR USE YOUR MAGIC TO WIN THE TALENT SHOW AND THE ICE CREAM?

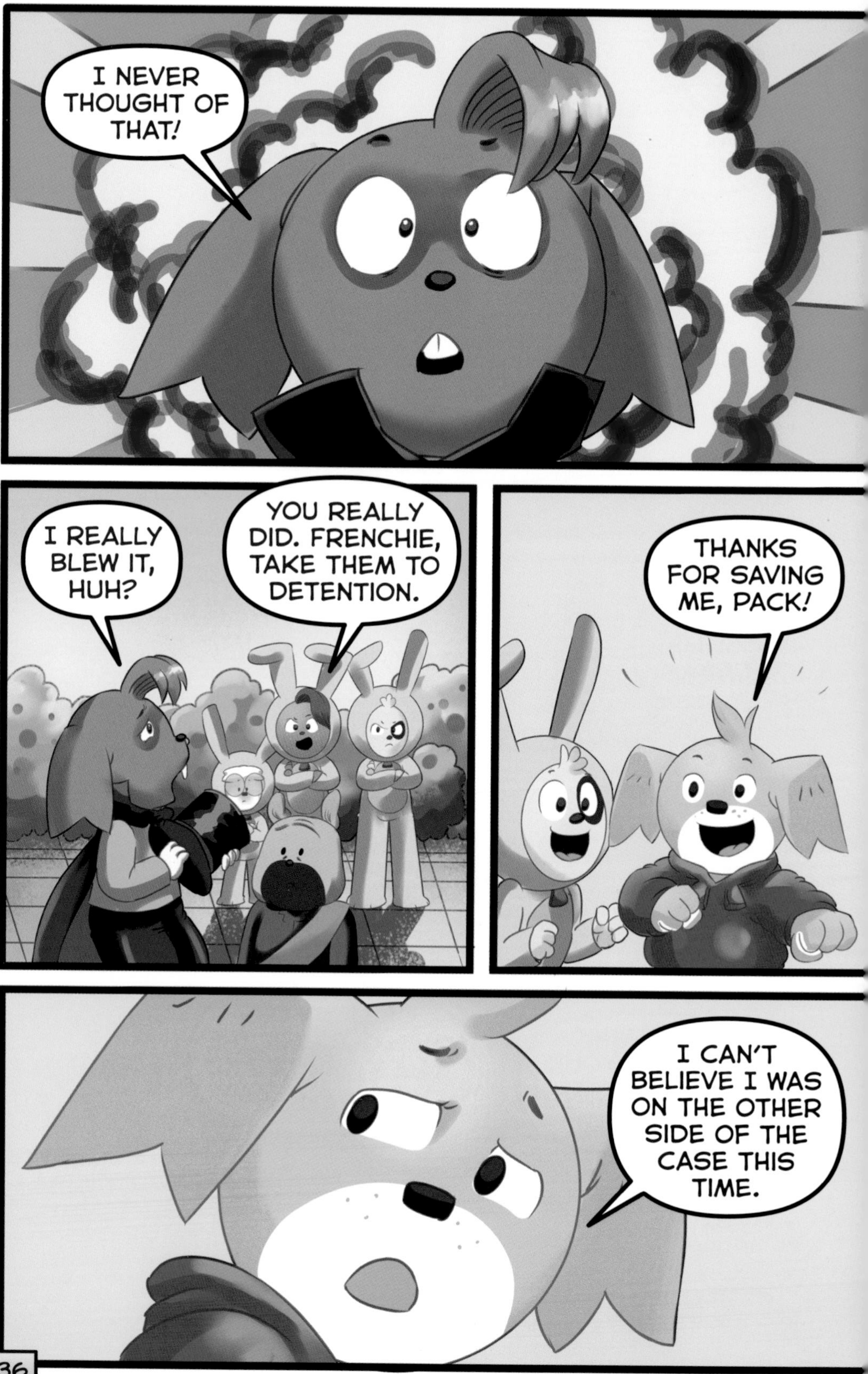
I NEVER THOUGHT OF THAT!
I REALLY BLEW IT, HUH?
YOU REALLY DID. FRENCHIE, TAKE THEM TO DETENTION.
THANKS FOR SAVING ME, PACK!
I CAN'T BELIEVE I WAS ON THE OTHER SIDE OF THE CASE THIS TIME.

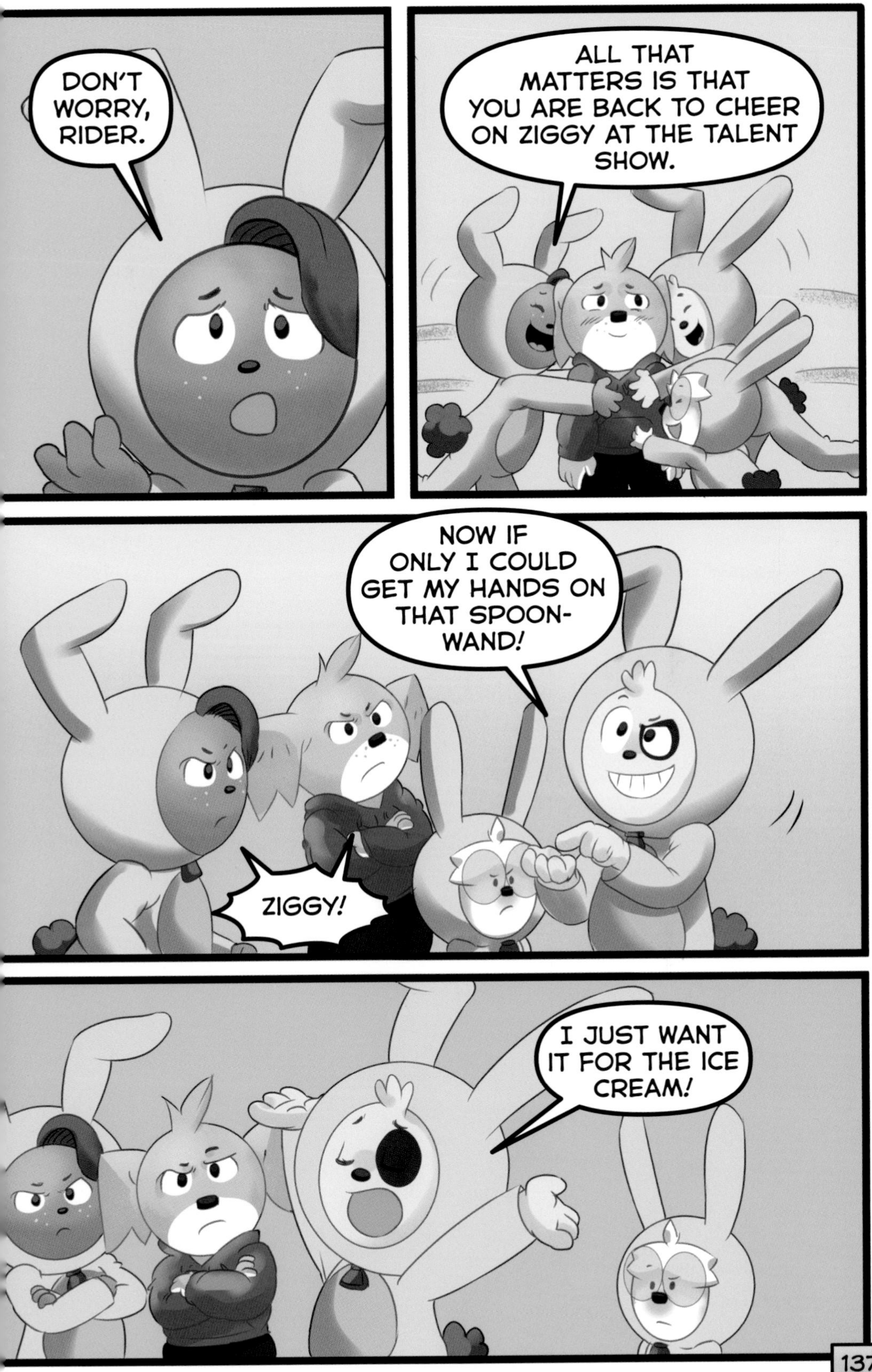

DON'T WORRY, RIDER.
ALL THAT MATTERS IS THAT YOU ARE BACK TO CHEER ON ZIGGY AT THE TALENT SHOW.
NOW IF ONLY I COULD GET MY HANDS ON THAT SPOON-WAND!
ZIGGY!
I JUST WANT IT FOR THE ICE CREAM!

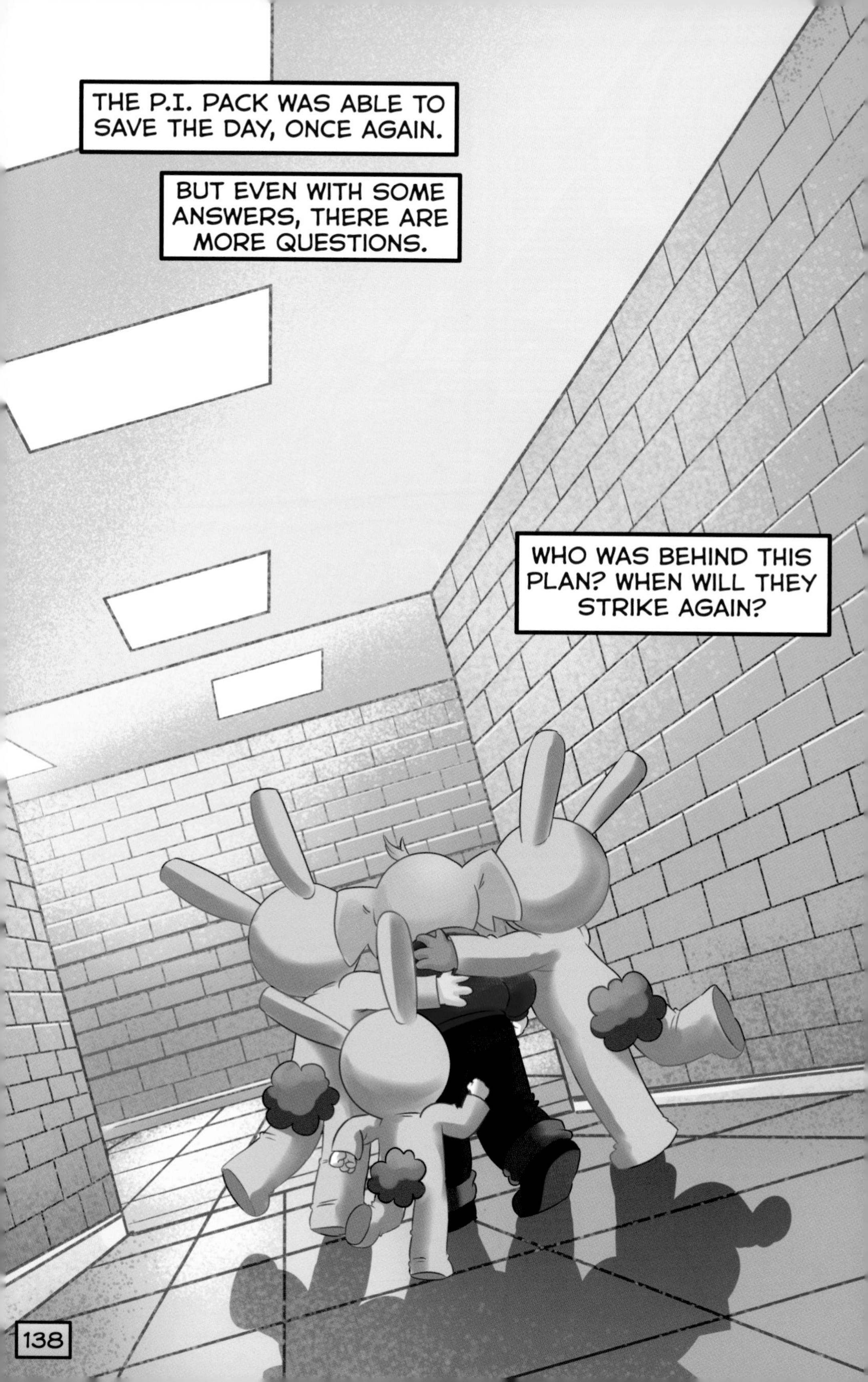
THE P.I. PACK WAS ABLE TO SAVE THE DAY, ONCE AGAIN.
BUT EVEN WITH SOME ANSWERS, THERE ARE MORE QUESTIONS.
WHO WAS BEHIND THIS PLAN? WHEN WILL THEY STRIKE AGAIN?

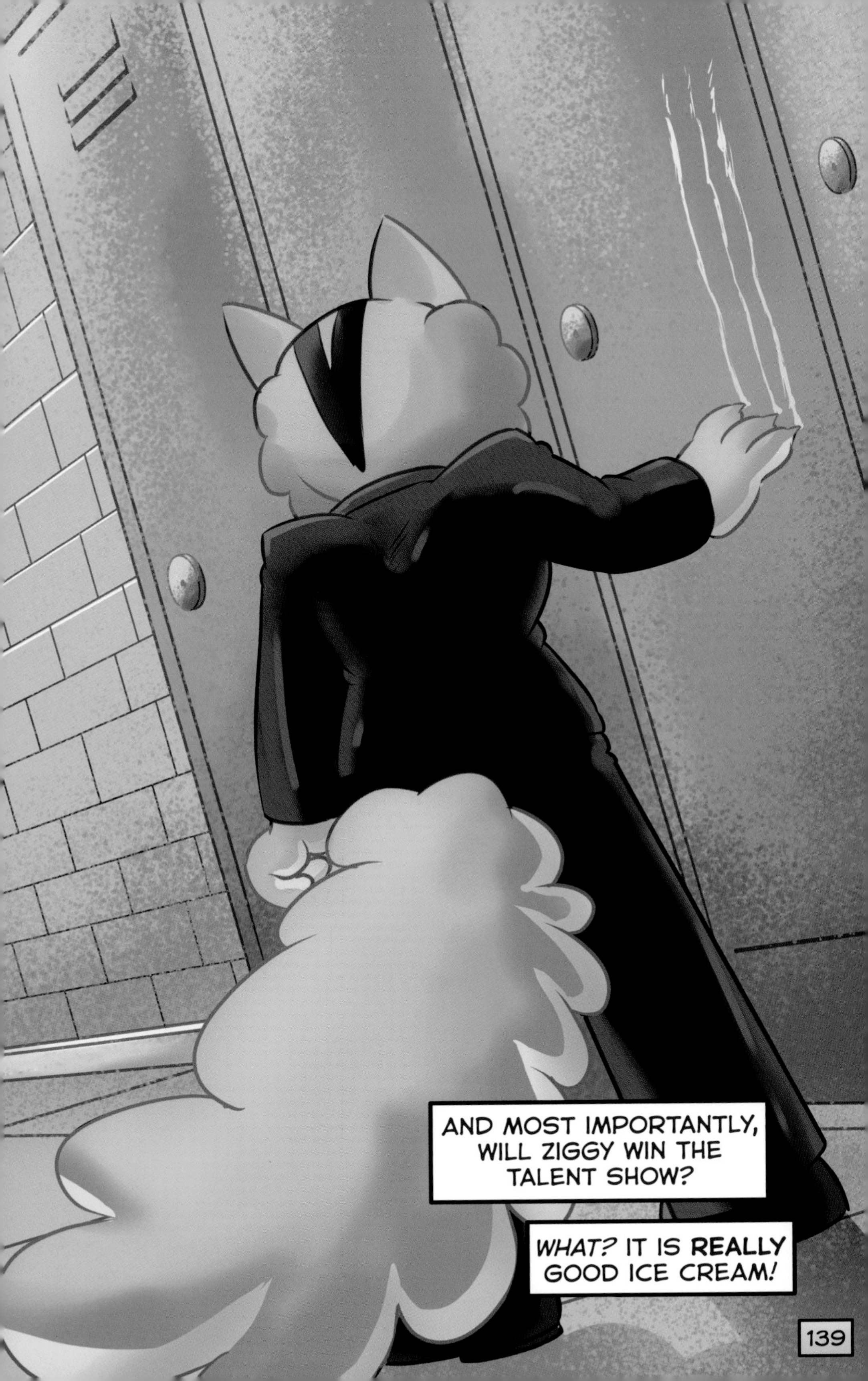
AND MOST IMPORTANTLY, WILL ZIGGY WIN THE TALENT SHOW?
WHAT? IT IS **REALLY** GOOD ICE CREAM!

A NEW CASE AWAITS IN THE NEXT INSTALLMENT OF

Graphic Novel
PUP DETECTIVES
FEATURING...
MYSTERY MOUNTAIN GETAWAY
PRINCIPAL
POPPA
RODERICK
PAWSTON ELEMENTARY · P.I. Pack · 900#
6

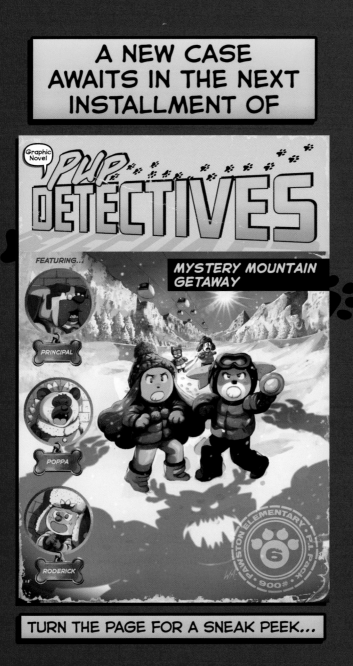

TURN THE PAGE FOR A SNEAK PEEK...

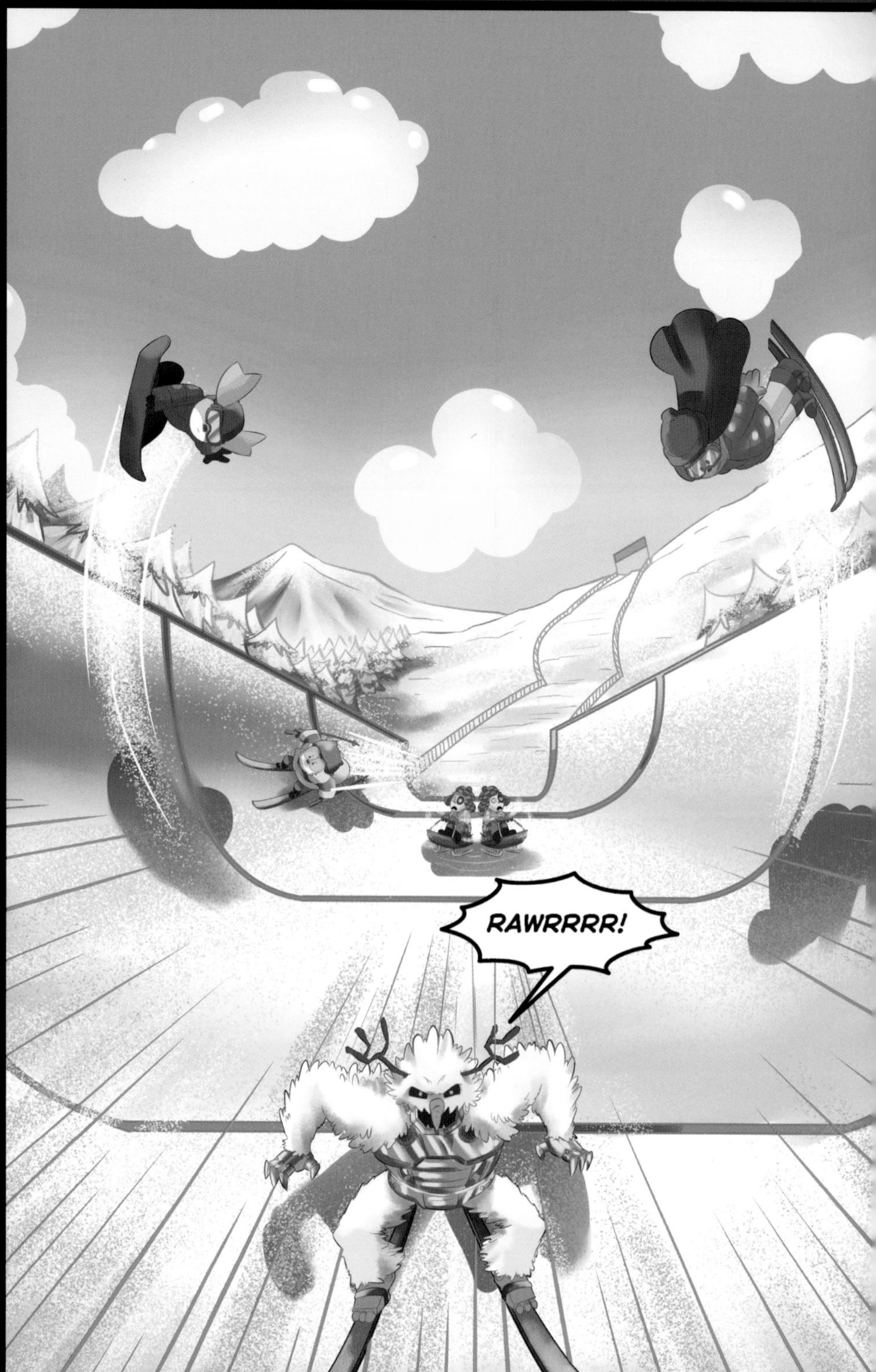
RAWRRRR!

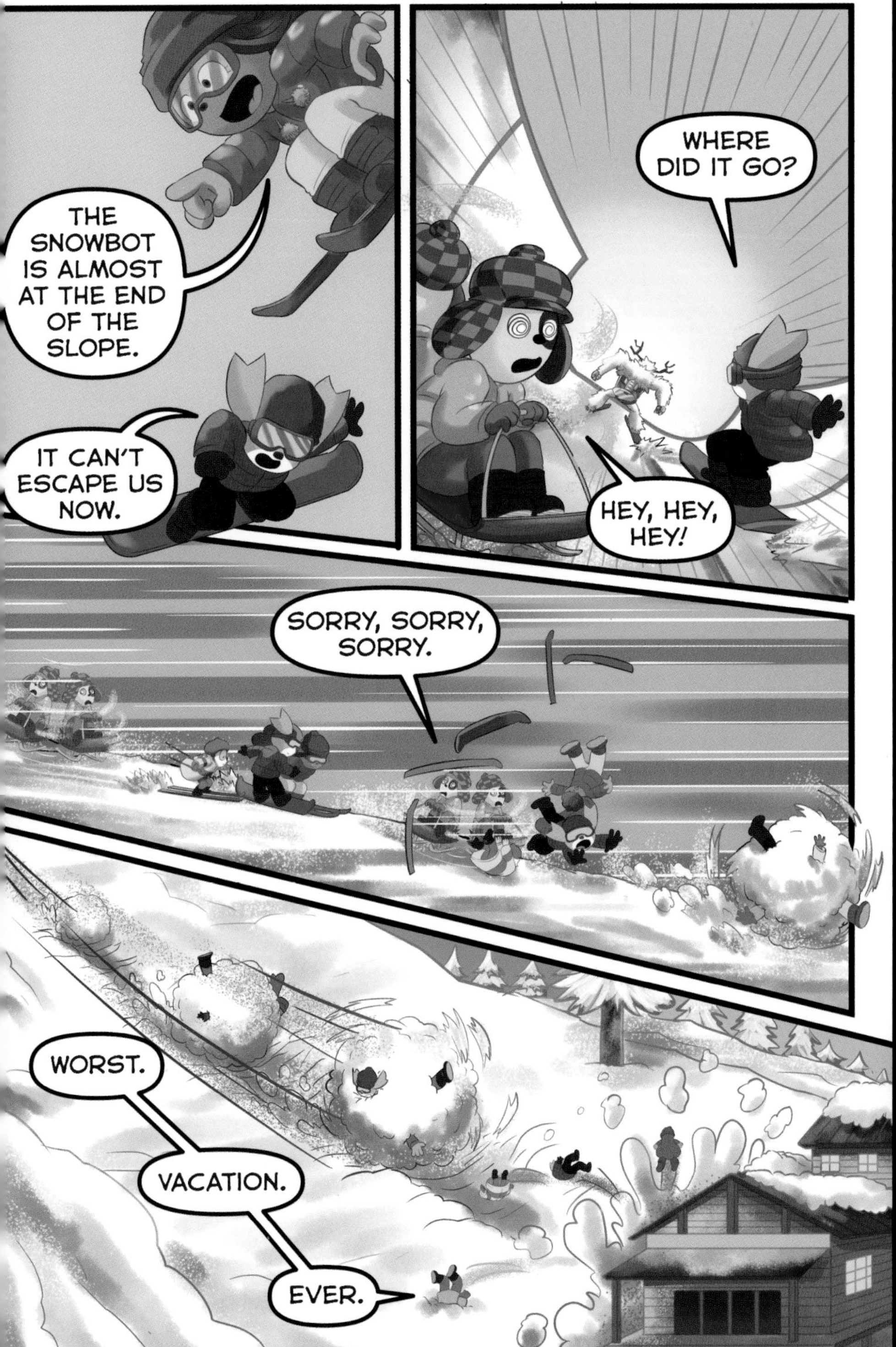
THE SNOWBOT IS ALMOST AT THE END OF THE SLOPE.
IT CAN'T ESCAPE US NOW.
WHERE DID IT GO?
HEY, HEY, HEY!
SORRY, SORRY, SORRY.
WORST.
VACATION.
EVER.